Sarah Zettel was born in California in 1966. She is the author of the acclaimed *Isavalta Trilogy* (*A Sorcerer's Treason*, *The Usurper's Crown* and *The Firebird's Vengeance*), a romantic fantasy based on the folklores of Russia, China and India, as well as the Arthurian romances *Camelot's Shadow*, *Camelot's Honour*, and *Camelot's Sword*. She has also written several science fiction novels and many short stories in various genres. Sarah Zettel lives in Michigan with her husband and their son.

By Sarah Zettel

A Sorcerer's Treason
The Usurper's Crown
The Firebird's Vengeance

Camelot's Shadow
Camelot's Honour
Camelot's Sword
Camelot's Blood

SARAH ZETTEL

Camelot's Blood

HARPER

Harper
An imprint of HarperCollins*Publishers*
77–85 Fulham Palace Road,
Hammersmith, London W6 8JB

First published in Great Britain by
HarperCollins*Publishers* 2008

This paperback edition 2008
1

A catalogue record for this book is
available from the British Library

ISBN-13: 978 0 00 715874 4

Typeset in Palatino by Palimpsest Book Production Limited,
Grangemouth, Stirlingshire

Printed in Great Britain by Clays Ltd, St Ives plc

Mixed Sources
Product group from well-managed
forests and other controlled sources
www.fsc.org Cert no. SW-COC-1806
© 1996 Forest Stewardship Council

FSC is a non-profit international organisation established
to promote the responsible management of the world's forests.
Products carrying the FSC label are independently certified
to assure consumers that they come from forests that are managed
to meet the social, economic and ecological needs
of present and future generations.

Find out more about HarperCollins and the environment at
www.harpercollins.co.uk/green

*This book is dedicated to the memory of
Catherine L. Moore*

ACKNOWLEDGEMENTS

I'd like to thank the Untitled Writers Group for their patience, and clear insights, as well as the women of the SF-FFWS list for their help and excellent advice. And, also, as always, my husband Tim for his support and patience.

Also, I'd like to once more thank Mr. Thomas B. Deku, who taught Writing for Publication at Trenton High School. Without him, none of these books would be in existence.

PROLOGUE

My narrow chamber seems a little darker today. Through my slit of a window I see the sky is clear and blue but daylight does not penetrate here. These stones in these walls are effective guardians, and in my fancy they lean a little too close, as if they want to see what I write upon this page.

I do not wish them to see. I do not wish any to see. This may be the final proof that my wits – in which I have taken such pride – have deserted me. Yet I do not pause in my writing.

It is also possible that this thing is true.

This is not the first time I have written of my wandering monk. A bluff, hearty man with a warrior's arms, and a pilgrim's staff. He visits me frequently, providing laughter for my old age, and an ear for my thoughts. Indeed, it is because of him that I have ventured to set these chronicles of lost Camelot down.

He came again today. I was sitting in one of my usual retreats, beside the hazel tree that stands hard by the monastery's stone wall. There is an old stone bench there where I like to rest, for the peace and the chance to let the sun bake some of the pain from my old, twisted bones.

The monk climbed through the breach in the wall, was tall and hale and smiling as ever, and his shadow was long in the evening sun as he strode across the grounds.

And I swear before God, this is a true record of the conversation we held:

'God be with you this evening, Sir Kai!' He is the last to call me by this title.

'And God be with you, Brother.' I paused and let us be silent for a moment. His silences are always comfortable things. Since I mean to record only the truth here, I will say that for one of the few times in my life I was afraid to speak. But at last my fear galled me too strongly, and I did speak again.

'A strange thought occurred to me lately, Brother.'

'And what is that, Sir Kai?'

'That for all the deep discourse you and I have held, and despite our many friendly meetings, you have never once told me your name.'

'Nor have I.' He smiled, a wry smile. He looked like a talespinner who knows his audience has anticipated his carefully crafted joke. 'But then, you have never asked me.'

Which was true, and until recently I had not stopped to wonder at it.

'I spoke to the Abbot about you. Do you know what he told me?'

'Should I?'

'He told me there was no such a one as you who came visiting here. He told me I should pray hard, for the Lord had clearly granted me visions, or perhaps the Devil had. He seemed unclear as to which it might be. He did say I'm often seen talking to myself, but no broad, bearded monk with a white staff had ever been seen, with me or without me.'

The monk nodded, judiciously, as if trying to decide the merits of my declaration. 'What do you think I am?' he asked.

'That, Brother, is an intriguing question.' I am amazed at how calmly I spoke. But then, I have seen many a strange thing in my long days. Usually, though, they came in far less mundane forms than this monk. 'I note you do not deny that you are a vision.'

He shrugged. 'We are all many things as we pass our time under Heaven.'

'This is so.' I loaded my final bolt. 'They tell a tale in these lands. It is of a man who came from the west of my own island, brought here as a slave from the Dumonii lands. He became a holy man, they say. They say he converted the heathen and the pagan here, and performed many miracles.' I narrowed my eyes at my companion. 'Might your name be Patrick?'

My monk laughed, loud and openly. 'It might, Sir Kai. It might.'

I should have been afraid. I had been afraid to begin this. Now that it was begun, though, it seemed right and natural that our conversation take this turn. How could I be afraid of this . . . this vision who had become both comforter and familiar gadfly? I admit that more than anything, I was rankled. No man likes his fellows – even taciturn monks of little imagination and less wit – to think he has lost his reason. I felt this companionable vision might have done me the courtesy of showing itself to the brethren so I would not be mistaken for a dotard.

'You are supposed to be dead.'

Patrick slapped his knee and got to his feet. 'Time will come, Sir Kai, when you are supposed to be a dream.'

Fear at last came on me. Not from his words, but from the thought that my words might drive him away, never to return. Age and loneliness pressed heavy on my head. 'Will you come back?' I heard the quaver in my voice, and was ashamed.

Patrick nodded, his face comprehending, but blessedly free of pity. I do not know if I could have borne that. He laid that warm, work-worn hand on my shoulder. 'Fear not, Kai. I will come back at the proper time.'

He walked away, stepping through the gap in the wall, leaving not even his shadow behind.

So, I sit here in this dark, stone cell, wondering what I have seen and why, and what this proper time might be. The pain in my legs is bad today. I feel the time of endings closing in on me like these too-close walls of my cell. I fear it, as men are wont do, and yet I welcome it too. I fear not seeing the days to come, and yet I fear seeing them, for I have already seen so much in my lifetime and I am so very tired of it.

So, to keep these great and terrible feelings at bay, I begin writing once more. I have not yet set down the tale of Agravain, the second of the sons of Lot. He is the one of my nephews to whom I was closest, which perhaps is why my hand shakes now that I think to write of him. But it was also he and his bride who brought about a great ending that was in itself a beginning, although none of us knew it at the time.

Here then begins the tale of Sir Agravain and the Lady Laurel Carnbrea.

Kai pen Hir ap Cynyr
At the Monastery of Gillean,
Eire

ONE

In the fortress of Din Eityn, the king lay dying.

Din Eityn squatted on a great black precipice, as old and as solid as if it had been carved from the living rock. Men who knew nothing but the working of stones and the worship of wells had once come here. They laid down stones without mortar to shelter themselves from the wind. Other men, ones who knew the working of bronze and understood the secrets of oak and mistletoe, came to cast these ancient ones out. They wove wicker fences and raised the walls higher. The the Romans drove all before them and took the great precipice after a bloody siege that was still sung of by bards and poets in both lands. They squared the walls of Din Eityn and built towers to better keep the watch.

That was four generations ago. The Romans were fled, but the rock and its many-layered fortress now called Din Eityn remained. The sons of the bronze-workers reclaimed the great place and they ruled on the thrones and the bones of their ancestors.

Now, Lot, the oldest surviving son of that lineage, screamed with the pain of his own passing.

The king's screams caused surprisingly little disturbance in that dark keep. Some men, drowsing in the court under the summer stars, turned and muttered beneath their harsh woollen blankets. Others, lounging on the parapets while drinking from their leather bottles or playing at bones beside their fires, cursed the noise and kicked the hounds who tried to howl in response.

King Lot had been laid in his great bed in his great hall. A fire burned brightly beside his resting place, and the linens tangled around his arms and legs were the finest that could be provided. These things brought him no comfort. Pain tossed him from side to side, dragging his cries and his moans from his ravaged throat. But none dared approach him. Not one of the cowering women who hovered in the dark doorway brought cloth or herb to their king, even now that the swelling in his legs had so greatly increased that he could not rise. None of the men slouched at the far end of the hall so much as looked up.

Only the two chieftains who sat on the other side of the fire from the bed made any move.

Lord Pedair rubbed his eyes. He was a grey, old man now, stooped by the weight of the years. The long nights of watching had left him weary and heartsick. He had known Lot in cleaner times, when they were both stronger, better men. It was a painful thing to see what Din Eityn had become, almost as painful as to see what had happened to Lot. The king's madness had driven away all men of strength and loyalty. Instead, he had surrounded himself with the corrupt and the cringing, who would follow any order, no matter how mad, as long as they could plunder the folk of Gododdin, and anyone else who crossed their paths.

'Will he hold long enough for word to reach Camelot?' Pedair asked.

'I do not know. They are laying bets in the forecourt now.' Ruadh's mouth curled into a sneer of distaste. Time had robbed Lord Ruadh of all the hair on his head and turned his long moustaches pure white. It had not, however, clouded his eyes nor his judgment. Like Pedair beside him, Ruadh had ridden to war with Lot in aid of King Arthur. He was the only other one who offered to take the night watches with Pedair. The king could not die without witness.

Lot kicked at his coverings. His feet were so swollen the skin on them had cracked and the wounds oozed with clear matter. The stench of illness hung heavily in the great square chamber. The swelling should be lanced. There should be hot cloths and poultices.

And I do not move. Pedair's hands dangled uselessly between his knees. *That is my king and my friend there, and I do not move.*

Lot writhed, his torso twisting and his arms flailing at nothing at all. His head fell towards Pedair, and Pedair saw the king's face contorted by pain and rage, his cracked teeth bared, his eyes burning.

'Traitor!' Lot roared. 'Stinking, whoreson traitor! Come to pick over my bones, Pedair? Come to dance on my tomb!' His mouth stretched into a horrible leer. 'Stay then, vulture! Maybe she'll take a liking to you next and you'll be dancing for the devil to her tune!' He laughed, a sound more harsh and horrible than his screams. 'Dance like me!' He lifted one grotesquely swollen leg and the words died away in a scream of pain.

'How much longer can he last?' Pedair whispered when he could speak again.

Ruadh shook his bald head slowly. 'Not long. God be praised.'

'Kill them!' bellowed Lot, his hands clenching into fists, strangling nothing but air. 'God rot them! Crush them!' In the next second, his hands fell to the furs and all the anger drained from his face. 'Water,' he rasped plaintively. 'I thirst. I burn. Mercy's sake, someone bring me water.'

Pedair looked sideways at Ruadh, spat into the fire, and slowly got to his feet. A pitcher and two wooden mugs stood between the men's stools. Pedair filled one with small beer, splashing dark droplets onto the stones. Slowly, shuffling from the stiffness in his knees, he brought it to the king's bedside. Lot looked at him, and for a moment, Pedair thought he saw his liege in the depths of those fever-bright eyes. He held the tankard to Lot's lips.

Fury distorted Lot's face again, and he lashed out, grabbing and twisting at Pedair's arm. Pedair cried out in pain, and dropped the mug, splashing ale everywhere.

'Poison!' bawled Lot. 'You'd poison your king, whoreson! I'll hang your head from my gate!' He shoved Pedair, sending him reeling back towards the fire. Ruadh caught him before he stumbled into the flames and helped him to his seat again.

'He still sees.' Rubbing his wrist and panting for breath, Pedair watched the king sink back onto his bed, plucking restlessly at the furs and muttering his curses.

'But what does he see?' asked Ruadh. 'We should have sent to Camelot before this.

Pedair watched his king lashing from side to side, as if to avoid a series of blows. 'Had there been any way to do so in secret, I would have.'

'I know,' said Ruadh. 'I know.'

The king groaned, a low, harsh horrible sound and for a moment, he strained to sit up, his eyes gleaming in the firelight and his mouth gaping in an evil grin. But his strength did not hold, and Lot collapsed back onto his bed.

'You come,' the words came out between Lot's gasps for breath. 'Even now you come to me.'

The wretched king paused, listening to that voice only he could hear, and his face twisted with a deeper pain. 'No. It is not true!'

Pedair knotted his fists. How much longer could he stand

to wait? It was obscene to sit here while a strong man writhed in pain, while his hands clutched the linens and sweat ran down his brow.

'It is not true! You are not she! You are not! Oh, God, no! Morgause! Morgause! Don't leave me!'

Pedair started forward, but Ruadh laid a hand on his arm. 'Do not let him come to grips with you again, Pedair. He's killed a man in his fits. He'll do the same to you.'

'Morgause!' the king shouted. 'Morgause where are you! It is not true! It is not true!' The last word choked Lot, and the scream faded into weeping, before rising again, a cry of rage and pain and the last strength of a man trying to hold back death and despair with nothing but his own broken will.

The old men bowed their heads and as best they could, they prayed for the dawn.

TWO

'My lady? Their Majesties summon you.'

Laurel Carnbrea, until lately the Queen of Cambryn, turned away from the window that looked over Camelot's yard. The sun was just setting and the rich light of the summer's evening warmed and gilded the world. The two girls sent up from the great hall were dressed to match, in fine linen and golden girdles. Their relative youth made Laurel think they must be new to their positions. Their youth, and the way they openly looked Laurel up and down, weighing her appearance against their own. Laurel smiled a little at this. It was not these two whose judgment she needed to worry about.

'Well, Meg?' she said to her own woman. 'Am I fit to be presented?'

Meg, an aging, bone-thin woman more soberly dressed in brown and cream, looked Laurel up and down herself. Her eyes narrowed to slits, the better to discern a wrinkle in sleeve or neckline, or an ill-considered fold of cloth in Laurel's trailing skirt. For the past three hours, Meg had circled the room like a hawk. Laurel's handmaids, Plump Cryda and little brown Elsa were both flushed and fluttery from Meg's constant stream of orders intended to make sure Laurel's layers of rich dress and ornament were displayed to perfection.

All of which had made Laurel feel like nothing so much as a horse being readied for sale.

It was, however, necessary. Cambryn, the land which Laurel personified at this moment, must make a good showing of its wealth before the great court. To that end, she wore an underdress of rich, black wool that turned her translucent skin nearly pure white. Over this was laid a gown of vibrant blue silk brought from Byzantium. The sea at midday never saw such a colour. Its sleeves brushed her fingertips like the lightest of whispers and trailed down to the floor. This had been one of her mother's treasures, laid away against such a time. A heavy golden girdle with links shaped into sun disks and studded with blue Turkish glass belted her waist. This matched the necklace at her throat. Golden cuffs circled her wrists and a gold band held the delicate black veil embroidered with bright blue thread that covered Laurel's startling white-gold hair, which itself had been braided with sapphire ribbons and golden beads.

Meg had tried to get Laurel to leave behind the ring of small keys that belonged to her dowry chests, on the grounds they made her look more like a merchant's wife than a queen, but Laurel refused. She had carried keys at her waist since she was nine years old. These few were all that were left to her, but she would not lay them aside. The idea made her feel as if she were being asked to walk into the court stark naked.

At last, Meg nodded judiciously. 'You'll bring us no shame, my lady.'

'Well then.' Laurel drew herself up. 'Let us go meet the man I am to marry.'

Trusting Meg to marshal Cryda and Elsa into a proper procession to carry the betrothal gifts, Laurel schooled her expression into one of calm dignity. She lifted her hems, and followed Queen Guinevere's ladies out through the corridors of Camelot.

This was not the first time Laurel had walked these arched and painted corridors. She had lived with King Arthur's court for three years as a waiting woman to the queen. She could have chosen to stay longer, but at the time she had thought her place and her duty lay in the land where her father served as steward. Queen Guinevere had respected that decision and let her return to her father's house.

Since then, the world had turned over. Father was dead, murdered by his son and heir. War had almost come to their home, but Laurel and her sister, in concert with the queen and the knights Lancelot and Gareth, had just managed to turn it aside. For this service, Queen Guinevere, heirless and likely to remain so, had given over the throne of Cambryn to the family line of Carnbrea. She had also given Laurel's younger sister, Lynet, in marriage to the newly knighted Sir Gareth.

This tumultuous progression of events left unmarried Laurel with the title of queen, but with no current means of producing a legitimate heir. Without an heir, she could rule, but could not provide long-term stability for her now royal family, or their fractious kingdom. Even before the high king's ambassadors had come with their marriage proposal, Laurel had made up her mind to abdicate the throne in Lynet's favour. She had not wanted to give their neighbors and chieftains the chance to decide they should make the change in a less civilized fashion.

'You're being a fool, Laurel,' Lynet had said. 'You are known and respected for your strength and your wisdom. No one would dare try to bring you down.'

'Strength and wisdom are all very well, but our allies and our lords want safety. You and Gareth can give them that. I, as I am, cannot.'

'Then marry where you may stay in Dumonii lands.'

'Who, Lynet?' Laurel had replied coldly. 'After what I have done, and what they have heard, which of our worthy neighbours will have me?'

Lynet had bitten her lip at that, and made no answer.

Laurel had left the bed chamber they shared, and went to meet Sir Bedivere, the high king's ambassador in Cambryn's great hall. There, she gave her assent. She would come to Camelot and give herself in marriage to Sir Agravain, King Arthur's nephew, the second of the sons of Lot, and heir to the throne of Gododdin.

Now, Laurel descended the curving stairs at a sedate pace, following Guinevere's ladies and attempting not to tread on her own hems. She tried once again to call Sir Agravain's face to mind, and once again, she failed. Sir Gawain, the eldest of Lot's sons, she remembered well enough. Dark-haired and handsome, with a ready smile, Sir Gawain was the subject of great gossip among all the ladies of the court, and not a few of the men. He had been the one to head the procession that met Laurel at the quay. There, Laurel found his smile and charm had not dimmed during her absence, and this cheered her nervous spirits.

Sir Geraint, the third of the brothers, Laurel remembered mostly as a figure in the distance while training for war, or participating in some race or game. He was silent to the point of taciturn, but if one looked into his clear blue eyes, one could see the depth of warmth and humour there. Sir Gareth, the youngest, and now her brother by law, was an unduly handsome, cheerful, surprisingly stubborn man, dizzy in love with her sister.

Laurel had asked Gareth about his brother Agravain. She watched his face while he chose his words with utmost care.

'His wits are keener than any man's I know. He is brave, in his way . . . He keeps much to himself.' Gareth hesitated.

His lower lip tucked itself beneath the upper, as if he had meant to bite it, but stopped himself. Laurel saw anew how young this husbandman was. 'He will not suffer any fool, and acts more on his own counsel than that of others. This makes him seem hard. It is to my shame that I cannot say whether this is real or merely what he wishes men to see.'

With all this echoing in her memory, Laurel Carnbrea allowed herself to be led to the doors of Camelot's great hall. The elaborately carved portals stood closed, flanked by an honour guard of six soldiers in shirts of shining mail with red ribbons tied about their spears. Between them stood four pages, all of them as nervously solemn as only young boys can be. This bright assemblage all bowed to Laurel and her entourage, and Laurel nodded solemnly in response.

Let this ceremony begin.

As if hearing her thought, the boys lined up and all four of them pulled open the doors to reveal the splendour of the great hall.

Dazzling light from torches, fires and tapers spilled out over Laurel in a wave of warmth. Gold flashed everywhere, reflecting the brilliant light and the stately music that rose in solemn and disciplined measure from harp, pipe and deep-bellied drum. Dazzled after the dim corridors, all Laurel could make out at first was a blur of scented colours; waxen scarlet, rush-tinged green, tallow blues, smoky grey and black, all the shades of stone and skin blended with lavender and lemon.

All this wreathed her round in a garland of heat and rustling cloth, setting her blood pounding. It seemed she had to step down a long way before the thin sole of her slipper found the mosaiced floor and she was able to walk forward. Laurel steeled herself and kept her pace stately. She knew her rank and worth. She was the one who had been entreated to do this thing. No one here would see her awed.

The whole of Camelot's court filled that hall. Where before

she had travelled dim corridors of stone, now Laurel walked down a straight aisle of particoloured humanity. Dark Britons and pale Saxons; the knights of the Round Table in their cloaks of madder red; lords and ladies in linen and silk, silver, bronze and gold. All of them watched her, craning their necks even as they made their polite bows. Despite the drum beats and lilting pipes, Laurel clearly heard her heart hammering.

What do they see, all these people? What have they heard of me?

It does not matter. I am here at the king's command and the queen's behest.

She fixed her gaze on the dais. It was no less crowded than the rest of the hall, but at least these were faces she knew. Her dazzled and unnerved eyes could rest a moment on Queen Guinevere. Dignified and tall beside the High King, the queen wore her raiment of scarlet, white and gold easily. Her swan crown circled her wide brow lightly, as the companion torque did her throat.

Arthur, High King of all the Britons, also wore his wealth and dignity with an ease that came from familiarity and assurance. The scarlet tunic, the dragon crown decked with rubies, and the dragon torque at his throat; these were symbols of a majesty that was both God-given and hard earned. Awareness of this truth gave Arthur his majesty as much as any show of wealth and temporal power.

At the king's left stood the crooked seneschal, Sir Kai. In his black garb and gold chain of office, he was a shadow waiting behind the light of kingship. The broad, handsome form of Sir Gawain, Arthur's heir, all but obscured the seneschal, but Laurel knew Sir Kai watched her approach carefully. Sir Kai watched all things carefully and did not remain silent about what he saw. A fresh, cold, finger of fear touched Laurel's spine.

Beside Gawain, stood Sir Bedivere, King Arthur's one-handed ambassador who had brought the king's offer to

Laurel, and beside him stood the bronze and gold form of Sir Lancelot whom she remembered well, standing like a living testament to knightly glory.

But beside Sir Gawain stood another man. He was as lean as the seneschal, but as straight and black-haired as Sir Gawain. A Round Table knight's madder red cloak fell across the shoulders of his green and silver tunic.

That was him. That was Sir Agravain, and Laurel had no time for more than that single glance. She had reached the dais now and must kneel in respect and obedience.

The musicians made their final roll and flourish. Her veil fell over her face, making a screen for her heated cheeks. Her breath was coming short. She needed to calm herself. She was no nervous child. She could not be seen to be afraid.

Footsteps touched against marble. A pair of embroidered slippers appeared in Laurel's field of vision. A fine hand, the palm marred by some old stain, reached down to raise her up. The smile Queen Guinevere gave Laurel was small but fond, and showed mostly in her shining grey eyes.

'My lord king,' said Queen Guinevere in her mellow voice. 'I ask you to make welcome Laurel Carnbrea, the lady of Cambryn.'

Arthur inclined his greying head regally. It was easy to discern the humour and sympathy in his bright blue gaze. 'Be welcome once more, Laurel Carnbrea. May God bless your arrival and the purpose which brings you here.' These words were pitched to carry, a speech for the court, but the understanding in his eyes was for her, and for that moment at least, Laurel felt some measure of composure return. 'Let me now make known to you Agravain *mach* Lot, knight of the Round Table, and heir to Gododdin.'

The brief calm the king imparted deserted her immediately. Laurel's pulse jumped and her breath stuck in her throat. Sir Agravain walked down the four dais steps and for the first time, Laurel stood face to face with the man who would be her husband.

Sharp as a sword, the thought flitted through her mind. All about him was wiry and lean, as if God turned miserly with this creation's flesh. Like his brothers, Sir Agravain was tall and had a wealth of raven-black hair, but where Gawain and Gareth were broad and open, Sir Agravain was closed. His face, while regular in its features, held no hint of either frankness or good humour. His dark eyes remained cool as they looked her over. Laurel was sure he missed no more details of her person than Meg had.

Despite her best resolve, Laurel's composure trembled. At once, she fell back on ceremony, and made a deep curtsey. 'God be with you, Sir Agravain,' she said, grateful that her voice remained steadier than her nerve.

Sir Agravain returned a deep bow. 'And with you, Lady Laurel.' His voice was lighter than she expected. Each word was clean and precise, with only a trace of the accents of the north. 'It is a great honour you do me and my house.'

She met his earth-brown eyes again. They seemed clear and honest, but she could see nothing deeper than his words in them. All about Sir Agravain was shut tight and bolted. She thought again of Gareth's words. Here was a man who would show no more than he wanted the world to see.

Manners. Manners. They are all watching you. Indeed, while she hesitated, the queen's smile had faltered the smallest amount.

'It is my hope you will accept this token from my house to yours.' Laurel signalled Meg to bring her maids forward. Between them, Cryda and Elsa carried a package wrapped in undyed cloth. This Meg unfolded to reveal a garment of saffron-dyed silk stitched over with costly threads in many colours.

Laurel had carefully questioned Gareth regarding Gododdin's

marriage customs. As it transpired, Gareth had left his home while still a child, and so knew very little first hand. He had, however, told her tradition dictated that the bride give her bridegroom his wedding tunic. So, with patience, if not with enthusiasm, Laurel set about making the garment. She now let Meg lay it across her outstretched arms so that she in turn could give it to Sir Agravain. Its saffron silk had come from Cambryn's treasury, of the same origin as her blue. She had seen it cut generously, broad-collared, full-sleeved, and long-hemmed. Under her direction, and with her help, it had been richly worked with threads of emerald, scarlet, cobalt and gold, to shape a design of open-winged falcons, which were the sigil of Gododdin's high house, and of sea waves, the sign of her own.

Agravain let her lay the garment in his hands. He looked down at this product of so much labour with his closed and shallow gaze. 'Again, you honour me, my lady. I thank you.' He bowed once more, and she made an answering curtsey, and then they looked at each other; the pair of them, surrounded by all the glory of Camelot's court, to be husband and wife before tomorrow was finished, and neither found a single word to say.

Blessedly, the queen broke the silence before the moment could become truly awkward. She took both Laurel's hands in hers.

'Come, Laurel, sit with us.'

So saying, Queen Guinevere led Laurel up the steps of the dais. The servants at once began their complex dance, moving the thrones back to their place of state, bringing the carved chairs for the guests who would eat at the high table. Laurel sat at the queen's right hand. Agravain sat at the king's left, after his brother, Gawain. This removal meant further conversation between them would be impossible for the length of the meal. Laurel found she was grateful for this mercy of

ceremony. Becoming tongue-tied in front of the entire court
had left her shamed. She sat on her softly cushioned chair
in uneasy silence while the trestles and boards were brought
and the richly embroidered cloths spread for the feast.

Queen Guinevere always seemed to have the gift of reading
thoughts, and Laurel's were no secret to her. 'Do not worry
yourself,' murmured the queen, touching Laurel's hand
lightly. 'You will find your way.' Other ladies and their lords
began to mount the dais, pausing to make their obeisance
before they took their place at the high table. 'Now, here is
one you must meet,' said the queen, brightly. 'This is the
Lady Rhian, wife to our Gawain.'

Lady Rhian was a woman of medium stature, no longer
young, but not yet to her middle years. What made her stun-
ning was her red gold hair that hung down to her ankles,
woven with gold threads and pearls. The lady looked fair
and open, a good match for her husband, but there was,
Laurel thought, something delicate about her, a hesitation of
movement and smile, perhaps or a faded colour to her eye
that made Laurel wonder if she was fully well.

'I am glad to meet you, Lady Laurel,' said Rhian as she
took her seat. 'As we will soon be sisters, it is my great hope
we will also be friends.'

The smile which accompanied these words reached Lady
Rhian's eyes, and Laurel dearly hoped this was not simple
politeness. She needed friends in this court to which she was
about to become even more intimately allied. The fact that
as the wife of Sir Gawain, Lady Rhian was heir to Guinevere's
swan throne as Gawain was heir to Arthur's dragon, was also
not to be lightly passed over.

It was high summer and all the bounty of the season was
brought forth to the table to the flourish of pipe and drum.
Laurel had lived before at the court, and her home was a
rich one, but she had never seen such a meal. She had not

thought herself to have much appetite, but was soon tempted
into tasting each dish that passed her. There was partridge
boiled in wine and vinegar and hare stuffed with nuts and
pine kernels. The puree of lettuce and onions accompanied
a dish of lentils and chestnuts flavoured so strongly with
cinnamon and pepper that Laurel's eyes began to water. There
was also roasted suckling pig, a patina of elderberries, and a
wealth of risen breads for sopping the gravies and jellies. All
this was followed by honey omelettes and honey cakes.
Ciders, wines and ales were poured out fresh with each
remove.

Lady Rhian proved a good table companion. She spoke of
small, light matters to which Laurel could give easy reply.
They talked of the excellent food and wines, the rigours of
the journey, of Laurel's time in Camelot as a waiting woman
and how it compared with Rhian's own. From the sound of
it, little had changed. The queen remained a good, if exacting,
mistress, and treated her ladies with the honour due to their
various ranks, but one could still find oneself surrounded by
more cackling hens than one might like.

Rhian's conversation was as welcome to Laurel as her own
unexpected appetite had been. The two combined to keep
her from casting too many glances towards the end of the
table where the lords and knights sat, trying to see Sir
Agravain. What attempts she did make proved all in vain.
The profiles of the queen, the king and Sir Gawain sheltered
her betrothed from her inquisitive, and somewhat furtive,
gaze. She could see nothing except a lean brown hand and
a green sleeve reaching occasionally for his cup or portion
of food.

Maddening. Despite the sweetness of the cakes, Laurel felt
her mouth pucker tartly.

A shrill twitter caught her ear. Laurel became quickly and
unpleasantly aware that down the length of the tables,

members of the beauteous flock of noble ladies smirked and
nudged one another, making certain she knew they shared
the joke made of her expression. Laurel's jaw tightened,
which only produced more smiles and winks from those
nearest. They touched and nudged their companions to make
sure this further bit of humour traveled the length of the
high table and back again. Someone let loose a fresh, trilling
laugh and Laurel winced as if it pricked her skin. Rhian alone
maintained her countenance, although a knowing light shone
in her eyes. Laurel tried not to let this evidence of suppressed
humour deepen her rancour. It was at least better than the
poorly smothered laughter further down the table.

With the feast now reduced to bones, rinds and crumbs,
Laurel hoped, more than a little desperately, that the tables
would all be cleared for the entertainment to begin in earnest.
The revelers would divert at least some attention from her.
She cast about quickly for a new conversation topic to raise
with Rhian. But before she lit on anything, fresh movement
turned everyone's attention to the centre of the high table.
Sir Kai was climbing slowly to his feet. Leaning hard on his
crutch, he raised his gilded cup high.

'With the permission of our king and queen,' he bowed
humbly in their direction, 'let me now offer up a toast to Sir
Agravain and Lady Laurel.'

Even as the cheer reverberated through the hall from all
assembled, Laurel's heart sank through the floor.

How did I forget this?

No great occasion, nor any light one, passed without Sir
Kai making a sport of it. His barbs and skewers had reduced
more than one proud reputation to a nine-days' joke. Laurel
had believed herself well-prepared for her return to court,
but her careful mind had not let her consider this tiny detail.
Sir Kai was sure to make one of his speeches on the theme
of her marriage.

Rhian touched Laurel's hand. 'Endure,' she whispered. 'It is expected, and soon over.'

Around her, the ladies smiled each according to their kind. Laurel saw superior sympathy, veiled anticipation, and open relish. Their knowing glances grew sharp, despite Rhian's frown, and the sterner, far more regal disapproval that had taken hold in the queen's manner. Sir Kai, however, was not looking at Queen Guinevere, or Laurel, or even at Agravain. He smiled out over the court and sipped delicately at his cup, a player ready to take up a much anticipated part. All the gathering settled back. No musician reached for his instrument. Every face turned towards the seneschal.

Beneath her silken sleeves, Laurel's hands clenched until her nails dug into her palms.

Sir Kai's smile broadened, and he began.

'What grander honour could be offered to a noble woman of the queen's own country than to be given in most holy matrimony to our mighty king's own nephew?' Shouts of assent rose up. Laurel's gaze flickered to where Agravain sat. She saw nothing but his hand on the table, the fingers curled, as hers were, into a fist. For the first time, she felt a slight chord of sympathy vibrate between her and her promised husband.

Sir Kai swallowed his wine, assuming an air of thoughtfulness. 'Though between the noble, varied and prolonged deeds of Sir Gawain and Sir Gareth, it's not surprising Sir Agravain had to send so far for a . . . suitable wife.'

Laughter rolled out warm, full and piquantly tinged. It was obviously an old joke, but still much appreciated. Even the king did not entirely suppress his smile. Gawain leaned forward so he could to roll his eyes and wink at Rhian, who blew out a long sigh.

'I would hasten to reassure the bride that no deeds such as those achieved by his roving brothers are sung of Sir

Agravain,' Kai went on. 'Knowing that such glory is a most oppressive burden, he has sensibly shielded himself from it. Much as an oyster shields itself from sea water by never leaving its shell.'

How did Sir Agravain receive all this? Laurel could not see. She could only see the king smile benignly. The queen, on the other hand, was making an attempt at good humour, but her brows drew more closely together as Sir Kai warmed to his recitation.

'But the trifling fact that Sir Agravain has remained his usual oyster-self about both bride and wedding, has in no way stemmed the flow of wise words through our court.' Sir Kai cast an owlish glance towards Laurel. Laurel could not keep her mouth from hardening, even while she prayed her cheeks would not shame her by blushing. The ladies tittered delicately, many making a great show of attempting to decently suppress their laughter behind jewelled hands.

'It is, after all,' he continued, his voice subtly changing, both warming and sharpening, 'absolutely necessary that both king and bridegroom have the finest and most learned of advisors to study such matters.'

There was a little more laughter at this, but it began to sound nervous. The glances between the ladies showed their humour growing uncertain. Laurel felt herself sit up a little straighter.

What is the man doing?

'Let me call your attention to the example of Lady Aylwen, one of our court's most tireless counsellors.' Sir Kai bowed towards a black-haired, round-faced woman with mottled skin and watery blue eyes who sat three chairs away from Rhian. 'By tireless exercise of her peerless wisdom, Lady Aylwen would have us all to understand, as she does, that this marriage was a love match conceived – forgive me, Lady Aylwen, perhaps one of us should have chosen a more fitting word –' A bark of laughter went up from somewhere in the hall. 'When Lady Laurel was here in Her Majesty's service. I must congratulate the lady on the keenness of this observation. So sharp is her sight, that she ferreted out the existence of a passionate affair without recourse to witness, or writing . . . indeed without reference to any communication of any kind between the principals that could be recalled by any other person. I am astounded!' Sir Kai laid his hand over his heart. 'However, I must say, it speaks well of Lady Laurel herself. That she struggled so long and so silently against such a passion as Sir Agravain is known to arouse in all tender hearts surely speaks of a strength of character seldom known in woman or man! Ah, well. The waters are cold in the Dumonii lands. Perhaps that accounts for it.'

More laughter rippled through the court, a little darker than it had been, and touched by the slightest edge of malice. Lady Aylwen's mouth pursed so tightly her lips turned quite white.

Sir Kai paused only a heartbeat to take in this seemingly satisfactory sight. 'But even more surprising were the deep observations of Lord Derryth.' The seneschal waved his cup towards a brown-bearded man in linens of fawn and ochre. 'Whom I confess that I had underestimated. So rare, and so sagacious a counsellor is he that he was able to accurately calculate the whole of the price the lady had paid to be married to the high king's nephew, and to whom she had paid it, without having been privy to any one of the negotiations. I am sorry to report, too, that Lord Derryth finds her a very poor bargainer as she could obtain no better set of goods for her outpouring of wealth than Sir Agravain. Indeed, he most generously offered himself as better suited to the exquisite tastes of so rare a bride.'

Fresh mirth erupted around the hall. Lord Derryth was elbowed in the ribs as he laughed, but it was plain from his thunderous expression that the laughter was forced. The king was looking on him with a mild and interested expression. Derryth did not miss this, and instantly hid his face by downing a large quantity of wine.

'Not to be outdone in these counsels – for you know, such counsellors must ever vie with each other like knights on a festival day – Lady Moire has added her considerable wisdom to the debate.' Sir Kai gestured broadly to a bony woman with a long, needle-thin nose who sat at a table below the dais, and who had gone as white as the linen of her embroidered veil. 'It is well known that when any find themselves considering matters for which no fact can be perceived by other, dimmer eyes, Lady Moire is the first who should be consulted. Where others see only air, this grave lady sees the whole of the tale pure and perfect laid out before her.

'Lady Moire tells us with absolute certainty that the bride is possessed of the power of witchcraft, and it is this that made the match, rather than the wisdom of their majesties. Witchcraft!' Kai spread his arms wide in astonishment. 'The signs and symbols of that science being known so intimately to Lady Moire that she can discern them across the length of our island. Such heights of wisdom are beyond the scope of my feeble imaginations, and I am left truly humbled in her wake.' Sir Kai set his cup down and laid his hand on his breast, bowing so deeply to Lady Moire that his hair brushed the tablecloth. By the time he straightened, Moire had gone from white to red. Indeed, thought Laurel, the lady looked in danger of succumbing to apoplexy.

'Think on it, as Lady Moire did, while the rest of us sat dumb and blind. Let us now think on this same Lady Laurel, who waits so patiently here. Lady Laurel, so obviously impoverished, and so enfeebled in her temporal powers by the great peace she and her sister wrought against the king's enemies. So crabbed and unlovely is she, with such squintings and pockmarks, that she must hunch over a bowl of herbs and mumble spells in order to captivate a man so rare, so highly prized, so besieged by lovers, as is Sir Agravain!'

The whole court was in stitches now, with ladies laughing into their sleeves, knights and lords slapping each other on their backs, their guffaws ringing from the walls. Queen Guinevere did not, however, join in the general merriment. Her frown had not changed, but it was no longer directed at the seneschal. Instead, she turned her quiet, even displeasure towards the Lady Moire. Moire did not miss this and attempted to hold herself upright under the double weight of the queen's glare and the court's laughter rolling over her. King Arthur leaned close to murmur something into the queen's ear. As Guinevere bowed her head to listen, Laurel was at last able to glimpse Sir Agravain.

Sir Agravain watched Sir Kai, his eyes narrowed, and his whole body tensed and ready. But ready for what? Challenge? Flight? No, not flight. There was none of that about him. Sir Agravain was holding himself ready in case he must act, while at the same time judging how to act, acutely aware of where he was and who he was. She felt certain of this, as she was certain of the stone floor beneath her feet. Then, Gawain and the king shifted their positions to converse with each other, and Laurel could see nothing but that lean, brown hand, still on the tablecloth, still curled into its fist. Still waiting.

Kai, evidently pleased by his success, had opened his mouth again.

'Enough, Kai,' announced the king firmly, and he raised his cup to the musicians who waited attentively near the hearths. They struck up a merry tune at once, and now the servants did come forward to clear away cloths and tables to make room for the brightly clad dancers to assemble in the centre of the hall. King Arthur gave his hand to the queen to raise her to her feet while their thrones were moved forward a little so they could better view the entertainment. The great crowd of the court stood as well, shuffling, murmuring, reassembling themselves into new, smaller gatherings for enjoyment and conversation. Rhian touched Laurel's hand and gestured for her to come a few steps down the dais to where she could stand amid the other ladies.

'May I ask what your impression is?' Laurel did not need Rhian's nod to know she meant her impression of Sir Agravain.

'I do not know,' murmured Laurel, but this was only partly the truth. 'You have lived beside him. What manner of man is he?'

Lady Rhian hesitated a long moment. *For my sake or for the sakes of all these listening ears?* Women pressed close. They were surrounded by rustling skirts and light ladies' whispers.

'He is an honourable man,' said Rhian at last. 'He will not give much demonstration when he is pleased, and that can make him seem hard.'

Laurel frowned. This was very near what Gareth had said, and she could see that like Gareth, Rhian held something back.

She could see Sir Agravain easily now. He stood on the edge of the dais in stern conversation with Sir Kai, who still had his crooked smile on his face. Gawain was there too, saying something, but whatever his brother was telling him, it did not effect Sir Agravain's wary and disapproving countenance.

What is it? What about you has everyone so careful of their words?

As this thought formed in her mind, Sir Agravain turned, and saw her watching him.

A flush instantly burned Laurel's cheeks, but she forced herself to hold steady. Sir Agravain's brows drew together, slightly puzzled. Displeased? She could not tell. She inclined her head towards him, and he did the same to her.

Rhian touched Laurel's arm, giving her a valid excuse to turn away. Two heavily carved wooden chairs with blue cushions had been set on the dais, two steps below the thrones. Sir Agravain caught her eye again, and somehow Laurel felt the slightest air of challenge from him as he walked down the dais steps to stand beside one. Head held high, Laurel allowed Rhian to escort her down the steps. She curtsied gravely to the knight, aware of the queen's eyes, the king's, the whole of the court's watching her every move. She took her seat, investing each movement with a lifetime's worth of practice at dignity. Although his expression did not appear to change, Laurel felt an air of amusement brimming just below the surface, and the corners of her mouth turned up in a tentative smile. Sir Agravain saw this, and bowed deeply, holding her gaze as he made the courtesy. Only then did he sit down beside her.

Once more Laurel found her heart quickening and a faint feeling, almost too tentative to truly be called hope, fluttered within her.

A clap sounded overhead, probably made by the king, and the musicians struck up a jaunty air and the assembled entertainers began their dance. They were a large troupe, six men in blue tunics and six women in cream gowns. They skipped and slipped through their formal patterns with merry grace, now bowing, now turning, all to the happy accompaniment of bells and tambours, cymbals, pipe and harp.

Beside her, Sir Agravain sat rigid, formal and correct. Now that the first tentative exchange had been made between them, Laurel found herself restless. Sitting still felt increasingly impossible. She should say something, do something, and yet she could not. Gathered about them was every listening ear and watching eye that could possibly be crammed into this suddenly too gaudy, too warm, too bright hall. All of them potential gossip-mongers with nothing better

to do than to note how she and Sir Agravain sat together
and did not speak, did not even look at each other.

Laurel had to stop herself from grinding her teeth in her
frustration.

At last, Sir Agravain broke the silence. 'I trust that your
journey was not overly difficult.'

'No, an' I thank you.' Laurel replied smoothly, ruthlessly
smothering the frustration that churned inside of her. 'We
had good seas, and your brother was well prepared to escort
us from the port.'

'Yes.' Sir Agravain's glance slipped to where his brother
stood at the side of the dais looking over their heads, probably at Rhian. 'Gawain is famed for his preparations.'

Silence fell once more. The dancers on the floor came
together, palm to palm, turned towards the dais and skipped
two steps forward and two back. Turned again, clapping
merrily as they did.

Say something! Laurel ordered herself. 'I have brought with
me a letter from your brother Gareth.'

Agravain's brows rose a hair's breadth. 'A minor miracle,
for Gareth to take pen in hand. The estate of marriage has
made a man of him.'

'Say rather he feared what you would think if he did not
write so manfully,' replied Laurel, unable to keep the tartness
out of her rejoinder, even as she instantly wished she could
take it back.

Whatever other effect they may have had, her words did
make Sir Agravain look directly at her. This time she thought
she saw a new expression there, a change in the set of his
shoulders and the way creases met at the corners of his eyes.

'You will forgive me, my lady,' he said softly. 'I am not
. . . I am not practised in the ways of courtship.'

'There is no need to make apology, my lord,' she said,
lifting her chin to hide the unexpected relief she felt at these

gently serious words. 'I fear I have never been able to master those arts of glancing and smiling that are considered necessary when responding to the attentions of gallants.'

'Good. Above all things, I feared to disappoint on the field of light flirtation.'

This was spoken with a humour so dry it might have crumbled to dust, but there was something underneath it, something tentative that might have been a crack in Agravain's shuttered self.

'I am in no way disappointed, my lord,' answered Laurel.

Sir Agravain remained silent for a moment at this, gazing down at her, his face set as stone.

'Thank you,' he said, at last.

Then, he turned back to the dancers, weaving an elaborate figure-eight pattern on the floor. He fixed his attention unwaveringly on them, looking neither left nor right, his mouth tightly closed. Sir Kai's image of the oyster flitted through Laurel's mind and she felt the breath of gossip curling around her neck like a cold draft. She gripped the chair arm tightly.

Mother Mary, why did I agree to this?

Memory overwhelmed her, in a single great flood, and suddenly she was in her home, in her private room, standing by the fire with Lynet at her back, flushed with her own frustration.

'Laurel, why are you doing this?'

Laurel just looked at her and said nothing. The blood drained slowly from Lynet's face. 'Oh, Laurel, not because I married Gareth.'

'No, sister, but because you married him under the aegis of a bargain with the sea. There is a spirit watching over you now, and if that spirit decides the bargain is not kept . . .' Laurel turned away. 'What then, sister? You will not even know you have broken faith until disaster falls.'

'I trust Gareth's heart, Laurel.' Lynet opened her arms. 'Do you not trust mine?'

Laurel did not move. Lynet wanted her embrace, to be told all was well. But Laurel could not give her that, not without her understanding. 'I trust you as I trust myself, Sister. It is the sea I do not trust. It is the blood we come from.' She watched Lynet's eyes dart eastward, towards the distant ocean. 'You see? You fear even now we are over-heard by the unseen. No. If we are to hold this land we've been given, we must have more earthly guardians, and we must have legitimate heirs who belong fully to the land, and we must have them soon.'

'Who belong fully to the land. What do you mean by that, Laurel?'

Laurel had not been able to answer, and Lynet had stepped forward. 'It's not me you're afraid of, Laurel is it? It's not anything I've done. You're afraid of yourself, that you might . . . that you might go back to our grandmother.'

For this was the secret between them, the truth that hovered just beneath the surface in their family. Their mother, the beautiful Lady Morwenna, was no mortal woman. Morwenna had been the daughter of the *bucca-gwidden*, the White Spirit of the Sea. The ocean itself was their lineage, and the power and the compulsion of it sang in each of them.

But most strongly in Laurel, for she was first born. It was the sea's lineage that gave her hair the colour of sea foam and eyes of pale agate green. It was the sea's heritage that allowed her to speak to the wind and to work upon the invisible world with a word and a gesture.

Laurel bowed her head, biting her lip. 'I will try, Lynet. I swear I will. But it has been hard.' She trembled. 'Since Morgaine the Sleepless forced me to draw on the legacy of our blood last year, the sea has pulled more even strongly.'

Last year Morgaine had attempted to overthrow the rule of Cambryn. She had succeeded in causing their father's death. She had almost brought open war to their country. It was their mother's legacy, and Laurel's workings, that had prevented that.

But it was a struggle to live in the mortal world while feeling the power of the immortal and the invisible. That struggle had weakened their mother, causing her to die after the birth of her third child. It was the struggle Laurel had felt in some form every day since then.

If that struggle was to end her life as well, it would not be before she had done all she could to secure their kingdom for Lynet and her heirs.

Laurel could not stand apart from her sister any longer. She moved close to Lynet, taking her outstretched hands and folding them closed. 'Lynet,' she spoke to those hands. She did not have the strength to meet her sister's eyes. 'Let me do what I must do, and let me face myself and my fate, as you must now face yours.'

'Not alone, Laurel.'

Now Laurel was able to look up, to show Lynet the tears shining in her eyes. 'No, not alone, my sister. Not while you live. But on my own nonetheless.'

Lynet embraced her, long and tightly, as if it was for the last time. When she straightened, Laurel saw in Lynet the queen she must now become. 'Make your contract, sister,' Lynet said firmly. 'I will stand by you.'

Now Lynet was scores of miles away, and Laurel sat amid strangers. The dancers had joined hands, women on one side, men on the other, to trip down the hall. Here beside her was the man she must depend upon to impart the safety she sought for her sister and her home, and she couldn't find a way to talk with him. Laurel was ready to curse each one of the dancers, and the whole of the court into the bargain. What way was this to begin? Surrounded by hawks, ravens and hounds in their gaudy clothes, waiting for any tit-bit they could snatch up to worry over and tear to pieces. How was she to understand anything of this man? How could he speak for himself, let alone have anyone speak about him? Tomorrow she would be married, married, before God and the law, and she knew nothing, nothing at all of the man!

The dance finished with a great ringing of cymbals and patter of drums, and all the dancers made their courtesies to the dais. Laurel was jolted out of her thoughts and her applause was tardy. Was Sir Agravain looking at her? She didn't dare look at him. She had already given the court so much to talk about . . .

'Now, my lord king, with your permission, I believe we should excuse Lady Laurel. It has been a long day, and she should be allowed to rest before the morrow.'

The queen. This was Queen Guinevere speaking and Queen Guinevere was excusing her. Laurel stood and turned, and for a moment, she met the queen's calm, empathetic gaze. Rhian stood beside her. Laurel had not even seen her move. She hoped both women could see the mute gratitude in her own expression before she knelt. She could go back to her room, to the company of her own women, back where she could think clearly again.

'Of course,' King Arthur was saying. 'I look forward to your attendance on the morrow. Sir Kai, escort the ladies back to their chambers.'

Sir Kai bowed as well as his crutch permitted and Laurel's fists tightened again. *What are you doing, Your Majesty?* There was something meaningful in the king's countenance, but she could not study it. She must curtsey to Sir Agravain, who remained correct and impassive, watching her with his narrow eyes.

Laurel made herself move. *Lift hems. Watch the steps. Don't stumble.*

Walk the whole, interminable length of the hall, feel the eyes, the endless eyes, watching and watching. Behind her, the order was given for more music, which muffled the murmurs, but they were there like a current of air, incomprehensible and inescapable. She breathed them in, they brushed her skin. She kept her gaze ahead. The doors got closer with every step. She felt, rather than saw, Meg and her handmaids walking behind. Loyal, intelligent Meg, guarding her back, and before her, moving briskly despite his crutch, walked the seneschal. His keen gaze slid this way and that, taking note of who was speaking, who was listening, and who was pretending to do neither. There was power in the seneschal's gaze. Wherever it lit, curious eyes turned away. Ladies ducked behind their lords, and lords behind their friends.

Sir Kai the Jester, and Kai the Cruel, she'd heard him called. Kai the Cruel who had nonetheless contrived to warn her of the worst of the gossip slithering through the stream of rumour that watered the high court.

The pages opened the doors, the guards saluted, the doors closed, and there was nothing around them but cool stone. Laurel walked forward into the blessedly dim and silent corridor. She drew in a great breath of cold, fresh air and let it out slowly.

Sir Kai cocked his head towards her. 'My lady seems a trifle piqued.'

'And what do you make of it, my lord seneschal?'

Kai shrugged one shoulder. 'That depends on what the reason may be. If it be the wine or the company I fear there is little that can be done. It was the best our poor house had to offer.' His face was utterly serious, but his eyes gleamed.

They walked on for a moment, his thumping crutch and

shuffling foot making a counterpoint for her rustling skirts and lightly pattering soles. If she had asked any in the glittering hall behind them, they would have said the last person she should confide in was this man. And yet his speech had given her warning about who she should particularly watch in the court. That would seem to mark him as a friend, and she very much needed friends. 'Perhaps,' she ventured, though it took every ounce of nerve she had left. 'It is because none here see fit to say more than two words to me about the man I am to marry.'

'Ah.'

He said nothing more for another score of paces. Long enough for Laurel's temper to reassert itself. 'What? Does the subject silence even you, Sir Kai?'

Kai's harsh features softened for just a moment. 'I fear it does,' he answered quietly. The keen edge was gone from his voice, as if he had just sheathed the knife of his spirits. 'You see, my lady, none wish to lie to you about Sir Agravain, but none know the exact truth about him.'

It was too much. At the foot of the stairs, Laurel turned and faced him. 'If you seek to soothe me, my lord, riddles are a bad way to begin.'

'It is not in my nature to soothe, as you may have noted. No.' He sighed. 'You want the truth?' He turned all the power of his gaze upon her. Laurel met it, matched it, and Sir Kai nodded. 'Very well. My nephew, your husband-to-be, is cold, difficult, acerbic, short-tempered and hard-headed. He is possessed of the second sharpest wit in the whole of Camelot, and cares little for whom he wounds with it if they strike him as foolish. This includes his brothers, and I would not expect it to except you. The only reason he is not possessed of the reputation for raillery that some are . . .' here Sir Kai smiled with bitter modesty, 'is that there are few he cares to talk to, or at.' He looked at her, waiting for her face to betray her heart. Laurel held herself impassive, waiting for him to finish. In response to her silence, Sir Kai's voice dropped to so low a whisper, Laurel had to lean close to hear it at all. 'He is also a man of deep and closely held feeling. He loves, my lady. Hard and fearfully. He would die for any of his brothers, without question, or for his poor, crippled uncle. He alone made a last stand to help his father who had gone mad. He failed, but he was the one who tried, and though I may be the only one who does, I believe it was done out of love.'

For a long moment, Laurel could not speak. When words did come to her again, they were only grave formalities. She hoped the seneschal understood she meant them. 'Thank you, Sir Kai, for your honesty.'

'I owe that much to my nephew, Lady. Let me tell you this, too.' His whisper was the soft sound of that knife sliding once more from its sheath. 'What I have never seen Agravain do is forgive.' He stepped back, bowing once again with too-elaborate courtesy. 'Now I beg your pardon, my lady. I must resume my duties.'

With that, Sir Kai turned, and left Laurel alone with Meg in the dim and empty corridor. Fear bit into Laurel then, fear and loneliness as she watched the lame knight limp away.

'Well,' breathed Meg. 'What are we to make of *that*?'

'We will see, Meg,' Laurel murmured. 'We will see.'

Laurel and her ladies continued up the stairs, and reached the shelter of the apartment they had been allotted. While Meg directed Cryda and Elsa to build up the fire and light the candles and braziers, Laurel drifted toward the window. The shutters were closed against the coming night, but she folded them open. She wanted the fresh air against her skin after being so long closed in the great hall. She wanted to think about what she had seen and done, and all the things that had been said to her.

The night was dry outside, but would not stay so. She could smell rain on the wind and the moon, a fattening crescent, was already drawing a veil of clouds across its face as if to make itself decent. The diamond stars shone dim from behind the high haze. There was little movement down in the darkened yard. The court was either at celebration, or asleep.

Then, a shadowed form caught Laurel's eye. It stood still, so it had taken her time to realize it was not a stack of wood, or a stock or stone. It was a man. Laurel looked harder. It was a man holding a white staff, and staring up at her window. At her.

Startled, Laurel looked down on Merlin the sorcerer.

He wore his black robes and cap, as he always did. His beard was as white as his staff. Laurel drew back, but he made no answering move, just stood like a forlorn lover gazing up at his beloved. She could not think what to do. This was so strange, so absurd, her thoughts refused to compass it.

Then, slowly, King Arthur's cunning man turned away, shaking his head. Stooped and slow like the old man he was, Merlin walked across the yard into the thickening darkness.

Laurel swallowed. Her throat had gone completely dry. She lifted her hands to fold the shutters closed against what she had just seen, and she saw her hands were shaking.

'Is something the matter, my lady?' demanded Meg.

'No.' Laurel collected herself. 'Nothing.'

She latched the shutters firmly and faced the warm and brightly lit room, and the familiar faces of her women. 'Nothing at all.'

THREE

Summer's short night settled in over the rough northern lands. In one of the country's few broad valleys waited a camp of armed men. They slept deeply, or kept watch beside their fires, making, mending and talking as soldiers at rest do. This was not a place for war, but an occasion of parley between would-be allies, and the men were easy in their minds and actions. They trusted their ultimate protection to their lady, though in the darkness none could see her. They knew she was with them, and that was enough.

A newcomer to the camp might have been hard pressed to choose which was the lady's shelter. There was no queenly enclosure, no bright flag or special guard, only a simple pavilion of wood and well-tanned leather. The lady, Morgaine, called Morgaine the Goddess and Morgaine the Sleepless, lay on a bed that was nothing more than a pile of furs. A fire burned in a brass brazier, producing a fragrant smoke to hang in the air over her. Its faint orange light shone in her wide open eyes. Morgaine the Sleepless lay still and staring, and she smiled.

After a while, the leathern walls stirred as the pavilion's flap of a door was unlaced. Morgaine neither blinked nor stirred any part of herself. The flap was lifted, and a youth stepped carefully in. He saw Morgaine and how she lay, but it gave him no pause. It was how he expected to find her.

The resemblance between the woman and the youth was strong. He had her black eyes and delicate bones. He'd begun to fill out early, though, and it was easy to see the sturdy man he would soon become. The dark dusting of his first beard coloured his chin. In his own eyes there shone a fierce intelligence, startling in one still so young. He dressed all in good black cloth with a black cloak trimmed in blue hanging over his bony shoulders. It was a quiet and dignified display of wealth, showing a surprising maturity for one who had not yet finished his sixteenth year.

Mordred caught up a plain stool, set it beside the brazier and sat down patiently to wait for his mother's return.

Eventually, Morgaine's eyes blinked, and then closed for a long moment. She stirred, sighing for all the world like one waking from a most restful sleep. She stretched luxuriously, and slowly opened her eyes once more. When she saw her son, her smile widened. Mordred stood and held out one black-gloved hand, helping his mother to sit up.

'And how fares King Lot this night?' Mordred asked as he poured Morgaine a drink of watered wine from the ewer that waited nearby.

Morgaine accepted the goblet from her son and took a sip. 'Poorly.' She blew out another sigh and shook her head. 'It would be that much easier on the man if he would let himself be gone.'

Mordred studied the toes of his boots for a moment. 'You know I do not question your wisdom in this matter,' he said, carefully. 'But it would have been simpler if we had killed their messenger. It could have been easily done.'

'That might have gained us Din Eityn, but it would not have weakened Camelot,' she reminded him. 'We must do both if we are to gain and hold the Gododdin.'

Mordred met his mother's eyes, a thing few men dared to do. 'Then kill Lot before they come. We can meet them from inside their own walls.'

She smiled over the rim of her cup at him. 'There is no need. If Lot dies before Camelot arrives, then Gododdin falls into chaos. This will aid us in our advance. If Lot lives, his son can take no real power without hastening his death. Every day the true seat of power is in question drives allies from the Gododdin to our side. The longer uncertainty lasts, the stronger our advantage grows.'

Mordred sat with her in silence for a moment, watching the coals burning in the brazier, considering these words and their wisdom. 'I hear what you say, but uncertainty is no friend in war.'

'Which is how a leader should think,' Morgaine nodded her approval. 'I must ask you to trust me in this, my son.' She stared at the brazier for a moment. There were no flames left, just hot, orange light and ashy shadows crawling across the surface of the coals. 'There are times when the greatest wisdom is knowing not to attempt too much.'

Mordred bowed his head over his cup, acknowledging this, and hiding the trace of impatience in his own eyes. 'Which son will it be, do you suppose?'

Morgaine answered with a light laugh, and drank off the rest of her wine. 'Oh, it will be the second son, Agravain the Sour.'

'Pity,' said Mordred, draining his own cup and gazing pensively at the pavilion's loose door flap where it fluttered in the night breeze. 'I would have liked to meet Gawain on the field.'

Smiling indulgently, Morgaine patted his hand, a gesture she no longer made when there was any other to see it. 'You will, my son. Gawain, and after him Arthur. But you must test your mettle against this other first.' She held up a finger, suddenly serious. 'Do not mistake him, or underestimate him. His wits are keener than the others, and less clouded by sentiment. He will give good sport, but he will be dangerous the moment you turn your back.'

'You see all this?'

She nodded. 'I do.'

Mordred's jaw shifted back and forth and he rolled the cup between his palms for a moment, watching the dregs swirl in the faint light. Then, as if reaching a decision, he set it down with a click on the table. 'They will not find us less than ready,' he said as he stood. 'With your permission, I will survey the camp and retire.'

'You go to meet with the Dal Riata again tomorrow?'

'One more exchange to seal the bargains.' Now it was Mordred's turn to smile with satisfaction. 'Their ties with the men of Eire are still strong. They do not like Arthur and his Britons, and are as eager to deal them a blow as the Pict men are.'

'Well done, Mordred. Well done.' Morgaine stood as well. 'Go to your duty and then take your rest, my son. I will watch here awhile yet. The night may yet have news for us.'

Mordred bent down, swiftly kissing his mother's hand. Then he backed away, executing a bow that would have done him credit in any court. Morgaine smiled at her son, grown so tall, as he strode from her pavilion tent to take up his duties as war leader for their people. Then, she turned back to the darkness.

Beyond the pavilion's leathern wall, the owls quarreled in the trees and the ravens croaked sleepily. There was a word on the wind. She could sense it. It told secrets to the trees and the trees murmured to each other, passing the news along. The smell of salt this far inland was rare, but it was there in the draughts that wormed their way through the pavilion's seams. The voices of the birds spoke of the distant sea, telling stories of water and sky, and the winds from the south readied their northern brethren for a new arrival.

'So,' said Morgaine to herself. 'She is to come too. Oh, very good. Very good indeed. We have a score between us, Laurel of Cambryn. I look forward to our debt being settled.'

Laurel Carnbrea dreamed.

She stood on the western-most watch tower of her home at Cambryn. The rain poured over her. It soaked her clothing and her skin. It flowed into her eyes and mouth. She was not cold. She was as warm and comfortable as if she stood in the sun on a spring day.

She was home.

She was home, and she opened her arms to embrace the rain that flowed down like a river from the silvered sky. The world rippled and blurred before her eyes, and she knew she was not alone.

A woman stood with her. The warm and giving rain filled Laurel's eyes so she could not see clearly, but she made out a form of translucent whiteness that rippled and changed as the wind blew. She was the rain, this other woman, she was the wind, and she was herself.

Grandmother. The *bucca-gwidden*, the White Spirit of the Sea.

'Congratulations my granddaughter,' said Laurel's grandmother. Her voice was the drumming of the rain and whisper of the wind. 'I wish you all happiness.'

'You do?'

Grandmother inclined her head. 'Even so.'

'But I left you.' In the manner of dreams, Laurel now stood with this woman of water beside herself and Lynet in their old chamber, listening to herself proclaim to Lynet she had no trust in their blood. She knew too well how a blood tie to the invisible countries could turn in the blink of an eye from blessing to curse.

'Who belong fully to the land?' Lynet asked. 'What do you mean by that, Laurel?'

Did I say all those things? She could not remember. She knew though that she had meant them.

But Grandmother was smiling. 'It is a fair choice, openly made with thought and foresight. Do not hold your doubts too tightly.'

'I did it for Lynet.' The words flowed from Laurel as if the rain that flooded her had lifted them to the surface, all unlooked for. 'I did it so she would be safe when I must leave.'

Grandmother cupped her hand. The rain filled up her white palm until it spilled out in thick ribbons of blue, green, brown and silver. 'Granddaughter, know this. If you leave the mortal world for reason other than the death which must come to all, it will be because of the choice you make. It is not your blood which compels you to forsake your sunlit country. It is your choice which will compel your blood.' She closed her fist, encasing the water within her ice-white fingers. 'Even the highest God leaves human kind a choice. It is this that changes and turns. It is this that robs and does not give back.'

'I do not want to leave.' murmured Laurel.

'And you fear to stay.' Sorrow tinged the flowing music of her voice. 'The future is long, child, and you must take care.'

For a moment Laurel felt the individual drops of rain, drumming each against her skin like fingers, each cold, fleeting pressure demanding her attention. 'I will remember.'

Grandmother smiled, and the safe, encompassing warmth filled all the world again. 'Then go on to your day, Laurel.'

'Wait!' cried Laurel desperately. The shining figure stilled for a moment, poised delicately between the worlds. 'Wait. Merlin was here. What is it Merlin wants of me?'

But Grandmother only shook her head. 'Choices, my child. Remember. There is always one choice left.'

The wind blew hard and Laurel opened her arms wide again, but the woman was gone. There was only the warm rain, drumming and tapping on stone and filling her up with itself. Then, even that was gone and there was only the darkness of deep, easy sleep.

It was barely light when Meg woke Laurel on her wedding morning. A grey light squeezed through the window's shutters, bringing the sound and cold scent of the rain drumming outside.

Is that you, Grandmother? Are you sending me some other message?

Laurel barely had time to blink her eyes before serving women flooded the chamber, carrying candles, carrying the great copper bath, carrying the bridal garments that were the gift of Queen Guinevere. Meg put a cup of warm posset into Laurel's hand and then snapped at the girls and women to hurry with the water. Laurel found herself helped from the bed, efficiently stripped by Cryda and Elsa, washed, doused, dried and clad in an undergarment of snowy linen. Her cup was taken and returned without a word whenever Meg thought appropriate, and Laurel drank the cooling posset as she was able.

Outside, the rain drummed down.

The queen had chosen an array of delicately dyed garments for this day. Laurel had never seen such colours in cloth and wondered where they had come from. The underdress was a rose pink so pale it evoked the thought of apple blossoms as it whispered lightly over her head and arms. The rich weight of the translucent gold overdress was increased by the stiff, scratchy scarlet and gold ribbons trimming its trailing sleeves. Her cloak was a pale green agate, a shade very close to her eyes, embroidered with elaborate chains of white blossoms and clasped with another apple blossom of gold at her throat.

Her white hair was woven with strands of silver and pearls, and left to hang down in a heavy maiden's braid for the last time, before the spring green veil was laid over it, pinned with gold pins and secured with a band of gold and peridots worked with the figures of leaping dolphins. A girdle of cloth-of-gold embroidered to match the headband secured her waist, and gold-embroidered slippers shod her feet. All perfect, all magnificent gifts signifying her worth to the High King. Under the weight of so much wealth, Laurel could rouse no feeling in herself beyond cold.

Am I afraid? she wondered distractedly. Her dreams of the night before were all about choice. But Merlin stood outside her window, watching in silence.

This was her choice. She did it to aid Lynet and Cambryn, but what if she did wrong?

'Now, my lady,' Meg came forward with a golden ring for Laurel's arm. Laurel seized Meg's hand suddenly, unable to do anything but hold it tightly and stare at the one familiar face in all this strangeness.

Meg covered her hand with her own. 'All will be right, my lady,' she said softly. 'The queen would not give you over to anyone who was less than honourable. Nor would I.'

These words gave Laurel the strength she needed to release Meg and stand still for the remainder of her ministrations. If the women of Camelot noted what passed, they were well-mannered enough to pretend they did not, for which Laurel was grateful. She felt strange in her own skin, as if she did not belong inside herself any longer, but instead was pushing and pulling to get out of this unfamiliar housing.

What is this? What is this? Nothing unknown is happening. This was all that I agreed to. It is already done. Today is only ceremony.

But it was not already done. Not yet. She could still put a halt to this. Return home, live cloistered the rest of her days, or walk into the sea's embrace if she chose. She could still choose not do this. Not give herself to a stranger among strangers. There was always one choice left.

A knock sounded through the door, and Laurel jumped half out of her straining skin. Meg shooed Cryda off to answer it while she brushed down the folds of the clothing Laurel had just unsettled. Laurel was certain Meg meant the motion to be soothing, but it could not reach her through the haze of embarrassment that seemed to have descended.

Lady Rhian stepped across her threshold. She was resplendent in green, saffron and gold for this day, her red-gold hair shining beneath a bright net of woven gold and a pure white veil that trailed down to the hems of her skirt.

'Are you ready, Laurel? They are waiting for you.'

Casting a glance at Meg, who returned the barest of nods, Laurel folded her hands. *I will give the semblance of dignity at least.* 'Yes. I am ready.'

'Let us go, then.'

As she had the day before, Laurel schooled her face into the calm she wished to be seen and stepped from the room, dressed in treasure, bearing legacy and bloodline, price and prize. She caught the approval in Rhian's eyes as that lady fell into step beside her.

Today, the procession down the dim, painted corridors and the cool, curving stairs seemed both longer and shorter than it had been before. Rhian walked beside Laurel in silence. Laurel found herself wondering what this woman's wedding day had been like, how she had felt, how she had carried herself and what she had done to keep her countenance. She bitterly regretted not asking while she had the chance. The sound of the rain followed them, growing louder at each window, fading away as the stone walls surrounded them again.

They passed the audience hall by today. As they did, Laurel heard the clamour of the preparations underway within. They would return there for the feast after the mass. They. Her husband and she. Agravain and she.

What were his thoughts this morning? Was he frightened and doubtful too? Did he want to change his mind about this bargain the king and queen had made of them and for them? Her stomach twisted.

She must have hesitated in her step, because Rhian touched her arm in reassurance.

Ahead of them lay another hall, the most famed in Camelot. Laurel had only entered here twice before. This was hall of the Round Table.

It was appropriate that it should be here. This was where Arthur's full council met, and what was done now was done with the approval and the witness of that council, but there was also the table itself, which had come from Cambryn along with Queen Guinevere. It was a moment of neatly staged symbolism, just as it was meant to be.

The doors stood wide open, revealing the hall in all its splendour, filled with the ranks of those honoured enough to be knights of the Round Table. Queen Guinevere waited at the threshold, and stretched her hands out to take Laurel's the moment she came within reach. Laurel received the kiss of peace, and the queen took her place at Laurel's right hand, with Rhian at her left, to deliver her to her husband.

The cadre was not seated at its table, but stood arrayed along the sides of the chamber, a guard of honour for Laurel's entry. The bright banners stitched with the symbols of their houses and their knighthood hung from the beams, with the banners of the dragon and the swan in the place of pride over all. To add to the authority of this ceremony, Laurel saw that the sword Excalibur had been laid upon the table. She knew it by its scabbard, which, like the table, had been brought by Guinevere as a portion of her dowry. It was a battered thing, the leather so old it had cracked and flaked, banded and shod in plain bronze. Unlike the elaborate and beautiful table, it was not at all what one would expect as a signifier of kingship. Still, the right of its possession had been jealously held by the women of Cambryn's royal line for more generations than anyone knew. As the last of those women, it was Guinevere who held it now.

Laurel saw all these things only dimly, crowding at the edges and filling up the back of her vision, for her eyes would not truly attend to anything but Sir Agravain, waiting beside the High King, who smiled benignly at her hesitating there on the threshold.

Sir Agravain wore the tunic she had given him. Cut to ample measure, it still hung well on his lean frame, which pleased Laurel strangely. The saffron cloth with its decoration of brightly coloured threads and ribbons brushed the tops of his boots and sat well across his chest beneath the red cloak he also wore. A belt of gold links shaped like hunting hawks circled his waist and a thin gold band circled his brow. Its red and blue gems shone brightly against his black hair.

Sir Kai stood on the other side of Sir Agravain, in his fine black, with his red cloak and gold chain of office. His eyes were keen, watching her. Sir Gawain was there as well, dressed in the green that seemed to be his favourite colour, and smiling his splendid smile. At her or at his own wife? She could not tell. She did not see any squire beside Agravain and she wondered at that, but she knew also her mind was simply delaying thought of what she must do next.

'Are you ready?' murmured Queen Guinevere.

No.

'Yes, Your Majesty.'

'Come, then.' The queen took Laurel's arm and led her forward, leaving Rhian to walk behind. The weight of the wealth and spectacle seemed suddenly far too heavy. Laurel tried not to shake, tried to understand where the fear had come from, tried to deny it, to put it aside. She tried to pray, tried to hear the rain reminding her of wind and water and who and what she was beneath the gifted finery. Who and what she had been.

I do this willingly. I do this willingly.

I do this because I can do nothing else to make Lynet and Cambryn safe.

Except for his dress, Sir Agravain was just as he had been the night before, sharp and shuttered, watching her with his impassive eyes.

What do you see in me, Sir Agravain? The table, beautifully crafted, cunningly wrought, unique among all things, a source of pride and honour? Or the scabbard, closely held only because it always has been, and of value only because it has always been closely held?

Sir Kai watched her over Sir Agravain's shoulder, his smile as crooked as his shoulders. The words he spoke echoed back to her at once. *He was the one who tried, and though I may be the only one who does, I believe it was done out of love.*

It was only then she realized who was missing from this great spectacle. Merlin was not there.

This made Laurel draw breath sharply, but she could do nothing more. She was at the edge of the table where her marriage contract and her husband both waited. She knelt to King Arthur and he raised her up with a warm and gentle hand, giving her the kiss of peace and an encouraging smile. Her mouth was dry. Her heart hammered at the base of her throat as he turned her towards her husband. She curtsied. Sir Agravain bowed.

What am I doing?

'You are most welcome to me, Lady Laurel,' said King Arthur. 'Of your courtesy, your name is required to seal the compact.'

Two white-robed monks waited nearby. One deftly unrolled the scroll of the contract. Laurel faced the table and the contract, blinking several times. Cloth rustled, mail clinked. Someone coughed. Sir Agravain was a space of warmth near her shoulder. Waiting.

The document had been written out on pure white vellum in many coloured inks; red, blue, green and gold as well as glimmering black marked out the terms of her marriage; the money and goods she brought, the duty of the produce of tin and other metals that would be owed from Cambryn to Gododdin, and herself. In return, from Gododdin, there would be arms and men, ships and sailors, the woollen cloth and hardy sheep for which they were famed.

All correct. All as she had negotiated with Sir Bedivere in her own great hall, so far away from here.

Laurel nodded. The second monk dipped a neatly trimmed quill into ink, and held it out to her. She took it between her fingers, feeling how smooth and delicate it was. Laurel watched her hand with interest, as if it was a stranger who wrote her name and title upon the page, *Laurel Carnbrea* verch *Kenan Carnbrea*. The scratching of the quill against the page sounded very loud.

Sir Agravain did not wait to be handed his pen, but took up the quill for himself and wrote in a bold clear hand *Agravain* mach *Lot, Equite*. Agravain, son of Lot, Knight. No other title. He caught her gaze as he handed the quill back down, and as she had the evening before, she felt an air of challenge surrounding him. Laurel did not know how to meet it, so she only returned his gaze as calmly and coolly as she was able. If this was how he chose to be known, what challenge was she to make of it?

With that silence hanging in the air between them, both Laurel and Agravain stepped back to make way for the king. Beneath their drying names, Arthur wrote his broad *Arturos Rex.*

'And may the blessing of God be upon it,' said King Arthur as he returned the quill to the monk. 'And upon you, my lady.' He took both Laurel's hands in his. His manner and countenance were calm and confident. For the moment he held her hands, Laurel knew he wished to impart that much to her.

'And you, Agravain.' On his nephew's cheek, the king laid the kiss of peace. Agravain returned the gesture, and as they parted Laurel found herself looking into Agravain's eyes again. It was almost a dare, as if he wanted to see what she would do now. What was he expecting? That she would show some sign of regret? Perhaps he thought she might be thinking of some lover left behind in Cambryn?

That last idea was ludicrous enough that Laurel felt a small smile form, and in Agravain's eyes she thought she caught a glimpse of that odd, dry humour he had bestowed the night before.

He loves, my lady.

Then, unexpectedly, Sir Agravain extended his hand. Laurel felt her brows rise a hair's breadth, and then she reached out. His was a hard hand, one that had known rein and sword and the work of war for many years. It was also warm and ever so slightly gentle, as Sir Agravain turned with her so that they might both make their obeisance to king and queen. There was no cheering from the assembled witnesses. It would not have been appropriate at this time, but Laurel thought she sensed a loosening of the air around them, as if the cadre had been holding its collective breath and now was able to release it.

With King Arthur and Queen Guinevere before them, and

the cadre of the Round Table behind, Laurel and Agravain emerged from the hall, where the whole of the court waited in the dim, grey light and the puddles left behind by the morning's rain. Now, brass horns blared out accompanied by the rolling thunder of drums. A huge cheer exploded from the gathering, ringing off the stones and making the ground shake as people stamped their boots and clapped their hands. Laurel walked through it all as if in a fog. The only real thing was the warmth of the man's hand holding hers; the utterly silent man who did not so much as look at her as they climbed the stairs to stand before Camelot's horse-faced bishop, resplendent in his robes of white and gold, flanked by his two priests in their black robes and caps.

The bishop looked down on them, first at Agravain and then at her.

Sizing us up? Deciding if we are worthy to be blessed?

'I do charge you, Lady Laurel, as you shall answer before God on the Day of Judgment, do you come here freely and of your own will to be given and blessed in marriage to the man Agravain?'

It was the last chance. Even now, with the ink holding her name dry upon the white vellum she could stop this thing. God and Mary could save her now if she but said the word. The clouds hung low, pregnant with fresh rain, waiting for her answer.

There is always one choice left.

'I do,' she said.

'And you, Sir Agravain, as you shall answer before God on the Day of Judgment, do you come here freely and of your own will to be given and blessed in marriage to this woman Laurel?'

'I do.'

Agravain bowed gravely. Laurel curtseyed, and did not take her hand away, partly because, if she were honest, she wanted to see what he would do, and partly because there was an unexpected reassurance in holding his hand as they together mounted the steps towards the chapel.

The contrast with the bright sunlight blinded Laurel for a moment, but her vision quickly cleared. With the gentle pressure of Agravain's fingers against hers, she walked up to the beautifully carved rail where the bishop took up the golden crucifix holding it high.

Agravain let go of her hand and stepped away so they could spread their arms wide in adoration and supplication as the right-hand priest anointed them with holy water from the silver bowl he carried, and the bishop made the sign of blessing. Around them they heard the shuffling and rustling as the other witnesses, and the king and queen, took their places.

'In nomine Patre, et File, et Spiritus Sancte . . .'

As she heard the stately and deeply familiar words of the holy mass Laurel felt the gaze of the painted saints and angels all around them. This was the second of the three acts that would make them truly married. They had the consent of their king and now called for the blessing of God. Laurel found her nervousness unaccountably redoubled. She had always entered into the ritual of church from duty more than from deep faith. She knew and had always known that the invisible world stretched beyond the teachings of the bishops and the Book. Now, though, she found herself yearning for some sign that God, to whom she was but another piece of creation, did indeed watch this as he watched the flight of the swallow, and approved.

She took the wafer into her mouth, and swallowed the wine, bowed her head for the final blessing and murmured the final amen of the mass.

'And as much as you, Agravain, and you, Laurel, have consented to enter into the sacrament of marriage one with the other, have you brought any token of the union sealed here before the eyes of God and Holy Christ and this royal company?'

Agravain turned towards his brother, and Gawain laid a ring in his palm. Even in the dim light of the chapel, Laurel could see it was a beautiful thing, an ornate band of gleaming gold surmounted by a square emerald the size of her fingernail that pulsed like a beating heart in the light of the tapers around them.

Agravain lifted her hand in his, and she felt again the determined gentleness of his touch. She watched him as he looked down at their hands lying together. For one moment, she saw the flicker of light behind his dark eyes, the fleeting warmth beneath the cold that lay like a private winter over his soul.

'May God find me worthy of this blessing,' he whispered, so softly she did not believe anyone else could have heard.

'May we both be so,' she whispered in return. Agravain made no answer except to slip the emerald band onto her thumb and fold her hand closed around it.

Hand-in-hand they walked from the dim chapel. Shafts of sunlight glittered upon the clean washed stones of the court-yard and all around the people of Camelot raised up a mighty cheer to greet the clearing day, and their place in it.

Laurel looked once more to her husband, who smiled a small smile that she alone was close enough to see.

FOUR

Had Agravain been able to work his will upon the world, the wedding feast would have been a simple meal held in private. Gawain had sobered in recent years and could be counted on to conduct himself with dignity. Rhian, Gawain's wife, understood propriety, and their uncle, of course, and the queen. Uncle Kai as well. But the rest . . . the rest would have been turned away.

But it could not be. The ways of courts and kings required he give the High King this opportunity to show himself generous, and the whole court turned out to take advantage of this. Only Merlin seemed to have absented himself from the throng, but he moved to his own rules and could not be counted on to observe the formalities of other men.

So, save for that one exception, around them swirled the pomp and luxury, and the increasingly raucous noise, of the court at feast, and Agravain felt himself stand in the midst of it all like a stone. The music was beautiful, and suited to a great celebration, with harps and pipes and drums pouring through the great hall for the dancers and jugglers to disport themselves to. Uncle Kai had omitted nothing from the feast. In all his years at Camelot, Agravain had never tasted the variety of spices that flavoured the array of meats; swan and peacock, lamb, venison and pigeon. The breads were white as snow and light as air, and the pastry melted the moment it touched the mouth. The wines came from all corners of the Christian world and ranged from a sweet gold to warm, rich red. Agravain held a goblet of that red wine now in his hand, untouched. In the midst of the pageantry and display, he could watch only one point, and that was the distant form of Laurel of Cambryn. Laurel of Gododdin, now. His wife.

My wife.

She was pale as ivory and dressed in clothing coloured as delicately as the first blossoms of spring. She stood beside Rhian at this moment, accepting praise and congratulations from the various women of the court. She nearly glowed with pearlescent light beside Rhian's red-gold form. Another lady, garish in a gown of too many colours talked to her animatedly. Blessing her? Warning her? Agravain felt his frown deepen. Laurel listened with an interest he was sure she feigned. Eventually, she inclined her head with the dignity with which she had borne herself since she had entered Camelot.

'Well, nephew?'

Agravain started abruptly, and turned to see Uncle Kai standing beside him, smiling his sharp and knowing smile. Agravain felt his brow furrow.

'Well what, my uncle?'

'What do you think of your bride?'

Agravain shrugged irritably. 'And how am I to know?' he snapped. 'You have spent more time in conversation with her than I have.'

'Yet there she stands.' Kai gestured broadly, indicating the whole space of the crowded court. 'While you, for some obscure reason, linger over here.'

Agravain felt himself scowling. He could not seem to help it. 'This is no place for such talk.'

'It is exactly the place. Here the whole court may see what a perfectly matched pair you are, and they will rejoice in it.'

'Do not mock me, uncle,' he muttered, more to the wine cup than to himself. 'I am in a poor humour for it.'

'And for anything else, it seems.'

The sly edge in Kai's voice cut neatly, and painfully, as Agravain was sure it was meant to. What a day it was when he could not even rely on his uncle to understand. 'I do my duty by the king and my own land. She is of worthy rank and good understanding.'

Kai quirked up one eyebrow. 'And nothing else?'

He looked across to Laurel again. Another gaggle of bright ladies surged up to her. She met this latest assault as she had met every other event of the day; with dignified grace and composed courtesy. If she felt at all fatigued, it did not show. She was tall, his wife, and the delicacy implied by her pale skin seemed deceptive. There was strength in her. He was sure of it. But what else was there?

'I don't know,' Agravain said, half in answer to Kai's question, but half to his own.

Kai clapped him on the shoulder. 'That, nephew is a good sign. I hold out hope for you.'

If Sir Kai was not in the mood to extend mercy, neither was Agravain. 'I will accept your guidance in all things, uncle, but not in the matter of women,' he said flatly.

An abrupt and unexpected silence fell at that. 'Perhaps you are right, Agravain,' said Kai. 'Very well. I leave you to your reflections.' Bowing more in mockery than in courtesy, Kai left him there, returning, Agravain presumed, to his duties. The whole hall needed to be served, and would for many hours yet.

Alone, Agravain felt exposed. He was watched, but most especially by Lady Laurel. What should he do? It was growing late. Voices were being raised to compete with the musicians, showing that the lavish drink was beginning to have effect, but also that more than he were thinking on what was to come next. What did Laurel think? How was he to know? She made such a mask of propriety for her finely sculpted face, he could read nothing in her.

Was there any other lady who had eyes of such a colour? Almost as pale as the veil laid over her white-gold hair.

'What, the bridegroom, all alone?' said someone mildly.

He'd been caught again, staring. Angry with himself, Agravain turned, a sharp retort ready on his tongue, and found Gawain standing beside him.

'Such feasts are far more to your liking than mine,' muttered Agravain, taking a swallow of his wine. He did not like the way Gawain looked at him. There were few moments when he cared for his older brother's scrutiny, and this moment was most certainly not one of them.

'Is there any matter you would speak about, Agravain?'

So, there it is. Agravain's jaw clenched. 'I told Uncle Kai that I would not hear his guidance in the matter of women and he sends you to me. I must remember to thank him for it.'

'God's breath, Agravain, that is cold even for you.' Agravain let it be. Perhaps the chiding was merited. It bothered him that he was not sure.

'What is it of the lady that worries you so?' asked Gawain quietly.

Agravain felt his spine stiffen and his free hand clenched reflexively. 'Gawain,' he muttered. 'I swear upon the Cross, if you've come to make mockery, I will forget you are my brother and your blood will run on these stones.'

'Nay, brother, never, and not at such a time.' Gawain's voice was mild, as was his expression. Any who came near them would think they were discussing nothing of import. 'I know well your worth.' The corner of Gawain's mouth turned up in a small smile. 'Whatever you may believe of me, I have never once forgotten the times you have been right and I have been so sorely wrong.'

Agravain met his brother's eyes and saw there none of Gawain's pride, and very little of his hero's certainty. For once, there was only his brother there.

Old habit warned Agravain to keep his own counsel. Old anger all but sealed that, but Agravain mustered his strength. Setting aside the heavy weights of the past and the future, he made himself speak.

'I . . . I am ill-acquainted with the ways of a lady.'

There. He had said it, and to Gawain, of all men, whose deeds among women were still the stuff of legend six years after his marriage. Agravain waited for his brother to laugh, and make some wry jest. His anger pulled at its weakening tether, ready to charge forward in an instant. He almost hoped he could be angry. The boyish nervousness he felt now sickened him. Anything must be better than this.

But Gawain kept his countenance, not even smiling in the depths of his eyes.

'Were I to counsel a man on such a matter,' said Gawain, clearly choosing his words with the utmost care, 'I would tell him to have patience, with the lady and with himself. I would tell him that it is a time when many men turn to brutes, and it is brutishness that many a woman braces herself for. I would say to look well upon her beauty, for she is a beauty, Agravain.' His voice dropped to the barest whisper. 'Study that beauty. Treat it as wisdom to be learned, understood and deeply cherished. There, you will find you will know all you need to of the ways of a lady.'

Gawain laid his hand on Agravain's shoulder, a touch of friendship such as he rarely suffered. Then, Gawain drifted away, leaving Agravain his private thoughts rather than risk drawing this moment out to become something either of

them might regret. Agravain found himself looking after
Gawain in some little wonder, thinking that things might
have changed within his older brother without his seeing
them. That in itself was a sobering thought.

Agravain straightened his shoulders. Laurel stood with
Queen Guinevere now, the pair of them encircled by
Guinevere's giggling ladies. Laurel's pale green eyes shone
with the light of the candles, a clear and golden light that
seemed to come as much from within her as without.

In the next moment, she looked up at him, and those eyes
widened just a little in surprise. Had she somehow felt his
gaze? She felt it now. A blush rose in her then, turning her
pale skin shell pink. Agravain's throat constricted. Gawain
was right. She was a beauty. Not just in face and form, but
in all her bearing, in the mystery she carried within her. The
sight of all that beauty seemed to root him to the ground,
and in that instant he knew something new was taking hold
within him.

Queen Guinevere spoke some word that sent peals of
laughter up among the ladies. The gaudy flock pressed closer
to Laurel, deliberately hiding her from him as they joined
hands in a ring to herd her away to the hall's main doors.
The move was highly visible, and meant to be so. Bawdy
cheers went up from all the men present. And, as if that
weren't enough, the flock began to sing:

'*To me a feast is a bore!*' they piped shrilly over the jangling
of tambourines and cymbals.

'*I favour a love-gossip more!*
I'm cool to a mere plentitude,
But the face-to-face, ah, that's good!'

The whole court erupted into shouts of laughter and long,
lascivious whistles. Agravain felt he could have easily killed
them all. Laurel glanced over her shoulder at him, and even
at this distance, he could see her expression twisted into

embarrassment and awkwardness. His own face burned. Without thinking, he made to stride after her.

A hand closed on his shoulder. Uncle Kai again, leaning lightly on his crutch, his eyes gleaming mischief.

'Not so fast, nephew,' Kai said cheerfully, but softly, Agravain noted. This was no jibe for the court to make sport of. 'Give the lady a moment to prepare.' With the barest twitch of his chin, he indicated the whole of the watching crowd, knights and lords and ladies, servitors, laughing and eyeing Agravain, some openly, some surreptitiously.

Agravain struggled to keep his countenance. 'I should go thank my uncle the king for the pains he has taken on our behalf.'

Kai nodded and backed away so he could pass. Agravain pulled the cloak of indifference that had served him so well for so many years into place. Under its shelter the sniggering and the ribald jests passed over him like a summer's breeze and he was able to let go of the foolishness surrounding him more easily.

But he could not let go of the memory of Laurel's cheeks so brightly flushed when she found him watching her. That was modesty, surely, injured dignity at the jibes that had been flying. Surprise. Anticipation.

It was not fear. It could not be fear.

Don't let it be fear. Please.

But this prayer, Agravain kept between himself and God.

'Come, sweetest, to you hear me call!
  'To you, loved by one and by all!
  'You're the light of my eye and a part . . .'
'Yes, but which part?'
'There's only one that interests her tonight!'

The song dissolved into shrieks of laughter as Guinevere's ladies hearded Laurel into her bed chamber. They'd been busy in here. They must have stripped every rose bush within a ten-mile square. White and pink flowers twined with ivy around the posts of the bed. Heaps of them decked every chest and stick of furniture and framed the window. The perfume was dizzying, as was the heat. The fire had been built up high and all four braziers blazed. Candles burned in bronze stands worked like leaves and branches. It was too warm. Perhaps it was just that she was too warm, with all these women filling the chamber, making lewd and intimate insinuations that she wouldn't have suffered from her sister.

And there stood the queen, smiling benignly on it all, so Laurel couldn't even say anything, let alone throw them all out the door.

One of them said tartly, 'My lord Agravain is more likely to have an icicle between his legs than anything fleshly.'

Another gave out a bark of laughter in reply. 'So speaks the woman who's found out what's between the legs of half the men-at-arms of Camelot. Were I to guess, I'd say you only curse my lord Agravain because he did not rise to your lures.'

'Stop it, you hens,' admonished Lady Rhian, waving them all back. 'You're terrifying the bride.'

Laurel could abide in silence no longer. 'The bride is quite composed, thank you,' she said frostily.

This drew another chorus of knowing *oh-hos*, accompanied by raised brows and widened eyes. Laurel clenched her teeth, remembering this was all to be expected, and that it was but a part of this final act. She glanced over the heads of the laughing women to see the queen, standing behind, neither participating in this, nor making any move to ameliorate their actions.

'*You're the light of eye and a part . . .*' Someone began the song again. '*The* far *better* part *of my heart!*'

They all circled around her, a cluster of eyes and hands and laughter. They pulled at her laces and clasps, stripping her of sleeves and overdress and jewels. She could not even see the queen. It was heat and damp, wine-soaked breath and constant jostling. Her veil was taken and her braid undone, so her hair tumbled free in a white wave. They were breathing all the air, and she couldn't tell who was who. They plucked at her laces, her sleeves, her jewels and skirts. Just as she thought she would have to scream, they moved back, leaving her standing alone in only in her white linen underdress and, to her shame, gasping for breath, and trying not to clap her hands over herself to hide what already felt like nakedness.

It was no comfort at all that now she could hear the ragged, weaving chorus of voices teetering up the corridor outside.

'. . . *Since on error bent,*
I've earned grave punishment,
Please, *O* seize *the penitent*
And lock him in your chamber!'

On this last exclamation, the door flew open so violently, Laurel could only assume it had been kicked. A flood of men spilled in, along with a reek of sweat and wine so pungent it threatened to overwhelm the rose perfume. Laughing, they seized the waiting ladies, pleading for kisses, pinching, and chasing them around the bed, receiving shrieks and slaps and curses in return. Only the queen and Laurel went untouched while the bacchanal current raged around them.

Swamped by the laughing rampage, it took Laurel a moment to realize that Agravain was not with these men. He still stood in the doorway, distaste stamped plain on every feature.

'*Out!*' he roared suddenly.

The single command rang through the room, freezing the whole riot in place for a single heartbeat, whether half-smothered in embraces, or ducking a slap, or leaning into a kiss.

'All of you!' cried Agravain, taking one step into the room, his fists clenched at his sides. 'Get *out*!'

The whole of the assemblage shifted their gaze from the red rage of the bridegroom, to the queen, whom he had presumably just ordered from the nuptial chamber along with all the rest of them.

But Queen Guinevere only drew herself up straight.

'Enough,' she announced to the gathering. 'My ladies, you will come with me.'

She swept from the room. Her ladies at once extricated themselves from the game and ran behind her, not without a few regretful backward glances. Agravain stayed where he was, facing the whole crowd of drunken men. At last, one of the lords gave a moan of disappointment and slouched out into the corridor. The others followed suit, groaning or chuckling however their mood took them. Not one met Agravain's gaze for more than an instant as they passed, and it was not until they were well out of the room that the songs and laughter started up again.

Agravain turned and closed the door, settling the latch firmly into place.

Agravain also had been relieved of a large measure of his clothing. He had on only his white under-tunic and a pair of hose. When he turned once more to face her, Laurel saw he was attempting to muster what dignity such a state of undress would allow.

There they were, the two of them, alone for the first time. Beside them waited the bed, its coverings folded back, and its posts hung with roses and ivy.

And neither of them seemed to be able to make a single move.

Ridiculous. 'Good evening, my lord Agravain.' Laurel curtsied. *Ridiculous,* she thought again. But she could not think of anything else to do.

'Good evening, my lady Laurel,' he replied, bowing.

They stood again, meeting each other's eyes. Agravain smiled a very little, acknowledging, she thought, the absurdity of the situation. It occurred to Laurel then, that he might be holding himself still to avoid giving her cause for alarm. It was plain to her that he was both sober and had no intention of turning this time into the sort of rout he had just expelled from the chamber.

What should she do? She knew nothing of flirtation. She knew what was to happen. It was impossible not to. She'd seen the act . . . and God knew she'd felt desire. She had secretly envied Lynet the attentions of her handsome bridegroom. Now it was her time to receive such attention. It was blessed and sanctioned, and she had not the least idea how to begin.

'There is wine,' she said, a little desperately, seeing the brass ewer and its matching cups on the rose-strewn table. 'Will you drink?'

'An' I thank you,' he replied.

She filled both cups with the amber brandywine, her mind working furiously, but to no purpose at all. Should she praise him? Remark on the feast?

What do I do? What do I do?

Laurel handed Agravain a goblet, grateful that years of practice at serving kept her hands from trembling.

'Will you sit?' she said, and in the next heartbeat she cursed inwardly. Some wit had removed the chairs.

Agravain looked about, and saw this too.

'If it pleases my lady?' he inquired, gesturing towards the bed with mock gallantry and the same dry humour he had displayed so briefly at the betrothal feast.

Keeping her countenance as grave as she could manage, Laurel curtsied once more. Agravain took the cup from her, and she sat down on the edge of the bed, smoothing her skirts and sleeves out fussily. Agravain stood there for one moment, looking from her to the wine cups. Then, he set them both down on a small table beside the candles. He sat down on the edge of the bed, a polite distance away from her.

'My lady. . .' he began, and then stopped, and began again. 'My lady, I had hoped that some words would come to me at this moment, but . . . but words were not ever my friends.'

'Then we find ourselves at the same impasse,' Laurel answered. 'My sister is the orator in our family.'

'She will suit Gareth well, then. He always enjoys a fine speech.'

Laurel's mouth was dry. She wished she could reach for the wine, but it was too far away. 'And you, my lord?'

'I, my lady?' he whispered to his hands, as if he did not dare to look at her. 'I would that I were mute. Then I would not have to struggle to say I am glad it is you here beside me at this moment.' Laurel held her breath, fearing that the smallest movement would break his determination. 'I have never cared what other men thought of me. But when I saw you . . . I became afraid I was not enough man for the honour that had come to me.'

He drew in a deep breath, but she could not breathe. Not yet. Not yet. 'But if you find . . .' he stopped. The words were too heavy for him. He was straining to bring them forward. 'If you find you cannot . . . like . . . me, I will ask nothing more of you tonight.'

He glanced at her, mistook her stunned stillness, and heaved himself to his feet. 'Forgive me,' he said, running his hand through his hair, and looking towards the door. 'I was counselled . . . I meant to be gentle, but it is not in my nature . . .' He was going to leave.

He was going to leave if she did not breathe, did not move, did not find what to say.

'My lord.' Laurel reached out and touched his sleeve of fine linen, feeling the strong, lean arm beneath. 'My lord, do not go.'

He stiffened. He was breathing hard, but he turned and met her gaze.

'Stay with me,' she said. 'I want nothing else.'

She meant it. She did not know for certain until the words left her, until she felt how her hand gently pulled him towards her, urging him to sit with her again, closer this time, so that she could easily hold both his hands. His was a warm scent, leather and strong soap, spice and gentle wines. The kiss he gave her was light, almost chaste. It might have been the kiss of peace between them. Laurel's newborn certainty faltered and she found she did not know what to do next. She could not stop or she would break this oh-so-delicate thread being spun between them.

Tentatively, awkwardly, she laid her hand on his chest, feeling the hard planes of its surface beneath the thin cloth. He pulled back, and regarded her a long time in silence. It was as if he would never have enough of looking at her. She did not move her hand, but left it there to feel his quickening breath rise and fall beneath her palm. She liked that feeling, that simple, warm sign of life.

He lifted his hand to her face, tracing her cheeks. His fingertips were calloused, and she felt the strength that waited in that hand, so controlled lest he be too rough. A kind of fear rose in her, for he was strong, far stronger in arm and body than she. His fingers brushed her chin, her throat, tracing the vein where her pulse beat so strongly just beneath her skin. His face tightened, the lines made by wind and care deepening, but his eyes shone more brightly.

Suddenly, Laurel realized her own breath was quickening to match his, and that in her fading fear was the desire that he kiss her again.

She leaned forward and he cupped her face with his rough-palmed hand, drawing her to him, lifting her chin so that he could kiss her again, and so that she could put her arms around his lean shoulders and bring herself closer still. His body was hard, his kiss was hard. There was no softness about this man, no spare flesh beneath the cloth, no featherbed of a body for her to lie against. Yet all she wanted was to press against him, to let his hands have the freedom of her body, to do all that she had known she must never venture until this moment, with this man, her lord, her husband.

'Agravain.'

She was not aware she had spoken his name aloud until he pulled away, holding her by the shoulders. In his searching gaze, she saw that he too was afraid of what he felt and what he wished for. He was afraid of what he would see in her. She made no answer. There was none she could make. She could only let him see her as she was.

His lady, his wife.

'Laurel.'

He kissed her again, caressing her, letting her feel the strength she knew was there. Her own hands seemed beyond her control, pushing at the fabric of his tunic, trying to find bare skin, to feel the heat of it, to know if he was rough or smooth there, if he was as strong and scarred on his body as he was on his arms. He was leaning her back and she was falling as if into the water to float free. Her hair spread out upon her shoulders, bare now as he pushed her lacings open and drew the linen down over her arms, down to her breasts which would be exposed to his searching eyes and hands in another moment.

'My lord Agravain! My lord!'

Agravain shot to his feet. Laurel scrambled backwards, snatching at linen and bedclothes, at anything that would cover her.

A man had broken into the room, not a reveller, a man spattered with mud and wet with rain, out of breath as if he had run for miles to be here, to see this. One of Camelot's page boys stood in the doorway, stark white with terror.

Agravain's face twisted in rage, flushing crimson red. 'Who in the devil's name are you!' he roared.

'Forgive me, lord, forgive me.' The man dropped onto his knees, and Laurel thought for a moment Agravain would have struck him but for that obeisance. 'I am come from Gododdin, my lord. The king is dying.'

Agravain froze. For a dozen heartbeats, a dozen breaths, he did not move. It was not that it took him so long to understand, Laurel was certain, but it took him that long to believe. He turned to stare at her there on the bed, half-undone by his own hands. While she watched, all expression bled slowly from his face.

Then he strode from the room without another word.

The messenger looked at her mute with apology and regret, and followed after.

And Laurel, crouched on her rose-hung marriage bed, was left alone.

FIVE

The king is dying.

Agravain strode down the dim corridor, with the messenger and the page both stumbling behind him.

'My lord . . .' stammered the boy, a rangy youth, not yet old enough to shave. 'My lord, I am so sorry. I never would have . . . but your standing orders said should any messenger come from Gododdin . . .'

The page was terrified, and that would not do. Agravain mastered himself and stopped in his tracks.

'You did right.' Colour rushed back into the boy's cheeks. Quite likely the page was afraid of being dismissed in disgrace. Agravain was known to be harsh in that respect. 'Take this man to the barracks,' he said gesturing to the messenger. 'Find him food and drink, and dry clothes. If he has any hurt, it is to be tended. Send two men to my chamber, immediately. Spread the word that any summons will find me there.'

The king is dying.

He turned to the messenger. Agravain could not see his face well in the corridor's dim light, but he could make out that the man sagged under the weight of weather and weariness.

In the old tongue of Gododdin, Agravain said, 'You will be called on soon to give your whole message to the High King. Be ready.'

The man did his best to bow, and Agravain nodded his acknowledgement. The boy also sketched a hasty bow, and, sensibly, offered the messenger his arm to support him down the corridor.

Agravain watched them go, briefly, before turning away.

His first instinct was to march into the great hall and drag Gawain out to tell him the news. But that would not answer, not in his current state of undress. Besides, Gawain might already know. So might the king. Someone had given this man entry. Sir Kai would have notified King Arthur of the arrival of such a messenger.

The situation rapidly clearing in his fogged mind, Agravain continued down the corridor. His stockinged feet padded ridiculously on the stones and rushes. It was cold. He was cold from foot to head. He had to stop every few steps to shake off the rushes that clung to the bottoms of his woollen stockings, and could only be grateful there was no one to witness his clownish progress. The soles of his feet cringed with each step on the cold stones. There might not have been a fire left in all the world, and the wind from outside found its way through the stones to touch his thinly clad back and brush his hands.

The king is dying.

His father, King Lot of Gododdin, was dying. Sharply and brutally, the image of how his father had looked the last time Agravain had spoken to him came to his mind; the wild blue eyes, unkempt hair and beard. His harsh voice had been a cracked and broken whisper, but he still had enough strength to all but crush Agravain's hand as he gripped it. Strong still. Lucid sometimes. Driven by his demons always. Driven now to death.

His eyes were stinging. Agravain wiped them hard with the back of his hand. He forced himself to continue towards his own chamber before any could come upon him to witness his lack of control.

It is good this is come at last, he told himself harshly. *Now all promises will be kept and all debts finally paid.*

That the summons should come tonight, at this time, was just one more black irony in the invisible battle consuming his past, and his future.

Agravain, by his rank, was entitled to a room within Camelot's main keep that was not far from the place he had just left.

Just left his wife. Laurel.

Agravain gritted his teeth against the memory of that interrupted moment. For all the tight, physical ache of it remained with him, he could not permit himself to think on it now. Laurel was of noble birth, raised to the royalty by the queen's hand, and by her marriage. She understood that duty came before all else.

If she does not now, she must learn.

The grim reality of that cut him unexpectedly, and Agravain winced. But he set that aside as well. There was nothing else to be done.

Agravain's apartment was small and spare, but not without elements of comfort. A woven carpet from the Pyranee mountains covered the floor. A shelf beside the carved bed held three books covered in wood and leather. A writing desk stood beneath the shuttered window. Beside that waited a flat chest specially made to hold the maps, charts, letters and documents that he had collected in his time here. The understanding of history was Agravain's special study. He pursued it whenever his other duties gave him leisure. He studied to understand the minds and movements of men as well as of armies. Without Gawain's happy talent for making friends, he must gather his knowledge of his fellow beings as best he could.

The silence of his empty room was deafening. It smelled of cold and damp from having stood unattended all day. Agravain uncovered the coals in his hearth and prodded the fire into giving up some feeble light and warmth. Then, he went to his clothing chest. His wedding tunic lay crumpled on the bed where it had been summarily discarded by the revellers. He did not reach for it. It would be inappropriate for this new turn of events. Instead, he donned trousers and tunic of plain blue wool, and reclaimed his boots and leather belt.

Dressed, Agravain felt calmer, more ready to face what would come next. Before anything else could be set in motion, he must speak with King Arthur. All the plans he had laid across the long years of his preparation must wait until he was given formal leave to go home.

Agravain looked again at his wedding tunic in its untidy heap. Its bright colours flickered in the firelight. With precise motions he smoothed the cloth down, looking for damage. If it had been marred in any way, he'd have words with those idiots who had tossed it so lightly aside. It was a rich gift, and painstakingly made. A gift to show respect and wealth. It should not be treated with less than care. He noted the close stitching and the fineness of the cloth as he folded it. He found himself wondering if Laurel's hands had worked the hawks that flew over the glittering waves.

A knock sounded on the door.

'Enter.' Agravain turned from the gift, his fingers trailing across the embroidery as he did.

The door opened. Leon, Gawain's oldest squire, came in, accompanied by two soldiers who were both far more tousled and bleary-eyed than they should have been. Agravain opened his mouth to deliver a reprimand, but remembered the feast. It was his wedding that had led to this state of affairs, and the men were not so far gone that they were unaware of their condition, and did their best to straighten themselves.

Leoan, looking alert and spruce beside these other two, bowed. 'My lord Agravain, the High King commands you attend him in his private chamber. My lord Gawain will join you both there.'

Agravain nodded. To the nearest, tallest soldier he said, 'Go and say I am coming.' To the squire he said, 'Go to my wife and tender my apologies. I may not return tonight.'

My father is dying, perhaps dead already. My new wife sits alone where I must leave her to attend this business. God above us, is there to be any part of this that is not cursed?

The boy kept his countenance firmly in check as he bowed and hurried away. Agravain found he had to allow his brother this much; Gawain trained his squires well.

'You,' Agravain said to the remaining soldier 'Go make sure that the queen has been informed as to what has occurred and request, in my name, that she send some competent woman to tend my wife.'

The soldier appeared less than pleased with this errand, but he too complied, which was all that mattered at this moment.

But I will remember that reluctant face, sirrah, for later days.

The proper messages sent, Agravain marched down hallway and stairway to wait upon the king.

The fire burned brightly in King Arthur's private room. Its gold light played across the richly carved furnishings and soft carpet. The High King stood beside the hearth and stared into the flames. Perhaps he divined omens, or perhaps he just visited the vast countries of the past that a king must carry within himself. King Arthur still wore his ceremonial wealth; the dragon crown decked with rubies weighed down his head, and the dragon torque guarded his throat. How long had he been standing there lost in thought, not bothering to change from his celebratory finery? The king was a man with a fine sense of ceremony and appropriate conduct. It was one of the things that made Camelot the great court it was. Disturbance stirred softly in the back of Agravain's mind as he moved to kneel.

King Arthur turned one blue eye towards him and stopped him with the smallest gesture of his hand.

'Your father was a great man and a good friend to me, Agravain,' said Arthur softly. The rubies in his crown shimmered like drops of fresh blood on his brow. 'I am sorry.'

Agravain felt a muscle high in his cheek twitch. It had been many years since Lot was either thing to Arthur, and they both knew it. Since Agravain's mother Morgause had vanished, Lot had become a madman. A ceaseless, unreasoning fire had burned in him, hot enough to drive him to murder.

Hot enough to kill a daughter and drive four sons away.

'There is no need, Sire,' said Agravain, keeping his voice sober and neutral. 'This has been long in coming.'

'Nonetheless, I am sorry.'

Agravain inclined his head, more disconcerted than he would have thought possible. Not only by Arthur's soft words, but by the way the king's face fell into deep and unfamiliar lines as he spoke. The red-gold of the firelight showed the grey in Arthur's hair and beard too plainly. Exactly what was he sorry about? Not this death. Lot was more a burden than an ally.

What, then?

The arrival of both Gawain and Kai saved Agravain from having to follow that thought any further. They too made to kneel and were stopped. Agravain met the seneschal's eyes and saw unfamiliar compassion in their usually edged gaze. Only then did he dare look to his brother. Gawain's eyes were dry, but red, and his face was flushed.

Agravain could not tell whether he was appalled at this evidence that his brother had so recently wept, or if he envied Gawain his ability to do so.

'Rhian has gone to Laurel,' murmured Gawain.

'Thank you,' Agravain replied, surprised at the depth of the gratitude he felt at this.

Fortunately, Gawain read his own mood accurately and did not now waste time on sentimental words. 'Shall we bring in the messenger?' he asked the king.

Arthur nodded, and Gawain moved back to the door, beckoning into the corridor. A moment later, the messenger from Din Eityn walked in to kneel before the High King. In the bright firelight, Agravain could see him better. He was not young. His hair and moustaches were still as wild as they had been when he burst into Agravain's wedding chamber, but his eyes were calmer now, and both his hands were swathed in clean white linens. Every part of him had been toughened by hard living in rough weather. The dirt rubbed into the pores and pockmarks of his face might have been part of his skin. Agravain could not put any name to him, but he discerned the marks of his unforgiving homeland in that tough skin and scarred cheeks.

The king raised him up courteously.

'What is your name?' Arthur asked in the Northern tongue. The man started a little before answering.

'Ros, my liege.' He had a rough, mumbling voice, weighed down by awkwardness.

'Who sent you? Was it King Lot?'

'No, my liege,' Ros shook his head heavily, his thick fingers knotting together in front of him. 'It was my lord Pedair.'

'He is with the king?'

'Yes, Sire.' Ros's gaze slipped sideways to Agravain. 'One of the last.'

'With your permission, Your Majesty?' said Agravain. The king nodded and Agravain faced Ros. 'Who else still stands with King Lot?'

'Lord Ruadh *mach* Keill. No one else who can in truth be called a chieftain.'

Which means there are others there who take the title without the right. God in Heaven. When Agravain had left, a full twenty chiefs had still called Lot king. 'How stands Din Eityn?'

'That's why I am sent, my lord. There is an army come from the south.'

The words drove straight to the centre of Agravain's soul.

'What army?' he barked, not even pausing to see how the king took this sudden news. 'Who are they? How close are they to the rock?'

'When I left, they were not more than six days' march, west and north, in the vale of Saint Isen's well. Some five hundred men. They travel under a raven banner.'

At the mention of the raven, all the men in the room went very still. There was only one person who flew such a sigil, and that was Morgaine, called the Goddess and the Sleepless.

Called enemy to King Arthur and Queen Guinevere and all who stood with them.

Agravain folded his arms over his chest, in part to keep his hands from clenching into fists. 'Moving how?'

Ros shook his head again and his fingers twisted and tightened, looking for something to hold onto. 'Not moving. Waiting. At parley, it's thought, with the Pict and the Dal Riata.'

So. It's come. It's come at last.

Although he was sure he already knew the answer, Agravain asked the next question. 'And no one has moved against it?'

'No, my lord.' Ros's voice changed tone subtly, becoming

not angry, but harder. Sour, as if he'd spit if he were not in such company. 'Our neighbors are all waiting to see which way the wind blows, Lord Pedair thinks.'

'Does a lady wait with the army?' asked King Arthur abruptly.

This took Ros aback. 'A lady, Sire?' Perhaps he had not heard the stories, although Agravain doubted that. More likely he had been so intent on delivering his news, he had not had the opportunity to think on what it might mean.

'Yes. She will have black hair and black eyes.'

Ros considered, searching his memory as well as the faces of the men around him. All stayed quiet, giving no hint as to the answer they wanted. 'No one has seen such lady. No one I've spoken to. The raven army is led by a man in black, though.'

'What man is this?'

Ros shrugged, seemingly abashed. 'He rides a black horse and wears armour all enamelled in black as they do in the eastern parts of the world. He is a shadow at midday, and they say he commands the earth underfoot and the skies overhead. I don't believe it myself, but I've seen him . . .' Ros faltered. 'Well . . . I've seen him.'

Agravain gritted his teeth briefly. 'What force is there left to Din Eityn?'

Ros licked his lips. He ducked his head for a moment, then seemed to remember some pride of place, and straightened. 'None, my lord,' he said and his voice was steady. Flinching from this truth would be useless. 'We're a hollow shell. We'll crack as soon as the hammer falls.'

The king nodded, tugging at his beard and contemplating the fire again. 'Thank you, Ros. Get some rest. We may send for you tomorrow to repeat what you have told us before the full council.'

Ros knelt again, and took himself out of there, not without

a backward glance at Agravain and Gawain. Agravain barely spared him a thought. All his attention turned towards the king. His frame thrummed with tension. Arthur must order him home. Now. At once.

Sir Kai shuffled past them and did what few were allowed. Without waiting for the king's permission, he sat, pulling his lame leg towards the fire.

'Forgive me,' he said. 'It has been a long night for these misshapen limbs of mine. What counsel then, my king?' He looked up expectantly at Arthur.

Agravain at first thought this was mere flippancy, but he watched how Kai's words made the king recall himself from across the distance his thoughts had travelled. It was no good road, but when Arthur spoke, his voice still held his familiar strength.

'So. The Dal Riata and the Pict are negotiating an alliance. If there were time, I'd lay another curse against Vortigern for inviting those men of Eire to our lands.'

History. History of battles that had left blood across the land and stained men's minds with hate. That hate moved them down the generations.

'We cannot believe that this new alliance, and these five hundred men from the south, will not be turned against us.' *Not with the raven flying over them.* But Arthur did not say that. 'And given the timing, we must believe its road south will lie straight through Gododdin,' he went on. 'Din Eityn and control of the firth are treasure enough to tempt any commander with a brain in his head.'

Arthur lifted his head and Agravain drew himself up, ready for the order. Requiring the order.

'What I ask now, Agravain,' said King Arthur, 'is that you do not go to Din Eityn.'

The words fell like blows against Agravain, wholly unlooked for and shattering all thought.

'What!' Agravain shouted before he remembered himself.
'My king, what . . .'

'We should not wait for the Dal Riata to make their move,'
Arthur went on steadily, as if Agravain had not spoken. 'A
force may still be assembled and moved in time to meet the
enemy before winter. The forts on the northern wall are still
sound. You, Agravain will ride out with me and we will end
this alliance of our enemies.'

Agravain looked to Kai, who only shrugged one crooked
shoulder, and to Gawain who stood silent and unsurprised.
His brother did at least seem to recognize this was perhaps
an awkward situation, and shifted his weight.

'If you go north without invitation, my king, it will be
thought you go to conquer,' Agravain said, forcing reason
back into his tone. 'It will infuriate the chiefs and lords there,
and call into question the open friendship you have offered.'

'It cannot be helped,' replied King Arthur. 'This alliance
and its architects must be broken.'

'You do not believe I can lead the army which breaks it?'
inquired Agravain. *It cannot be you do not trust me. It cannot be,
my king, you doubt my ability or my loyalty.*

Arthur faced Agravain fully, and Agravain found himself
assessing the king almost as he would an opponent before
battle. Arthur was old, but still straight, still strong of arm
and body. He met Agravain's eyes with the certainty that
must belong to a king.

'I believe I do not want you to go alone to the place where
your father was driven mad by Morgan the Fey,' said Arthur.
'It would be too dangerous to us should the same fate befall
you, Agravain.'

Morgaine. There it was. The name no one in the whole
of Camelot dared to speak aloud. The name of the one who
was nemesis to King Arthur and Queen Guinevere both.

The name of his mother Morgause's twin sister.

'We cannot leave Din Eityn kingless,' said Agravain doggedly. 'It commands both the old Roman walls.'

'Which mean far less than they used to with all the quarrels that have sprung up between them, unmediated,' said Gawain slowly. 'Let the dogs fight over the bone a little, while the true threat is dealt with.'

Agravain stared at his brother. Gawain could not really be thinking this way. It was Gododdin he spoke of. It was their place, their land and their people. It was the place that made them princes, and the place that they had been robbed of, and where their father was prisoner. He could not seriously be considering waiting one more day to take it back.

But as he stared at his brother, Agravain saw Gawain was not thinking like a man of Gododdin. He was thinking like the one who must be the next High King. As Arthur's heir, Gawain must consider all the lands and peoples that had entered into the Pax Arturus. Gododdin was but one piece in that puzzle.

Would you sacrifice our north to save your south, Gawain? It was not a question he had permitted himself to ask before, and in that he had clearly been foolish. When Gawain had left Gododdin, he had left the whole of it behind. He was fully a man of Camelot now, and would not be anything else.

It occurred to Agravain then that Gawain and Arthur might have spoken on this very subject.

Spoken on it, and not told me.

He felt anger take hold. Its grip enfolded his reason, cold and unyielding. He looked at his brother and his king, and saw how their plans hid behind their calm eyes. What was his kingdom to them? What care had they for the men of Gododdin? Leave them to the wolves, and while the wolves worry their bones we stay safe.

'There is another way.'

Kai spoke the words judiciously, craning his neck to look

up at the men who stood around him. The gleam in his eye pierced Agravain's deepening anger like the light of hope.

'What is that?' asked Arthur.

'If Your Majesty is already mindful to strike first, do not go to the north. Strike in the west.'

Arthur stared at his foster brother. In return, Kai smiled, the sly, crooked smile that so many in the court knew and mistrusted. 'The cat's away, my king. Why should we not take her mice to play with?' His eyes sparked with mischief, but his words were sound. *How long have you contemplated them, Sir Kai?* 'If this is her army, it came from somewhere. Wherever that is, she has left those places only lightly defended.'

Agravain stared stupidly at his uncle. *Why did I not think of this? We were all of us so blinded by fear of her.*

Kai sat further back in his chair, rubbing his chin with his long hand. 'Gareth is in the west. So is Geraint. Send them word. Our nephews can send men to their neighbour countries more quickly than we could move a southern army to the north.'

The High King blinked, like a man rising from a heavy sleep. 'Could it be done?' he whispered. 'Has she bared her heart at last?'

Agravain seized the opening. 'It may be so. Geraint and Gareth can tell us for certain. They can find where the men have moved from. We can determine which lands have given her their alliance and attack there.'

He could not see the king's eyes for the shadows that puddled in them, and Agravain found he was glad. He did not want to see Arthur's fear. Each time Morgaine's name was uttered that fear was there, and it changed the king, wearing him down like any heavy burden must at last wear down the strongest man.

The king shook his head, wagging it slowly back and forth,

uncertain what to believe. Agravain felt a different cold overtake him. Fear trickled into his veins. It was not like Arthur
to display uncertainty in a matter of war. But talk of attacking
Morgaine who had plagued them all like a demon for so
many years made him hesitate. How could this be?

What has she done to you? Has she already taken you? The
thought constricted Agravain's heart. If Morgaine had sunk
her invisible knife into Arthur, they were all lost.

No. Merlin protects him. But Merlin was not there and
Agravain looked again at the king's eyes, so distant and so
suddenly old. The cold within him deepened.

'She may still be in the West Lands,' said the king uneasily.
'Her reach is long. That she leads in the north does not mean
she is there. It may be a trap.'

'Let her be in the west,' Agravain said flatly. 'She has left
herself without her usual guard, and will come the more
easily to the sword.'

The doubt did not leave the king's countenance. He fell
back to studying the fire again, watching for omens and
answers in the bright flames. Agravain cast a glance at
Gawain. *Will you strike this blow if the king cannot?* Agravain
asked his brother silently. Gawain's face was hard and grim.
With a brother's sympathy, Agravain felt the heat stirring in
Gawain's blood. Oh, yes. This much he could trust Gawain
to do.

'Let me go to Din Eityn, Sire,' said Agravain. 'Let me go
at once.'

'Not alone.'

Agravain's focus was so intent on King Arthur, it took him
a moment to realize it was Gawain who had spoken. He
turned to his brother, the cold of anger descending over him
once more. 'This is mine to do.'

Gawain stood solidly, but the fingers of his right hand
rubbed together. Itching for action. So, he did remember this

was their home, and how it was taken from them, and by whom. He did want to strike a man's blow in that place. 'This is not a quarrel between us, Agravain. The security of all our lands is in jeopardy.'

'Nothing could be worse than sending the High King's heir up at the head of a southern army. It will be the excuse Morgaine needs to bring those gore crows on our borders to her side. Think, Gawain!' he ordered, for all the good it would do. 'Do we want her to be able to stand up and shout that all Arthur seeks is conquest?'

He made no apology for these words, nor sought to soften them. They must speak plainly here. The time for obfuscation and hesitation was done. *And if you are going to be the southern king, my brother, you cannot also be the northern. You must accept that.*

'Five hundred men,' Agravain said slowly, clearly. 'If she can take Din Eityn, she will be able to stand any siege we can mount next spring.'

Pain flickered behind the king's eyes. 'We thought we were encroaching on her domains from the east, and she was already embracing the north. Too slow, again,' he breathed hoarsely. 'Too late, again.'

'Not this time,' said Agravain. 'We know her object. She can be stopped, and she will be.'

Arthur rubbed his eyes. His old, tired eyes. 'I will think on this. We will hold further council in the morning.'

'Sire . . .' began Agravain.

But Sir Kai got ponderously to his feet. 'Go, you two. I will keep the king's company for a little while yet.' More softly he added, 'Go back to your wife, Agravain.'

And that was the end of it. Agravain and Gawain bowed, and walked into the corridor, and the door shut behind them, leaving them in the dim and flickering torchlight. Agravain glowered at the blank wood.

What is the matter with you, my king? he demanded silently. *Where is your heart?*

There was no answer here. There was no answer anywhere. Agravain turned on his heel, and strode down the corridor. He had no destination in mind. He just needed to be away from there. Away from the voices of men which he could no longer understand, out from the closeness of the walls.

He needed to be home, but home was days and years away.

'Agravain, do we know it is her?' asked Gawain softly.

Agravain rounded on his brother, glad to have a vent for the frustration pressing hard against his heart and thoughts. 'Are you calling me a liar?'

Gawain did not flinch. 'You have often complained that King Arthur does not keep the northern borders well enough. If you thought it would spur him to greater action, you might speak of suspicion as certainty.'

Agravain felt his mouth tighten into a hard line. 'If I wished to spur the High King on, Morgaine is the last name I would invoke.'

'That is unworthy.'

Agravain's brows arched. 'Is it?'

'You know that it is.'

Perhaps, but it is true all the same. Agravain folded his arms, blowing out a sigh. He could not stay here bantering with Gawain. There was something else that needed to be done at once. 'Is there anything else you have to say to me, Gawain?'

'Much, but very little you'd hold still for.' Now Gawain sighed, and he ran his hand through his hair. He also was tired. Dark circles showed under his eyes. Was his brother beginning to age as the king had aged? 'Look carefully to your own need for revenge, Agravain. It will lead you down the false path she lays.'

'You counsel me thus?' Agravain held his ground. He would give Gawain no excuse to accuse him of running away.

'Yes, brother.' Gawain nodded, absolutely sober. 'I do, and I have cause to know.'

Agravain felt the corner of his mouth twitch. 'I will bear your words in mind. Now, I ask your pardon. I have other business I must attend to.'

'God be with you, Agravain.'

Agravain did not answer him. There was no answer that needed giving. All that he required now was that Gawain not follow him.

The corridors here were empty, and he could make out no sound of celebration as he passed the main hall. Good. He had no desire to meet up with any of the court now.

Go back to your wife, Kai had counselled him. Perhaps he should. When he had laid these plans, there had been no wife in them. Laurel was not something he had even imagined.

No. If I delay in this matter, I may never find the heart, or the time, to pursue it.

The coldest part of the night had settled in. The damp wind smelled heavily of more rain to come. Agravain's skin prickled beneath his woollen tunic and he wished briefly he had thought to get his cloak. But there was no time to waste on minor discomfort. This needed to be done before the whole hall roused itself, before rumour had the full and open light of day to play in. One last secret to be acquired while there was still time. He did not delude himself. His was an audacious request, and he might be refused. If he was successful, he would need time to add what he learned to his current plans.

The plans the king might yet destroy. Agravain's fist clenched and he strode across the quiet yard.

Near the southern wall of Camelot's great keep waited one

humble edifice set apart from the others. It was a thatched cottage, its wattle and daub walls washed over with lime. But rather than belonging to a herdsman or kitchen woman, it was the chosen dwelling of the king's chief advisor.

Merlin's home glowed white in the waning light of the stars, and the door was ajar. Agravain did not bother to knock or to announce himself. He pushed the door open and stepped across the threshold.

A fire burned low in the hearth, giving barely enough light to see by. Shadows filled the cottage. They hung from the rafters with the drying herbs. They lurked on the long work tables amid the plants and earths, clay vessels and pots of inks and dyes, carefully obscuring the drawing instruments required for charting the course of the heavens. They scuttled around the walls like rodents and squatted at the foot of the broad, covered well like toads. They crept close, brushing Agravain's ankles and leaning over his shoulders.

Merlin stood before one of the work tables. Shadows gathered behind him, like servants waiting for their orders. The sorcerer appeared as he always did, in his robes of unadorned black, a black cap on his sparse white hair. He did not look up at the sound of Agravain's step. Instead, he stared at a great sheet of parchment, covered in carefully rendered lines and perfect circles. Agravain knew enough to see it was a star chart, an elaborate and detailed horoscope, obviously many days, if not weeks, in its making. But it was ruined now. A huge puddle of black ink crept across its surface, a shadow in liquid form, trickling across the illustration of the future and blotting it all out.

Merlin made no move to rescue the document. He just leaned on his gnarled hands and watched the stain spread.

'You're late,' said Merlin heavily. 'I expected you before.'

Agravain walked forward warily. He had never known Merlin to be at all unsettled, no matter what came before him. Had he been wearing it, he would have laid his hand on his sword.

'Then you know why I have come?'

'In part.' The sorcerer ducked his head. It was difficult to see in the encroaching shadows, but Agravain thought he closed his eyes. He did sway on his feet, as if exhausted almost beyond endurance.

Agravain waited. The shadows waited too, but restlessly. The firelight pushed and pulled them, holding them back just a little although they were anxious to surge closer. Loyal servants, their master's distress disturbed them.

'What is the matter?' asked Agravain, although a deep part of himself that was either a coward or a wise man hoped Merlin would give no answer.

That part was not disappointed. Merlin just shook his head, turning from the ruined horoscope, shuffling to his chair like an old man, like a blind man. He laid one hand on the carved back. The shadows pressed close, warning, supporting. Merlin looked at his shuttered window. 'Speak, Agravain.'

Why won't you look at me? What have you seen? 'I have a request to make of you,' Agravain said bluntly, attempting to crush the uneasiness these unwelcome questions raised.

Merlin nodded. He swallowed. Agravain could see his withered Adam's apple bob clearly beneath his beard. 'You are the last man I would have expected to seek guidance by such uncertain means as prophecy.'

'Morgaine holds sway in the invisible countries. I would look into them before I face her.' Merlin knew of the messenger and message. Of course he knew Morgaine was responsible for the army that threatened Gododdin.

Agravain held his ground while the sorcerer contemplated his shutters. The shadows pressed heavily at his back. They would not hurt him. They existed to frighten the fools and the weak who were not certain of what they did here.

Merlin sighed so deeply his bent shoulders shook. 'Very well.' He turned, shuffling again, looking with regret at the horoscope, still not looking at Agravain himself. 'Give me your question. I shall see it answered.'

'No,' said Agravain.

All the restless shadows froze in place, startled. 'No?' repeated Merlin softly.

'I cannot begin this war by shrinking from the invisible. I will do this thing myself.'

It was as if those words were finally too much. Merlin lifted his lined face and met Agravain's gaze. To show his determination, Agravain looked long and hard into the sorcerer's eyes. Danger waited there, even now, when Merlin was exhausted and unaccountably afraid. Danger old and deep, going back more years than should belong to mortal man. Agravain felt his resolve tremble.

'You do this at your peril, Agravain. This is a thing which will dull wits even as sharp as yours. You are not trained to this. It is beyond your understanding.'

Merlin's eyes were clear blue, like the king's, but in that moment, it seemed to Agravain that all the room's shadows looked out at him through that ancient gaze.

'I will do this thing myself,' he repeated.

He felt his past stripped from his skin, and folded around his future. All his shields of indifference, pride, reason and isolation were gone in an instant. He felt his self standing naked before the old sorcerer and all his unseen familiars. For one dreadful instant, Agravain knew clearly that Merlin could choose not to give those shields of soul and self back.

But Merlin lowered his gaze, and all disturbance was gone. Agravain was able to breathe again.

'So it must be,' he whispered. 'Come then, Agravain. I can give you three answers only.'

Slowly, Merlin walked to the covered well. A strange chill

of anticipation ran down Agravain's spine. None had ever
seen this thing opened. Gareth swore he'd looked once, on
a dare, but he was never able to satisfactorily describe what
he had seen.

Merlin laid his hands on the heavy lid. He leaned his
weight on his hands and stood like that for a moment, his
eyes closed, his lips moving soundlessly. Agravain felt
suddenly heavy, as if he were being pushed into the earth
by the restless shadows around him.

Then, in one surprisingly swift move, Merlin heaved the
cover aside, revealing a light more steady and golden than
any flame. 'Look on what you would see, Agravain. Speak
your questions as you will.'

Fighting against the unnatural heaviness, Agravain moved
forward. He steeled himself, and looked down.

It was no true well, only a shallow depression filled with
some clear golden fluid that made him think of honey, save
that this shone like the sun made into liquid form, although
its light gave no warmth at all.

In this thickened light lay three human heads.

All three rested on their backs, so that he could clearly
see the stumps where their necks had been severed from
their bodies. They had all been dispatched with clean blows,
his reeling mind noticed distantly. All three taken with a
strong arm and a sharp blade. There was a man, in the prime
of his years, his beard full and his face strong. There was an
ancient woman, her eyes wise, her long white hair waving
in the subtle currents of the light that surrounded her. There
was a youth, younger than even Gareth, his pale face terrible
with pain.

Their eyes were open and milk-white with the film of
death. They all looked directly at him.

'Hail Agravain, King of the Gododdin,' said the man. His
voice was the whisper of a sword against skin.

'Hail Agravain, Heir of Lot and all his deeds,' said the crone. Her teeth were grey and broken, and her voice trembled but still held an awful strength.

'Hail Agravain,' said the youth, his voice light and fragile as a bird's. 'Hold your heart close. You will see far worse than us ere long.'

Fear shook him hard. He had been ready to face a demon, an elf-lord or some other captive spirit. Something with which he could match his wits. Something like the creatures his brothers had already faced and defeated.

This . . . these . . . were unnatural, terrible things. Death should not be so violated. These were souls dragged from the ground, hidden from God himself. What power, what blasphemy, could do this? Could mock what was granted only by the Word? What devil had made them? Merlin. Had Merlin's hand struck the blows so clean and swift as to trap the soul itself?

'Speak Agravain,' said Merlin. 'You have three questions.'

How could he seek truth from such abomination? Agravain groped after his carefully laid plans, but his thoughts had all flown and there was nothing left but shadow. He was blind while these things looked at him, waited for him. Blind, lost, alone.

'What do you see for Agravain?' His voice croaked awkwardly, but he did not think it mattered. Surely these three could understand any word. It was their function.

The man answered. 'War,' he said in his soft, death-sharp voice. 'It comes on the raven's wings. It comes with bloody vengeance and conquest to the walls. It seeps into the stones like the lightest wind and it lurks in the shadows.'

Agravain's mouth was dry. Sweat sprang out on his brow. His skin itched and crawled from the voice and the gaze of the blind white eyes that saw far too much. Wasted. A question wasted. He must think, must clear his mind and find understanding. He must remember who he was, what brought him here.

'Who . . .' he began, and stopped, and began again. 'Who is the man in the black armour?'

The crone spoke, clicking and snapping her broken teeth. 'He is Mordred.' The words pinched and clutched, leaving cold behind to prick his very heart. 'Arthur's bane, Arthur's son. Morgaine's hope, Morgaine's son. Born of prophecy and vengeance, his is the hand that ends the world and begins it again.'

Arthur's *son*?

Arthur had no son. Morgaine's son? No. No. This could not be. Morgaine was Arthur's sister, his *sister*. It could not be. He would not, and she, even as she was, she could not have.

No. No. Not even she would do that . . .

Agravain's gorge heaved. He gripped the side of the well, digging his fingers into the stone. He could not think. He could not speak. It was too much.

God! God help me! God save me! Take this from me!

'You have one more question, Agravain.'

'No!' Agravain cried out, squeezing his eyes shut. He could not look, could not face what was before him. 'No more!'

But Merlin's living voice was harder and more pitiless than the mocking voices of the dead before him. 'You have begun this thing, Agravain. You cannot leave it until it is done.'

No! No! I will not. But his mouth moved. He could not stop it. Words would tumble out of him, whether he willed it or no. He must find a question. There must be one last question, one way to find out how to put right this terrible, unimaginable wrong.

Agravain had faced death. He knew it, but it was an ending, all pain all horror gone. Death was not supposed to give back, God was not supposed to let go. How could the king keep near him one who had done these things? The king who had lain with his own sister . . .

His voice trembled as badly as his hands, and he could barely force out the words. One question. One last chance. And there was only one question, one real question. It had haunted him for ten years, and it was what he had come here to learn.

'How can Morgaine be defeated?'

The youth spoke, and Agravain heard his brothers' young voices there, and his sister's, and his own lost childhood. All crumbled to dust, dragged up again and made to serve when they should have been left to lie in peace.

'Only her own deeds can defeat Morgaine. Her pride is great, Agravain *mach* Lot, greater than yours. Only when she forgets she is bound by the laws of men and gods will she fall.'

That lightest of voices pressed against his skull as if to crush it. It fell against his back and shoulders with a grave's worth of weight, bowing him down. Sweat rolled down his cheeks and a groan escaped his clenched teeth. He closed his eyes. He could look no more on this violation. He heard wood grate against stone, and the light winked out.

'Sit down, Agravain.'

Agravain groped blindly and found a chair's arm. He slumped into it, his head in his hands. Shame filled him, and disgust, and bewilderment. He looked up at Merlin, as mute as a child who sees death for the first time.

Merlin stood over him, leaning on his white staff. 'And now you know what few others do. Arthur and Guinevere know. Morgaine who brought this thing into being, and Mordred himself.'

'How?' Agravain's voice cracked on that single word.

'By trickery,' said Merlin with weary simplicity. 'How else? She heard the prophecy that Arthur would be killed by his own son, and she was determined that such a son would be born. It suited her fancy that Arthur's doom should be conceived by a change of shape, since that was how Arthur himself was conceived.'

Not his fault then. Agravain drew in a long, shuddering breath. It was easier to bear knowing that. One more sin to lay at Morgaine's door. It was not the king's fault. He had only been tricked, as others had. He had not sought out this sin. Merlin would not lie about such a thing.

Merlin would not lie about such a thing.

Agravain lifted his head. Merlin had returned to his chair beside the window and slumped into it, turning his staff in his crooked hands. 'Bespeaking the dead is a hard and terrible thing. You bore it well.' He was not looking at Agravain. He was looking again at the shutters, as if wondering whether they were stout enough to keep out the night, lest it swallow his guardian shadows in its greater darkness.

Is this what disturbs you so? Did you know I'd find out? Or is there something else?

But he could not make himself speak these new questions. Though his reluctance sickened him, he knew one more heavy truth would break him in two. Agravain rubbed his palms on his trousers. 'I suppose I should thank you for your help.' He got to his feet. 'You did try to warn me.'

'Agravain.' His name spoken as a plea stopped him halfway to the door. 'Do not discard what you have heard. Once prophecy has been spoken, there is danger in ignoring it.'

Agravain laid his hand on the door latch. 'I will remember.' He could not make himself look back at the shadows, at Merlin hunched beneath the weight of his unnatural knowledge. Instead, he walked out into the clean night and looked up at the fading stars.

He did not know where to go. He did not know what to

do. A year seemed to have passed since Ros first stumbled into his room.

His room. His wedding chamber. Laurel. He looked across at the main keep. A few lights flickered behind some of the shutters. Was one of them from her window?

He walked across the courtyard, empty and silent except for the forms of the watchmen on the walls. He moved quickly, to get away from all he had seen. He would not ignore it, but he could not think on it. Not yet. It made the very stones beneath his boots feel fragile with rot.

Mordred. The Black Knight. Arthur's son. Morgaine's son.

Up the stairs and down the corridor, Agravain came up to Laurel's door. He scratched at it softly, and pushed it open.

A fire burned low in the hearth. In the chairs beside it dozed not Laurel, but her woman Meg, and Gawain's wife Rhian. Rhian started and looked up as the door opened. When she saw him, she got to her feet.

'What news, Agravain?' Rhian asked.

'Not much,' he said tersely, looking past her towards Laurel where she lay on the bed, stilled by sleep. 'There will be more council in the morning.'

Rhian followed his gaze. 'Do you want me to wake her?' she asked softly.

Agravain looked at Laurel lying in that bower they had been meant to share. Her face was troubled in her sleep, her white brow furrowed just a little, as if she must concentrate on the dreams that bore her away. The braid of her white hair lay across her neck and shoulders. As he watched her, her brow smoothed, and her hand lifted, brushing the braid back, exposing her throat, reminding him of how warm and delicate her skin had felt beneath his touch, of how she had laid her hand on his chest. On her other hand, lying on the coverings, he saw the green and gold gleam of the wedding ring he had given her.

He had thought to go to her, to sleep beside her at least. But even as he looked down at her, his skin crept and crawled over his bones, shivering from the memory of what he had seen and done. It filled him with the sense of having been made unclean. He could not go near her, not yet. Not until he mastered himself.

He would master himself. He must. Nothing had changed save his knowledge of what he faced. He had sought that knowledge and could not shrink from it.

But neither could he move towards his pale, beautiful wife where she lay.

I'm sorry. His chest tightened now and he swallowed.

'Let her sleep,' said Agravain, and he turned away and left her there.

SIX

Laurel woke slowly. Groggy, she sat up, shoving her hair out of her eyes to see Meg and Lady Rhian sitting beside the low fire. Cryda and Elsa were busy beside the hearth, obviously taking care not to make any noise.

Meg was on her feet in an instant to twist Laurel's hair back from her face and help lace her underdress up around her shoulders.

Rhian also came to the bedside. 'Meg, will you go and see what there is to break your lady's fast? The queen has sent word, Laurel. You are to come to her, but only once you have eaten properly, and had time to dress yourself.'

Laurel nodded absently at this, and Meg excused herself, bustling out the door.

'And my lord Agravain?' Laurel asked.

'It was he who made sure we were sent for. He apologizes for this necessity and prays your patience with his absence.'

'That was not what he said.' It was strange how certain she was.

Rhian lifted her eyebrows. 'No,' she admitted. 'But he did tender his apology.'

Laurel made no answer to this as she pushed back the

covers so she could climb out of the bed. The roses and ivy had been taken down at some point, much to her relief. This was no longer a celebration of marriage, but a crisis between kings. Summer's flowers had no place here.

Neither do bare feet and a thin, linen underdress. 'I must get decent. There is a long day ahead.'

Rhian wasted no more time on conversation. Instead, she summoned Cryda and Elsa from their work with the fire and kettles. Soon, Laurel's face, hands and feet were washed, and her hair was brushed and braided. It was strange to feel the air on the back of her neck as her braids were coiled and pinned in a style befitting a married woman. She was dressed in a rich but sober gown of forest green trimmed with brown and white ribbons. A matching veil was secured over her hair. Meg arrived shortly after that, leading a trio of kitchen girls who carried trays loaded with frumenty, milk, honey, fresh strawberries, stout bread, salt herring, small beer and cider. As soon as she smelled the food Laurel realized she had an appetite. She had been able to eat almost nothing at the feast the night before. Now, she sat herself willingly at the trestle table. Meg, as had become her habit it seemed, vented her personal worries by harping after Cryda and Elsa, who in turn passed the frustration down to Camelot's fair-haired kitchen daughters as they laid the cloth and the dishes.

As Laurel opened her mouth to invite Rhian to sit down with her, a footfall in the corridor made her turn her head.

Agravain stood in the threshold.

'Forgive me, my lady,' he said, bowing. 'I heard you were awake.'

Laurel rose, taking in the sight of her husband. Agravain had dressed, but not slept. His eyes were hollow and dark, and his hair disordered. Black stubble turned his chin, and much of his throat, sooty. Their eyes met. She saw there the memory of all that had, and had not, passed between them the night before, but what ease they had created between them had vanished with the night.

Which left Laurel feeling nothing so much as frustration. 'There is no apology necessary, my lord,' she said. 'Will you break your fast with me?'

He looked at the table and its fragrant burden. Emotions she could not read flickered across his pinched face. For a heartbeat, she feared he meant to refuse.

'An' I thank you,' he said at last, taking a step into the room.

'Meg, a place for my lord.' Laurel looked past her waiting woman towards Rhian, hoping the other woman was as quick as she seemed.

She was not disappointed. 'You are well looked after here, I see,' Rhian said briskly. 'And I am required elsewhere. God be with you, brother.' She nodded briefly to Agravain as she swept past him.

While Meg bustled about helping retrieve a chair and an enamelled bowl, Laurel took the silver cup and jug from a waiting tray. Her mother had always served her father's first drink of any meal with her own hands. She could think of nothing better than to revisit this courtesy now. Laurel poured out a measure of fragrant cider and set the cup before Agravain as he sat down. He watched her with a mild surprise, but accepted the cup and drank deeply.

Like Rhian, Meg understood there was a need for privacy at this time. She saw to it that all the bowls and cups were filled and that all the necessary implements and comforts were at hand, and dismissed all the other maids. Without another word, she retired discreetly to sit beside the fire with her own bread and porridge, waiting to be needed.

The food was warm, fresh and good. Laurel found it easy to help herself and eat with relish. Agravain ate in silence but with deep appetite. If he did not quite enjoy the repast, it was plain he at least appreciated it, and the colour strengthened in his sallow face.

But for all her careful watching, it was not until the meal
was almost completed that Laurel could move herself to
speak.

'May I ask what further word the night has brought?'

Agravain set the last bite of bread down in his bowl, as if
suddenly unable to finish. He looked towards the door, and
the window. *Searching for listening ears or looking for his words?*

'There is . . . much debate as to what should be done next,'
he said slowly.

Laurel felt herself frown. 'Surely you must return to
Gododdin.'

Agravain pushed his bowl back, scowling at some memory.
'Nothing is sure. I hope . . . I hope that I will be given permission to go within three days. There is war to come, but there
is disagreement over how it should be met. The king has his
doubts . . .' He stopped himself. 'Should I leave to return to
Gododdin, it is my wish that you should come with me.'

That startled Laurel. She had assumed her role would be
to wait in Camelot and be sent for once the throne was
secured.

'If that is your wish, I will come,' she said. 'But I do not
understand. You tell me there is a war to fight. I can do
nothing to help in this, and may weaken your side.' *I am
your outsider bride, and rumoured to be a witch as well.*

'That I bring my bride will show that I mean to make
Gododdin my home. It also . . .' He stopped once more, and
for a moment watched his own hands flexing open and
closed. When he spoke, it was clear he had reached some
decision. 'There is also one of the reasons for which I agreed
to this marriage.'

Laurel's throat tightened, and she felt suddenly cold. 'What
reason is this?'

Agravain raised his eyes. He had closed himself away again, as if that would make it easier for him to speak. 'You have almost as much reason to hate the sorceress Morgaine as I do. The heritage of your blood may give you ways to stand against her that others lack.

'It is Morgaine's army I go to face.'

Morgaine. A flood of memories tumbled through her thoughts, sweeping them all away; a black-eyed woman standing before her in the great hall, Laurel's brother in chains at her feet, that woman beside her father's grave, offering her . . . offering her all that she thought she wanted and the power to keep it.

Blood. The itch and stink of blood on her hands, which could not be removed for the weight of that memory. Her father's blood. Her father killed by her brother, at Morgaine's urging and instigation. Her sister white with exhaustion, reclaimed from the death Morgaine would have purchased for her.

The thought that the sorceress had entered into the calculations Agravain had made in accepting her was like ice in Laurel's veins. He had accepted her not in spite of her heritage, but because of it. And he was not telling her everything. There was more waiting in that closed-off part of him. It had aged him overnight, this unspoken thing, and it waited silently in this room with them now.

Set it aside. Speak to what was said. 'You see Morgaine's hand in this?'

Agravain nodded stiffly. 'Her sigil has been seen, and even if it had not been . . . Her hand pressed on Gododdin for a long time, on the king most of all.' The king, not 'my father'.

Grimly, Laurel willed her hand to reach for the cup in front of her and lift it to her mouth so that she could swallow the cider down and clear the way for her voice again. 'Why? Gododdin is far from her lands, and farther from Camelot.'

'Because of the war between herself and her sister, who was my mother. I am Morgaine's nephew as well as King Arthur's.' Agravain's brown hand curled up on the table-cloth. She was not sure he even knew he had made this new fist.

'If it is true she is responsible for this new war,' began Laurel, setting the cup down carefully, 'how can there be disagreement about whether you should return to Gododdin? The fortress and the land must be made ready.'

Agravain grimaced. 'Because it is Morgaine, and because it is my uncle.'

'The High King . . .'

'Can do nothing,' said Agravain flatly, harshly. 'Nothing.' With that last word, he slammed his fist against the table so the dishes rattled. Meg started up and Laurel waved her back.

'Forgive me,' he said. 'Forgive me. It has been a long night.' He glanced towards the door. 'I should leave you.'

I should not speak at all. She heard this in the current of feeling underneath his words. *I should not trust anyone with this counsel.*

Secrets. New secrets come from somewhere. He did not yet know how to shut them all in. If he dwelt on them another moment, he would leave, and she could not let him go yet. It would be that much harder for him to speak next time.

'What is the nature of this disagreement over tactics?' she asked, praying she did not sound too hasty. 'If you do not return home, what other course is there?'

Agravain did not answer immediately. He only watched her, deciding. He would either speak, or leave. Inwardly, and absurdly, Laurel cursed Lot, and Morgaine. They should not have been talking like this. Not this soon. They should have been strolling through the orchards, speaking of small matters, beginning to learn each other's natures and ways.

In the end, Agravain chose to speak. Methodically, he laid out the three separate plans, his own, the king's, and Sir Kai's. Laurel listened in silence. It clearly nagged at Agravain to have to admit his uncles disagreed with his wish to assemble a small retinue and leave at once. It was a reasonable and obvious plan. It was, perhaps, the only plan he had ever had for the time when this message should come. But there was deep merit in Sir Kai's plan. It could be made to work, if Morgaine's all-seeing eyes could be deflected for long enough. The war itself might not be enough . . .

An idea came to Laurel then, fully formed, and audacious. She sat frozen for a moment under the weight of her thought. Seeing how rigid she had gone, Agravain paused in his narrative and his brow furrowed.

'Meg,' Laurel's voice rasped as she spoke. 'Leave us.'

Agravain's brows furrowed more deeply, as did Meg's, but the waiting woman did not question the command. She made her curtsey, and walked out of the room. When the door shut, Laurel still kept her silence, to give Meg time to remove herself a little down the corridor.

Agravain waited, not with good humour, but he did at least wait.

'There is another way,' Laurel said. 'To claim Din Eityn and lay a trap for Morgaine.'

'What is that?' Agravain narrowed his eyes, suspicious, surprised, and something else she could not name.

'Let it be seen that you leave in opposition to the king.'

Agravain drew himself up. It was strange to see the anger, and the relief at being able to be angry at the same time. 'You say I should stand out against my uncle?'

'No,' replied Laurel calmly. 'I say you should be seen to. Let it be rumoured, and talked over and descried, that you quarrelled with King Arthur, and then returned home without his permission.' She swallowed. Agravain had gone hard as flint. But she was right. This was the way. 'If Morgaine has any strategy, it is to create dissent.' *Dissent and death. But secretly. Let any hand get bloody but hers.* 'She works by dividing people from each other and annihilating trust.' *Even between father and son, and brother and sister.* 'Then, she lets those she has split in two destroy themselves by whatever means comes most easily to them.

'If she believes there is a break here in the heart of Camelot, she will not watch it as critically. She will rejoice over any dissent and believe it must work in her favour. Believing you will arrive already weakened, she will turn her attention to this war for Gododdin, to be ready to properly welcome you. That will give Lynet and Gareth, and your brother Geraint, time to determine where her western lands are the weakest.'

Would he dismiss her out of hand? No. His eyes flickered back and forth, hearing her words repeat inside his mind, weighing and considering, adding them to what he already knew and seeing how the totals stood.

'And if this contrived rumour reaches Geraint and Gareth before the truth does?' he asked.

'I will send Meg home to Lynet. She was nurse to Lynet and myself, and lady to our mother before that. Lynet will know she can believe any message Meg carries. It need not even be written down. Gareth can then send word to your brother Geraint by whatever means he thinks best. No other instruction need come from Camelot. King Arthur will be seen as disregarding any counsel save his own, and send his army north, to try to meet the Dal Riata, who will hasten to take Din Eityn, before they are fully ready, the better to meet Arthur from inside Din Eityn.'

'And while they are rushing themselves, Arthur can swing west as soon as Gareth and Geraint have useful intelligence,' murmured Agravain. His fingers drummed against the table cloth, making a sound like muffled rain. He looked past her, to the wall, to the fire, to how this plan might play out in the waiting future. 'Were we to do this thing, you must be seen to choose where your loyalty lies.'

Strange that this is what should concern him now. 'Yes.'

'If you stand by me, it will open you to great censure.' He was thinking of the rumours Sir Kai had alluded to at the welcome feast. Those would come back, and double, and redouble, including the allusions of witchcraft.

'It is better than leaving Gododdin and Camelot open to conquest by Morgaine.'

He was watching her closely, adding her to his calculations. *What is it? What are you thinking of?*

Then she saw it, slowly, that opening behind his shuttered eyes to show her the thin thread of self that was trust inside Agravain. It was fragile and new, the tiniest green shoot of spring, but it was trust nonetheless.

'I will speak to my uncle,' he said softly. 'You will know which way it is decided when you hear the outcry.'

Laurel inclined her head. 'I will be ready,' she said and she hoped that was the truth.

She expected him to get to his feet then, but he hesitated. 'Will you go to Din Eityn or stay here?'

Laurel blinked. 'I have already said, my lord . . .'

Agravain waved his hand dismissively. 'You spoke dutifully, my lady, without all the facts in hand. Now that you know more of what surrounds you, it may be that you would make another choice. If this is so, please speak. I will not require you to go.'

Trust waited. Fear waited. This was a test of sorts, and she knew it. That angered her, even though she understood why he put her to it. It was not the wife he doubted. It was the new ally he was uncertain of.

As he should be. Laurel smothered that thought as quickly as it came to her.

'Thank you,' she answered. 'But I will go. Gododdin is my land now. I will not neglect it when I may be of service to its peace or to the king, my husband.'

One muscle in his cheek twitched. 'Thank you, my wife.'

For a moment, she wondered if he would make some mention of their night which had been so swiftly and thoroughly interrupted, but he did not. He got to his feet.

'Please excuse my haste. I must confer with the king. If your . . . plan is put into action, there are many things I myself will have to arrange.' He bowed, and once more he left her there.

As the door closed, exasperation, irrational to the point of being ludicrous, swirled through Laurel. Was this what it would be to be queen of Gododdin? A series of hasty exits that left her agape? Laurel rubbed her eyes.

Patience, she counselled herself. *He goes to meet a dying father and a kingdom at war.*

And what do I go to meet?

To her shock, Laurel found her hands trembling. One way or another, she would be leaving. She would go farther from home and family than she had ever been. No ally waited for her there, only strangers, and war, and enmity in the shadowed form of Morgaine the Sleepless.

Laurel had been born with the power of the unseen in her blood. She had always known it was there. But her mother who might have taught her the ways of the invisible and the divine had died when she was eight years old. So, she was left alone. She could hear the voice of the wind, and she could use it to carry word for her, making someone go or stay, though they knew not why they did so. Men spoke in her presence sometimes things they would rather keep silent about. She could see what was hidden if she tried, and she could bring fear if her anger reached deeply enough, and the sea would answer her if she spoke.

But for all that, she was not learned, not practised, not truly, not as Morgaine, who was as skilled in her art as any master smith or veteran soldier.

Laurel closed her eyes, and swallowed hard.

If you have no stomach for action, you should have kept silent, she chided herself. *It is too late for your qualms now. You have begun. You must go on.*

But how?

Laurel licked her lips. Steeling herself, she walked gingerly to the window, undid the latch and folded back the shutters.

The day beyond was bright. All the smells of the yard rushed in: straw and animals, hot metal and the distant stink of the tannery. The wind brushed her face. She smelled rain, and earth on it. Cold to come, perhaps, even at the height of summer. She reached within, opening the doors of her mind, letting the wind pass through, pass through blood and spirit and self. Let it see her questions, let it carry answers as it carried the scents and sounds of the wide world all around.

Too far, the wind and her own quieting heart told her. She looked too far. She needed to look closer. Look to herself, look to her own, to the woman of her home, the man at her hand, the one whose eyes had seen the most of this war that had been brewing for decades now.

Laurel closed her eyes, letting understanding and relief both seep in. The woman of her home. That was Queen Guinevere. The man at her hand. Agravain. The one whose eyes had seen the most . . . King Arthur? Sir Kai? No. That last meant the oldest of the players in this deadly game. The one she had not seen since the eve of her wedding.

Merlin.

Laurel breathed the fresh breeze deeply, thanking it, releasing it.

'My lady?'

Laurel opened her eyes. Meg stood behind her. Annoyance flashed through Laurel that Meg would have come back without being summoned. But in the next heartbeat, she realized Meg would have seen Agravain leave, and rightly assumed that she might be needed.

'My lady, the queen is waiting for you,' Meg reminded her diffidently.

Laurel shook herself, ashamed at having forgotten so important a fact. 'Yes, of course. Do we know where?'

'In the library, my lady.'

'Then let us go,' she said. *I wish to speak with you as well, my queen.*

The great library at Camelot had always been a wonder to Laurel. There did not exist in the whole of the isle another room such as this one. It rivalled the Round Table's hall for size. Scores of books bound in wood, bronze or leather lay on long tables. Box-like shelves held scrolls written in Greek and Arabic as well as Latin. Letters between kings, lords and commanders were bound with ribbons and wax and laid on its shelves in meticulously ordered piles. The silent, brown-robed monks sat at their high tables beside the open windows, carefully inscribing sheets of vellum and parchment with coloured inks. This was the place where her marriage contract would have been drawn up, and a copy would be left here as the official record of the act.

Queen Guinevere herself sat at a writing table, somewhat apart from the industrious monks. A beautifully drawn map of the Isle of the Britons was spread out in front of her. Each of its kingdoms had been picked out in a separate hue. The Dumonii lands, Laurel noted, were tinted blue and decorated with swans, the queen's own sigil. Yellow coloured the broad lowlands that were Arthur's native country, and a scarlet dragon wound through them. The valleys and broad firth overseen by Gododdin were all in green. Falcons dived there, wings folded, stooping to strike.

The queen turned her head towards Laurel, and belatedly Laurel moved to kneel. Guinevere, though, stopped her with a gesture.

'I am sorry this came upon you when it did.'

'It is not for us to order such things, Your Majesty,' replied Laurel. She had readied this polite piety while Meg braided her hair, anticipating she would need it as soon as she left her room. 'We must trust in God's time.'

'Sometimes, however, one could wish the Almighty showed a little more delicacy.' Queen Guinevere's mouth twisted into a wry smile. 'There. Now I will have to make confession to the bishop for blasphemy. Again. Sit, Laurel. Tell me what I can do to help you.'

A chair had already been brought, and Laurel sat down. She faced the queen, folding her hands in her lap. So decorous, so polite. So different from the matters she needed to discuss.

'I have only one question, Your Majesty, ' she said. 'Why is my husband so haunted by the sorceress Morgaine?'

Queen Guinevere stared at Laurel for a long moment. Then, the queen drew in a long breath through her pursed lips, letting it out again slowly.

'I should have known.' Guinevere's wry smile returned, but this time it did not reach her eyes, nor smooth the worried creases in her brow. 'You were ever one to strike straight for the heart of the matter.' The queen eyed the library door, as if to satisfy herself that it was indeed closed, and was the only entrance to the place. The monks paid not the slightest attention to their queen. They bent to their work, their pens squeaking and scratching, accompanied by the soft click and clink of the nibs touching the ink pots.

'You should know this. It is right you know,' Queen

Guinevere muttered, clearly attempting to convince herself. She twisted her fingers restlessly together. The queen's hands were long-fingered and strong. Some old, dark stain marred her soft palm, and had as long as Laurel had known her. Laurel had never been able ask what made the mark. It was not a question one addressed to the High Queen.

When at last Guinevere spoke, it was not in the language of the court. The words she chose were in the Dumonii tongue that she and Laurel shared. 'You must bear with me, Laurel. What I say now I have never told another, saving Arthur and Agravain.

'You know that the daughters of Ygraine and Goloris of Tintagel were brought in secret to foster at Cambryn? I was seven years old when they came. They were a strange sight to me: two girls of my own age with features so exactly matched, one might have been a reflection of the other. The only difference between them was that Morgause had blue eyes while Morgaine's were black.

'But I soon came to see that their natures differed as entirely as their eyes, and those differences broadened as they grew older. Oh, they remain fiercely devoted to each other for many years, but when womanhood came, the breach broke open so wide there was no crossing it.'

Queen Guinevere watched her own hands as she spoke, rubbing her thumb back and forth across the darkened patch of skin. It was strange to listen to her halting words. Laurel had never known the queen to be less than confident in her ways. Harried yes, but never unsure.

'The wedge that had been planted between the girls was the death of their father, Goloris. My father said he was a hard man, a jealous man. He turned against the whole nation of the Britons because he believed his wife Ygraine had been disloyal with Uther Pendragon.

'Morgause grieved for her father, but found room in her

heart to forgive, and to live with the scars. Morgaine could not do that. She nursed her hate. She would have vengeance.'

Laurel found herself once more in memory's grip. She stood beside the dais in her home hall. Her father lay sprawled on the stones, her brother's knife in his guts and the red blood pouring from him. She remembered looking into her brother's eyes and feeling the inferno of rage. She would have killed him, could have killed him easily, if law and imagination had not found a worse punishment.

'But it was more than that.' The queen's gaze was distant, looking out of the arched window down to the orchard beyond. Laurel saw blood, blood on her hands, blood on her sister's dress, on her father's corpse. What did the queen see? 'Morgaine would have power. The workings of the world would never again sweep away what she wished to keep hold of.'

Laurel's hands closed in sympathy. She knew this too. Only power could meet power, only strength could stand against strength. After all, what did she fear now but her own weakness?

'I remember when word came that Uther was dead,' the queen whispered. Her voice was harsh and Laurel felt her own throat tighten. 'Morgaine wept bitterly. Not because of the death, but because it was not her hand that struck him down. I think that was when I first truly became afraid of her.' Guinevere's hands stilled for just a moment. *Are you relieved or startled by this understanding?* wondered Laurel.

'After that, everything dissolved into chaos,' Guinevere went on, and the restless motion in her hands returned. 'The Saxons were everywhere, burning, raiding, slaughtering. We withstood one siege, then another. We starved and we held, and there was talk that the Dal Riata and the Eire-landers would join the Saxons, and it seemed like the world must end. Then, the rumours began. There was a war leader, a young man, a true *dux bellorum* in the old Roman style. Some said he was the bastard son of Lord Ector. Others said he was the son of Lady Ygraine, raised in secret to protect him from the traitors and poisoners who had murdered his father, Uther.

'Morgaine listened to all of these rumours hungrily. She sought them out, collected them, stored them as another young woman might store up tales of the man she was to marry. It was horrible to see the light burning in her eyes whenever she heard word of this warrior.

'I spoke of this to Morgause. We were close friends, she and I, true sisters though we shared no blood. I was lonely. My brothers and sisters had all died so young . . . Morgaine accused me more than once of stealing her sister's love. Perhaps I did. I don't know.' The queen shook her head. Her eyes were bright. *Will you cry?* Laurel had to keep herself from cringing, selfishly not wishing to be near any tale that would cause the queen to cry.

'Then Arthur came to Cambryn, to seek my father's allegiance. In that moment, I saw my heart's love.

'Morgaine saw her enemy made flesh and brought within reach of her hand.

'It was then that Morgause had to make her choice. Would she choose to aid her sister or me? I don't know what road she walked to reach her decision . . . I never had the strength to ask, but in the end Morgause chose to side with me, and with Arthur.' Queen Guinevere slumped back in her chair, passing her fingertips over her brow. 'What followed was a long and dark war between the sisters. I only knew some of it. Much of it was waged far outside my ken. I do know that it only ended when Arthur and Merlin worked with Morgause to deceive Morgaine, and trap her. Merlin and Morgause together bound her in the earth, for all time, so we thought.'

'Why did you not kill her?'

Guinevere's face tightened. 'Merlin would not permit it,' she spat the words. 'He claimed it would bring about a worse evil. I hope he was right, because what evil has been brought is fully bad enough.

'It was not until some years later that we found out Morgaine did escape her confinement. Morgause, her sister, my sister, left her husband and four sons and went to face her. Alone, this time. I do not know what happened to her.' The queen spoke these words so softly Laurel had to strain to hear them over the rustling and scratching of the work going on around them. 'I do know she did not return. Since then, Morgaine has taken out her revenge upon Morgause's husband and children, upon myself, and upon Arthur. Her revenge is pitiless and brutal and will not be slaked.

'We believe she is responsible for King Lot's madness. He was broken when Morgause did not return, and we knew he would never fully heal, but he began a descent into darkness so rapid, it seemed as if he were driven, or pushed.' She twisted her hands together once more. 'We did not know it was her for a long time. None of us knew. All we knew was that he travelled so deeply into despair that he murdered his unwed daughter when he found she was with child.'

Laurel was cold. It was as if her bones had become stone, lest she bow down under the weight of what she had heard. All this and more for the death of a father, for the blood spilled on the stones. It was abomination. It was unforgivable, and yet she could understand it so well. She remembered looking into her brother's eyes while pronouncing his banishment, remembered the calm place beyond anger where her spirit had gone when she realized he was not sorry, and never would be.

When she knew he had sided with the one who would bring their whole family down.

She could not sit here any longer. She looked left and

right, seeking escape, only belatedly remembering who sat in front of her.

'Forgive me, Your Majesty. I . . .'

'There is no need,' said the queen. To Laurel she seemed relieved not to have to go on. 'You are excused. You have much to consider now. I only ask that when you are calmer, you return to me so we can talk further. You are part of this war now, and there is much you have yet to understand.'

Laurel knelt swiftly, and swiftly departed. She had to get out. Now. She could not be smothered by stone anymore. A doorway loomed in front of her, someone opened it, and the wind, sweet and fresh and heavy with rain's promise, rushed over her, wrapping her like a cloak. She breathed it in, letting it run through her veins, cooling her, calming her.

So, this was what it was. So simple. Revenge. The coldest, darkest canker ever born in human heart. A single word. A single thing, a lightning stroke, a knife, a stone. Revenge.

She had not thought to understand Morgaine. She knew to hate her, to beware her, but she had not thought herself capable of feeling as the sorceress felt. Father, dead on the stones, the murderer there, in reach, yet out of reach. Her own failure to stop him. Her own shame. That was what birthed it. That shame at having not seen. Shame and blood begat revenge and revenge begat madness.

Oh, yes. She understood this all very well.

Laurel wrapped her arms around herself and stared across the courtyard, seeing nothing. Her new understanding blinded her. But for fate's glance, the flicker of the hand of God, she could have been just as Morgaine was.

Why didn't they kill her? Why in God's name didn't Merlin want her killed?

'My lady, my lady, come in. You have no cloak. You cannot stand here like this.'

Meg. Eternal, vigilant Meg. The present world came slowly

into focus. The yard was filled with busy life, with men and women, animals, passing by, and pausing to stare at Sir Agravain's new wife standing in the arched doorway, alone and purposeless.

Pride came to her rescue. Laurel drew herself up and turned to brush past Meg. She would return to her chamber. She had no purpose there, but at least it gave her a path to take. She could walk decorously down the broad corridor, fix her aim upon the stairs. There were others passing, men and women both, of the several ranks that dwelt at Camelot.

Do not think of them. You should be used to being looked at by now.

She would return to her chamber. She would calm herself. She would think reasonably over all she had heard. Even so light a purpose could mask the turmoil inside her. Nothing had changed, she told herself sternly. Not truly. She had only learned a very little.

Only a very little. I will calm myself. I will return to the queen. She is right. There is much yet . . .

Then, in front of her, a door slammed open. Agravain marched out into the hall. Laurel had to pull back in mid-stride to keep from running headlong into him.

'Stop!' thundered Arthur.

Agravain did stop, from the king's command, and from seeing her there so suddenly. His face was cold as winter's soul, and his eyes shuttered tight as he turned to face the High King.

Every person in the hall knelt, heads bowed. She could hear them all breathing hard, feel them all straining not to look up in improper curiosity.

She should kneel too, but she could not make herself move.

'Be very sure of what you do, Agravain,' said Arthur, his voice stern and clear.

'It is you who should be sure.' Agravain's words rang

smooth and cold as steel. 'Forsake one of your kings, you forsake them all. I will not permit my people to be used as your catspaws.'

'Agravain, don't be a fool!' Gawain strode past the king, his hands trembling at his side. He looked as if he wanted nothing more than to seize his brother by the shoulders. Desperation choked his voice, and drew deep lines into his handsome face. 'You'll cut yourself off. You will be absolutely alone.'

Agravain ignored him. At first she thought his attention was all on the king, who stood there, straight and tall, but with a deep pallor beneath his sun-bronzed skin. But no, he truly watched Sir Kai. The crooked seneschal had come to stand at the king's shoulder. Agravain's face was a mask, but the seneschal's showed a thousand things; cold anger, bitter humour, hard promise, and admiration as steel-sharp as all the rest.

'If there is no other way,' said Agravain slowly, to brother, seneschal, and king. 'Then so be it.'

Arthur's mouth moved, but Laurel could hear no sound. It came to her that he was praying. For guidance? For strength? She could not discern fear in him, not truly. But there was sadness, and there was a profound concern, and the weight of years grown suddenly heavy indeed.

'Go, then, Agravain,' King Arthur said. 'And unless it be that your heart changes, do not return.'

Dismissed, Agravain should have knelt, but he did not. Neither did he bow. He turned his back to Arthur without any sign of acknowledgement before his king. Laurel heard the rustlings at her back, horrified murmurs and whispers as Agravain strode past.

'It is begun,' he murmured.

Alone amidst this disbelieving crowd, Laurel looked to King Arthur, his eyes filled with sadness, and to Gawain, his chest heaving and his face gone pale, and last of all to Sir Kai. Sir Kai met her eyes. There beneath all the show of strength and anger, she at last saw the fear she had been looking for, and it ran deep into the seneschal's heart. Kai's fear chilled her worse than the king's would have, for it was Kai who understood Agravain best.

But she also saw determination, and calculation. He was already deciding how he would help this plan succeed, how he would spread the word of what had come to the shocked ladies, to the stunned lords and outraged knights. They in turn would spread word of this thing through the world beyond Camelot faster than bird could fly or wind could blow.

Slowly, it seemed Arthur realized she was there, the only one before him still on her feet. He regarded her with lidded eyes, as if trying to decide what to do with such an object.

But it was Sir Kai who spoke. 'And you, my lady?' he inquired. 'What will you do?'

'What I must, my lord seneschal.' Laurel curtsied deeply to the king. Then she straightened, turned, and followed her husband.

Agravain did not look back to see Laurel behind him, but marched forward steadily, his shoulders hunched against some invisible blow. All those they passed stopped to stare, to wonder, Laurel was sure, what trouble plagued Sir Agravain now.

They'll know soon enough. Far too soon.

When Agravain reached his chamber, he moved to shove the door shut, hard. Laurel caught it with her hand. Only then did he look back and see her. His face creased, trying to hold back the flood of feeling within him. He let go of the door, stepping back, turning away, not giving her permission to enter, but not denying it either.

Laurel stepped softly into the spare chamber, closing the

door behind her and securing the latch. Agravain drifted to his worktable, and stood beside it, staring down at the smooth, dark wood. Laurel waited where she was, uncertain what to do next.

'That was . . . more difficult than I expected,' he said at last. He ran his hand through his hair. His face was pale, pinched and drawn, as if he had just come out of a violent storm. 'Gawain doesn't know.'

'What?'

He let out a brisk sigh and scrubbed his face hard with his palm, as if he thought he could wipe away all trace of the emotions that now filled him. It was strange to see him making so much purposeless motion. 'He is a poor liar, my brother. There was some question as to whether he could maintain the ruse . . . He will be told later, but . . . but for now my brother believes me a cold-blooded traitor who has turned against the great and blessed king who has been a second father to us all.' She would have expected those words to be spoken in anger, but there was only wearied bewilderment in them. He leaned both hands on the tabletop, pressing down, trying to regain his hold on himself, trying to believe somehow that Gawain could not possibly come to believe this much of him.

'I had wondered how it would be.' The words were harsh, breathy, and he looked up. He tried to give her his ironic smile, but his mouth would not shape it. 'For you, so far away from all you knew, without family. I felt some pang about taking you so far away . . . and that was right. I know now. We are both alone.'

'No.' She crossed the space between them swiftly, without pause for thought. 'No, Agravain.' She laid her hand on his. 'We are not alone. Not now.'

He stared down at her white hand where it lay across his brown one. His hand was cold beneath her palm. He was trembling.

Slowly, he reached up and cupped her chin with his free hand. His touch was weaker than it had been. His strength was drained away by what he had done, what he must do next. Gently, his thumb stroked her cheek while his gaze met hers, not holding it, there was no strength there either, just searching, looking for the truth of what she said, needing to the depths of his soul for it to be true. For this one moment, he had lost the ability to hide.

She lifted her own hand, mirroring his gesture, cupping his rough face, feeling the hard line of his jaw, feeling the muscles taut beneath the flesh. She kissed him. She wanted nothing more. To kiss him, to bring him close, to wrap her arms around him and ease the tremors that shivered through him.

Slowly, he was able to respond. He answered embrace and kiss, awkwardly, each movement, each hesitating touch, a confession from one whose ingrained habit was silence. She could not lead him. She did not know this road. Blind together, they clung to each other, restoring strength, restoring warmth, beating back years of determined loneliness with a new torrent of feeling. For how could either of them have expected anything but loneliness? There was no one who would take so much danger and uncertainty, so much secrecy and fear, into themselves. It was too much to ask. There was no one who would, who could, answer that asking. But such a dream was now made real, and lay clasped in the embrace of arm and heart and aching need.

There was no grace to this. Need left no room for courtesy or play. His weight bore her down onto the bed and his hands – warm now, and filled with the strength she remembered from the night before – shoved up her skirt to caress her bare legs. She burned bright with her own wanting, with the heat of his body that she drank in through her hands, through her mouth. The scent of him, the salt taste of his skin, only fuelled the fire in her blood. Giddy with the power of it, she gave herself over to all; to Agravain, to herself, to the moment she took him inside her and felt the pain, and the ending of pain. She held him tight, able to answer his strength with her own, able to kiss and cry and press and hold, to exalt in this tumult where nothing was forbidden and nothing was withheld. They were both free here, finally free.

When all was spent, and they both were at last able to be still again, Agravain gathered her into his arms. They were completely dishevelled. Their clothes hung off them and were crushed up between them. His sweat was harsh on her skin, and she was flushed and out of breath. Her hair trailed in damp elf-locks about her face.

And she did not care. All she cared for was that Agravain cradled her close, gentle for the first time since they had begun. She closed her eyes, resting in the warmth they made, listening to his breath, feeling his heartbeat.

With the hesitant caress of Agravain's hands against her shoulders, Laurel drifted into sleep.

SEVEN

The morning sky hung low and grey overhead as Mordred and his men rode up to the edge of the Dal Riata camp. Two spearmen, dressed for war after the fashion of their people, with striped cloaks and bare chests and bronze bands on their arms and legs, round shields in their hands and bronze helms on their heads, stood guarding the rough trail. They crossed their iron-tipped spears in a show of barring the way.

In keeping with that show, Mordred, encased in his gleaming black armour, swung himself off his stallion and came up to them on foot.

'We are summoned by Lord Olcan to his council,' he intoned in the Dal Riata's own lilting tongue.

The spearman who stood at the right, a hulking, ungainly fellow with moustaches so long he could almost tuck them in his belt, looked over Mordred and his retinue of five horsemen. His weathered face showed in equal measure how he both coveted the animals and cursed the trouble it would be holding onto such mettlesome beasts while the high and the mighty held their conference.

Mordred let him look. There was no harm in it, and the

greater the impression they made on these men, the better.

At last, the spearman remembered his manners and bowed. 'You'll follow me, my lords.'

At Mordred's nod the men dismounted. In a neat double column, they followed the moustached spearman through the camp. Fragrant smoke rose up from the many fires. The men at leisure hunched over them, their striped cloaks pulled close against the damp. They talked in the low, grumbling voices of men forced to wait with ill patience. They gnawed bread, or attended to the hundred small tasks of living beside their raw-boned women who tended the food and the fires, or stood in knots exchanging their own grumbles and gossip. They glanced up at Mordred's passage, and then turned straight back to their own business. The Britons had become a familiar sight. If they were cause for any comment, it was the wish that the mighty chiefs would get their bargain struck so they could move out of this mud hole.

We will have to hope Lot has the sense to die soon. It rankled Mordred that nothing could be done until that moment came, but it would rankle these already impatient nomads more. He would have to press his case to mother more firmly. It was not often Mordred felt the lightness and unsteadiness of his youth, but it came to him now as he thought of facing her down again. That too would have to end soon.

If Mordred strained his eyes to the east towards the hills, he could see the forms of the Pictish watchmen standing dark against the grey sky. These two peoples might agree to fight together, but they would not live together.

It was the clearest sign, if any were needed, that no alliance formed today would outlast the war, if it even lasted that long. One more reason to press for haste.

There was only one real pavilion in the whole of the Dal Riata encampment. It was a crude construction of wicker and mud, closed over by a length of tanned leather. Smoke rose through a hole in that low roof. Dogs nosed around in the trampled mud outside.

Because of the formality of the day, no less than four men stood guard, also in full warrior's regalia, with broad knives hanging from their belts in addition to the spears in their hands.

Olcan is in a mood to show his teeth.

'The Lord Mordred, son of Morgaine, answering the summons of Lord Olcan of the Fionan,' announced their guide, who spoke up clearly and proudly now that he was in earshot of his chief.

The first of the guards bowed his head in curt acknow-ledgement of the rank of the visitors. 'And you come in peace, be welcome here.'

'We come in peace.' To demonstrate this, Mordred removed his helmet, and then unbuckled his swordbelt, passing both arms and helm over to the guards. All his followers did the same. Only then did the guard step back from the door and allow them entry.

Mordred stooped as he crossed the low threshold into the pavilion's twilight. A fire burned merrily in a central ring of stones. Warriors and witnesses stood by the walls. Their masters sat on piles of fur close to the fire: four Dal Riata chiefs, grim, hirsute, greasy men; and two sleek brown Picts with their raven-black hair limed into the likeness of spikes and feathers and their bodies traced with bright blue ribbons. Only Olcan had a stool for his use.

For his kind, Olcan was a quiet and subtle man. He was powerfully and flawlessly built, as a Dal Riata chief must be. The clay noggin in his dirt-stained hand looked as fragile as an egg. Unlike most of the others here, he wore a woollen tunic beneath his blue and brown cloak. Though his torque and clasp were worked bronze, the cuffs on his wrists were simple tooled leather. He'd gone bald many years before and his pate was as tough, bronzed and mottled as his hands were. His innate vanity showed in his moustaches that were well groomed, twisted and tipped with bronze beads where they hung down past his chin.

He lifted up the hand of friendship as Mordred entered, and Mordred clasped it. 'Welcome to you, Mordred Morgaine's son. Sit and be my guest.'

Mordred settled himself cross-legged on the thick pile of fleece. His men arrayed themselves along the walls with the followers from the other chiefs gathered there.

Thus far every motion was familiar ritual, but that did not lessen their importance. If anything, today it was more vital than ever that all formalities be observed.

Olcan's wife, Eanna, was there too. She was a woman worn as hard as her stone and leather man. Her eyes glittered as she handed Mordred a welcome cup brimming with clear liquor, showing something very like hatred.

He nodded to her, acknowledging both the welcome cup, and what he saw in her. Her eyes remained hard as she turned away.

Mordred raised his cup to his host. 'May blessing be upon this assembly, and may strength, honour and wisdom flow from the words we speak here today. I give my thanks to Lord Olcan of the Fionan for the good welcome we have been given here.'

He drank the cup off smoothly, although it was like downing a measure of pure fire. The men he now sat with grunted and nodded giving their approval for his words and his conduct.

'Now, honoured chiefs, honoured friends.' Olcan rested his hands on his thighs. 'We come here to make our final answer to Mordred, Morgaine's son, in his offer of alliance, of war, of treasure and of land. Let him say his final words, and then he will have our answer.'

Mordred inclined his head in thanks. He had thought to stand, but he stayed seated. He did not want to appear at all agitated, and he did not want to display before these men the measure of his youth any more than absolutely was necessary.

'There is little I can say here that I have not said before. While Lot remained strong, it was prudent to leave the fortress rock and the firth of Gododdin in his hands. But he is dying now. We have a moment, a single heartbeat during which we may decide whose hands that fortress shall pass into.

'The southern men, of course, want it for themselves. They want to use it as a base to harry lands they have not yet conquered, and they want to use it to spy upon those peoples of the north who still remain free.

'I say we do not permit this. We are enough here to over-whelm Lot's little force and take the rock for ourselves. In so doing, the Dal Riata secure for themselves and their friends the North Lands from shore to shore, as well as the means to defend them. We will keep the southern men from harrying us any further, and we will bring to ourselves the chance to push them back onto their plains where they belong.'

Mordred paused for breath, looking around at his audience. They listened intently, making no sound, either of approval or the reverse. He could have wished for more show of agreement, but at least they listened.

'It will not be without cost,' he went on bluntly. 'Even now, Arthur the Bastard sends the sons of Lot, who he has held hostage these long years to Camelot's greed. He means for these false sons to take the rock for him. They will fight, and they will fight hard.'

No one moved. No one made any sound at all, but Mordred felt the change in the air. They wanted action, these men, after all this waiting, and that was what he promised them now.

'Each man who joins in this effort will be sung of in glory and in honour. Each man who lives to see the victory will have his worthy and equal share of the treasure. That treasure will not just be what Lot hoards in Din Eityn, but the riches and arms that Camelot sends to secure what they would steal from us.' One of the Picts stirred at this, his thin mouth turning up in the smallest smile. Some of the Dal Riata, though, frowned in scepticism, having been cheated by their allies one too many times.

But Mordred was ready for that too. 'Lest any think they will be cheated of what they and theirs will bleed for, I promise now that this council will oversee the division of the spoils, and no other.'

There. He was done. He wished he had more words, grander words, of glory and bravery that might bring the heat to men's blood, but he was no bard or orator. He could only make his case in the plainest terms. But they were fair terms, and spoken honestly.

It had to be enough. It had to.

'Well said, Lord Mordred,' said Olcan. 'You have treated with us openly, and with wisdom beyond your years. We have consulted the gods. The oracles speak favourably of your victory. The promise of taking the rock is a fair one. A risk, but a grand risk and the gain will be great if we succeed. We will rid ourselves of Lot who has worked so much grief upon us, and deal a blow to the Bastard that will make him think twice about coming up here to trouble us. It is much in my mind to give you the pledge of the Fionan.'

A loud snort sounded from the back of the pavilion, and all heads turned. There Eanna stood with her round arms folded. As gloomy as the pavilion was, the shadows were in no way thick enough to hide the disapproval stamped hard on her weathered face.

Mordred expected Olcan to censure her, but he just cocked his brows towards Mordred.

So. Not ready to leave this bargaining to your men. 'You do not like this decision, Eanna?' Mordred inquired mildly as his mind raced, searching for the best answer to this unexpected challenge.

'No, Mordred, guest of my husband, I do not,' she said flatly.

Mordred opened his hands. 'Share with me your wisdom. Why does this undertaking not have your approval as it does your husband's?' After years of his mother's tutelage, Mordred understood how heavily a woman's words could weight a man's decisions. He had no real pledge from Olcan yet, only the pledge of a pledge. Eanna could still make trouble.

Eanna shifted her gaze to the assemblage. Both the Pict men were grinning, nudging one another at the prospect of hearing this outlander – either Olcan or himself, it didn't matter – taken apart by the sharp tongue of a woman.

'Oracles and omens may also be just bones and flame,' she said flatly. 'The gods speak to their own purposes. So too do allies. And hate,' she narrowed her eyes to keen slits as she said this last word, 'is a poor reason to go down a hole after a badger.'

Which seemed to be as much leeway as Olcan was ready to permit. 'Enough, Eanna. If your heart is weak for this, you can stay behind.'

At this, the woman all but reared back. She was tall enough that her braided head brushed the leather roof.

'When has my heart ever been weak, Olcan?' she demanded. 'Where you go, I go, but it does not follow that we will be alive to enjoy the victory our blood will purchase.'

She folded her arms across her breast. 'In four generations, no one, *no one* has been able to take the rock. Even though it has been held for ten years by a madman who doesn't know an enemy from his own shadow. Bands of men break like water against those cliffs, and they leave their blood splashed on its sides while they creep away in shame!'

Mordred spread his hands again. He needed to stop this. The Dal Riata were looking towards each other uneasily and the Picts had stopped smiling.

'What you say is true,' he acknowledged, inclining his head. 'It will not be easy what we intend to do.' Satisfaction glinted in Eanna's eyes. 'But it is not impossible. Din Eityn has never been so lightly defended. They have few spears, and fewer horse. Their storehouses are near empty. Should they try to wait out a siege, they will not survive. Should they come down and meet us on the valley floor, we will outnumber them. Should the day go badly, we can withdraw, reassess, regroup, and return like the fall of the smith's hammer, again and again. They have nowhere to go but an empty fortress that can give them shelter, but not the sustenance of life.'

'A pretty story,' muttered Eanna.

This pricked Mordred's temper, but he held it tight. 'Have we not been generous with you?' he asked. How much gold and how many swords and rings had they poured out over these people? Enough to buy a hundred cows and more. *What more do you want?* 'Have we broken faith with the Dal Riata?'

'Oh, you have been generous with all manner of things,' she acknowledged in a sneer. 'Save perhaps the truth.'

'Eanna, do you call our guest a liar?' There was anger in Olcan's voice, but not, perhaps as much as there should have been for the insult offered. Mordred looked from one of them to the other, and it occurred to him that this could be a game.

Olcan using Eanna to say things he could not, or would not say himself, to judge Mordred's reactions, and those of his own men.

'I wonder how it is he can know so much about what goes on inside Din Eityn.'

Very good. Very clever. But now Mordred knew how to answer. 'Do I guard my secrets, Eanna?' he inquired, keeping his words soft, his tone filled with reason. 'So I do. So do the Dal Riata. But I do not ask after those secrets. I do not ask what missives you send back to the kings of Eire. I do not ask what your plans are for the day when you hold this land from the east to west, although perhaps I should.' He let himself glance at the Picts as he said this. The pair of them sat as still as two stumps, listening. 'I know that your people are strong and that you are the best of fighters. Beyond that, I care not.'

'Why, Lord Mordred?' she demanded. 'If you believe we will be here tomorrow, after we have all heaved Lot's body over the cliffs, why do you not care what we might mean to do next?'

'So now I will tell you my secret. It is because I am desperate. There.' He sat back, keeping his gaze on hers, speaking to her alone, though he did not forget for one moment all the others who listened to his words. 'That is the truth. Arthur the Bastard has been readying himself to move against my lands for a year and more. His father killed my grandfather, and he cannot bear that our family, our nation, did not fall when he fought his twelve battles to wrest the island from its ancient peoples. He has built himself a treacherous kingdom in the south, buying and bribing what alliance he could, slaughtering kings and putting in his puppets where he could not. I could tell you tales of the lands just south and east of us, once proud and free, now conquered and divided up for Arthur's closest kin.'

Mordred let his voice drop, almost to a whisper, making all strain forward to hear him. 'He has been patient, but there are signs that that patience is at an end, and I am afraid. If I do not prepare myself to meet him, if I do not gain allies who can stop him, my people, and I myself, will be pushed into the sea. I cannot reach south to where the Saxons wait, so I must reach north, to you. Without you . . .' he sat back, and made his voice go cold, grim, final. 'Without you, I go home to die.'

He had them. He could feel it. These men might sing of the glory of thievery, of death in the course of honour, but when it came to the moment, they would all lay down life and limb most readily to save their families, their wives and sons and broad clans. They all knew what it was to live in an enemy's shadow and to fear his tread on the hilltop. He had just told them the enemy was in the next valley, and they believed.

It was the silent Pict men who made the first gesture. Brude Cal, their chieftain, and Fidach, his brother rose smoothly to their feet, clearly in some silent accord and came towards him. Together they drew the stone hammers from their belts and laid them at Mordred's feet. Mordred bowed deeply, humbly before these two in their leather kilts and they bowed silently in return. But Mordred's inner smile trembled when Brude Cal caught his eye, and he saw in the mountain chief a spark of edged humour. It said plainly that though the Dal Riata didn't see they'd just been herded into this alliance by some clever talk, the Pict men did.

The moment passed in a heartbeat, and the Picts backed away to make room for Tean of the Brinath, and Shora of the Dan Tuegh, and all the rest. One by one the Dal Riata's lords rose and laid their weapons at Mordred's feet.

Last of all Lord Olcan of the Fionan put his great axe in Mordred's hands.

'We are your men now, Mordred Morgaine's son,' Olcan said. 'Use us well or the gods themselves will know of it.'

Eanna watched from her shadows and said nothing at all.

There was more talk afterwards, of course. Hours of it, of men and numbers, of how the new allies would work together, and how the command and resources would be distributed among them. It was past noon before Mordred stood to receive Olcan's embrace and to clasp hands with the other lords. To Brude Cal he bowed, and received a consenting nod. Mordred told himself that would be enough for now.

Olcan himself led Mordred and his men through the camp. This time, everyone they passed stood to watch. Loud cheers raised up to shake the low clouds and sandalled feet stamped on the ground. The sight of the two of them together meant the wait was over. There would be action. There would be victory and treasure, and all the gauds and goods that came with war.

As he mounted his horse alongside his men, and once more donned his black helmet, Mordred looked out across the milling camp, hearing the shouts and the cheers. Beneath the noise of celebration, though, he still heard the echo of his own words.

I am afraid . . . without you, I go home to die.

He had begun the speech as a tactic, a move in the game of bargain and diplomacy that was necessary to persuade the Dal Riata chieftains to fight willingly. But as the words had fallen from his mouth, he felt the deeper truth of his admission.

He was afraid. They had laid their plans carefully, and had backed a score of battles and more secret deaths, but never had an open fight. That had until now all been left to others.

Until this moment, Mordred would have sworn all he felt

towards Arthur was hatred. He would have spoken of what had been done to his family; the treachery of Uther that laid his mother low and raised up the Bastard and his supporters, including the fickle and honourless woman beside him now as queen, rewarded for betraying her foster sisters. It was not right that such treachery should hold the throne of kings. Without vengeance, he would have no rest in the world to come, no honour to pass to his own sons, and be condemned to live his own days in hiding and poverty, perhaps even hunted, from the shores of the land of his birth. No. It would not be.

But now the war of arms would truly begin. War against the High King Arthur, who held the South Lands so long with the aid of his rich and well-trained knights. Who had won twelve battles begun when he was still younger than Mordred.

Fear is part of courage, his mother had told him, and he must remember that now. He had his alliance, and they must set all things in motion or he would meet dishonour by his own doing. The only choice was how to face the battle to come.

Mordred turned his horse's head south and rode down the slope. It was time to tell the Lady of their success.

Laurel woke alone. Aghast, she sat up at once, to see Agravain, dressed only in his undertunic and stockings, sitting on the broad sill of the shuttered window, watching her. He had one leg crooked up and rested his elbow lightly on it. It was the most at ease she had ever seen him. She marvelled at this for a moment before absurd modesty returned and she gathered the bed coverings around her with one hand and smoothed back her hair with the other.

'God be with you this evening, my husband' she said.

'And with you, my wife.' He inclined his head as if they

were meeting in the most public of places. But there was a subtle warmth she could feel across the room. Whether anyone else would have noticed this, she did not know, but to her it was as bright as the shaft of sunlight that streamed between the shutters.

'And how was your sleep?' Laurel inquired.

'Most pleasant, an' I thank you,' Agravain replied soberly.

They looked at each other for a moment, but only a moment, before Laurel had to clap her hand over her mouth to stifle the laughter that bubbled out of her. Agravain chuckled, low in his throat, and a thin, but real smile spread across his lean face.

'I am sorry,' he said. 'I am most . . . unfamiliar with how to greet the morning after . . .'

'We will become used to it in time, I should think.'

'It is my hope,' he answered softly.

'And mine.' They met each other's eyes again, and again Laurel could not help but be amazed by the simple warmth so new and unfamiliar in his dark brown eyes. Had this man, relaxed and easy, with his dry humour and his thin smile, been inside the closed and forbidding Sir Agravain all the while?

Then, Agravain sighed, and laid his hand on the shutter slats. 'I am inclined to stay here awhile yet,' he said. 'Most likely, these are the only pleasant words either of us will hear today.'

And we have kept the world at bay as long as we could. A strange bereftness crept over Laurel. She realized she did not even know where Meg was. 'It is no good asking, I suppose, whether you must leave.' She climbed out of the bed, smoothing down her skirts, setting her bare feet on the rush-covered floor. Her laces were loose, some might be torn. Her stockings were not anywhere to be seen.

He shook his head. 'There are preparations that must be

set in motion. I must find out if any here are willing to come with me, as things stand. If nothing else, I must go down into the city and hire messengers.' He swung his long legs down, getting ready to stand.

Laurel took a deep breath, trying to put her determination in order as she had her clothing. If she was to take part in this, she must begin, and begin now. 'My husband . . .'

'Yes?'

'I . . . I must speak with you about something you said yesterday.'

'I said many things yesterday.' Wariness crept back into his voice. Laurel hated the fact that she had invited it there, but she did not let herself falter. 'That you entered into this marriage in part to have an ally against Morgaine.'

His gaze did not flicker, nor his expression change. 'It is so.'

'Then there are some questions I must ask you.'

'Very well.' Agravain settled back, leaning against the window frame and folding his arms. His permission was given, but his ease was gone. He was already retreating from her.

Part of her said she should have picked her time better. She was dishevelled, undignified, still flushed. But there could be no other time. There was no knowing what would come next.'I need to know why you left Din Eityn. No one else can tell me.'

Agravain held his peace for a long moment, deciding. She let the silence stretch. The floor was cold beneath her feet.

'I left because the king, my father, banished me,' he said softly towards the writing table.

'That is not the whole of it.'

'Do you say I lie?' he snapped.

It was a reflex. He was glad to be angry because it might

prevent him from having to speak the whole of his memory. Laurel's certainty of this made it easier to hold her ground.

'No, my lord,' she repeated calmly. 'I have been told of your sister's death, and your father's madness. But it does not explain why you, the heir of Gododdin, left your kingdom when the king fell mad instead of taking the throne, a move that would have been supported by Arthur, as well as by your own lords and chiefs.'

Agravain looked at his writing desk, at his piles of maps and letters, scowling at them when they offered neither answer nor shelter. She could see him considering his options. He could leave. He could order her out. He could maintain this silence. But none of these things would make the question go away. It would hang in the air between them until he did answer. A draught worked its way thought the window, smelling of cooling earth and approaching night.

'After . . . after my father . . . threw my sister down, Gawain left. I don't know that I have ever forgiven him for that.'

And with this between them, he cannot tell Gawain what he's doing now. Was that Arthur's idea? God and Mary, kingship is cruel.

Laurel did not speak this thought. Agravain was forcing himself to speak, convincing himself one word at a time that he should continue. She could give him no reason to change his mind.

'Some nights later, Geraint came to me and said he had seen our mother walking the corridors. Our mother had vanished utterly five years before. We were certain she was dead.

'I remember hoping that he was lying, or dreaming. After all, he was a boy, and had been our mother's favourite. He doted on our sister. At the same time, I feared he was showing signs of the madness that consumed our father.

'I sat watch with him the next night, so I could find out for myself.

'I did not see her. I did not . . . do not have such gifts. But Geraint did, and he described her carefully.' His fist curled as he spoke the word, clutching that fact to himself, as if he might have to protect it from grasping fingers. 'What I did see was our father grovelling where Geraint said she stood. I saw him curse and swear and cry out in his torment while Geraint, tears pouring down his face, repeated to me her mocking of him.' His voice fell to a whisper. 'He was a boy. He would not have thought to invent such things as she said.

'But this . . . thing that mocked and abused our father was not our mother's shade.' Agravain crossed his arms again, shielding himself from the truth that he must speak. 'It was her sister, her twin. It was Morgaine.'

Laurel had been expecting this, since the moment he spoke of a shade, but expectation did not keep her throat from tightening around her breath as he spoke the name.

'I knew then it was she who was to blame. She had driven our father mad, or deepened the madness brought on by our mother's disappearance. It was she who had killed our sister as surely as it is the man holding the sword who slays his enemy. And she who was driving our father towards his own death.'

Her father's bloody corpse on the floor, the knife in her brother's hand . . .

'I sent Geraint and Gareth away,' Agravain went on. 'Down to Camelot and safety. They were boys. They could do nothing.'

And what were you, Agravain? You could not have been more than fourteen when this happened.

'I swore I would find a way to save our father. I knew what was happening now. I would not fail him, as I had failed Tania. But what was I to do? There was no one I could

consult, no warrior, priest or sorcerer whom I could reach.
The malaise that had taken hold in Din Eityn had made it
difficult to tell friend from foe. What was I to do?'

For the first time since he had begun his narrative, he looked
at her, openly pleading. She did not know whether he was
hoping she had an answer for his tormenting question, or to
see that she had none, and would have had none then.

'I waited, and I watched. He had lucid moments sometimes, most often at midday. At this time his melancholy
would be at its greatest, but his wit would also be most clear.
So, it was at midday I went to him. I told him I knew what
nightmare was riding him, and I begged him to tell me how
she could be fought.

'He grasped my hand so tightly I thought he would crush
the bones. But he looked at me, and he knew me, and I saw
all the terrible fear in my father's eyes.' He saw it again now,
as clearly as she saw him. Agravain's whole frame tightened,
trying to stand against the memory of these horrors.

'He said, "You think I do not know what I have done?
Whose hands struck Tania down? I am lost. I am damned.
Leave me."

'I answered I would not leave him to her. "You must," he
said. "You and your brothers must grow to be men. It is only
as men you will be able to defeat her. She means to destroy
us all. While I live, she stalks me. While I live, you have
some shield. Go. Live and keep our secret. She must never
hear how much you know."

'I left him at dawn the next day.'

These last words were spoken in a rush. This was the real
pain, the knife that dug most deeply: that there had been
no other choice.

'You never told anyone,' she murmured. 'That your father
was standing between you and Morgaine. Not even your
brothers.'

'How could I?' He flung out his hands. 'The very wind could be her spy. And even if I could speak in safety, what then? Gawain would go charging back and get killed for his pains. Geraint would follow because his sense of duty would override his judgment. Gareth was little more than a child.'

Laurel did not remember crossing the room, but she found she was suddenly beside Agravain, taking his hand and holding it between her own. They stood like that while he collected his wits again. In truth, she also needed time to let the pieces of his narrative fall into place in her mind.

It changed everything. Everything. She had seen Lot as a villain, a barbarous northern lord driven to madness by over-weening love for his wife, without the faith or wisdom to cling to polity and reason. She had thought to hear that Agravain had left after cold, hard words had been exchanged. Perhaps Agravain had been driven out by a torrent of insults and, left alone by all his sons, Lot had been seduced by Morgaine.

She had been wrong. Completely wrong.

Agravain pressed her fingers gently before he withdrew his hand. 'May I now ask why you needed to know this?' he inquired with studied blandness.

'Because you said Morgaine had some long hold over Din Eityn.' *Do not say over you, or over the king.* 'To secure the fortress, that hold must be broken. I could not do this unless I understood the nature of it.'

'Can you break her hold?'

How to answer? 'I will do my best, I promise you.'

To Laurel's utter surprise, Agravain kissed her fingers lightly. When he raised his head, she saw, all unlooked for, that she had given Agravain hope. Her heart swelled with emotion, unfamiliar and tremulous, but also with fear. Should she fail . . . should she wipe that hope from him . . .

I will not. I cannot.

'Thank you, Laurel,' he whispered. He straightened then. 'And now, I must go to play my part. What will you do, my lady?'

'I will go to visit Merlin.'

Laurel did not know what she expected in response, but it was not Agravain jerking backwards as if he had been stung. 'Merlin? Why?'

'Because he once trapped Morgaine, but did not kill her. I would know why. It may become important to us.'

With obvious effort, Agravain brought himself back to some semblance of calm. 'Of course. Of course, you are right. I . . .'

'What is it, my lord?'

Agravain watched his hands flexing for a moment. *What are you trying to grasp?* 'Do not inquire too deeply there, my lady,' he whispered. 'Do not . . . do not stray from your path. Merlin's knowledge is not all . . . wholesome.'

Something had happened to him last night. It occurred to Laurel he might have spoken to Merlin, and got more than he had bargained for. The thought chilled her. 'I will be careful. These ways are not unknown to me.'

'No.' He was looking at her afresh, but he was not reassured, and she did not know how to make him so.

'Forgive me.' Agravain straightened and lowered his restless hands, bringing himself fully back to the task of the moment. 'Now, perhaps you should wish me luck.'

'Good luck, my husband,' replied Laurel gravely.

Agravain bowed in solemn reply. As she watched, he schooled his face into its habitual sour expression, closing himself away behind his sturdy shutters and lowering the latches into place. Within a handful of heartbeats, he was Sir Agravain once again; cold, alone, acerbic, inscrutable.

Without looking back, he strode from the room.

Alone, Laurel blew out a sigh and looked around

Agravain's spartan room, shoving her disordered hair back from her face. It was all so strange that for a moment she did not know what to do. Then, she caught a glimpse of her rumpled sleeve.

First I must get decently clothed. She too had this day to face, this role to play. She could not fail to see it through.

Back to my own room. Get washed and some order made from this disarray. Make sure Meg and the others are all right. Her responsibilities to her husband did not negate her responsibility to her own women, and this she had neglected over the past several hours. Cryda and Elsa at least, would be going out of their minds wondering what would happen next.

Fortunately, the dim corridor remained empty as she hurried down its length to her own chamber. She pushed the door open, and warmth wafted out over her along with a stench strong enough to make her clap her hand across nose and mouth.

'God Almighty!' she cried as she pushed the door shut behind her. 'What is that?'

Cryda looked to Elsa, and then to Laurel, tears shining in her eyes. She gestured helplessly to a pair of buckets that stood beside the bathing basin. 'It is the wash water. It's been . . . fouled.'

So it had. What should have been clear water was muddied, greasy and malodorous. In fact, judging from the straw that floated on its surface, it had been used to swill out the stable.

Laurel felt her stomach tighten. *So, this is how Camelot shows its displeasure.*

'Meg's gone to find out who was responsible,' said Elsa. Her tone said she didn't hold out much hope.

Laurel put her hands on her hips, trying to keep her breathing shallow, and her mind calm. *First things first.* 'Well, there's no point in keeping this. Throw it out the window.'

Cryda and Elsa glanced uneasily at each other. 'Meg told us to keep the windows closed.'

Laurel looked steadily at her maids for a moment. They, in turn, both studiously looked at the floor. Then, Laurel walked over to the shutters, undid the latch and pulled them open.

Her window overlooked the broad yard at the centre of Camelot's keep. She could see the stables and various outbuildings, and the busy, dusty expanse of the yard itself stretching towards the chapel and the walls beyond.

But not everyone was busy today. A small crowd clustered beneath her window. As soon as she opened the shutters, these idlers let out a rude hissing and shouting. Laurel, unable to believe what she heard, froze for a moment. This gave one of them time enough to pick up a clod of dirt and hurl it upwards. Fortunately, his aim was off, and it smacked against the wall beside her head.

'Hey!' shouted another voice. 'You there!' A man-at-arms wearing a leather coat strode up to the jeering crowd. 'Get back to your work! She's the king's guest!'

The idlers scattered before his order, quickly at first, but then – as it became clear he was not going to chase after them – more slowly. The man turned to glower up at Laurel. She nodded her thanks. In reply, he spat into the dirt, and sauntered away.

So. Laurel sighed. 'Well, they're gone for now. Let's get rid of this filth.'

Cryda and Elsa obediently emptied the buckets into the yard. Now there was no water at all. Laurel turned about, taking stock of the rest of the room. The fire was low, but the basket for fuel was empty.

'Do I need to ask?' She rubbed her forehead.

'No one has brought any today,' said Cryda. 'We've been afraid . . .'

Laurel didn't make her finish. 'Yes, I can see why. All right. We will not remain here much longer. Three days at the most. We must make do for ourselves as best we can. We are still the king's guests, and there are limits to what outrages may be performed against us.'

'My Lady . . .' began Elsa, twisting her plump, capable hands together.

'Yes?'

'My Lady, what's happened? They say your . . . Sir Agravain has turned traitor against the High King.' Her face had gone ghostly white. 'My lady, is it true? What's to become of us?'

'You hold your tongue, Elsa.'

It was Meg. She shouldered the door open with the yoke she wore around her neck. Two buckets full of fresh water hung from its ropes. 'You have no business pestering our lady. She will tell us all we need to know in due time.' Meg set the buckets down firmly, splashing water onto the hearth-stones. 'Now help me with these, you fool girls.'

Cryda and Elsa ran forward at once, removing the yoke and lugging the buckets nearer to the dying fire.

'Now, my lady, do you wish to change?' inquired Meg, sounding for all the world like this was any other day.

'In a moment, Meg. I need to speak with you all.' Laurel licked her lips. *How do I begin?* Cryda and Elsa turned to her, hungry for explanation and reassurance, and she had so little she could give. 'There has been a disagreement between Lord Agravain and the High King. Lord Agravain will be leaving at once for Din Eityn. He does this in defiance of King Arthur's orders.' She drew a deep breath. 'I will be going with him.'

'Oh, my lady, not if he . . .' Cryda clapped her hand over her mouth.

'In this, I may choose to side with the king, or with my

husband, Cryda. I choose my husband.' Cryda bowed her head humbly, whether that was from her words or Meg's uncompromising glower, Laurel could not tell. 'It is difficult and uncomfortable now. Perhaps things will smooth out over then next day or so. Perhaps not. I am sorry you must suffer for this,' she added softly.

Believe me, my women, if there had been another way, I would have taken it.

'And that should be more than enough for you,' snapped Meg, setting her fists on her hips. 'Now, you can surely brave the yard long enough to find our lady some fuel for the night. Stay together and keep your mouths closed. Go!'

Cryda and Elsa both made their curtsies in acknowledgement. Then, keeping huddled together, as if hoping to go unseen, they slipped out into the corridor.

When she could no longer hear their footsteps, Laurel turned to Meg. 'There are some things I must say to you, Meg, that cannot be repeated to any living soul.'

Meg folded her hands calmly in front of her. Laurel realized she had been perfectly prepared for this moment. It might even have been the reason she sent the other two away. Softly, carefully, Laurel told Meg of the plan, and of Meg's own part in it. Meg listened without interrupting until Laurel at last fell silent. Then, Meg lifted her chin.

'I will not leave you.'

Laurel stared. 'Meg,' she said softly. 'You must.'

But Meg shook her head and turned away, dipping her hand into one of the buckets to check the temperature of the water, and then lifting it a little closer to the fire where it could warm more fully. 'You go to a foreign land.' She might have been speaking to the fire as much as to Laurel. She lifted the second bucket, all but setting it in the coals. 'To God alone knows what place . . .'

Laurel waved her words away impatiently. 'Meg you must

stand messenger for me to Lynet. There is no one else to send.'

In reply, Meg took up the poker and jabbed it angrily into the coals, breaking them open to release fresh flames. 'Then you find must someone,' she said doggedly. 'Won't it cause yet more talk if I abandon you now?'

'Yes,' replied Laurel firmly. 'That will only strengthen this illusion we seek to create.'

Meg straightened up, keeping her back towards Laurel and her face towards the dwindling fire. When she did turn, she looked Laurel directly in the eye. It had been a long time since Laurel had truly seen her woman. Meg's stern face was brown and seamed from the years of work and care. Her once dark hair had all faded to grey. The skin bunched and sagged on her strong hands. Meg had served Laurel's mother, had served her, since she was a girl. She had denied herself husband and children to remain in that service. She had never done one thing that did not protect and strengthen Laurel and her family.

Humbled by this knowledge, it was Laurel who bowed her head this time.

When Meg spoke again, her words shook with anger though she remembered to keep her voice low. 'I will not send you into danger alone. Let the others be seen to desert you. I will not do it.'

'Meg,' Laurel began again. 'You do not desert me. You are my only steady friend, and the hope of my lord and our king. If you do not do this, then the whole enterprise will fail. Lynet will not accept the word of anyone else once the rumours begin to fly.' She stepped forward and took Meg's trembling, workworn hand. 'I'm begging you, Meg. For Lynet's sake. For mine. Take this message home.'

Tears glittered in Meg's eyes, born of fear, of weariness, of anger that this new place which had promised honour had begun to drag them down. But this time, Meg kept both her tears and her thoughts to herself. Instead, she made a deep curtsy.

'It shall be as my lady requires.'

When she rose, they embraced, as they had not done since Laurel was small. *God grant it is the right decision*, Laurel prayed fervently. The thought of going alone into the north terrified her, but she could not show that. Not now. Perhaps not ever.

She pulled back. Meg was still visibly on the edge of tears. She could not be made to stay here, not without a real task.

'For now, Meg, I have another errand. Cryda and Elsa can dress me when they return. I need you to go down to the thatched house that belongs to Master Merlin, and say I would visit with him in the morning.'

Meg curtsied and relief was plain in her voice. 'Yes, my lady.' She turned away, wiping at her eyes, adjusting the set of her shoulders as she closed the door behind herself.

Finally alone, Laurel collapsed into the chair. Her knees were shaking from too many waves of overwhelming emotion. She felt as if she had been scooped hollow and nothing remained to stand before the world but the shell of her skin.

Partly, it was hunger. If her maids came back undisturbed from their quest to find firewood, she must send them out to find something to eat. Or perhaps she should just give herself over to fasting. Given the little demonstration in the yard, she could not be sure how the kitchens might express their disapproval.

A fast can be my penance for causing so much trouble. She slumped backwards, staring at the little fire. Earthen coolness oozed from the stone walls around her. She could smell evening in the draught that slipped under the shutters. She wondered where Agravain was, and what was being said to him, or about him.

Will he come to me again tonight? I should be ready. She stirred, but somehow could not bring herself to stand. *Perhaps, when I'm decent again, I should go wait in his rooms . . . No. Let him be alone if he needs to.*

She rubbed her hands together. The chill settled more heavily against her skin. Why did it make her so uneasy? She was used to the cold of night. This was more than that. It felt like prophecy, like the promise of grim news to come. Something was happening. She could tell in the prickling on her arms and the restlessness that spread from the back of her neck. Something had gone very wrong.

Agravain?

Even as she thought this, Meg burst into the room. 'My lady!' she gasped. 'My lady, the sorcerer, Merlin. He's gone . . . he's gone, and his house is destroyed!'

EIGHT

In an instant, Laurel was on her feet. Forgetting place and appearance, and all other delicate decencies, she hiked her hems up around her ankles and barreled down stairs and corridor, out into the yard. Probably Camelot's folk stopped and stared. Laurel heeded none of them. She ran across the yard towards the low, lime-washed house that was home to Merlin the sorcerer.

Her first thought was that Meg was wrong. The low, white cottage stood whole and sound, with its window was tightly shuttered. Her woman had made some mistake. Everything was clearly all right. The nervous, shifting crowd in front of the open door was there because she, Laurel, had dared to come to this place.

But as she circled the edge of the crowd, she saw this fleeting hope was mistaken. What she had first taken for a stick of firewood dropped across the threshold was Merlin's carved staff, lying like a fallen branch.

Fury moved Laurel forward, shouldering the gawpers out of her path. How could all these fools just stand about like sheep? Never mind that this was Merlin's house, never mind that no one dared enter here without permission even in broad daylight, let alone with night approaching, something was wrong!

She pushed her way out of the crowd and caught up the staff, shoving the door open wide.

All at once, Laurel found herself in the midst of a ruin.

Overturned tables lay like driftwood in the sea of smashed crockery and trampled herbs. Inks and dyes ran in rivulets down the walls. Precious books lay trampled on the dirt floor, their pages torn and scattered. The well's cover had been tossed aside and the well beneath was dark and cold. Laurel thought of death as she looked at it, but did not know why. Then she realized the curved grey fragments beside the wall were not broken crockery, but broken skulls. Skulls someone had thrown against the wall.

What had happened here? She turned slowly, looking at the whole of the ruined cottage. *What could do this while Merlin . . . ?*

God and Mary, is Merlin dead? The sight of Agravain so worried about her coming here returned in a rush. It could not be possible he had a hand in this. It could not! Suddenly ice cold, she gripped Merlin's staff and crossed herself with one shaking hand.

'Do not distress yourself, lady. I am here.'

Laurel whirled around. There in the threshold stood Merlin, silhouetted against the dimming evening light. He hunched over, bracing himself against the door frame like a crippled old man. One shuffling step at a time he walked into the wreckage of his house.

'That is mine, I believe.' He held out his crabbed hand, and she put the staff into it. He drew it to his chest, embracing it like a child might a favoured toy as he gazed around at the devastation.

Laurel forced her mouth to move. 'Where have you been, Master?'

Merlin smiled grimly. 'Can you not tell?' He spread out the hems of his black robe. On the rich cloth, Laurel saw the wavering white line that was unmistakably the stain of salt water. The thought of him up to his knees in the crashing waves came to Laurel and she frowned.

Merlin reached one shaking hand down to pull a stool out of the flotsam and stumbled. Laurel grabbed his shoulders to help steady him, but he shook her off angrily. She backed away. Merlin set the stool down, and set himself on it.

'Why did you go to the sea?' she asked softly.

The sorcerer's mouth twitched. It was terrible to see him this way, so weak and dishevelled in the midst of the ruin of his home, which he did not even remark on, as if it was no surprise to him.

'To ask her to take you back.'

Her? Grandmother? He asked Grandmother to take me . . . It was too much. Her thoughts could not compass it. 'I do not understand.'

'No. No you don't.' He lifted his face and his eyes glittered brightly with the cold light of anger. 'You careen into the middle of this war, hazarding everything, bringing death with your every act and you do not understand!' He slammed the butt of his staff against the floor and Laurel jumped. She could not help it. But she did not retreat. She must understand what had happened here.

Slowly, the burn of anger dimmed and Merlin's face fell, all violence in him changing into simple grief. 'Leave here,' he pleaded softly. 'Return to your home. Let you yourself be the one who delivers the message to Geraint and Gareth.'

Laurel could barely breathe. Her hands knotted in her skirts. She wanted to run, to flee Camelot altogether, just because he spoke. She wanted with a terrible force to abandon Agravain, and the whole of this suddenly cursed place and go home.

She swallowed hard. 'Master Merlin,' she croaked. 'Master Merlin, please, tell me what you know.'

To her horror, a laugh bubbled out from Merlin's throat. Shaking as if fever gripped him, the sorcerer threw back his head, howling with horrifying mirth.

'What I know? Ah, lady ask anything but that! Anything at all!' Tears streamed down his face and the laughter dissolved becoming a hiccoughing sob.

'What is this, Master?' Laurel dropped to her knees beside him. 'If there is anything I can do, tell me, only speak plainly!'

'Speak, speak, speak! When will I be bid to keep silent!' Merlin wagged his head, his face flushed, his eyes fevered. 'I destroyed everything here, the charts, the oracles, so I could give no more answers.'

You *did this, Master? Oh, God and Mary no . . .*

'Even as I did it, I knew it wouldn't be enough. I meant to kill myself,' he whispered. 'I stood there in the sea. I could have thrown myself down, drowned in the waters. Could have . . . could have done any of a thousand things. Except . . .' He turned the staff in his hands, gripping it until his knuckles turned as white as the wood. 'Except I could not. It would have changed nothing. All still would have unfolded, the only difference would be that I was spared having to watch, and I found . . . I found I had just that much honour left.'

Laurel gripped his arm. This time he did not shake her off. She doubted he had the strength. 'Master Merlin, if my presence will bring harm to Agravain, to this war he must wage, then tell me. I will leave, at once. I swear it.'

Merlin's mouth moved. He chewed at his own lips, bringing blood. Laurel's mouth spasmed with pain in sympathy. *He's mad, he's mad*, whispered a voice in her head. But he was not mad, and she knew it. He had just seen too much.

At last, Merlin leaned forward, his face alight in a dreadful parody of a child who is about to tell a secret. 'Do you know what it is to be a prophet, Laurel?'

'No.'

'It is to give up your freedom to do what is most human.' He smiled broadly, delighted. 'I cannot lie. I cannot even keep silent. I made myself a vessel years ago, when I thought . . . when I thought I could hold enough knowledge to shape the world.' His voice grew hoarse, and the levity bled away from them, bringing the weight of all his long years crashing down like a stone. 'The oldest sin,' he whispered. 'The sin of Adam himself. And for it, I pay, and pay, and those better and stronger and greater than I am pay with me.'

She could not speak. All her words had turned to sand in her throat.

'Will your presence bring harm to Agravain?' He grinned, showing her his teeth, gone grey with age. 'Oh no. It is you who save him. You who wins his war.'

Then why do you wish me gone? 'How?'

'You bring him the thing Guinevere brought to Arthur.' He leered at her. 'The thing most precious but least regarded. Riddle that, Laurel Carnbrea!' he cried triumphantly.

'Master.' Laurel took his hand. It was hot and light and dry. Instantly, she remembered her mother on her death bed, and the child inside Laurel struggled not to cry. 'Master, why didn't you kill her? Why did you let Morgaine live?'

Merlin's face twisted and contorted. He tried to hold back his flood of feeling and failed. The ancient sorcerer bowed his head as weakly as any old man, and wept. Laurel sat back on her heels, stunned for a moment. Then, she wrapped her arms around his shoulders and held him while he sobbed for the loss that tore at his soul.

'I could not . . . I could not kill . . .'

The light was blotted away. Rough hands grabbed Laurel's shoulders, jerking her backwards, spinning her around.

When her sight cleared, Laurel found herself face to face with Sir Gawain.

'What are you doing here?' Gawain demanded, his face flushed red. 'What have you done!'

Behind them, Merlin had not ceased to weep. It was as if he could not stop.

'I have done nothing, Sir Gawain,' said Laurel carefully. 'I only sent to find if the master would speak with me. When I was told his house had been broken, I came to see.'

'It was not your place!' His grip tightened on her shoulder, his blunt fingers digging into her flesh. 'You should have sent for me!'

'Perhaps I should,' replied Laurel, struggling to keep her voice even. 'I did not think of it.'

'Gawain, take your hands from my wife.'

Agravain stood behind them in the courtyard. The crowd of witnesses gathered around the door had trebled in size. The courteous, civilized folk of Camelot had all grown dark and staring. All their watching eyes tallied the ruin they saw, their minds running far ahead of what was known, straight into the worst conclusions they could imagine.

If Agravain was aware of all the people at his back, he gave no sign. He was looking at his brother. He stood easily, his feet apart, his arms at his side. He wore no sword, but that did not seem to matter.

Laurel felt a cold bead of perspiration trickle down her cheek as she saw Agravain so ready to work cold violence upon his brother for her sake. Agravain and Gawain stared at each other for a long moment, the air thrumming with tension between them. All the crowd at Agravain's back silently, urgently wished for something to happen, and the only sound was Merlin's wordless lament.

Gawain let her go.

Laurel's arm hurt where Gawain had gripped her, but she

did not rub it, or give any other sign. As calmly as she was able, she walked across the yard to stand beside her husband. Agravain held out his hand, the meaning of the gesture plain, although he did not let his attention flicker from Gawain. Laurel took Agravain's hand and let herself be drawn to his side.

'You are still kin and guest, Agravain,' said Gawain. 'I would not break the king's courtesy and quarrel with you in his house.'

'No, you would not,' answered Agravain flatly. 'And it is as well.'

Agravain turned away from Gawain, turning Laurel with him. It required all her force of will not to look back at Gawain and Merlin, but to instead face the storm darkness of the gathered crowd. She thought Agravain would walk around them, but he did not. Instead he met their collected gaze with his own, these people he had known for much of his life but who now saw him as an enemy. Knowing he was right, and in his rights, he stood and waited in absolute silence, daring them to act.

In the face of this, they backed away, falling apart into a dozen smaller knots. Saying nothing, Agravain unhurriedly walked her between them. It was a dreadful parody of their wedding march and Laurel's shoulders twitched and trembled from the force of their stares. She bit her tongue so that the pain would help focus her mind on the way ahead and keep it from straying to all the varied wrongs they left behind.

Agravain kept to his deliberate pace, so it took a long time to cross the yard and travel the corridors, but at long last, he walked her into his chamber, rather than hers, and shut the door. Only then did he let go of her hand and step away so he could look at her better.

'What,' he said, folding his arms, 'was that?'

He would not criticize her in front of others, but his tone and stance made it equally plain he assumed she had just done something foolish in the extreme.

And should I explain myself to you? Laurel thought with a kind of numb anger. She wanted to sit down. She wanted something to drink. *God Almighty, where is Meg? Where is anyone?*

Agravain's jaw shifted, and his mistrust slipped. He pushed the chair beside his desk forward and held out his hand once more. She took it gratefully and let him sit her down. He brought a long-necked jar down from a shelf and poured some of its contents into a cup, which he handed to her. Laurel smelled brandywine and sipped sparingly. The warmth traced its way through her blood, calming and clearing her thoughts.

Agravain nodded, apparently satisfied. 'Of your courtesy, my lady,' he said, setting the ewer down. 'Tell me what brought you to the state I found you in?'

It was not a patient request, but it was an attempt at courtesy and understanding, and she accepted it as it was meant. Stopping every so often to sip more of the strengthening brandywine, she told him how Meg had come rushing into her, and how she had gone down to Merlin's house. Though the words came to her slowly and with difficulty, she told him all that Merlin had said to her. These were not matters she would have willingly discussed with anyone, but she knew full well she could only do damage by being less than honest with Agravain at this moment.

At last she was done with both words and wine. Agravain watched her in silence for a moment, arms folded, slowly digesting all she had said.

When he did speak, his question surprised her. 'Could he have taken you away? To . . . to the sea?'

'I don't know,' she admitted. She had not had time to

think about it. No, that was not true she had not wanted to think about it. Merlin, Arthur's cunning man, Arthur's astrologer and sage adviser, had gone to the sea, to petition her immortal kindred to take her away. Away from the land, away from her life.

Away from Agravain. He had said she was to win Agravain's victory, and he still wanted her dead or gone. How could that be?

Her hand trembled. She stilled it. 'Most likely not. I am not . . . I was born of earth, as others are. It is not enchantment holds me here.'

'Good.' He pushed himself away from the desk and walked to the shuttered window. It seemed to her he meant to open it, but thought the better of that.

'What was it you think Merlin meant?' he asked harshly. The harshness was not for her, but for their circumstances. She could hardly blame him for that.

'I don't know,' she said again. 'I will have to think on it.'

'Yes.' He curled his hand into a fist and raised it to the shutters, and struck them lightly, making them rattle against the hinges. 'What can any of us do but think, and wonder if it will do any good . . .' He shook himself and faced her again. 'You should not be alone,' he said briskly. 'Your women can make shift to bring your things here. There is not much room or comfort for a lady, but . . . I would rather you were with me.'

Relief washed through her. At that moment Laurel was not certain she could have stood, let alone walked. 'Thank you, my husband. I would be glad of it.'

'Good. I will go get Meg. You rest here.' Agravain laid his hand on the door, and then looked over his shoulder. 'Gawain would not have hurt you,' he said softly, then opened the door and left.

Gawain would not have hurt you. He meant two things,

and she understood them both. Sir Gawain, prince and gallant knight, would not have hurt her. It would have offended his sense of right. But he also meant that he, Agravain, her husband, would not have permitted any hurt to come to her, even from his own brother.

It might have been honour which made Agravain speak this way, but as she sat alone in his private room, she remembered the flash in his eyes, the strength in his words, and Laurel found she did not believe it was honour alone that made him defend her. Not anymore.

Much later, Laurel lay in the darkness, with Agravain's arm wrapped around her shoulder. He snored, her husband, and did not respond even when she elbowed him in the side.

Meg had been nearly melting with gratitude when she helped Cryda and Elsa to carry Laurel's chests into Agravain's chamber. The three of them had wrestled with trestles and slats, but managed to assemble a bedstead large enough for two, with mattresses and covers enough.

Sir Kai himself had brought up food and drink for them. Whether Agravain had been required to speak with his uncle about the state of affairs, or the seneschal had seen it for himself, Laurel didn't know and did not feel it necessary to ask. The stuff Sir Kai brought was plain; he went through great and acerbic pains to let the pages who carried up tables and trays know it was only the castoffs and leavings from the tables down in the hall. For all that, the food was wholesome and unsullied and she and Agravain ate together in peace by the light of a fully adequate fire.

Laurel tried to follow her husband to sleep, but in vain. With her three women asleep on their pallets, the room felt stuffy and overfull. She wanted the fresh wind against her skin. She wanted to be alone with Agravain so he could drive away the restlessness in her with his kiss and his caress.

She wanted to do anything but lie there with the memory of Merlin's words and his weeping running back and forth in her mind. But they would not leave, and she could not rest. She kept turning the words over, looking at them from every angle, taking them apart and knotting them together again, trying to see if the new pattern might make any sense.

You bring to him the thing Guinevere brought to Arthur. The thing most precious and least regarded.

What did that mean? Guinevere was the king's helpmeet, his council, his friend. All this was reassuring, but none seemed to apply directly to this riddle. She brought her dowry, of course, much wealth from her father's kingdom, the lands of the Dumonii. Alliance in a time of war. But that was hardly least regarded. There were her jewels as well, but they were Agravain's for the asking already.

The thing most precious and least regarded.

Guinevere also brought Arthur the Round Table, of course. It was a masterpiece, but Laurel doubted many thought what a triumph of craftsmanship it truly was. In her mind's eye she saw the Round Table again, with her marriage contract waiting on it beside the magisterial presence of Excalibur in its worn leather scabbard.

Its scabbard.

Laurel's prowling thoughts paused over this, showing her again the stained and flaking leather bound in battered bronze. Could Merlin mean the scabbard?

Excalibur's scabbard was a symbolic thing, without the objective worth it would have had, if, say, it had been gilded or bejewelled. That, though, did not sit easily. No symbol was truly worthless, no sigil completely hollow. The scabbard had belonged to the royal house of Cambryn since before the Romans came. Surely, it was not simply an empty vessel.

The thing most precious, but least regarded.

Again, her thoughts paused, backtracking, casting about on ground already travelled, uncertain they had caught the right scent.

The empty scabbard had belonged to the royal house of Cambryn. Her house was now that royal house. Her line the line of its kings. Queen Guinevere had given the land and its wealth over to her family a year ago now. This meant that the scabbard, the property and symbol of the royal line, belonged, by tradition, to her bloodline. Belonged to her.

This did not make easy sense, but neither did Merlin fallen into distraction and speaking in prophecy's worst riddles. And neither did the scabbard itself make sense. It never had. Why would an ill-fitting, ancient scabbard of so different a vintage from the blade of Excalibur be gifted apart from the sword itself, much less be worn and used by so meticulous a warrior as King Arthur was said to be?

The thing most precious, but least regarded.

Mystery upon mystery, and only one way to find any answer. She would have to play out one more scene in this painful mummery and seek an audience with Queen Guinevere. If the queen was able to give the scabbard over easily, it was nothing of genuine importance, and surely then not the thing Merlin spoke of in his broken prophecy.

If, however, the queen refused and denied the request of a traitor's wife, then the scabbard was a thing worth having.

And Merlin knew it was what I should take to bring victory, and yet tried to prevent me from doing so. Why? Why?

What else will I do when I take the scabbard from Camelot?

Laurel shifted uneasily. As if her distress touched him where her annoyance could not, Agravain's snore broke and stopped, and his arm tightened around her.

'What is it, Laurel?'

'Nothing, Agravain.' Laurel laid her hand on his chest. 'I think I now know what I must do next.'

He was silent for a moment. 'Is it something you can do?'

'Yes. It will not be easy, but I can do it.'

'Can I help you?'

'I don't believe so. I must ask the queen to give me a part of her dowry. How she parts with it . . . that will tell me whether it is what Merlin meant I must bring to you.'

She heard his head rustle on the pillow. She wished she could see his face. His breath trembled once under her hand and then eased. 'God be with you in this, my wife.'

'Amen, my husband.'

Agravain drew her closer then, and Laurel pressed against him willingly. This time, lulled by the rhythm of his heart and the shelter of his arms, it was she who drifted away into welcome oblivion.

The morning began with Ros making an appearance, his clothes torn, his nose and knuckles bloodied and one eye swollen shut. Agravain examined his messenger's injuries. Another man might have cursed but Agravain kept all his anger close behind his eyes.

'Who were they?' he asked quietly. Ros gave what names he could, and Agravain nodded. He would, Laurel had no doubt, remember each one of them for as long as it was required to bring them to account. Even if it took another ten years.

'All right.' Agravain folded his arms. 'We cannot all stay crammed in here, and I cannot leave yet. My lady, can you manage for a day or two without a woman to attend you?'

'I can, my lord.'

'Very well. Ros, you will escort these women down to the quay. I will give you a letter that will allow you to find them a ship and send them home.'

Ros opened his mouth, and Meg started forward immediately. Agravain held up his hand, stopping them both.

'You can both serve best by leaving now, and doing so quickly and quietly. No hurt will come to us here. I have alerted the seneschal. He will take it on himself to make sure we are properly served, and that courtesy is not broken.'

Meg's gaze slid sideways to Laurel. 'It is for the best, Meg. The sooner you are gone, the less time rumour has to outpace us.'

Meg made no move to argue. Cryda and Elsa, for their part were plainly delighted, although they did their best to conceal it as they ran at once to gather up their few belongings. As they did so, Agravain gathered a thick stack of letters and put them in a satchel of waxed leather for Ros.

'You know where these must go.'

'My lord.' Ros knelt and Agravain touched his shoulder. Laurel was sure she heard him whisper 'good man', but was uncertain if anyone else would have. Then he sent him down with the maids to see to the outfitting of horses for riding and for the baggage.

Meg, on the other hand, was not about to begin making ready until she saw Laurel washed, dressed, laced, brushed, braided, pinned and veiled. Only then did she fold her spare dresses and brushes into her leathern satchel and turn to Laurel.

Laurel took her woman's hands and looked into her worried, stubborn eyes. 'Meg, make sure Cryda and Elsa get home safely,' she said. 'When you arrive, this is what you tell Lynet. Say, Morgaine has left the West Lands. Now is the time those countries may be taken. Tell her I go with my lord to defeat Morgaine in the north. She is to believe no other truth until it is sent by myself, my lord, or the High King.'

Meg nodded once, and then she too knelt. Laurel raised her up and embraced her, giving her the kiss of peace.

When the door closed behind Meg it made a hollow sound, and Laurel found herself blinking away tears. Agravain's silence gave her the time necessary to collect herself, so that when she turned to him, her countenance was as composed as she could manage.

'Will she be able to remember your words exactly?' he asked, in a tone of carefully neutral inquiry.

'Without doubt. I have trusted her with far more complex messages, and she has never forgotten so much as a syllable.'

'A valuable woman.'

'Very much so.' She sighed and set her loneliness aside for later. 'I must go to the queen soon. This is when she is most likely to be in her court. With all due respect to the seneschal, I think it would not be good for me to have to hunt about Camelot for her.'

'As you see fit, my lady.' He hesitated for the space of a heartbeat. 'Do you require escort?'

Laurel gave him a small smile. 'I do not believe so, and this matter is between her and myself.'

Agravain gave a small bow in acknowledgement of this. 'You will find me here on your return.'

He sat down at his desk, and began carefully rolling his maps up to make room for a stack of closely written letters. Intent on his task, he did not look up to see her stand there a moment, watching him. Each movement Agravain made was careful and competent, spare and deliberate. He was comfortable in this place, inside these walls, sitting at this desk like a cleric, without servant or squire. Yet he bore the title of knight given by a king who did not give honour without merit. She had already seen danger in him, felt the raw strength of his arm, but neither was his power, nor his personal study. This was. This patient concentration over ink and paper which most men-at-arms would scorn.

Softly, Laurel stepped through the door and closed it behind her, feeling that she had witnessed a mystery.

*   *   *

When Laurel had been lady-in-waiting to the queen, it had been Guinevere's habit to spend a portion of fine mornings in the Queen's Court, a mosaiced and pillared yard that was part of the Roman villa Camelot had once been. Like the king, Guinevere also had her work to do. The provisioning and maintenance of the walled city that was Camelot was her responsibility. She must hear daily from seneschal and chatelaine, from the masters and mistresses who oversaw the weavers, the dyers, the tanners, the smiths, the orchards, the cattle, sheep, pigs and fowl, the kitchens, and even the monks who made sure of the king's charity. She must meet with the merchant men who travelled from Londinium and places further afield yet with goods bespoke for Camelot's use, or who wished for writ and permission to sell their goods inside Camelot or in the city below. She must meet with those who petitioned for her mercy or intervention, and judge which cases she could mediate, and which must be left for the king.

Laurel made her way down to the Queen's Court. On the way, she met with nothing worse than stony glowers and even the lowest of serving women drawing their skirts aside lest they accidentally brush hers.

My thanks, Sir Kai.

She found herself in good time. Guinevere sat in her carved chair, dressed simply in shades of blue girdled with gold and lapis. Her golden torque and rings glittered in the sunlight as she bent to examine the wax tablet handed her by a stout, mottled-skinned man Laurel thought she remembered as the master of the ovens. Her ladies surrounded her, spinning, embroidering, working at their hand looms or sewing, all this accompanied by the music of the fountain that splashed merrily in the sunlight streaming down from the uncommonly blue sky.

Lady Rhian stood at the queen's shoulder, alert for any order or errand that might be given. It was she who saw

Laurel hesitate in the shadowed threshold. Even across the court, Laurel could see the controlled fury in Rhian's face. She caught her skirts up in one hand, and strode across the court to block Laurel's way.

'How dare you come here?' Rhian hissed. 'What right have you to stand before our queen?'

She has not been told. She knows only what she sees, Laurel reminded herself firmly. But oh, it hurt. Was it really so easy for this woman who had been her friend just two nights before to believe she and her husband ingrates if not actual traitors?

Be calm. Agravain has faced this and worse. If he can brave it, so can you.

'I remain the queen's subject. It is my right to be heard by her majesty,' replied Laurel evenly. Rhian's green eyes were a deeper shade than her own, and burning like dark emeralds. 'It is not for you to refuse.'

She was within her rights and they both knew it. Nonetheless, Rhian spoke only with great reluctance. 'Wait here.'

But though she turned, she did not need to go any further. The whole of the assemblage in the court, Queen Guinevere first among them, had looked to see what had caused Rhian's hasty departure from their side.

'Let her come,' said the queen crisply.

Head properly bowed in respect, Laurel walked forward to kneel before the queen. It was only when she was bid to rise that she met Guinevere's grey gaze. It was stern and searching, looking, perhaps, to see how well Laurel weathered this storm of her own making.

Does she know the truth? Laurel realized with a shock that she had neglected to ask. She could not imagine Arthur failing to tell his queen of such an important plan. But then, he had not told his heir.

'With respect, Your Majesty, I have come to ask for a thing that is rightfully mine.'

'You should speak carefully of right, Laurel Carnbrea,' the queen's words were clear, clipped, and ice cold, 'when you aid in the commission of great wrong.'

'It was Your Majesty who gave me in marriage to Sir Agravain,' replied Laurel. 'Do you now say I should renounce this royal gift?'

It was a hard blow, and the ladies whispered to hear it fall. A single straight line appeared between the queen's arched brows.

Laurel licked her lips, glancing at the icy women surrounding the queen, and at the suddenly too-alert soldiers of her guard.

'If it please Your Majesty to speak of this in private?' she asked, hoping she did not sound frightened.

'It does not please me,' replied the queen, stonily. 'You must say what you have to say before witness and peer. What is it you lay claim to?'

Very well. Laurel steeled herself. 'The property of the royal line of Cambryn, which was this past year made my line. I ask for the scabbard of Excalibur.'

'What!'

'False jade!'

'It is Sir Agravain urges this on her, mark me.'

Exclamations and whispers flew up in a great cloud until Laurel could hear none clearly, but not one came from the queen. Guinevere sat rigid as a marble statue, and as white.

'Leave us,' said Queen Guinevere to her assembly.

For a single heartbeat, Rhian looked as if she might refuse, but only for a heartbeat. She made her obeisance and gestured to the other women. With many a glare of contempt and poisoned whisper, the ladies retreated to the shadows in bright, rustling procession. The soldiers too followed, but did not, Laurel was sure, go so far away that a shout would not be heard.

After that, the only sound in the court was the endless, mindless splash of the fountain at her back.

'Gawain came to us greatly agitated yesterday,' said Queen Guinevere at last. 'He told a fantastic tale of finding you in the ruins of Merlin's den.'

The queen had never liked the sorcerer. She had always met him with perfect courtesy, but there was never any warmth between them, nor were their meetings ever voluntary on the queen's part. With what she now knew, Laurel found herself wondering once more how this dislike had come about. Was this yet another wound from one of Morgaine's many blades?

Or was it that Merlin had refused to kill Morgaine when there was the chance?

'I did go to Merlin's house, and Gawain did find me there.' Laurel found herself searching the queen's clear eyes for some sign, any sign that Guinevere knew the truth, and was only playing out her role. But the queen gave away no such sign. She sat on her throne, imperious and distant as a goddess from the ancient days.

'You wished to hold some discourse with His Majesty's cunning man?'

Laurel folded her hands properly in front of her, and made sure her spine and shoulders were straight. If she must face the queen's approbation, she would do so correctly. 'I did.'

Guinevere's grey eyes narrowed slightly. 'I would not have thought you required recourse to such.'

'Of your courtesy, there were things he could tell me of Morgaine and her wars that Your Majesty could not.'

It took the queen a handful of heartbeats to digest this. 'I see.'

Conscience stirred in Laurel, and sympathy for what she had seen before. 'He was most unwell when I left him. Is he better now?'

Guinevere's sigh was curt and dismissive. 'So says the king. I do not know.'

Knowing the queen to be a dedicated and competent healer, this startled Laurel more than almost anything else could have. 'Why is it you hate him?'

'That is a question I am not required to answer. It has nothing to do with this brazen request you have made.'

Laurel bowed her head once more in a show of humility she was certain the queen would not believe genuine. 'I am sorry if I have offended Your Majesty.'

'But you do not withdraw your request?'

'No.'

'Did Merlin tell you to do this?'

Laurel lifted her gaze to look directly at the queen and spoke the truth. 'No,' she said.

Guinevere set her jaw. Laurel could see swift calculation in her eyes and in the shifting lines on her broad brow. For all that, she was still startled when the queen stood abruptly.

'Come with me.'

Guinevere swept from the court, leaving Laurel little choice but to follow. All they passed stopped to stare and point and whisper, and Laurel felt her ears begin to burn. Was this Queen Guinevere's revenge for what she had asked? Exposing her to further humiliation and censure?

A page opened the outer doors and the queen walked out in to the main yard without pausing. Hoods were doffed and heads lowered. If the queen noticed this propriety she gave no sign. She strode in a straight line to the chapel steps, where Laurel had stood so recently with Agravain, and this game had begun.

The lone priest sweeping the floor in front of the altar rail looked up, sincerely startled, as the queen entered. He made awkwardly to kneel, obviously uncertain as to whether he should put his broom down first. Guinevere stopped him with a gesture.

'I would pray alone for a few moments, Father. Please excuse me.'

The priest looked towards Laurel, who waited uncertainly in the doorway, but he did not question the contradiction, only bowed, and, clutching his broom, retreated.

A few fragrant lamps illuminated the holy place. The saints and angels looked down from the walls, but the Christ in his agony had his face turned towards Heaven. Guinevere dipped her hand in the font and crossed herself, before holding out her arms before the altar. Laurel bowed her head in respect to the prayer, but did not move to enter the church. She did not understand what was happening, why she was being made to witness this. Impatience warred with a growing uneasiness. She felt as if storm clouds closed over her head. She had known it was no small thing that she did, but now she had the growing sense of a previously unguessed enormity.

'Amen. Amen. Amen,' whispered the queen. She lowered her arms. 'Come here,' she snapped.

A chest waited beside the altar. As she approached, Laurel smelled cedar and saw it was bound, not in bronze, as she had first thought, but in gold worked with the sign of the cross that had been fashioned of many ribbons. The queen knelt before it. She lifted the ring of keys at her waist, and took out one that was small and gold and also fashioned into a cross's shape. She turned it in the golden lock. When she raised the lid, the hinges made no sound. A cloud of fragrance wafted up, and Laurel for only the second time in her life smelled bitter myrrh and sweet frankincense.

The inside of the chest was lined in shimmering white

samite. In the centre of this precious nest lay a bundle of white silk wound like a shroud. This Guinevere carefully turned over, unfolding the fabric to expose the battered, flaking, stained scabbard. The queen laid her right hand on the long, dark stain that travelled half the length of the sheath, and Laurel to her astonishment realized the colour and shape of it matched the stain on the queen's palm.

'You do not even know what this is, do you?' Queen Guinevere spoke in a whisper that was at once reverent and angry. 'Let me tell you. This scabbard belonged to a Roman soldier in the holy land. His duty was to watch over a place called Calvary during an execution. That soldier took a spear and pierced the side of a certain carpenter who hung upon the cross, to end his suffering which had gone on for three days. Some of the blood that flowed free then was caught in a cup. Some clung to the lance that struck the merciful blow.

'Some rained onto the sheath that held his sword.

'And since that time, no one who has carried the scabbard has fallen in battle. It is said they will not even bleed.

'This is what you are so bold to lay claim to. This is what you ask me to take from my husband before he goes off to war.'

Laurel felt herself rooted to the spot. As soon as the queen spoke, she felt she should have known. Perhaps in her heart she had always known, but nothing short of pride had kept her from understanding. It was wrong what she had done, what she did now.

No one who has carried the scabbard has fallen in battle. Life itself lay in that casket. Life for Arthur.

Life for Agravain.

You must bring to him what Guinevere brought to Arthur. Laurel's eyes closed. She could not look any longer at the queen's weary, frightened countenance, at her stained hand laid upon the Blood of the Saviour.

Help me, Laurel prayed. *Give me some sign.*

But perhaps signs were not for such as she. She only heard the words again. No one who has carried the scabbard has fallen in battle. She saw Agravain at his desk, his strong, careful hands working with paper and ink.

What if Merlin is wrong? She asked herself desperately. *He was not in his right mind yesterday. What if he did lie, or make a mistake? He has made others.*

She saw Morgaine's black eyes shining in triumph. She saw her father's corpse at her feet and felt his blood on her hands. She saw her brother's hand closed around the knife.

But what if he was right?

If he was right and she did not do this thing, Agravain would die. If Agravain died, the protection Gododdin brought to Cambryn would fail. Her land, her people, hated by Morgaine would fall, and fall fast.

Her little sister Lynet would die, would end in a pool of her own blood as their father had.

Laurel opened her eyes. She made to speak, but found she could not raise her voice. She could only whisper hoarsely. 'This is my right, and the property of my lineage. Your own doing made it so.'

'I could refuse you.' Queen Guinevere spoke to the scabbard, not to Laurel. 'I could give it formally to the mother church to hold, as perhaps I should have done years ago.'

'My request was witnessed. If you refuse me, it will be known that you broke faith, as did Arthur with Agravain.'

Guinevere closed her eyes for a moment, swaying on her knees as if gripped by terrible pain. Laurel's heart strained inside her and all at once she hated herself. But she did not speak to stop it.

Hands trembling, tears shining on her cheeks, Guinevere

wrapped the silk around the scabbard, lifted it free from the chest, and handed it to Laurel. Laurel received the gift. The silk was cool and slick against her palms. She knelt before the queen, before Christ on his cross, before the understanding of that enormity she had only sensed before.

Guinevere touched her head, and Laurel knew then the queen had been told the truth. She did understand why Agravain and Laurel acted as they did, but that made this no easier.

'Go,' Guinevere whispered.

Laurel did not hesitate. Cradling the scabbard in both arms, she ran from the chapel, leaving the queen to pray and weep as she must.

She was barely aware of the world around her as she hurried back to Agravain's chamber. She was aware only of the weight in her arms and the soft slip of silk against skin. She was out of breath by the time she opened the door, darting inside like a thief.

Agravain looked up at once as she stood there, panting.

'What has happened?'

Wordlessly, Laurel held out the silken package. Agravain's brow furrowed with impatient incomprehension, but he stood and unfolded the silk without lifting it from her hands. When he saw the scabbard, he frowned. He picked it up and examined it with a soldier's eye, seeing a piece of equipage that was too ancient and too worn to be of any use at all.

'Why this thing?' he asked.

She swallowed hard to ease the tremor that robbed her of her voice, and she told him.

All anger and all impatience drained from Agravain's face, leaving him nearly as pale as the silk still draped across her hands. Slowly, he set the relic back on the virgin bed she held out for it. His hands free, Agravain crossed himself.

Then, he lifted the trailing silk, wrapping the scabbard once more.

'Take it back,' he said.

'What?' Laurel stared at him.

He did not look at her. He looked only at the silk that concealed the scabbard. 'I believe I spoke clearly,' he said, his implacable certainty returning to him now. 'Take it back to Queen Guinevere. I have no right to this holy thing.'

Unexpected relief flooded her. And yet, the vision of Merlin's blue eyes returned to her, and the touch of his hot breath on her cheek. 'Merlin said . . .'

Agravain shook his head. 'I do not care. This is not yours to take, nor is it mine to keep. It should be held by the bishop and the High King. You will take it back.'

It is you who saves him. You who wins his war. You bring to him what Guinevere brought Arthur. 'My lord, without this you may very well fail in all you now attempt.'

One muscle twitched high in Agravain's cheek. 'That shall be as God wills,' he whispered. 'I have seen what comes of defying the divine order.' She opened her mouth once more, but Agravain held up both hands, as if to wave her back. 'You will not argue with me in this thing, my wife. You will return this relic to the queen's hands and have nothing more to do with it.'

He meant it. His gaze was completely closed as he looked at her. Slowly, holding that gaze, Laurel curtsied to him. Without hesitation, he nodded, distant and formal, accepting her gesture of obedience.

Laurel walked from the room, the silken bundle cradled like a babe in her arms. Relief still ran through her blood. She did not have to do this. She could give this back to God to whom it belonged. But with each step, that relief ebbed and a tide of fear spread through her to take its place. She could not rid herself of the echo of Merlin's words.

They drummed in the rhythm of her footsteps against stone. She felt them in the cool of the silk against her palms and arms.

She could not rid herself of the understanding that without this, Agravain would fall, and without Agravain, Cambryn too could be so easily lost.

A draught curled around the back of her neck, curious, comforting.

Grandmother? Grandmother? What do I do?

Tears threatened. Laurel hardened her heart. She must decide. If she obeyed, she and Agravain kept their honour, but if he lost life and war, if Morgaine raised her arms in triumph over his corpse, and what then?

Relief fled her, but so too did anger. All that was left was a stone in the depth of her heart weighted with decision and determination.

She took my father and my brother. Cost what it may and the sin be on my head, she will not have my husband nor my sister.

I must find Sir Kai. Her mind raced. The sun had been low when they crossed the courtyard. It wanted but an hour or two before the evening meal was laid in the great hall. The seneschal would be in the cellars, supervising the selection of the wines and ciders for the high table.

Blessing her knowledge of Camelot's workings, Laurel hastened her steps. She held the scabbard closely, draping her sleeves and veil over the white silk to hide it from the eyes of those she passed.

Down the stairs and down the halls. Ignore the stares and the mutters. Hurry, hurry.

Hurry. Before I change my mind.

The corridors grew darker. She heard the kitchen's shouts and thumps and smelled the roasting meats for the dinner. Her stomach growled. She could not remember when she last ate. But all this was distant. Only the weighted silk in her hands, and the stone of determination in her breast were present. They drove her need to hurry to the soot blackened door, and pull it open before anyone in the busy, kiln-hot kitchen saw her fleeing form, and shouted to stop her.

And she found herself face to face with Sir Kai, coming up the steps, a red clay crock in his free hand. Their eyes met, and she moved forward, closing the door a little behind her. The seneschal, obligingly, awkwardly, backed down two steps.

'Well, well. It is our noble Lady Laurel. Full as noble as her new husband.' His dark eyes glimmered and his words let her know they could easily be overheard. 'Why come here, lady? Is the wine I sent up not to your liking?'

'Sir Kai,' Laurel murmured, looking over her shoulder at the door, half afraid it would be jerked open. 'Uncle Kai.' *You are also my uncle now.* 'I have a grave favour to beg of you.'

He regarded her silently, his wariness plain even in the darkness of the cellar stairway.

Laurel shook her hand so her sleeve and a corner of the white silk fell away from the scabbard. Kai's eyes widened just a little. 'You know what this is,' she whispered hastily. 'Merlin has prophesied it is necessary for Agravain's victory. Agravain has refused it, and ordered me to return it to the queen.' She held it out. 'I beg you, see it put into my trunks when they are loaded onto the cart.'

Eternity passed in a handful of heartbeats while the seneschal held her gaze. Then, Kai wrapped one long hand around the scabbard and lifted it away.

Laurel dropped a deep and heartfelt curtsey to him. If Kai even nodded she did not see. She only heard the scrape and thump of his crutch as he turned and limped away down the stairs once more.

Forgive me. Forgive me. Laurel was not certain whether her plea went out to Kai, Agravain, Arthur, or God. *It is what I must do.*

Laurel rose, alone in the darkness now. She brushed down her skirts and sleeves and turned to face the other way, to open the door full and let in the light, and return once more to her husband's side.

NINE

Mordred reined his black gelding to a halt and stripped off his gloves so he could blow on his hands. The mists had kept dawn's twilight lingering in the valley, and stopped the sun's rays from warming the world. There was just light enough to see, but it was still cold as midnight.

Mordred had gone out early to talk with the men who had the unenviable, and cold, dawn watch. It was unlikely in the extreme that Din Eityn should try to strike at them, but not unthinkable, so he would not have the watch neglected.

The Westmen and the Dal Riata now camped side-by-side in uneasy neighbourliness. The Pict men consented to come down from their hill, but still kept their faces to the rest of the camp, and their backs to that same hill, as if they thought they might have to retreat quickly.

So far the guards were all men they'd brought up with them. That arrangement would have to change. But the Pict men . . . they were proving difficult. They did not like the idea of guards at all, alternately boasting that no one could sneak up on them awake or asleep, and demanding to know why they couldn't drift in and out of the camp as they pleased, as they had neither horses nor cattle, nor much of anything else that needed guarding. The Dal Riata would be marginally easier, but they were already bored, and as a people seemed to lack the talent for patience. But they had to be made to feel they were truly a part of this company, this fight. If nothing else, it would help maintain their friendship and keep them convinced that this squatting in the mud was the prelude to something much more.

Because the Dal Riata were beginning to doubt that, with the slow marches, and the long stops. It was not only the Dal Riata either. The mists were excellent for concealing the presence of listening ears, and Mordred had heard more than one uneasy grumble coming from his own men.

The addition of a crowd of restless strangers was no help at all.

'My Lord Mordred!'

Mordred turned his head to see one of his captains, Corryn ap Rhys, striding out from the teeming mass that was the new encampment. A small crowd of men followed him, all with an air of excited expectation about them.

Mordred watched their approach through narrowed eyes. Corryn was a broad, bluff man. He wore his moustaches long with red and blue threads twisted into them. A little more intelligence gleamed in his stone-brown eyes than in those of most of Mordred's men. This made it right to put him in charge, but it made him less willing to take orders based on faith and friendship.

And, unfortunately, it meant that when it came to patience for their slow progress, Corryn was almost as bad as the Dal Riata.

Corryn stepped up beside Mordred's horse and bowed. 'We have word from Londinium. Ros, the messenger from Din Eityn, he's back. Sir Agravain is to meet him there soon.'

Agravain. As she said it would be. 'Any word about how many men might be coming up from Camelot with him?'

Corryn stuck his thumbs in his belt. 'We may be in luck there, says our man. Seems there was a falling out with Arthur, and the Bastard let no one come with him. He's travelling alone.'

A smile came to Mordred as he turned his face eastward. 'How sad!' he announced, pulling his gloves back on. 'We must be sure to give him good welcome!'

The men grinned knowingly at each other. Only Corryn failed to smile. 'My lord . . .' he began.

Mordred raised his eyebrows. 'Yes?'

Corryn shifted his weight. From his height on horseback, Mordred watched his face closely. Corryn was coming to a decision. He had not come to make this announcement in public because it was important news. Rather, he wanted to see what Mordred would do with it.

No. He wants the other men to see what I do with it. 'What is it, Captain Corryn?'

Mordred had calculated his overly mild tone to produce a reaction, and he got it.

'Why do we not move now?' Corryn demanded. 'We know Din Eityn is all but defenceless. We could go in there, slaughter their mad old king and be in charge of the place by the time they sail round the point.'

'That is not what we have planned.' Mordred allowed the smallest hint of severity to creep into his voice. He paused. 'You're frowning, Captain. Why is that?'

Corryn's eyes shifted sideways. 'Nothing, my lord.'

Mordred sighed. This had to come. It was inevitable, given the nature of the men he must lead. He found himself genuinely sorry it must be Corryn of whom he had to make the example.

Mordred dismounted, tossing his reins across the saddlebow. His horse stamped once, restlessly, sensing his master's change of mood.

'You do have something to say, Captain.' Mordred faced Corryn, waving his hand languidly. 'I'd like to hear it, if you please.'

Mordred's dismissive tone made the captain bold. 'I say perhaps we are ruled too much by a woman's plans.'

Ah, Corryn. I thought you better than this. 'Do you?' Standing at his full height, Mordred was as tall as the captain, but Corryn was still a full two stone heavier. It was like being a willow sapling beside the venerable oak.

'And perhaps you think I am too much a child to be leading this army?' Mordred cocked his head, keeping his inquiry soft, almost gentle, but his tone had changed from silk to steel. The men at Corryn's back shifted uneasily as Mordred stepped forward. 'Perhaps I should still be sucking at my mother's breast?'

Proving he had ears, and some idea to whom he spoke, Corryn hesitated, and made some attempt to duck back after having stuck his stiff neck out so far. 'I did not say that.'

Mordred took another step forward. 'But it shines in your eyes, Captain Corryn,' he said softly. 'You question our lady's judgment; what was she thinking to put a stripling boy in charge of matters best left to men. That he is her son only makes matters worse.'

Mordred laid his hand on his sword. *How far are you ready to take this, Corryn? Have sense, man, and beg forgiveness.*

But sense of that kind seemed to have deserted the captain. He was determined to take Mordred's measure. What goaded him so? They'd just had the best of all possible news. Agravain was on his own. With no army of knights behind him, he could not hope to hold the rock. They only needed a little time and everything would fall into their hands. Mother would have the death for Lot that she wanted so badly, and they would still have their victory.

I understand it is hard, I do. Make a show at apology, Corryn, and all is forgotten.

But Corryn's hard hand also wrapped around his own sword hilt. 'You may put words into my mouth, my lord, and insult me by doing it. It does not make this plan we follow any better.'

They were alone now, even while the crowd of men grew around them. It was a strangely intimate thing, this matter of insults and accusations, the necessary preparation for the first and last dance of a fighting man's life. Despite his heart's whisper of regret, Mordred found himself savouring the moment. This was where he and Corryn would show who they truly were. Some of Corryn's comrades had backed away, forming a circle around them. Others came up. Shouts sounded in the distance, letting the whole camp know what was happening. Mother herself would know soon, if she did not already.

But she would leave it to him. This was his test. Corryn was intelligent, but he was angry. His strength was a bull's strength, direct and brutal, with no subtlety or strategy.

You hesitate, Corryn. Afraid? Is that caution in your eyes at last? Very well. You've done good service for me, so I will make it easy for you.

'You say I am not fit to lead, Corryn.' Mordred made voice and eyes leaden. He let the words roll out, implacable and unstoppable. 'I say you are not fit to follow. How dare you question your betters? You are a pig-skulled wastrel, fit only to sit in the mud with one thumb in your arse and the other in your mouth . . .'

It was too much. Far too much. Corryn's sword flashed out and he charged head-on. Mordred had his own blade up in an instant and they came together with a ringing clash. Corryn had a heartbeat's worth of time to look into Mordred's eyes and see the pity there before Mordred's boot lashed out to catch Corryn directly on the knee. The instant he felt the captain crumble, Mordred swung them around, bearing Corryn to the ground. Shouts sounded behind them, and warning gasps, empathetic cries.

Mordred did not give Corryn a chance to rise, but kicked again, this time to his skull. Corryn's head snapped back, and he grunted, sprawling dazed in the dirt. Blood made a gnarled scarlet flower to decorate Corryn's brow and flowed in red threads down his cheeks.

Mordred laid the tip of his sword on the captain's throat. Bending over carefully, he took up Corryn's weapon in his free hand. He straightened then, and gave Corryn a good long moment to let his eyes focus, so that he might understand where he was and what was happening.

At last, Mordred saw comprehension take hold in the other man's eyes. 'Look about you, Captain. What friend have you here now that you have spoken against my leadership, and the wisdom of our lady? Who raises a hand to help you?'

Mordred spoke clearly. This was as much for the crowd as it was for Corryn. Mordred scanned the faces of the men who stood silent and stolid at the captain's defeat. None of them met Mordred's gaze. If anything, they sought to back away, to get more distance between themselves and this fallen man who many until this moment had indeed called friend.

The sight sickened Mordred. Any enjoyment he had felt at weathering this test of his authority drained away.

Corryn lifted a shaking hand and wiped at his temple. 'Mercy, Lord,' he croaked. 'Please.'

'You shall have it.' Mordred sheathed his sword. 'Come here, Durial.'

Durial was Mordred's other captain, a small, stony, silent man with a bushy beard and sharp eyes. Mordred had seen him among the crowd, but he had not come with Corryn. Come to see, but not to support.

It was time to warn him against taking such action as Corryn had.

'This is your slave now,' said Mordred, waving contemptuously at Corryn. Gasps and murmurs rose from the watching crowd, but no protests. None at all. Mordred wiped his brow on his sleeve. 'Do not let him linger too much in idleness. It is bad for a brain prone to fevers, such as his.'

Durial bowed low in acknowledgement, but not in thanks. He understood then that this was a burden, and a lesson. Good.

'Get up, then,' said Durial to his former war-brother.

The new-made slave still had dignity enough to obey without begging. He rose, and staggered, wiping the blood from his face. Corryn met Mordred's gaze for an instant. Mordred watched his former captain's pride flicker and die just before Corryn dropped his gaze as was appropriate for one standing before his lord. One heavy step at a time, Corryn moved to follow his new master.

The men parted for them, muttering, shaking their heads. Mordred stayed where he was, head up, waiting. Would anyone be bold enough to make objection? Had Corryn any comrade to make an open challenge? The idea brought a fresh sweat to Mordred's brow. If things were so bad that he must face two challenges in the same hour . . .

But the men only fell away, turning back to their work, talking in undertones. Word of this would spread in its own time. It was a hard punishment for a man such as Corryn. Mordred expected he would put an end to it by his own hand, and soon.

What a waste.

Mordred swung himself back up into his saddle. He had meant to finish riding the edges of the camp. But the import of Corryn's challenge settled into his stomach, leaving him with a taste like lead in the back of his mouth. He swung his horse's head around and set it walking back towards the centre of camp, back towards his mother's pavilion.

As he passed the clusters of fires, the men and their women going through the motions of the morning, they looked up at him. They nodded, or bowed their heads in respect, but not one watched him without a question in their eyes, and for each of them the question was the same.

When do we begin this war? When do we *move*?

Mordred gritted his teeth as he reached the leather pavilion. He tethered his horse loosely and pulled back the flap to duck into the dim interior.

'Ahhh, my son.'

Mordred blinked hard, his eyes adjusting to the sudden lack of light. His mother stretched luxuriously on her simple bed, gazing up at him. Mordred stared back, barely able to believe what he was seeing. He was used to the satisfaction and lassitude her workings could bring on her, but now she lolled on her fur bed all but drunk, looking at him with the misty indulgence of a doting mother for a toddling babe.

'Mother!' he said through gritted teeth, barely remembering to keep his voice down. 'What have you been doing?'

'Nothing, my dear, nothing at all. Just . . . enjoying.' She sighed wistfully. 'I will miss him you know. In his way. He was quite strong. Quite strong.'

In another moment she would giggle. Frustration roiled Mordred's stomach. He strode to her bedside. She sat up as he approached, her face full of innocent surprise.

Anger, brassy and unfamiliar rose in his throat. 'Mother,' he said by way of greeting. 'I just had to enslave Corryn for saying what the whole of the host has been thinking.'

She smiled as if he had just brought her the finest possible news. 'And what might that be, my beloved one?'

'Listen to me, my lady. These new men we have brought in to make up our numbers will not sit still for this plotting.

They are not yours, not ours. They want war and they want plunder, and they will not wait here while you nibble on what's left of Lot's sanity!'

She cocked her head, judging his words with the mildest of temperaments. 'You are the commander here. What do you say should be done?'

Does she make a game of me? Mordred turned the thought away. He could not, would not let such suspicion take root. Those roots would poison every other thought in his heart.

'I say we do as Corryn said. We take Gododdin now. Damn prophecy, damn Arthur, and damn Agravain. They will fall in good time, if we but make ourselves ready and fight this war with skill and science.' He dropped onto one knee to bring his eyes level with hers, pleading for her to understand. 'Sitting out here waiting for Lot to die is nothing short of foolish, Mother. It weakens us.'

He searched her black eyes, the eyes that were twins to his own only so much deeper. There was no light to reflect in them, only pools of night, fathomless, unreachable.

Slowly, Morgaine surfaced from that blackness, the lady who had led her people so well for so long, whose watch never tired or faltered.

'I hear what you say, Mordred,' she told him, her voice firm now that her inmost self had returned to the present and mortal world. 'I can only ask you to be patient, to trust me this much longer.' She sat up, her skirts and sleeves falling decently over her bared limbs. 'Victory will only come if we drive Agravain from his senses as we have driven his father. If he remains cautious, he will win. This is what all the signs say. He must see what his father has become, must know intimately what has been done and what surrounds him and his.' His mother laid her hand lightly on his. 'Then we may take him, quickly, cleanly, and for all the world to see, but Arthur especially.' Her eyes sparked at this, and Mordred found he could not help but smile in return.

'As for the fact that these new men have no faith in me or my words.' She drew herself up. 'You are right, and that must be remedied. I will consider how it may best be done.' She smiled, and it was with relief Mordred saw it was her own sober, edged smile. 'Do not worry, my son. It will be done very soon.'

She meant that to close the conversation. She did not wish him to stay any longer. More, she did not wish him to make any mention of how he had found her.

'Thank you, Mother.' He bowed, obedient as ever. 'Now I must finish my inspections.'

She nodded and he left her shadowed pavilion, stepping once more into the daylight, straightening his shoulders. The mists were lightening, and day's warmth touched his face, but it could not warm his thoughts. He looked around him at the camp, the people moving to and fro, tending fires, horses, and oxen. They talked, perhaps of food, or weather, or what the next day might bring. Nothing he could see was wrong.

But he knew the wrong was there now, both without, and within. He had spoken the words in her presence, and he had believed them. All this waiting was pure folly. All his mother's reassurances could not wash it away. It had been growing in him for some time, this niggling, nagging suspicion that it was not his mother's visions, or even the revenge he wanted as badly as she did that prevented them moving against the living King Lot.

What if, what if she enjoyed her nightly visits to him too much? Got some woman's pleasure out of it that she was loath to give up, the way a drunkard could not give up his whisky?

What if he, Lot, had managed to seduce her somehow? He had done as much to her sister . . .

Mordred's jaw clenched. He should not doubt her. Shame crawled through him at the very thought. But he did doubt. He had seen her power, knew its strength and its worth better than any man living, but the deeper they drew themselves towards the reality of war, the less he liked depending on it. What was done in smoke and darkness could be undone by fire and daylight. It was not foolishness to make sure they had a position to safely fall back to.

This was his war. He could not leave victory to the whim of his mother's need and power, however strong those might be. There was far too much that could go wrong here, now, in the visible world.

'You,' he said to a passing man with the raven's silhouette on his leather jacket. 'Find the messenger from Londinium and bring him to my fire.'

The man bowed and strode off on his errand. Mordred took up his horse's reins again and led the beast through the maze of the encampment, trying not to look like he was leaving in haste. He hated the feeling that his mother could hear his thoughts, the idea that she sat in her shadows this very moment, frowning at the turn his ideas had taken.

Mordred had no pavilion for himself. The only difference between the place beside his little fire and all the others surrounding it was the blue banner with its black raven fluttering in the morning's fitful breeze. He wanted to be sure his command was respected because of his actions, not through display of wealth or rank. He had enough wealth to be generous when occasion demanded, but otherwise, he lived as his men did; sleeping out in the open and caring for his horses and his gear himself. When it rained, he was wet. When it was cold, he huddled beside his fire and sent up his curses in white clouds of frozen breath.

Mordred removed his horse's saddle and bridle, hobbled

it loosely, set down some oats for it to graze, and squatted down beside his fire to lay on a handful of extra fuel.

'My lord, here is Oeric.'

Mordred stood, dusting his hands and nodding his thanks to the soldier. Oeric could not have been hard to find. His hair shone like gold amid the sea of muddy brown and midnight black heads belonging Mordred's company. Likewise his skin showed bright red where the sun had burned it and his eyes icy blue. Oeric had a sailor's hard, crooked hands, bulging arms and straight legs. He looked Mordred up and down, weighing and judging, and not thinking much of what he saw.

That was all right. 'Do you go back to Londinium now?' he asked in the Saxon's language.

The man's eyes widened, startled to hear his own harsh tongue in a Briton's mouth. 'I do,' he answered. 'Got my own to keep, haven't I?'

Mordred nodded. 'So do we all. Well, I thank you for the pains you have taken so far.' He slipped the silver cuff off his own wrist and held it up. 'For you, for what you've done, and for another service I'd ask of you.'

Oeric took the ring, openly weighing it in his hand as he had weighed Mordred in his gaze. Evidently, both satisfied him, and he slid the cuff onto his own wrist. 'What can I do for you, Lord?'

Mordred took the gold ring from his finger. It was decorated with a midnight black stone, etched with a raven in flight. It had been his since he had come to manhood. He did not like the thought of parting with it now, but it was the most recognizable sigil he had about him.

'Take this ring to the *Jarl* Sifred of Londinium. You tell him that Mordred ap Morgaine pledges him twelve rings of gold, and lasting friendship besides, if Sir Agravain never leaves his city.'

Oeric closed his hand around the ring. 'It will be done, Lord.'

Mordred nodded. 'Good. Tell him to send me word by you when it is.'

Oeric made his salute and tucked the ring into his broad belt. Mordred watched him march away with the rolling gate of one who lived more on water than on land.

And it is done. If Agravain gets himself killed in Londinium, everything just becomes that much easier. If he makes it out alive, well, we will be here waiting for him.

It was not really betrayal. Not really doubt. He was aiding the cause of their family, as he had always done. That was all.

That is all. Mordred turned to his fire again and tried his hardest to believe that.

Agravain held out his hand to help Laurel step from the boat onto the stone slab of the quay. She lifted her brows at this courtesy – it was not as if she must worry about her stout boots taking a wetting – and received the slightest quirk of his mouth in reply.

It had taken three days to sail from Camelot to Londinium. Their single-masted, round-bottomed boat was crewed by a pair of dour men; an uncle and nephew as near as Laurel could make out from their infrequent comments. What she did know was that Ros had hired them, and they had, it seemed, been waiting for Agravain impatiently for some three days by the time he and Laurel arrived at the harbour from Camelot.

It had been an easy voyage with fair winds and a calm sea. Laurel felt certain this was a gift from her grandmother, but she had not been inclined to call attention to the fact. They spent the nights in fishing villages on the shore where the headmen were more than willing to host a prince on his way to his own country, especially one who would freely reward such courtesy with a ring of bronze or silver, or a length of good cloth from his wife's chests.

The days were spent mostly sitting side-by-side in the prow of the boat, keeping out of the way, and singing.

This had been Agravain's idea, his way of teaching her the language of his home, of which she knew precious little. He would sing a verse of an old ballad, tell her what it meant, and sing it over again with her, until her pronunciation met his exacting standards. For all that, he was a surprisingly patient teacher, and his voice was of a pleasant, middling range. They even laughed sometimes when her tongue stumbled in a particularly egregious fashion, or, far more rarely, his memory failed him.

Sometimes at night when he held her, he hummed beneath his breath, so that this was the last thing she heard before she fell asleep.

Laurel found herself looking at him with growing wonder. She suspected not even Sir Kai knew this part of him. But as with the serene weather, she feared to call attention to it, lest somehow she break the peaceful spell that swaddled their voyage.

Despite this pleasant idyll, she was not at all surprised to see Agravain's more familiar, more wary aspect take firm hold as they slogged up the muddy shore of Londinium's low, broad river. Here, he had said, was where they began to learn how well his long preparations had taken hold.

Londinium was a strange place. The riverbank had become a kind of permanent market. Men of a half-dozen lands – Aquitaine, Bretagne, Languedoc, Andalusia, even one or two of Byzantium and Rome – moved about between crowds of yellow-haired Saxons. All the voices, all the languages mixed together with the calls of hundreds of animals into an indecipherable gabble. The whole world seemed occupied in either getting cargo off ships, or loading it on, where they were not sitting down with jugs of liquor. Men hefted jars, chests, and bulging sacks. The scents of spices and spirits rivalled the smells of sweat, manure and mud. A trader with earth-brown skin led a string of horses with such delicate legs Laurel wondered how they could bear their own weight. Other men herded fat, red cattle that the chieftains in her home country would have traded their daughters, or perhaps even their sons, for. Still others held the leashes of huge, shaggy hounds that could bring down an elk, or even a bear.

The few women in evidence were dressed in the plainest stuff, their braided hair decorated with baubles of bronze or brass, or a few bright ribbons. They tended fires and pens, and poured out measures of liquor for the men. They cast as many measuring glances at Laurel as their menfolk did.

What was truly strange about the place was the way it was even now taking shape over the bones of the older city. Broken walls stuck out of the mud here. She could see the remains of Romanish carvings, tiles and mosaics, but all of them seemed to be incorporated into something else. A wattle and daub hut had been built on a floor of baked bricks. The field stone and timber watchtower that rose up to dominate the scene owed its neat square to the smooth Roman stones at its base. A design in shining blue glass gleamed under the muddy boots of two men sitting under no more roof than the sky, sharing a jug. A curving wall carved with dancing women was now part of a crude warehouse, and a fluted column made one pillar for a pen for squealing, brown pigs.

None of this mis-matched enterprise, nor the crowd and crush of those who on other ground would gladly run him through, seemed to give Agravain any pause. He craned his neck this way and that, plainly looking for some person or thing, frowned because it was not instantly in evidence.

Then, Laurel saw a slender man in a forest-green tunic,

his left arm crooked strangely against his chest, making a beeline toward them. She touched Agravain's arm and pointed. Agravain did not smile, but she knew his face well enough to see that he did relax, just a little.

'Sir Agravain,' said the man in court Latin as soon as he was close enough. He bowed deeply, if not gracefully. 'It is good to see you, my lord.'

'Squire Devi. You are in good time.'

Squire?

Laurel found herself staring at the man. Devi was a brown-haired young man, but no longer a youth. Indeed, he looked perhaps only a year or two younger than Agravain himself. Like his master, he dressed plainly and went clean shaven. His only ornament was a bronze brooch in the shape of a soaring falcon, the sigil of Agravain's own house. What set Devi apart though, was that his left arm had met with some accident of birth or misadventure, and the fingers on that hand were twisted twigs, and plainly useless. His good hand, which Agravain now clasped, was stained with an odd mix of mud and ink.

Agravain turned to her. 'This is the Lady Laurel,' he said to Devi. 'My wife.'

Devi stared at her, exactly as she stared at him, plainly stunned to find that there existed such a creature. He swallowed and bowed hastily. 'God be with you, my lady.'

'And with you, squire,' she replied gravely. 'I am glad to meet one who has plainly looked after my husband's business so ably.'

The squire flushed a little, but at the same time his hunched shoulders relaxed. 'It has been my privilege, my lady.' From someone else, this might have been mere politeness, but Devi spoke the words with a wealth of feeling.

It was loyalty. Pure and simple. It shone in the man's eyes. She had never yet seen anyone show this towards Agravain, with the single exception of Sir Kai. *What else are you hiding out here in the hinterlands my husband?*

This, however, was all the time Agravain was prepared to allow for courtesy. 'How much is ready?' he asked Devi.

'Everything, my lord,' answered the squire, his chest puffing out with pride. 'We can begin loading as soon as we have the ships to take the cargo.'

Agravain nodded once in sober approval. 'Have you found us some likely masters?'

'I have, but they were reluctant to believe one such as myself,' he shrugged so that his withered arm jerked a little, 'could give them something worthwhile for their troubles.'

'Well, we shall see if we can change their minds on that score. We must find . . .'

The squelch and slap of sandals in mud cut off Agravain's words. A boy splashed through the crowd, dodging men, beasts and drowning cobbles, but plainly heading towards their little gathering. His fair hair and blue eyes marked him as Saxon and his deep blue tunic spoke of some wealth or rank.

'*Jarl* Agravain *mach* Lot?' the boy asked breathlessly, giving Agravain's title in their guttural tongue.

'I am,' Agravain acknowledged in the same language.

'I am sent by *Jarl* Sifred Hunwald, the holder and protector of Londinium. He welcomes you to his city, and salutes you in brotherly greeting. He invites you and yours to share bread and hearth with him tonight.'

Sifred Hunwald. Laurel knew the name. Sifred was the one who made treaty with Arthur and ended the war between the Britons and the much-diminished band of Saxons. He had not joined the Great Peace, neither had he disturbed it. There were many who said the High King was a fool to allow him holding on the island, especially one encompassing this rich river port. But once given, Arthur would not break his word, and so far, Sifred Hunwald had not broken his.

Agravain's face remained neutral upon hearing the invitation, but Laurel could all but feel the quick calculations thrumming through him. This was unexpected, but having come, could not in courtesy, or indeed safety, be refused.

'Tell *Jarl* Sifred we will not fail him.'

'Then you will know his thanks, worthy sir.' The boy bowed hastily and loped off once more, expertly dodging men, carts and animals as he made his way back up the long, shallow slope.

'And his purpose too, I hope,' murmured Agravain.

Laurel considered. 'Perhaps he hopes to find out what yours is, now that you are here.'

'It may be.' But Agravain was plainly not convinced of this. 'However, it makes us more formally guests here, at least until we have heard him, and that is no bad thing.' Having determined this, he set it aside at once. He was itching to get to his main business. 'My lady, I fear I must ask you to wait with the boat. There is no suitable escort or company I can leave you with while Devi and I see to what is needed.'

'Of course.' In truth, Laurel was not sorry for the excuse to retreat. She had not been prepared for this teeming, stinking, half-built place, and neither was she ready for her own reaction to the sight of so many yellow Saxon heads, or the flash of light in their clear blue eyes. Anyone who saw her white hair and pale skin might think her at home here, but these were not in any way her kindred. These were the enemy, who crashed up against the bulwark that Arthur and his knights made. These were the ones, who, if allowed, would flood the whole of the isle and leave no more alive than they needed for slaves. Laurel had found herself moving closer to Agravain, trying hard not to cringe as so many curious, hard blue gazes lit her way. The ship's master was at least a known quantity. If he was silent, he was steady and exacted steady work from his nephew.

Agravain walked Laurel back to the boat, and helped her over the rail. The master heard his charge of her without either complaint or enthusiasm. As soon as his nephew came trudging back with two bowls of a powerful smelling eel stew, the two of them hunkered down on the quay to eat, and block the way of anyone who might approach with business or mischief in mind.

Without looking back, Agravain, with Devi all but running to keep up, strode into the surging crowds of Londinium, and was lost to her sight.

Laurel let out a sigh and brushed her trailing veil back over her shoulders. The boat rocked under her as she sat down on the bench, gazing out at the rippling brown water. *Abandoned once again.* The thought flickered through her mind, and she swatted it angrily aside. It was unworthy. If she chaffed at idleness, she should find some way to busy herself. It was not Agravain's role to always provide her company.

But it was more than that, if she admitted it to herself. The whole journey had been strange, not like the feeling of homecoming she was used to when she travelled the water. It was as if she must hold some part of herself back, in defence or deference. But in deference to what? Agravain? The marriage? She twisted her hands together.

And is it really me that holds back, or is it you? She wondered towards the river. *What did Merlin say to you?*

The water made no answer. It lazily rocked the bobbing boats, lapping at both ship and shore, its soft voice unheard under the roar and gabble of so much mortal activity. Even by her.

It occurred to her wonder if Agravain's ease had been bred by the water itself. She had been so caught up in wondering what her oath of marriage meant for herself and her future, she had forgotten to wonder if it worked any change in him to now be blood of her blood and flesh of her flesh.

It was a strange thought, and not entirely a comfortable one. Laurel shook herself. She could not sit here and brood. That Agravain must now plunge back into preparations for Din Eityn after their brief interlude should not come as any shock to her. She was no whey-faced child bride. She was wife of a prince, soon a king. She must start to act like it.

Laurel looked left and right, seeking some way of distracting herself. The only means that came to hand was her chests. She'd had no opportunity to inspect their contents on the journey. Now, she opened them, shifting the contents carefully, examining fabric, ornament and treasure for signs of damage from insect or, more pertinently, from water.

That, and the evidence of Agravain's labours kept her from having to dwell too much on her own thoughts. Their quay quickly became its own small market. An hour or so after he left with Agravain, Squire Devi returned and stationed himself at the foot of the dock. Every few minutes another man would come up and greet him, usually a trader or merchant with a stylus and a tablet hanging from his belt. Ships lifted their anchors, moving themselves closer to their tiny craft. These were not little cogs like the one they travelled in, but great, oared long ships with square, striped sails. They let down their gangways to allow the merchant's crews to begin their lading.

And what they loaded! Laurel forgot her own work to stand and stare: great timber beams that had been squared off and notched; hogsheads of water and beer; swords and armours; oxen, ponies, ingots of iron, bars of steel. There were far stranger things as well, clay jars, some empty, some sealed in wax that nonetheless stank of pitch, piss or sulphur. Caulked barrels carried disgusting messes of hair and sinew.

These were wrestled aboard beside shapeless bundles of leather and canvas, some so huge it took three men to lift them.

With these outlandish objects came an equally outlandish host of men; thin, pale boys Devi greeted as brother squires. Ancient men with gnarled hands and sharp eyes. Men with soft, scholar's hands but crooked backs, or lame legs. Old soldiers with missing limbs. Blacksmiths, woodwrights and wheelwrights. They barely had a sword or even a knife among them. Instead they brought hammers and saws, augers and adzes.

Ten years of work. Not cultivating loyalty or friendship. Ten years of quietly buying and storing, and hoarding. She had been surprised, in her brief time at Camelot to find how meanly her husband lived. Now, she saw where his wealth had gone, and she found she understood none of it.

But wonder palled, and modesty reasserted itself. Laurel could not stand there endlessly gaping like a raw maiden. She busied herself again with her chests, counting, folding, examining, airing. The clang, clatter and chatter of the other ships washed over her.

It was in the last chest she found what she was truly looking for. This was the smallest, most stoutly built box, made to hold the precious store of watered silk. She folded back a length of garnet red to find a flash of pure white. It was laid out neat and smooth, and had not been there when Meg had packed this chest under Laurel's supervision.

So, this is where you hid it. Well done, Sir Kai.

She laid her hand on the cool silk. It seemed as if the sounds of the world dimmed just a little, and a strange mix of feeling seeped into her blood, some of the comfort she had missed, but also the sense of things changed and changing, and of that change being both feared and welcomed.

Laurel found herself wondering for the thousandth time

about the nature of this sacred thing, of why Merlin's shattered vision showed him that this was what would turn the tide for Agravain, and for herself.

As she sat there, lost in this inner sea of thought and sensation, a ripple of movement in the muddy water caught her eye. Laurel lifted her hand away, and quickly slammed the chest's lid shut. Around her, the world continued on, nothing pausing or even hesitating.

But she saw it again. A golden ripple in the lee of one of the jutting rocks that made navigation in these shallows so treacherous. As she frowned at it, a dark head lifted from the waters. Had anyone else noticed it, they might have taken it for a seal come too far up the river from the sea. But Laurel knew at once that was not what it was. Long, dripping locks streamed across its naked shoulders. Its eyes were too dark for any animal's, the skin too smooth and its face too flat.

Morverch. Laurel's throat tightened.

The *morverch* were the sea-women. Mermaids some called them. Bards spoke of them as beautiful women with sparkling fish's tails where their legs should have been. They had never seen one of the corpse-grey beings before Laurel now, her hair tangled with weeds and strange flowers and a narrow slit in place of her nose.

Greetings, sister. The voice insinuated itself into Laurel's mind like the first cold trickle of water that said the dam was cracking.

Laurel nodded in return. She glanced to either side. The sailors and the workmen went about their business without hesitation. Probably they could not even see this creature if she did not wish to show herself to them.

What are you afraid of? The *morverch's* silent words spread themselves out in a long sneer in Laurel's mind. *You don't wish that man you've snared to see you greeting your kindred?*

'I did not snare him,' Laurel snapped back before she could stop herself.

The *morverch* grinned. Her teeth were needle sharp. *No? You brought him all the wealth that land could offer. You promised him power, but didn't tell him the first thing about what it means. Gave him your body, but nothing of your true self.*

Laurel felt the blood drain from her face and the *morverch* laughed, a sound like rain spattering into a pond. *So stricken. You have all those thoughts swimming on the wind, why should you be surprised they got tangled in another's net?* She lifted her hand plucking at the air with her long, thin fingers.

Laurel bit her lip. 'You are wrong,' she murmured, knowing full well the *morverch* would hear her no matter how softly she spoke.

Am I? That red blood of yours is all but still now. I can feel it. The tide of it is ebbing. You're terrified of what he will do when he truly realizes you have your beginning in the countries where he cannot see or walk. You are as weak as your mother, and just as afraid he'll leave you when he finds out.

Anger tightened Laurel's jaw and her hands gripped the rail. 'You have no right to speak of my mother.'

Who has more right? I clung to her, I cried for her. I begged her not to go. But she went to the burning sun and the scorching air. She let herself die for a man of flesh and blood, and she left her children in ignorance. All this out of fear of what that man would do if he saw what she truly was. If he knew that union with her would change him, change their children forever.

'No,' whispered Laurel. But the denial fell flat.

The sea-woman slid forward, her pale shoulders disturbing the muddy waters. *Yes. Yes. And you know it. You cannot stop looking over your shoulder. You cannot bring any warmth to your flesh because you are too close to the truth here.*

Laurel's fingers ached from gripping the wood so hard, but she could not loosen them. 'You lie,' she said through gritted teeth. 'You think you can trick me like some sailor in a storm.'

The sea-woman's grin was as sudden and terrible as a light-ning flash.

Very good. Very good. You have not forgotten everything, sister. Nor will you forget what I've said. I will be here to welcome you home, Laurel.

Between one eye-blink and the next the *morverch* was gone, leaving behind nothing but a rippling ring in the water, and the memory of her moonlit grin and her cold voice.

Laurel bowed her head and dug her nails into the splin-tering wood. She did not try to deny that the sea-woman's words had dug deep into her. That was folly. She was afraid. Every day took her further from all that she was. The only familiar place she had was the sea itself rolling beneath the fragile ships, and that familiarity was treacherous.

Well? She asked herself stonily. *What are you going to do? Jump in after her?*

Laurel stayed like that for a long time, with no real answer to her question.

TEN

The long summer day was dimming towards twilight when Agravain walked up to *Jarl* Sifred's house with Laurel at his side. Four of the stoutest men Devi had gathered into his service followed behind them. They were a decent guard, but they did not make much show in their plain clothes and with only knives and hammers in their belts.

Like King Arthur, *Jarl* Sifred housed himself in a villa that had once belonged to some wealthy Roman. Unlike the High King, however, Sifred did not appear to have made any effort to maintain his dwelling, let alone improve on it. Soot and mud dimmed the flaking murals. The mosaics and tile patterns had great gaps where precious stones had been dug up, or portions had simply crumbled away. Dogs and pigs roamed the court, and a good deal of the house, freely. The wind from the river blew hard through the airy building, which had been designed for a friendlier climate. The two roaring fires Sifred commanded in the square audience room that served as his great hall did little to blunt its edge.

There was one area in which Sifred was diligently making improvement. Like the city itself, the villa was getting a new set of defensive walls. Great piles of stones sat in the villa's shadow, waiting for the mason's chisel and mortar to be applied.

Jarl Sifred clearly does not expect the peace between himself and Arthur to last forever.

A wizened old man waited at the bottom of the steps to serve as porter. Agravain passed the man his sword, and charged him to take good care of their followers. The fellow bobbed his head repeatedly and waved them up the steps, but did not follow them.

Alone, Agravain and Laurel walked up the cracked marble steps to greet their host. Agravain would have believed her lost in thought, were it not for how quickly her gaze flickered here and there, taking in every detail of this place and its inhabitants. As was the custom among the Saxons, separate tables had been laid for the men and the women. Laurel's arm stiffened against his as she took the measure of those whose company she would bear. They looked at least as rough as their men. Their woollen clothing was well-dyed, but unpatterned, and trimmed with furs rather than ribbons. They had some gold ornamentation, and some silver, leavened by the flash of coloured glass and the odd rare gemstone, possibly stolen from the ravaged mosaics.

Londinium's port might be busy, the wealth of empires might flow through here, but little of it was staying here or at least not with those who inhabited Sifred's shabby court.

Sifred himself sat between the fires on an ivory inlaid chair of Roman make. Cuffed, collared and belted by broad links of bronze, he wore his beard forked. His straw-yellow hair had been streaked with white and red, then braided so it hung down past his shoulders.

'*Jarl* Agravain!' Sifred surged to his feet, a sturdy mountain of a man, holding out both hands to take Agravain's own. Agravain suffered this because it was the courtesy of

Sifred's people. 'Let me look on the man who has sent so many of his own to walk among us!'

With this, Agravain received a kiss of peace that smelled less of liquor than he would have expected. Sifred wanted to come sober to his business. That in itself was telling. This meal was not to be a mere politeness, one lord to another.

'And your good woman!' Sifred's blue eyes suddenly looked piggish in his red face as he took in Laurel's delicate green dress, translucent veil and gold girdle. She dressed herself fairly plainly from her stores, but even so, she shone brightly among these worn-down women.

Agravain felt his shoulders stiffen. 'My wife,' he said firmly. 'Laurel Carnbrea of Cambryn and the Dumonii.'

'A stout race,' allowed Sifred. 'Brave fighters and rich by all accounts, but I'd not heard tell they bred such beauty among them.' Sifred tried, and failed, to make his smile something less than a leer. Laurel bore it all with a straight back and untroubled countenance. It occurred to Agravain that he had failed to ask whether she understood the Saxon language. She remained silent as she made her shallow curtsey to Sifred, but her gaze in the moment before she modestly dropped her eyes was keen, and not at all confused.

What are you doing, my lady?

'Let me make you known to my women. None so fine as yours, *Jarl* Agravain, but they suit me well.' Sifred beckoned to a pair of women in plain blue woollen gowns trimmed with furs. The first was Sifred's match; broad and strong armed, with a round face and keen blue eyes. A necklace of gold and garnets shone on her ample bosom. The second was far smaller and her sunburned face served to brighten her spun-gold hair. The scowl that marred what could have been an otherwise fair countenance spoke of a hard life at the hands of the more powerful woman.

'This is my Hilde, and that little mouse there is my Tatae.

They'll give your wife good welcome, *Jarl* Agravain, while we tend to our meat, and our business.'

'You are most welcome among us,' announced Hilde in an awkward but determined Briton dialect. Laurel raised her head at this and curtsied briefly.

'I do thank you.'

So. Agravain did not let his expression change. It was a good device. Her feigned ignorance would encourage the women to speak freely in front of Laurel, believing she could not understand. He nodded in answer to her cautious glance, and received a reassuring press from her hand as she turned. But he could not help but stare after her a moment as Hilde steered her to the trestle table beside the blazing fire where the women of the house sat.

'Now!' Sifred clapped him on the back, and Agravain suffered this too without comment, not having any choice. There were a thousand ways, he knew, to insult Saxon honour. The trick throughout this meal would be in not stumbling over any new ones.

Sifred led him to a curved table, obviously another artifact salvaged from the Roman times. Their companions were a dozen men cut after Sifred's own model: bluff, hard-bitten and bright-eyed. More than one was scarred from fighting. Many had lost some part of themselves to violence, whether a finger, half a hand, a piece of ear, or, in more than one case, an eye.

They were survivors, these men, and they sized him up as instantly and intently as he did them.

'Meat!' bellowed Sifred, clapping his hands loudly over their heads.

The servants came forward at once. It was, by Camelot's standards, a crude feast, but summer's bounty was not wasted or dismissed even here. Stews of eels and fish were served up with rough breads and accented by the spices of Andalusia.

Great salmons were served up whole in their own sauce. There was, unexpectedly, wine. This was clearly a nod to his presence among them. The Saxons, Agravain knew, greatly preferred their own subtle, lethal honey meads.

Courtesy, and plentiful food, gave Agravain good cover for keeping his silence. There could be no 'business' discussed until after the meal. It also gave him ample opportunity to observe Sifred and his men. His command of their language was good, and he could follow most of what was said. They spoke of common matters, of the weather and trade. They exchanged what were plainly old jokes and favourite stories about long ago fights, wonders seen on voyages, and life in their homelands.

They seemed content and collegial enough, but there was an undercurrent running between them all. Agravain had expected there to be matters that would not be broached casually in front of him. He had no illusions as to his status. He was a stranger, and an enemy. He had been suffered here because of Sifred's agreements with King Arthur, and because he had made sure that all the men he sent to sift through the Roman ruins, or to find ships from Greece and Byzantium, brought with them rich gifts for Sifred, and whoever else might demand them.

What he sensed, though, was more than just the restraint that came when entertaining a not-entirely-welcome guest. This was sharper and more brittle, the feeling that the whole gathering walked across thin ice while feeling the sun hot on the backs of their necks.

It was the women who waited on them that gave the game away. Some of them had not yet been cowed by Sifred's glares or by the hard-handed woman who could have been Hilde's mother. These all shot glowers at the scarred, determinedly bluff men. Their grim expressions spoke of old wounds, and promised new ones if they were ever free to work their will. They were not happy, or even stoic. They were furious, and they were hiding it badly.

Whenever he could do so without being too closely attended, Agravain looked across to the women's humbler table. Laurel sat flanked by Hilde and Tatae, a shaft of silver among the gold. Modest, decorous, silent, she ate and drank little, but smiled much. If she spoke a single word, he could not hear what it was.

He itched to be near her. He did not like what he sensed in this place. He did not like having her out of arm's reach, or being without his sword. Men such as Sifred had been known to turn feasts into brawls deliberately, the laws of guesting not being seen to necessarily apply to those they considered outlanders and strangers, no matter how many fine words they spoke.

You should have considered that before you walked in here, he said sourly to himself.

'Now then, *Jarl* Agravain.' Sifred topped up Agravain's gilded wine cup from the leather bottle of rich, Languedoc wine. 'There are some matters I'd discuss with you, if you're willing to turn your ear to them.'

'Of course, my host. As you please.' Agravain sipped the wine in judicious appreciation. It was unwatered, and traced a fiery line down his throat. Sifred had been filling his cup all night, urging him to drink. It was a transparent ploy, but Agravain did not let this deceive him. The man had not kept his grip on Londinium's Saxons by being a strong-armed fool who thought he could get what he wanted from a wary visitor simply by getting him drunk.

Sifred tossed the wine jack on the table and lifted his own cup, settling back in his chair. The other conversations drifting languidly about the table stilled slowly, and all attention turned to their headman.

'Now, you know,' Sifred gestured to Agravain with his

brimming cup, 'and I know, that Arthur intends to swallow us as soon as he can. He'll lull us with sweet words and good gifts until we may as well be blind drunk. He'll then take us with treaty if he's able, with swords if he must. I cannot blame him for it,' Sifred added, holding up his hand to forestall any remark Agravain might have been about to make. 'What man leaves an enemy unchained and unchallenged like a starving dog on his doorstep?' He spread his hands. His men took the signal and chuckled darkly.

'But I've no desire to be swallowed,' Sifred went on, taking a deep draught of his wine as if to illustrate his point. 'So, I'm minded to make a bargain with you.'

Agravain carefully and deliberately set his own cup down. 'Why should I wish to enter into any bargain with you?' he asked, keeping his tone mild, merely inquisitive. The room had gone silent. There was some muttering and snapping over at the women's table, but the laughter and gossip there had died away too. Everyone was listening, and listening close.

Sifred leaned forward, planting his oaken forearms on the table. 'Because, *Jarl* Agravain, word has flown ahead of you. You and your uncle the High King have quarrelled. I was not inclined to believe what I'd heard of the severity of this quarrel, but you've come to us with little more than what you've got on your back. Knowing the sort of man Arthur is, I'd say it would have had to be a bad quarrel indeed for him to turn you loose all but naked to make your own way home.

'You're an intelligent man, Agravain. You know the fact that you've lost Arthur's blessing will make it difficult for you to command men and stores from the Britons who hold the coast you must pass by. Especially when their promises were given reluctantly to begin with.' He grinned up at Agravain.

So, you keep your ear open to the doings of your neighbours. Very good, Sifred.

'I, however, seeing your circumstances, feel no such reluctance. It is in my power to place three hundred men at your command, all armed, all spoiling for a fight. In return, I ask that if Arthur attempts to make me another of his vassals, you'll work to stop it.'

Sifred sat back, folding his arms across his broad belly, his whole manner that of a confident trader. *There! You cannot say fairer than that!*

'And how would you be sure I'd keep my end of this . . . bargain?' inquired Agravain.

Sifred grinned broadly and waggled his finger. 'Firstly, because I see you're a city man, a Romanish man, who honours the agreement he puts his name to. Secondly, because you would of course show your gratitude for my three hundred men by giving them each three or four hides worth of land around that great fortress rock of yours.'

'Of course,' Agravain replied blandly. 'It would be only fair.'

'So, what say you?' Sifred didn't move, but his eyes narrowed.

Agravain lifted his cup, he inhaled the warming scent of the wine, and sipped, setting the cup down again.

'I say that a man could do far worse than have such a promise at his back during his travels.'

A spasm of annoyance crossed Sifred's red face. 'Come, come, Agravain,' he beckoned impatiently. 'This is not a time to mince words. I've made you an open proposal, one man to another. I must have a more certain reply than that.'

Again, Agravain felt that brittle undertone. It was not desperation, but rather a kind of hope. Sifred needed things to go his way. He needed this offer to be accepted. Something was riding on this, and it was much more than aid in a war that might never come.

You said your men are spoiling for a fight. How badly? Badly enough to decide you should not be their leader anymore?

But before he could speak, a crash sounded from the women's table. Agravain jerked his head around. Laurel lolled forward in her chair, a cup of wine at her feet spilling out in a pool of blood red across the muddy flagstones.

He was on his feet before any of the other men moved, and across the room before Sifred could open his mouth and remind him this was a matter for women's hands.

Agravain took Laurel's hand, and she gripped his hard. She felt neither cold nor fevered and the glance she shot him through her separated fingers was firm and clear.

'Are you ill, my wife?' he asked softly.

'Only a little, only a little, my husband,' she answered, but she did so in court Latin, and she slumped towards him as she said it.

He laid one hand on her brow, and looked into her bright eyes.

'Our host is not one to speak softly,' he murmured also in Latin. 'What do you think of this?'

Laurel removed his hand, patting it, a gesture of conciliation and reassurance. 'I think Lord Sifred is most likely an honest man after his kind, but I think he should watch his back, and I think we should leave here now.'

Agravain frowned. 'How so?'

'The women I sat with are most . . . opinionated. Their insults ranged from me and my appearance, to you and your heritage.' She made a fair show of a brave attempt to sit up and smile. 'They also had much to say about their overlord. They sighed after the dream of being led by a real man, not some . . . fat horse-trader, I believe was how one of them put it.'

'So.' Agravain lifted her hand to his mouth and pressed the back to his lips. 'I think I must go make my excuses to our host. Thank you for your . . . caution, my lady.'

A slight smile flickered across her face. 'You are most

welcome, my lord. It was . . . instructive. I believe I have improved my knowledge of their tongue significantly.'

The corner of his mouth twitched as he turned back to Sifred and the waiting men. The air about them had chilled considerably in his absence. Some of them, at least, suspected something of the little mummery he and Laurel had just staged. Sifred however, looked nothing so much as mildly amused.

'Is your woman – pardon, your wife – well?' he asked, raising his brows.

With some difficulty, Agravain shifted his expression to one of embarrassment. 'You must forgive me, my host. She is taken ill, and we must depart.'

'Ill? She should not be moved then. Let you stay here and my women will care for her.'

'I thank you for it, but this illness is not unexpected, nor is it anything that time will not deliver her from.' He made himself smile, hoping Sifred would catch the play on words.

He did. 'Ah!' Sifred slapped the table jovially, making all the cups rattle. 'Well, my best wishes to you then. But you cannot go from me without some answer to my offer.'

Their gazes met, and Agravain once more felt the keen awareness of every man around the table waiting to measure his words against their own desires, and whatever promises their lord had made to them.

'My host, your offer is generous, and your warning about what I will find waiting for me further northward is well taken. But you will understand that I must see this for myself.'

Sifred's face fell fast, but he made a great effort to recover himself. 'It will go hard on you when you do.'

'As you say,' agreed Agravain. 'I will tell you this much. I go to a war I cannot lose. I will not give my home to the Dal Riata or the men of the west, whatever the cost. Whatever bridge I must burn, whatever aid I must beg or buy, I will not give over to them.'

'Well, *Jarl* Agravain, if that's what you'll give, then that's what I must take.' Sifred heaved himself to his feet. 'This is no place for a city man such as yourself to be roaming alone at night. I myself will return you to your boats.'

It was a courtesy Agravain could have well done without, but he could not turn it down without giving offence. Less so because it was true. Londinium was a place where wealth changed hands, and not always as the bargainer might wish. Alone he had no fear, but he had Laurel to protect and could not unnecessarily court danger.

Besides, the current of anger that ran through the house was now so palpable he could feel it beating against his skin. It was not directed at him though. This was all for Sifred. It might be that the Saxon lord of Londinium had some word to speak or promise to make in private, away from those whose loyalty was so plainly weakening that a stranger could see the cracks.

Given this, it was perhaps not strange that he did not ask any of his lords to accompany him. Hilde shoved a lit torch into the hands of a stripling boy, who looked nothing so much as sulky at being sent on such an errand. Agravain reclaimed his sword from the old man beside the door who stood in place of a porter or seneschal. The men of his motley guard left the fire they clustered round with badly concealed reluctance and ranged themselves behind him. As they did, Laurel laced her cloak more tightly, as if armouring herself against the darkness. He did not miss the fact that she laid her hand on the small knife that hung beside her ring of keys.

Laurel's eyes narrowed, and Agravain followed her gaze. Sifred and Hilde faced each other, glowering like roosters about to fight over a portion of the yard. Though not a word passed between them, Hilde gave a mighty snort and turned on her heel, stomping back to the fire and the grim party of women she presided over.

Sifred seemed to find the incident amusing and was still chuckling as he passed Agravain and Laurel. He gestured broadly to indicate they should follow him down his crumbling steps.

Londinium at night was like no place Agravain had ever been. It was not wholly a city, though the moonlight picked out the silhouettes of great houses and some new storehouses, but neither was it a village with the closeness that came of common family and common labour. It sprawled on the river banks, but it still felt huddled under the scudding clouds, ducking itself under the wind that filled with the scents of water and waste. What dwellings there were rose up in clusters, leaning towards each other for companionship because there was no one else to turn to. Fires lit the night at random, futilely driving back the river's chill air and the great masses of midges and flies that feasted among the reeds, giving it the look of a soldier's encampment, but it was not that either.

This place knows it picks over the bones of giants, and the giants still might return.

Voices rang out at random in the darkness. To the right, a wobbly, drunken song broke out, the words so slurred Agravain could making nothing of them. There was no bond of discipline or purpose here. Each man's work was his alone. All alliance temporary, and correspondingly fragile.

Agravain was glad of the weight of Laurel's hand on his arm. He did not want her out of reach in these smoky shadows. He was even more glad of the men at his back, and knew without seeing that more than one had his hand on knife or hammer.

Sifred, however, showed no fear. His men might have their doubts about his leadership, but it was clear he still saw this misshapen place as his, and his alone. He wore the smoky darkness as lightly as a good cloak and stumped along in the wavering light cast by the boy's torch, whistling tunelessly through his teeth. No random voice distracted him. None of the noises, shuffles, clashes or footsteps, near or far, gave him pause.

Are you truly that secure in your person? Agravain wondered. His own sword hung heavily at his hip, and he was as glad of its closeness as he was of Laurel's. The back of his neck itched. He did not like Sifred's silence. He did not like how they walked unescorted in this place, even if they did bring with them Londinium's only lawgiver. The smoke, the stench and the unseen, unknown motion in the dark worked persistently on him.

Laurel felt it too. She walked stiffly, her pale green eyes flicking this way and that. She was afraid. Tension stretched out of her, as if she wanted to grab the wind because there was nothing else to hold on to.

Then, unexpectedly, Sifred stopped, holding up his hand in a way that brought Agravain instantly to a halt.

'Draw your sword, *Jarl*,' Sifred said, loosening the axe he carried in his belt.

Agravain drew, signalling to his men to spread themselves out, and cursing the fact that though there was a broad-armed smith and a wiry tanner, none of the four was a trained soldier. Sifred slipped his axe from his belt, and Agravain shifted to a fighting stance, putting his back to Laurel and his face to the dark.

Sifred whirled, swinging his axe down towards Agravain's skull.

Agravain had just time enough to throw up his sword to ward off the blow, but no time to block the knee that drove up into his guts, doubling him over. The next blow would be on the back of his skull, and he made himself fall into the mud ahead of it, rolling over, feeling the hard length of his sword under his back. Half-a-dozen men rushed out of the darkness, grappling with his guard, swatting them swiftly down.

Breathing shallowly against his pain, Agravain rolled again, grabbing at his sword hilt, and miraculously finding it. He stabbed upward, and felt the soft jarring of flesh as his opponent swerved too late. It gave him just enough time to get to his feet, to swing himself around, sword up and ready. Two ox-built Saxon men faced him, stark and plain in the torch light, one with a short bronze sword, the other with a fat axe, both grinning at the prospect of a good fight. None of his guard was left standing, although they'd taken four of their attackers with them.

He was alone.

Agravain shifted his weight to his toes and took better hold on his sword, all but daring them to come to him, not daring to look away, but needing to see where Sifred was, where Laurel was . . .

'Hold there, Sir Agravain.'

One glance told him all that had happened. Sifred held Laurel's arm twisted up behind her back. Her knife was in Sifred's fist. A long red score marred his face and the blood dripped down to darken his beard. Laurel met Agravain's gaze, her own face filled with a mixture of pain and apology.

Rage. Perfect as glass, deep as a well, it filled him like the soul's own killing frost. It rooted him straight to the heart of the earth. It filled him with such impossible strength he knew that if Sifred had been in arm's reach, he could have dug his hands into the Saxon's flesh and torn his guts out. As it was, his sword all but vibrated in his hand, razor sharp, hungry for blood. Agravain could see with perfect clarity how Sifred's pulse beat in his delicate veins, how his fragile joints held legs and arms together.

'Drop your sword, Agravain,' said Sifred. His voice was tinged with sorrow and he shook his head. 'You should have taken my offer, man. Then I could have turned down the other.'

Agravain licked his lips and tasted blood. Stones littered on the ground at his feet. Shafts stuck out of the broken fence to his left like swords. They were all weapons. His arms, his legs, they were weapons. Even if he robbed Agravain of his sword, Sifred stood in the midst of a hundred possible deaths.

But he held Laurel out of reach. It would take Agravain three heartbeats, four, to get to her. It would take Sifred a single heartbeat to stab her through with her own knife.

Laurel shone pure and perfect in the middle of the mud, with Sifred holding her as close as a lover. It was unthinkable that this creature should hold her that way. He would die. Now. Agravain would kill him.

'Your sword, Agravain. Now.'

Although he could not take his eyes from her, Laurel was not looking at him. Her gaze was distant, unfocused, as if listening to a sound only she could hear. For a heartbeat, Agravain thought it was fear that drove her so far away, but that was not it. She strained with her whole being, reaching out, reaching beyond, straining with her very soul towards the unseen.

Agravain's rage did not ebb, but it loosened, flexed, becoming less a fist of ice than a hand readying itself to strike. He could think again. He could buy time.

It took him a moment to make his hand obey, but Agravain unbent his fingers, and let his sword fall to the ground with a dull thud. He brought his feet together and spread out his hands on either side.

Look, I have no weapon.

'Listen to me, Sifred,' Agravain said softly, clearly. 'No

matter what quarrel exists between myself and Arthur, I am still of the High King's blood. When he hears a tale of murder in the dark, he will crash down on you like a mountain. What you have built here will be burnt to the ground and all your people driven into the sea. You will have no warrior's death. He does not allow such for murderers. You will be hoisted from a tree limb and your body left for the ravens to make sport of.'

Sifred did not move. His bemused and sorrowful expression did not change, but neither did he interrupt.

Laurel lifted her head. The distraction was gone from her. She was back with him, whole, and a new light sparked in her eyes.

Agravain did not understand it, but something sparked in him as well, working in his mind. It raised a new readiness in him, and brought words to mask this.

'You think it has already gone too far, that you will lose your honour before your own. Fight me, and you will be dead sooner or later. Kill me, and your sons and your hope of a holding in this island will be dead with you. There will be no more plots, no more plans, no more chance ever of turning any Briton to your side.

'Let me and mine go, and you will only have to fight your own kind, and they are men you have already beaten.'

Something new. Some new sound, new scent. A distant thumping that should have been familiar to him, was familiar, a sound he knew like he knew his own heartbeat.

Hooves. Horses' hooves.

'You may also want to think on this.' *Look at me. Attend my words. Don't hear that other sound. Don't hear it.* 'I am in no mood to let you die without letting the men here see what a terrible mistake it is to lay hands on that which is mine. It may be I will leave some portion of you alive to make clear this point in their minds.

'What is your decision, *Jarl* of Londinium?'

Sifred shook his head. 'You're a brave man, Agravain of Gododdin, to threaten a slow death to the one who holds your life in his hands. Still, it is better to die with words of courage in your mouth.'

He raised Laurel's knife in salute and in signal. That briefest of pauses was long enough for the new sound, the frantic pounding of hoofbeats, to penetrate Sifred's hearing. The Saxon whirled around in time to see the red roan bearing down on him. Laurel threw herself forward, tearing free of his loosened grip the instant before the horse reared up and came down, and Sifred fell hard.

Devi.

Agravain's squire wheeled the horse clumsily around, and charged again, screaming like a madman, galloping straight for Sifred, groping and struggling in the mud. Agravain's surprise lasted only an instant. He launched himself forward, diving for his sword and coming up again, spinning as fast as the mud would let him. Laurel was standing on her own, the torch held in her fist. The boy had vanished. *Smart boy.*

Sifred, bowled down by Devi's charge, lay still and bloody in the mud. Agravain dismissed him. The two other barbarians had jumped back, and were spreading out at arm's length in front of Laurel, deciding how to dodge round her makeshift weapon.

Agravain gave them no warning. They deserved none. He charged silently, knowing exactly what he would do before he struck. The right-hand brute he sliced through the side, letting the blood and guts spill out of him. With the backhand, Agravain blocked the blow from the other, grabbing his long beard and jerking him forward, ruining his balance and his ability to stop Agravain's sword arm as he swung it down and stabbed deep between the ribs. The man fell in a fountain of black blood.

Agravain stepped back, breathing hard, his mind calm and settled as he watched long enough to be sure that none of the three was going to rise again.

When he was sure, he turned to see Laurel beside Devi, holding onto his horse's bridle. She appeared quite calm, holding the torch high to give Agravain light. They were not alone. Two other men, two of the old sailors Devi had recruited, waited with them, also on horseback, their faces grim and, for all their age, their eyes bright and ready.

Voices rose around them. Of course, this had not passed without notice. They could not stand here a moment longer.

'Quickly.' Agravain wiped his sword roughly on the hem of his cloak and sheathed it. He took the torch from Laurel and gave it to one of the stout old men, what was his name? He'd have it from Devi later. What mattered now was helping hand Laurel up to his mate, and then swinging up in front of Devi. Agravain touched up the horse, which did not like the idea of another quick run through the dark, especially now that it had two men to carry. He did not give the beast the opportunity to protest, but dug in with knees and heels until it gave a squeal of protest and cantered forward.

The quay was but moments away at this pace, and a good thing too. Shouts filled the darkness now, and more torches and fires were blazing up high. Agravain dropped onto the stone almost before the horse halted.

'Wake up! Wake up!' he shouted, adding his own voice to the growing din. 'Get ready to sail! Now!'

To his great relief, he soon saw his words were unnecessary. Lamps and lanterns were hoisted up so Devi could lead the horse forward to join the others hobbled and roped on deck. All the sailors were already busy with the anchor ropes and oars. The old man handed Laurel down to him, and she had wit enough to clamber swiftly over the side of the nearest ship. He followed at once, turning back to the shore.

'Dead! *Jarl* Sifred's murdered!' came the shouts.

An answering cry went up, much closer and far more welcome. 'Pull, you whoresons! Pull for your worthless lives! Pull!'

'Camelot's treachery! Stop them! Stop them!'

But they were already too late. The pull of the oars sent the ship lurching away from the shore, where the current, sluggish as it was, could catch them. The master angled his oar, heading them straight downstream. Torches lit the bank, showing a growing crowd of Saxons, staring after them. A few feeble shouts went up to the nearest boats, but the oarsmen were strong, and they wanted to live.

Before any of the Saxon boatmen could make any sense of the shouting and the sudden light, Agravain's fleet was gone.

Agravain let out a long, shuddering breath as the darkness wrapped around them. Thanking God for the full moon, he leaned over the rail and strained his eyes to count the ships following them. Five dark shapes sailed in the darkness. Five. They'd all made it. Probably they were not fully loaded, but they would have most of what they needed. And they were alive and underway.

For now, it was enough. Or almost. There were questions remaining.

Agravain picked his way amidships to where Devi sat among a pile of ropes, clutching his withered arm to himself. He struggled to stand, but Agravain bid him stay as he was.

'How did you know to come and find me?' he asked, squatting down beside his squire.

Devi shook his head. 'It can only have been God's grace, my lord. I was waiting with the boats, and I . . . I can barely describe it.' His face creased, searching for words. 'A restlessness seized me. I was sure, down to the pit of my soul, that something was wrong. The feeling would not leave me, no matter what I tried. In the end, I took your horse, and followed my nose. I . . . am glad that I did.' His smile was bashful, as if Agravain had caught him making some shameful admission.

'As am I, Devi,' replied Agravain, utterly serious. 'When we reach Din Eityn, you will be knighted for all the work you have done. That is my promise.'

Stunned rapture slackened the squire's face. 'Thank you, my lord,' he managed to stammer.

Agravain nodded once more and left him there. The oarsmen had all found their stroke, and the oars struck the water in perfect time, setting the ship's timbers to a rhythmic creaking as they glided into the night. He moved carefully, lest a misstep send him toppling into one of the men, walking towards the prow, and Laurel.

She sat on the bench nearest the prow, straight as a willow wand, staring into the night ahead. She must have caught his movement in the corner of her eye though, for she turned her face towards him, watching silently as he sat beside her.

In truth, he was not sure how to break that silence. He settled for a direct question. 'Did you bring them?'

She inclined her head once, ducking her eyes and hiding her face as if in shame. He breathed out again. He had suspected, but there had been no time to think on it. He should feel something, think something. He had known she had the blood, and the power, of the invisible countries in her, but now he had seen it at work. And he could feel nothing, nothing at all. It was as if it was beyond him, and he had no desire to reach for it at all.

So, he did not ask after it.

'Sifred said he had another offer,' he remarked, casually, as if it were nothing more than the day's smallest business. 'I would I knew who it came from.'

'I know.' Laurel's voice was hard. 'I saw it on his hand.

He wore a ring with a black stone, and that was carved with a raven. I told myself I was being a fool. How could that be her device, worn so openly? She does not permit such carelessness of her secret allies.' Laurel rubbed her hands together. 'If I had spoken. If I had told . . .'

'It would have done very little. They would still have tracked us. They had the whole long way to the river to stalk us and pick their ambush.'

She looked up at him, mute. Then, slowly, her face crumpled and twisted as if in great struggle with herself. Two tears slipped from her eyes, and in the next instant she buried her face in her hands, her sobs shaking her shoulders.

Agravain found himself staring, helplessly stunned as he had never been in battle. Laurel, his wife, was sobbing beside him as if her heart would break, and he did not know what to do. His mind had gone utterly blank.

After what seemed like an eternity, he thought to put his arms out, to draw her close against his breast. She pressed her face into his shoulder now, still weeping. He stroked her shoulders, wishing frantically he knew what to do or say that would end this. He had nothing to give her, nothing at all to offer this need.

Despite that, her sobs gradually eased, and she was able to sit up.

'Thank you,' she whispered, mopping at her flushed cheeks with her hands. 'Forgive me, my lord. I don't know what came over me.' She was trying to hide behind her hands. She did not want him to see her face.

He caught her hands and gently lowered them. 'It does not matter, Laurel. You did right. You acted bravely. It is over, and we are still here.' He brushed her wet cheek with his fingertips, and found himself wondering again at its softness. She was smiling and the sight of it went straight to his heart. 'I have seen grown men weep over far less.'

She leaned towards him and he gathered her once more into his embrace. He held her close, letting the motion of the ship rock them both, lulling the last fear of their escape from them.

You are safe now, he promised silently. *God and Mary be my witness, I swear you will always be safe beside me.*

ELEVEN

It was twilight when Morgaine emerged from her pavilion. She wore a simple gown of rich blue girdled with a chain of silver. A silver band circled her brow, holding back the water-fall of black hair that was otherwise as loose and uncovered as any maiden's.

She came without any announcement, without anyone to cry out her name and open the way before her. She walked silently through the camp on her slippered feet, seemingly unaware of the damp, or the cold wind blowing down from the northern mountains. She trod gently on the stony ground, looking neither left nor right. Her face was tranquil, as one in a dream.

All the people who saw her stopped their tasks and their talk. They turned their heads to see where she went. Their neighbours also stopped what they were doing to better see what distracted those nearest her. In this way, silence spread out from around Morgaine's path.

Almost without thought, her people laid down their tools and moved to follow her. They did not question their actions. They only wanted to follow where she went, and see what she would show.

Slowly, the silence and strange motion spread from the westerners' side of the camp. A few Dal Riata lifted their heads to see what extraordinary thing made their allies so quiet. As they looked, they saw the lady of whom they had heard so many rumours, but only distantly. To them, she was a vague figure of blue and silver gliding through the world of green and grey.

Curious, the Dal Riata stood, first one, and then another. They craned their necks, and began walking forward, inquisitiveness turning to fascination as they drew into the silence trailing in Morgaine's wake.

The Picts noted the spreading silence as it lapped up against their own encampment. They glanced uneasily at each other, and at their headman, Brude Cal, who was methodically smoothing the head of his stone hammer with a curved whetstone. Brude Cal looked up sharply, as if catching some familiar but unwelcome scent. Ponderously, he got to his feet. He motioned to his brother to stay where he was. Looping the hammer's thong around his belt, he ambled down the hill.

A bonfire burned at the crux between the various camps. Mordred had ordered it to be established as a place where the leaders of the uneasy alliance could all meet without any having to stand under the shadow of another captain's banner. This was the place to which Morgaine directed her soft steps. The fire had burned low over the long day, and a pile of brush and tinder waited beside it to feed new life into the coals as the slow summer darkness deepened.

Mordred waited there in his gleaming black armour, a figure cut from the fabric of the night. Where before he would have knelt to her, she now curtsied to him. She wanted no misunderstanding from those who witnessed this. Her son would lead. He must lead. He was the keystone of promise and prophecy.

Mordred inclined his head, accepting her gesture. Morgaine

straightened, turning at once to the fire. The heat from the coals made a mask for her face while the cold wind wrapped around her shoulders. The contrast made her skin shiver, but she held herself still. She gazed unblinking at the coals, letting their heat sink into her, letting the orange glow dazzle her. She breathed in the heat and the scent, drawing it into herself, making it part of her.

Willing it to grow.

One coal broke open with a snap and a shower of sparks. A flame leapt up, then another, and another. Petals of gold and white unfurled, stretching up, swaying in the wind. They danced over the bed of coals, multiplying and melding into a single mass of flame without a hand or a breath being raised to aid them. They fed on their own coals, on the very air. They rose, knee high, waist high. Head high, cracking and roaring and vibrantly alive. Heat and light tumbled over the gathered crowd.

Morgaine lifted her head, stretching beyond the fire. She let her expanded and expanding self seek beyond the scrawny trees scattered throughout the encampment, down to the thicker forest, until she touched there the slow, hungry thoughts she needed.

Morgaine bid these to follow.

Back in the blood and bone of herself, Morgaine lifted her right hand. As she did, the brown owl descended. Around her, she heard the sharp intake of a breath. Owls foretold death. The cry of a hunting owl meant sacrifice and prayer to try to ward off the disaster that was imminent.

The great bird settled heavily on her wrist. Its claws dug nervously into her flesh, sending the heat of pain to join the heat of the fire burning in her blood. The owl blinked its round, yellow eyes at her, confused to find itself here. Morgaine took her free hand and wrapped her fingers gently around the hooked beak.

'Hush,' she said, clearly, so that all the assemblage could hear her. 'Now you carry no message but mine.'

Sighs and whispers filled with furtive wonder flitted through the crowd. *No message but mine. She's forestalled death's harbinger.*

She let go of the beak and raised her wrist. Silently, the owl flew away.

Do you see how she commands the gods' messengers?

Then, Morgaine raised her left hand. She hardly had to stretch at all. The raven, her raven, was always within reach. Her ambassador, her familiar and her second self when she required its shape. It waited hidden in the oak tree growing at the edge of the encampment. It was not silent like the owl, that was not its nature. It dropped out of the encroaching dark with a rattle of wings, alighting comfortably on the familiar perch of her wrist. It cocked its head towards her and made no protest as she curled her right hand lightly over its eyes, though she could feel its amusement at her sudden need for such display, and gave a croaking laugh.

'Hush!' Morgaine commanded. 'Now you spy for no one but me.'

The raven, naturally mischievous, bobbed its head, and took wing immediately. Every eye watched it fly westward, toward Din Eityn, toward the coast where Agravain would be landing.

'Do not fear.' She spoke softly, but she had no doubt that everyone heard her. She stretched herself out to them all now, letting her will carry the words as far as they needed to go. 'Do not fear. The enemy comes in darkness. He thinks he is unobserved, but we see him. He thinks his swords are sharp and his allies strong.

'But we are greater than he, our numbers far more than his. He comes to establish an outpost for the invader, to betray his own ancestors to the southerners. This will not be permitted. Together, we will defeat this traitor and we will cast him into the sea that bears him onto our waiting knives.'

There was no cheering, nothing but the rustle and sigh of a people breathing out their wonder and breathing in her words. She could feel their spirits lifting, their fears and their struggles calming. They remembered, all of them, that this was a holy cause. What they did was right and their vengeance was just and warranted.

More than this, they saw that she would not abandon them to any fate. She stood with them, and she brought the blessing and the power of all that was unseen to their side.

Morgaine had no more need to dismiss the assemblage than she did to call it. All her folk drifted away of their own accord. They went almost as quietly as they had come, walking in close knots of threes and fours. Some held hands. Some wrapped an arm around the shoulder of a brother or comrade. Some walked alone, their heads sunken beneath the weight of their thoughts.

Even the Dal Riata wandered away without questioning, their whispers brushing her with excitement and warmth. Morgaine let them all go, drawing her spirit back into the confines of herself, releasing wind and fire to make their own way in the world again. Mordred alone stayed beside her, watching his followers disperse and holding back his own smile.

But one among them did not leave. Morgaine felt him unmoving like a stone in the middle of a stream. She lifted her gaze to the hillside, watching until her eyes became dark adapted. There, she saw the square, brown figure standing above her with his thick arms folded across his chest.

So. 'Do you have something to say to me, Brude Cal?'

The Pictish man chuckled low in his throat and made his easy, confident way down the hill. He was a full head shorter than she, and had to look up to meet her gaze. He might have been moulded from the earth itself, he was so small and so brown. White lime made twisted peaks out of his thatch of hair and the flicker of the fire made the blue tattoos which obscured his face writhe eerily. But there was no mistaking his clear cunning as he met her gaze without fear, and without reverence.

'A good show, Morgaine,' Brude Cal said softly, speaking in his own tongue which he knew she well understood. 'I see why you are a great priestess. Few would dare the gods' wrath so casually, and with so little reason.'

Disquiet rippled through Morgaine, and a little anger. 'My reasons are my own, Brude Cal.'

'I am sure.' His smile was indulgent, and it was brief. He took a step closer. Morgaine smelled earth, sweat and stone. 'Hear this, Sleepless One.' He raised his hand. 'I and mine have come to enrich our clan, and to rid ourselves of an enemy who would steal our herds and their grazing land. That is reason enough for us to fight. Let it be reason enough for you.'

So. Morgaine let her brows rise. 'Your words are too deep for me to follow, Brude Cal.'

'Then I will be more plain.' He laid his hand on his stone hammer. She felt Mordred start forward, and then think the better of it. 'Morgaine, do not try to awe my people. Do not try to take them into yourself. I will not permit it.'

She nodded, acknowledging the truth of the accusation. She could not, would not hide from it. 'You see far, Brude Cal. But is it far enough?' She opened her eyes wide. 'Do you understand what we truly do here, you and I?'

His curiosity was roused by her words. She could feel it. He wanted to understand this little riddle she posed.

If you wish to see, come closer, Brude Cal. Look deep. She smiled just a little, showing him the challenge, and in less than a handful of heartbeats, he accepted, and he looked into her eyes.

For a long moment, Brude Cal met her gaze fearlessly. Indeed, he was slightly amused. Caution held him aloof, but pride and curiosity both prodded him. He reached with his spirit, testing his limits and striving to find hers, like the warrior he was. She fell back before him, retreating slowly, one tremulous step at a time. He followed, going ever deeper, farther from himself, into a familiar warmth that held no fear for him. He was strong. He was well-guarded with the charms and wardings impregnated into his very skin. He understood the ways of god and man. He had held himself steady while all others had been fascinated by a little trickery, by the most paltry of magics fattened and gilded for show.

She depended on his strength. He knew that. She needed him. He could leave in a moment, and ruin her hopes, her plans. She bowed before that reality, yielding to it now in spirit. He felt her weakness and it drew him on, like the touch of a hand, the press of lips. The depth of her need of him and all he could bring her surrounded him. It was a warm cloak, a woman's willing embrace. It lulled and excited, soothed and enflamed.

It wound around him tighter than any iron chain, but Brude Cal did not feel that. Against iron he would have struggled. Surrounded and soothed, filled with the certainty she poured into him, he never felt the shackles close.

Satisfied, Morgaine took his rough, fire-warmed hand in hers. 'Do not desert me, Brude Cal,' she whispered. 'I need you.'

She kissed him then, softly, chastely, the kiss of peace and friendship.

When she drew back, Brude Cal bowed his head. 'I will not fail you, Sleepless One.' He smiled at her. With that smile he acknowledged the depth of her dependence on him, but told her this knowledge would go unspoken, for the sake of her dignity and for the sake of the promise he believed she had given.

'Thank you.' Morgaine let Brude Cal's hand go, and watched, as it strayed first to his cheek, then to the hammer at his belt, then to the blue ribbons on his arm. Perhaps he sensed vaguely that their charm had unravelled, but that thought did not take hold. He turned, dazed, but not hesitating. He had been dismissed, and he would go now. Back to his people, where he would speak in awe of the Sleepless One.

Morgaine smiled at his back. *Now you truly understand, Brude Cal.*

Around them, the noises of the camp revived themselves. Fires sprang up, lifting their smoke and light to the lowering clouds. Voices also lifted up too, a noise as easy and reassuring as the rustle of leaves and the creak of branches in the woods. Morgaine sighed, suddenly tired. She turned her gaze towards the clouds and found herself wistfully wishing for a sight of the crescent moon they obscured.

'Well done, Mother.'

Mordred. Morgaine sighed again. There was one other thing to be done tonight. 'Thank you, my son.' She faced him. He was smiling, the confidence she so loved to see filled him. 'They are yours now. I trust you to make good use of them.'

That smile broadened as he savoured the possibilities, and betrayed his eagerness for the beginning of the open battle. 'Oh, I will, you may be sure.' He gave her a sweeping, showy bow that at another time would have brought her own smile out.

Not tonight. 'Mordred?'

'Yes?' He looked up without straightening. It was a vaguely ludicrous position, and she found it easy to frown.

'I know what occurred in Londinium,' she murmured. 'Your plan failed. Sifred, who might have otherwise become an ally, is dead in the mud.' Slowly Mordred straightened. The golden firelight did nothing to restore colour to his white cheeks.

'Do not question me again, Mordred. We stand on a knife's edge. If we stray in either direction we can still fall. Do you understand me?'

Mordred swallowed hard, the disguise of manhood cracking open to show the boy who still waited beneath. To his credit, he did not try to argue or make any excuse, he just bowed low to her, a spare and serious obeisance devoid of all his previous foolishness.

Morgaine touched her son's brow in blessing and forgiveness. *It is a hard thing, Mordred, to know when to lead and when to follow. But you will learn.*

He straightened again, and she smiled up into his eyes.

'Now, you have your chance to solidify your command. I trust you will use it well.'

'And you?'

Her smile sharpened. 'Agravain has most helpfully separated himself from his best source of support. Now it is time that I do the same to Laurel Carnbrea.'

Mordred nodded, and left her there, walking into the dusk to take the opportunity she had given him. She watched his straight back and confident gait for a moment with sober pride. Then, she turned to face the east, the direction of Din Eityn, and the direction her raven had flown.

'Find her for me. Let us take the measure of the new Lady of Din Eityn.'

Laurel's first impression of Gododdin was of a grey place. The rich green of the grasses and trees seemed to have a darker tone than she was used to, as if the Creator mixed some heavy silver into his paints before he applied his brushes here. In the misty distance she could see the great fortress atop its wedge of black rock. A hooded crow called once, welcoming her, warning her.

They arrived as the long, slow summer twilight began to stretch its shadows towards the stony shore. The ship's masters shouted and cursed and strained their eyes, but there was no way between the rocks. So, their heavily laden fleet was forced to anchor a good dozen yards out.

Now, those men who could do the work formed long lines in the foaming surf, passing chests, bundles, barrels and jars from hand to hand to stack on the shore out of reach of the waves. The men-at-arms worked to lead the skittish horses through the waves up to dry ground.

Laurel stood on the sloping shore, wringing the water from her trailing sleeves. Agravain had insisted on carrying her, an exercise Laurel found faintly ludicrous, but she did not argue because of place and rank. Beside her, Agravain, oblivious of his soaking boots and trousers, looked inland, scanning their jagged, grey-green surroundings. The ground folded deeply in on itself to make a channel for the great river that fed the firth. Smaller wrinkles cradled the numerous streams that fed the river. Cliffs thrust suddenly out of the smoky emerald ground, tearing it as roughly as a knife thrust through green fabric.

Even in these first moments, Laurel could see how this land had formed Agravain. It was stark, stern and strong, with nothing to offer the careless but its harshest edge.

As they had approached this harbour, Agravain had grown steadily more silent, steeling himself. When he spoke at all, it was one or two words. He had warned her of this.

'I do not know what waits for me when I go home,' he said. 'I do not know what I must become to face either my father or my enemy. It will take much from me, and it may be there is little left for you.'

He whispered this to her as they lay in the bed loaned to them by their hosts the second night after their flight from Londinium. As the honoured guests of the well-settled clan, their bed had been by the fire, and most of the rest of the folk snored and shuffled around them. He had done no more than hold her close in that overcrowded darkness, and whisper that warning. In return, she had answered, 'Do not fear for me, my lord. You must do what is necessary.'

The truth be told, she was grateful for a little distance, a little time. They were all on edge, constantly watching for pursuit from Londinium. Pursuit never came, but that did not lessen their troubles. By now, they had discovered Sifred had spoken the truth.

When they landed at Gariannum, Lord Isean had greeted Agravain with a heartiness that was coloured by fear. Ros was waiting there, his wrinkled, leathery face long healed from his altercation at Camelot. Laurel now knew he had been sent ahead, to do more than get away from the hostile attentions of the men of Camelot and alert Squire Devi to his lord's imminent arrival. His main task was to remind the lords of the coasts of promises made years before. Promises that they would supply Agravain with men and arms to shore up his fallen throne whenever he should come and ask.

But one look at Ros's crestfallen countenance, and Laurel knew the news was not good.

Lord Isean and his fellows, whose halls dominated the coastline on the route north, had made their promises with the implicit understanding that Arthur too would send a levy of men, and, more importantly, of knights from the Round Table cadre to lead them. When it became clear no aid was coming from Camelot, it was only the threat of war sweeping down on their borders, or in from their coasts, that kept the chiefs from finding a way to refuse absolutely.

For the first time, Laurel saw Agravain as a leader of men.

He shouldered the blame for the loss of Arthur's support without flinching, but sternly reminded the nervous chieftains that it changed nothing. The Picts and the Dal Riata were still in alliance with the men of the west. The southern wall with its neglected and dilapidated forts, half of which were now the halls of cattle thieves, would stop no one. If Arthur had to ride up to meet the enemy next summer, their lands would become the battlefield.

It was a speech he was forced to repeat time and again as they made their halting way up the coast.

In the end, his efforts raised one hundred men. This small company, along with Agravain's collection of ancients, scholars and misfits, arrayed itself on Gododdin's ragged shore in the deepening twilight, waiting for their orders.

'We are too late to make the climb,' muttered Agravain, jolting Laurel out of her thoughts. He glared at the deepening blue of the sky, as if angry at the sun for daring to sink at its normal pace. It was plain he itched with impatience. He did not want to be separated from his home a moment longer, but his responsibility was to make sure that all with him arrived in health and strength. Every hand would be needed for what was to come.

Agravain turned, reluctantly and faced Devi and Ros, who were now constantly at his side. 'We must camp here tonight.'

The two men made their bows and began shouting their orders to the men. At once, the shore was full of noise and motion. Men called out to each other as they shouldered their burdens and began trudging up to the most even ground.

Agravain turned to watch the progress, and as he did seemed to see her for the first time since their landing. The shadow of a frown crossed his face.

Wondering what to do with me.

'By your leave, my lord, I'll go see to the women.'

He bowed briefly to her, with the punctilious formality that had become an odd, subtle jest between them. 'And I thank you, my lady.'

It was not only men who came from the holdings and little kingdoms where they landed, but wives and mothers, sisters and aunts. They came to 'do' for their men, to get away from others they left behind, or out of simple, stubborn family loyalty that dictated no one should be sent away alone.

This was far from the first campaign for most of them. As seasoned as their soldiers, they set about the business of building fires, unpacking and examining gear to see what was dry, what was wet, what remained whole and what needed mending. They fetched their buckets and began trudging upstream to find the place where the broad river's water turned sweet.

From this flock of hard-scratch hens, Laurel had picked out two girls for her own. There was little Jen with her sparrow-brown hair and small hands, and tall Cait, who looked as though given time she might grow up into a second Meg; lean, leathery and sharp both in her bones and in her wit. Laurel chose them not because they were experienced in this life, but rather the reverse. Both came with distant relatives. Jen followed a cousin and Cait a man she called 'uncle', though it was doubtful the connection was that close. Laurel had yet to learn why either of them came, but it was plain from watching them that these rough circumstances, and these men, would soon run roughshod over them. There was little enough that Laurel had been able to do on this voyage since the disaster of Londinium. She could at least keep these two whole.

'Well, my women,' Laurel said as she stumped towards them. The little sparrow, Jen, particularly relished that designation. 'Let us see what we can bring out of this chaos.'

Even though there was much to be done, there was, it transpired, little for her to do. A patch of ground had been set aside for her, to be improved by the addition of a pavilion (a concession to her delicate status as noble lady), a fire, and the small mountain of her dowry chests. But Cait, Jen and two old but hale sailors handled most of the physical labour, leaving Laurel to stand and give what little advice they needed.

She should be grateful, she told herself. She was tired. The voyage had not been hard, but the anxiety was wearing. Rest had been hard to find, despite the wind and the water surrounding her. She could not lose the sense that she was followed, and closely watched. But whether she feared pursuit from Londinium, or by the *morverch*, she could not tell.

Laurel rubbed her arms, casting about for something to occupy her mind. But despite the activity surrounding her, she could not settle on anything. She tried to tell herself she was simply infected by Agravain's impatience. But that was not true. It was her own thoughts that would not let her rest. She turned her gaze up the broad valley, looking towards the looming fortress where it stood stark against the darkening sky. What was happening there tonight? Where was the king and where were his men? More importantly, where were their enemies, and the one enemy most particularly?

Does Morgaine walk in spirit tonight? What will she do when she sees us here?

Laurel heard a throaty croak behind her. Up the slope a rock thrust out of the thin soil, like a finger pointing the way to Din Eityn. On its tip perched a glossy, black bird. For a moment, Laurel took it to be a crow out scouting for its flock-mates.

Then she saw by its size and its straight, heavy beak, it was a raven.

Warning sounded low in the back of Laurel's mind. Her first thought was to frighten the ill-omened creature away.

But days of ill-defined fear set her anger smouldering at the sight of Morgaine's sigil made flesh. Probably it was only a bird. Probably it was only seeing if there was some dainty to be found among this gathering of busy men. More likely than not, her own need to be useful spurred her to a conclusion that was not warranted.

But perhaps not. The Sleepless One had many spies, in many shapes. It might be she wanted to look on her enemy's arrival, perhaps the better to take them unawares.

'Cait,' Laurel called softly, keeping her gaze on the raven.

The tall girl came running at once. 'Yes, my lady?'

'Have they brought the chest with the lock and hinges worked like oak leaves yet?'

Cait cast a glance backwards over the neat pile of dowry chests, which she had become almost as familiar with as Laurel. 'Yes, my lady.'

'Good. Here is the key.' Laurel unhooked the bronze key from the ring at her girdle and pressed it into her maid's palm. 'I wish to be alone for a few moments. If . . . if you should see me stagger or fall, or if anyone should call my name and I do not answer, you are to open that chest and take out the bundle of white silk. Do not unwrap it, but press it into my hands. Do you understand?'

'No, my lady,' Cait confessed, with a frown. 'But I will do as you say.'

'Thank you, Cait.' *A second Meg indeed.* 'I will rely on you.'

Cait made a brief curtsey, and went back to her work setting their few sticks of furniture in place, and handing Jen the bucket so she could join the parade of women heading upstream for fresh water.

Laurel looked about for Agravain. He was down by the waterline, in conference with Devi and a man who might have been one of the smiths. If he were going to come and find her, it would not be for a while yet.

In all this while, the raven had not moved. Laurel's suspicions settled in more strongly.

A low, round stone hunched nearby. Laurel sat slowly down on it. She breathed deeply of the fresh wind, so heavy with the sea's salt scent. The wind tugged at her hood and hems, as restless as she. She considered the bird carefully, reaching out to the wind. She pictured the raven in her mind, forming the thought of it lighting down near her. This idea she gave to the restless wind, and the wind in turn bore it aloft to the raven, ruffling its feathers, calming its fear, carrying the simple notion of flight and destination to merge with its own thoughts.

The bird croaked once, and rattled its wings. With a hop, it took wing, gliding down to perch on one of the smaller stones near where Laurel sat. It cocked its glossy head towards her, and Laurel met the wild gaze of a single, round, red-rimmed eye. Looking deeply into it, she found there the blur of flight, delight in the company of bird and wolf, and the simple hunger that seeks endlessly to be filled.

But there was something more as well, something distant and strange.

She has touched you. What does she know of us, little friend? What has she sent you to look for?

Laurel reached out towards the bird, her will carried forth by the wind blowing through her white hair and the bird's black feathers. She felt a questing curiosity about the men below far beyond the instincts of hunger and hunting natural for such a creature. How many were there? What was their appearance? Was there one among them who was tall and lean with hair as black as the bird's own body?

Laurel felt her jaw tighten. *Get you gone, get you gone,* she ordered the spy, her silent command heavy with blossoming anger. *There is nothing here for you. Nothing at all.*

The bird croaked again, cocking its head this way and that.

It was hungry. It was hunting. It wondered about her too with its unnatural curiosity. The wind blew hard, and Laurel thought she felt a warning in the gust.

But before she could move, she felt another touch, as delicate as a petal, falling over her thoughts.

Greetings to you, Laurel, wife of Agravain.

Fear flooded hard behind the first shock. Laurel suppressed it, drawing outrage up to shield her.

I did not expect courtesy of you, Morgaine.

As clear as day, a picture formed in her mind of the sorceress, standing beside a bonfire.

Morgaine smiled up at the twilight sky. *What need is there for enmity between us? There should be friendship between like and like.*

Laurel closed her eyes to hold onto the picture, cutting off her own sight so that Morgaine could not use it against her. *Only when their ends agree.*

And why should our ends not agree? You wish your lord to have his due. I wish the same for my son. There is no reason why both our wishes may not come true.

No reason, save that you wish my lord's destruction. In her own secret mind, Laurel strained her will. *Look about, look about.* She reached for the wind, sending the wish on. *Find me some landmark, some sign to show where she is.*

I wish Agravain's destruction? False surprise filled Morgaine's reply. *Never. We are blood kin, he and I.*

Anger bit at the edges of Laurel's concentration, almost opening her eyes. *Do you believe I came here ignorant, Morgaine?*

Ignorant, no. Only naive.

Laurel felt her nerve and patience shiver. This was a mistake. It gave the sorceress a chance to joust with her, to plague and play with her, as the *morverch* had. Morgaine loved her games, and Laurel must refuse to enter into them.

Get you gone from here, Morgaine. This place is closed to you.

Is it? asked Morgaine. *Because you say?*

Yes. Because I say.

Foolish, foolish child. Morgaine's insult grated on Laurel's mind. *You think this is some strange dream. You believe you can banish it just by willing it so. You know nothing of the sacrifice to be made for power. You think your mortal heart and immortal blood will grant you strength enough to face me. You have never stood before true power, never had to fight for your self and what is right-fully yours against those who have turned traitor against you.*

Words only, Morgaine. You do not frighten me.

Then I must teach you fear.

The raven in front of her laughed, and launched itself at her. Laurel raised her hands to shield her face, and in a moment, she was seized tight. Not in body, but in spirit. Her innermost soul was clutched tight in a force beyond her ken. She struggled, frantic, but it was no good. She could not discern the force that held her. She could not touch it with any force of her will, though her thoughts flailed wildly. It was like trying to touch panic itself. She tried to call to the sea wind, but she was mute and helpless.

The pounding of the bird's wings filled her and surrounded her, a living, throbbing wall between her and any help. Her spirit eyes, blind before, were now forced open. She saw all the land below her, wrinkled green and stone grey.

See what is to come for you and yours, little girl.

It was not Gododdin she saw spreading beneath her with its frozen waves of earth and stone stretching out from the ocean's shore. She knew this land like she knew the shape of her own bones. This was the high tablelands and sheer valleys that belonged to the Dumonii. This was her home.

Battle raged below. Knights on horseback clashed together, wielding sword and spear amidst a sea of men on foot with their poleaxes and cudgels. The roar, the heat and stench; the mud and blood and death and confusion; the screams and the shouts; the endless clash like a thousand blacksmiths hammering at once, it all surrounded her, shattering all hope of thought or struggle. All her senses were smothered over by the terrible morass of war. Horses danced and reared, torn between their master's commands, and trying desperately not to tread upon the bodies of the falling already sinking into the mud. Overhead, the ravens laughed, urging on the battle, cheering for the slaughter.

Then, for one instant, the unfathomable riot of war receded, and Laurel was able to discern a single knight in the middle of the bloody storm. He was a bright, bronze man, on a huge, red horse. His blue and white shield had been splintered and battered. A second man strode towards him, a young man with black hair and red arms. His face, though contorted by rage, was familiar but she couldn't remember why.

Gareth. God above, it was Gareth, Lynet's husband, who charged the bronze knight. He swung his sword wildly, crying out like a man driven insane. The bronze knight blocked the first blow and the second. His face was almost languid as he thrust once, and Gareth looked surprised for a single instant.

Then, Gareth fell back from the horse to sprawl in the mud.

A howl rang out, torn from some maddened throat. Now Laurel saw Agravain urging his lean brown charger forward. His sword high, Agravain bore down on the bronze knight, who only smiled to see who came now and raised his own sword.

All Laurel's spirit struggled to scream some warning, but Morgaine's power held her mute. The battle blurred before her, and cleared, to be replaced by the aftermath of carnage. The bodies of men, broken and mauled beyond recognition, lay in the drying mud. The flies and ravens swirled around, looking to drink their fill before the worms came wriggling out of the earth for their share.

Gareth was there, but not alone. Oh no. Agravain's corpse lay beside his brother's, his head lolling loose on the red and black stump of his neck. Laurel's mind swayed and swirled. Had she been fully in her body, she would have fainted.

A woman's scream tore the world. Lynet, Laurel's sister, whom she had left flushed with love for her new husband, struggled across the muddy field, stumbling over the dead, fighting to reach Gareth, stone cold and dead beside Agravain.

Where am I? wailed Laurel. *Where am I in this madness?*

Long gone, Lady Laurel, came Morgaine's cruel whisper. *You fled back to the sea ages since.*

Laurel felt herself sinking into terror and heartbreak. This was the future. This death, this blow. This was the end of the world, and she, Laurel, had run away.

No. No, Laurel told herself desperately. *This is only Morgaine's future. Only Morgaine's wish.*

No. This is my work. I spun this destiny before your birth, little girl. It is wrought of blood and fire, and the stuff of my very bones. My hands spun its threads, measured its length and tied its knots. My knife will cut its threads. Every step your man takes, every breath he breathes, binds him more tightly. I have him already, and having him, I have all the rest.

You were too late already when you took your vow of marriage, when you lied and told him you had the strength to stand against me. It would have been better for him had you put a knife to your throat than his ring on your hand.

But even as despair crushed Laurel down, warmth touched her, distant, but real. It flowed through her, reminding her of another place, of time outside this bloody vision. It spoke of life and hope, and the freedom of self. It snaked through the deathgrip that held her, prying it open, as if a shaft of sunlight had thrown open a locked shutter.

What is this! cried Morgaine. *What have you done!*

Laurel fell. The whole of her spirit dropped into the waiting warmth as suddenly as if she were a stone cast away. Her eyes flew open.

She was where she had been, on the hillside with the busy sounds of the new encampment swirling around her. Cait hovered over her, holding her hands closed. Laurel felt the slick, cool touch of silk against her palms, and she knew by what blessing she had been freed.

Humbled Laurel bowed her head at once.

'Thanks be to God,' she whispered. 'And to you, Cait.' Her hands shook. With an effort, she made herself let go of the silk, handing it back to her maiden. 'You may return this to its chest. Carefully.'

'Yes, lady.' Puzzled but obedient, Cait did as she was told.

Could Cait feel it? Laurel wondered as she watched her maid returning to the pavilion. Could she feel the blessing she held and the power that had coursed through this place; power of despair, and of hope, of death and life? The reverberations still shuddered through Laurel's bones.

'My lady?'

Agravain. Coming up the darkened slope with his long, swinging stride. She stared, relieved, confused, her thoughts teetering between reality and nightmare. Here was Agravain, whole and unbloodied, but the horrors Morgaine had forced on her were so fresh in her heart, she could barely see him as he was.

'You are pale, my lady,' Agravain said as he reached her side. 'What is it?'

Laurel drew in a breath, gathering all the strength she had left to her. *It was only Morgaine's lie.* Laurel's fingers knotted in her skirts. *It is nothing but a lie. I need not burden him with it.*

'It is nothing,' she whispered. 'It is only the cold.'

His brow furrowed. 'Are you certain?'

He did not believe her. But what could she tell him? Not

what she had seen. She could not tell him she had met Morgaine, and failed utterly, that it was only because she had disobeyed his express wish and brought Excalibur's scabbard that she survived sane and whole. Pride, cold and comfortless, but inseparable from the rest of herself, would not permit so much.

'Forgive me if I worried you,' she murmured.

'There is no need. Our pavilion is ready. That will give you some shelter from the wind at least.' Agravain extended his hand and she took it, letting him help pull her to her feet. Together they picked their way between the rocks and puddles left over from the recent rains to the little leathern shelter waiting for them.

Hidden among the looming stones, Morgaine's spy watched them walk away. Hidden in her distant valley, Morgaine the Sleepless smiled in her waking dream. The girl had escaped, but not unscathed. The seeds of fear were sown in her heart. She would not forget what she had heard and seen. It would colour every move she made in the coming days, and blind her to the truths that might have saved her and her so-beloved husband.

In the thread of her mind, Morgaine tied another knot.

TWELVE

Morning came, late and grey with mist. Laurel woke alone, her breath steaming in the damp air. Now she could clearly hear the clashes and thumps of the encampment, accompanied by staccato shouts, and the grumbling of sleepy men.

Packing to travel already.

Sparrow Jen had woken before Laurel, but just barely. The girl was still yawning prodigiously as she helped lace up Laurel's sleeves properly, brush down her woollen dress and pin up her braids. As soon as she was decent, Laurel pushed her way out of the tent.

The sun was barely over the horizon, and the place was already a hive of activity. Laurel easily picked out Agravain sitting above the purposeful chaos on horseback. If he had slept at all last night, it was only a little. She had been aware of him a few times, coming in to sit beside her, but not to lie down in their makeshift bed.

To her shame, she had been glad. She needed the night to regain her composure, to understand what had truly happened when Morgaine had taken possession of her. She had made the gravest mistake. She had underestimated the Sleepless One. No more. It would not happen again. The kernel of fear that nestled beneath her heart would not have the chance to grow. She would never leave Agravain to the nightmare future Morgaine had planned for him. There was no disaster that could drive her into the sea.

Looking at Agravain now, a wave of pure wifely concern mixed liberally with annoyance swept over her. *He surely has not eaten.*

Cait stooped beside the fire, tending an iron kettle. Devi and Ros hovered beside it, torn between wanting whatever smelled so appetizing, and wanting to rejoin Agravain. They shuffled aside politely when Laurel approached, and Cait handed her a bowl of plain pottage and a hunk of bread. Bowl in one hand and hems in the other, Laurel picked her way through the swirl of activity to Agravain's side, where he looked up towards Din Eityn as if he thought it might have moved under cover of darkness.

'Has there been any word, my lord?'

He looked down, startled to see her there, and she handed up the bread and pottage. For a moment he stared at them, as if they were foreign objects and he did not know their purpose. When he did take them, she saw a flicker of gratitude.

'I am hoping word comes now.' He nodded up the slope, and scooped up some pottage with the bread.

The mists had lifted enough that Laurel could see a column of tall shapes moving deliberately down the rocky path. After some straining, she counted four men, all on horseback. One carried a long pole that might have held a banner, but in the dank, still morning it was impossible to make out its sigil.

Greeting or warning? Agravain's face was creased and his gaze never left the approaching column, even while he shovelled his hasty breakfast into his mouth. They had not spoken of it aloud, but they both knew it was possible that the fortress had already fallen to internal strife, and that there was no welcome for them there.

Laurel took Agravain's bowl when he was finished, handing it off to Jen who had come up beside her. Her own hunger stirred uneasily inside, but she could not make herself move. Whatever was coming, she would not wait for the news any longer than necessary.

Slowly, slowly, the little procession wound its way in and out of the dissipating mists. Then, all at once, Agravain stood up in his stirrups.

'Pedair,' he breathed. 'Thank Christ. Devi!' Agravain shouted. 'Devi!'

The squire had just accepted a hunk of bread from Cait. He shoved the morsel back into her hands and ran up the slope, bowing hastily.

'Get Ros to carry the banner, and run up to greet Lord Pedair and bring him to me.'

'My lord.' Relief loosened Devi's brown face, and he hurried to put the orders into action.

'Pedair would not have left if there was not at least some semblance of order in the fortress,' murmured Agravain, not looking down at Laurel. 'That is something, at least.'

Laurel nodded. She had known he was worried, but she had not guessed how frightened he was of what he was walking into. Seeing him relax, sit back on his saddle and wait with something approaching patience allowed her to breathe more easily.

Pedair and his three men-at-arms rode into the camp on sturdy dappled horses with blankets striped blue and grey beneath their plain saddles. Huge, heavy-jawed hounds trotted beside the horses and laid down obediently at their master's commands. The smallest of them stood as high as Laurel's waist. These were more than hunting dogs, these were war hounds.

Lord Pedair himself was an old man, his hair and moustaches gone fully grey and his eyes nearly lost in the
weathered folds of his face. His blue tunic and leather trousers
were worn, and his striped cloak had seen hard use and little
washing. But he dismounted his horse easily and bowed
before Agravain.

Agravain also dismounted, and grasped the man's forearm
to raise him up.

'Pedair,' he said, warmth and relief plain in voice. 'Thank
you for being here.'

'It was my honour, Your Highness.'

Highness. There it was, and for the first time; Agravain
greeted not as Arthur's man, but as the king's son.

This did not seem to give Agravain any pause. He turned
at once to her. 'This is my wife, the Lady Laurel Carnbrea
of Cambryn and the Dumonii lands.'

Pedair bowed to Laurel. 'I am sorry we could not give you
better welcome, my lady.'

'It is of no matter, my lord.' Inwardly, Laurel cursed herself
for allowing her greed for news to cause her to neglect her
proper duties. She should have had welcome cups prepared
for these men.

Agravain, however, seemed in no mood for the delays of
courtesy. 'We are almost ready to leave here. How does the
king?'

'He lives,' replied Pedair with a glance up the slope to the
looming fortress. Laurel thought she saw him shiver slightly.

If Agravain saw this, he gave no sign. He only nodded
curtly. 'We will go at once.'

'Yes, Sire,' said Pedair. There was a martial acceptance in
his reply, but there was also a small hesitation. 'You should
know, much has changed since you and your brothers left.'

Agravain's expression did not change. 'For the worse, I am
certain. What loyal man would stay to serve madness?' The

tone was neutral, but he was holding back a flood of feeling, Laurel was certain.

Pedair dropped his gaze, unable to make any answer, and hiding his own feelings of shame.

How many failures and how much desertion have you faced these ten years?

'Who have you left behind?' Agravain was asking.

'Ruadh *mach* Keill. He is a good man.'

Agravain nodded curtly. 'We should delay no further, unless there is something more you would tell me before I enter the fortress?'

'No, Sire.'

Did Agravain see how far the other man's eyes were sunken in, and how he swallowed hard before he spoke? Oh, yes. He surely did. He was watching this chieftain as closely as he would an enemy who challenged him. With his searching gaze he hunted for lies, or for hidden truths.

Agravain nodded once more. He was not satisfied, but he was not in any mood to delay further so he could quiz Pedair more completely. Whatever waited at Din Eityn, they would find it out soon enough.

'Let us go.'

And it was done almost as quickly. Three of the captains were detailed to supervise the remaining decamping, and Ros formally given the role of messenger which he had already carried out so ably. Laurel sent Jen running for a horse, and turned back to see Agravain gazing down at her thoughtfully. But he made no objection, and by the time his chosen guard was formed up in a processional line, Laurel was on the back of a steady grey mare, stationed immediately behind Agravain. Neither Jen nor Cait were happy about her order for them to stay behind and accompany her chests up along with the main body of men, but they acquiesced when she gave them no choice.

Lord Pedair went before them, the hawk banner of Gododdin fluttering weakly on its staff. The drumming of the horses' hoof beats on earth and stone was the only music to herald their march.

The way up to Din Eityn was no smoother than it looked. Though the valley was broad, it remained stony. The earthen blanket was thin and torn in many places. There were many homes here, but nothing Laurel would call a village, let alone a town; just scattered clusters of houses made of thatch, wicker and stone, joined by strange sunken walkways, some of which were roofed over as scant protection against this land's harsh weather. The fields looked to be little more than gardens between the stones, but the sheep and the goats were well fleeced and well penned. Beside every house waited at least one boat, or the frame of a boat, all turned over to keep out the frequent rains.

Their passage was not unmarked. Folk came out of every doorway to gawp at them. Murmurs passed between the people who stared in slack-jawed in surprise. Then, slowly, here and there, one began to kneel. A shout rang out. Then a cheer. The cheer drew yet more people out of the scattered dwellings and in from the scanty fields.

Soon the folk of Gododdin came running, men and women, children hurrying up on round, sturdy legs, or hoisted in their parents' arms. Whatever else they wore, they were all wrapped in lengths of sturdy woven wool against the perpetual cold and damp, the women swathed head and shoulders, the men swaddled around their waists and across chest and back.

They came down the slopes and out of the valley's little green hollows to stand beside the route the procession travelled and lift their hands.

'Lord Agravain!' they cried. 'Prince Agravain! God bless your coming! Thank God! Thank God!'

Agravain lifted his hand, acknowledging the tribute, and the folk who dropped to their knees. This outpouring startled him, but did nothing to lighten his demeanour. His attention drifted between the gathering, cheering crowd and the square, black fortress above. His jaw worked itself, tightening and loosening.

Wondering just how bad things have been that so many are so glad to see you, thought Laurel.

What troubled her was that none of the folk who cheered their progress and called out blessings followed them. She would have expected a joyful parade to the fortress that was the high house of this place. But not one of these people fell into their wake. They only watched, crying out their hopes and their prayers, and let the armed men and their returning prince go on ahead.

Soon, their climb began in earnest. Din Eityn stood on a mighty stone prominence that thrust up from the centre of the valley bowl. More hills, larger and rounder, loomed in the distance, but it was plain why this place had been chosen for the fortress of Gododdin. There was only one easy way up for a man on a horse, and that was a narrow, painful pass that snaked crookedly up the uneven side of the hill. There was, Agravain told her, a footbridge over a gap at the back of the rock, but no horse could travel that steep path.

Even on this easier way, no speed was possible. Laurel knew herself to be no great horsewoman, but, fortunately, strained as she was, her light mare remained steady of foot. Even so, the sturdy animal was blowing and sweating before they were half-way, and she had to pat the animal's neck constantly for encouragement.

At last, the gates of Din Eityn loomed before them. The stout, black timbers banded with iron stood wide open to welcome their returning heir. Beyond them waited a courtyard so neatly squared it had to be of Roman making. But

its lines were the only thing about it that was neat. The ground
was pot-holed and puddled, with wisps of ancient straw
sticking out of the thick layer of mud. The long hall made of
unadorned, grey stone dominated a loose flock of smaller
anonymous buildings that might have been dwellings, or
storehouses or stables for all Laurel could tell. The only one
bearing any markings at all was the chapel with its deeply
incised cross.

No cheers greeted them here. An untidy gaggle of men
lurked in the shadows, uncertain what to do as these snorting,
panting horses clopped into their yard. A few faces peered
out from the open doors of the hall. No one looked down
off the walls, though, and it was clear that despite the fact
an enemy approached, no watch had been set.

The only woman Laurel could see was an ancient dame
in a corner of the hall, throwing out crumbs to a scattering
of chickens. She hunched low in on herself, in the manner
of one who hopes not to be noticed.

Agravain's skin drew so tightly over the bones of his face,
Laurel thought for a moment it would tear like cloth. He
looked on each of the staring, straggling men, and his flat,
black eyes promised silently to remember them, all of them.

'Anden! Donal! Come take your lord's horse!' barked
Pedair. 'Iain! Spread the word that Lord Agravain has come
home! Find Lord Ruadh and bring him here!'

Sluggishly, reluctantly, the men began to move in response
to the orders. Their calculating eyes looked Agravain up and
down, wary, wondering if this was real. They looked at Laurel
too, measuring her probably for position and worth. She
returned their gaze coolly, showing her own strength for any
who cared to see. One seemed inclined to smile at this lofty
response to so rude an inspection, but he wavered.

*Yes, it is a true lord come again to this ruined place. You'd do
well to think on that.*

One of these slouchers took the reins of Agravain's horse. Her husband's whole face bent into a deep scowl as he dismounted.

'Pedair, you see to the horses yourself, and wait for the men. I can still find my way, I think.' Agravain came to Laurel's side, his glower turning away the sly-eyed man who was first to approach, and helped her down from the horse. 'You there!' he called out towards the woman feeding the chickens.

The crone looked up, eyes wide, as if she just now saw her yard had been invaded. With a speed that showed she was still spry under her shapeless, undyed dress, she scrambled to her feet and scurried forward, scattering chickens as she did.

'My lord, my lord,' she bowed. Her voice was high and rusty. Laurel guessed she did not speak much. 'Welcome home, my lord Agravain.'

Agravain's face shifted, uncertain what to make of this first acknowledgement of his arrival in his father's house. 'My lady Laurel needs a woman to guide her about here. You will take that role until her own maids arrive.'

'My honour, Your Highness,' the woman said with wonder in her voice. She dipped a stiff-legged curtsey.

Agravain did not waste another word, but strode into the dark hall.

'Will my lady . . .' began the old woman.

'No,' said Laurel curtly. She strode after Agravain, leaving her new waiting woman no choice but to follow.

It was like walking into a cavern. The air was damp, stinking of mould, and fouler things. Stone walls pressed close. No tapestry or rug softened them. No light alleviated the darkness.

Ahead, someone screamed, a hoarse, horrible sound. Agravain broke into a run, and Laurel, hiking up her hems, followed fast behind, her heart filling her throat.

Within a few paces the dank entranceway opened into the great hall. It could have been a regal chamber, had there been any dressing, any banner or flag to confer stature on it. Instead it was an empty, echoing cavern. The three fires that blazed along its length did nothing to lighten the chill. Slovenly men in dirty leathers, and a few slatternly women in stained wool dresses lounged here and there. They looked up dully at this interruption of a man and woman clattering into their private cave.

In the centre of it all, the king lay in a richly carved bed beside the central fire. The sight of him stopped Agravain dead.

Laurel had seen illness many times, but nothing like this. Lot's skin was so yellow he might have been dyed with saffron. Fever slicked his skin with sweat. His legs were swollen to the size of tree limbs. He writhed in a nest of soiled blankets. A draught crossed the hall, bringing the sick-sweet stench of illness.

Lot screamed, his whole face twisting until his eyes screwed shut. His scabrous hands clawed at the blankets. The slovenly and slatternly around him looked up, but did nothing.

Agravain took a step forward and stopped. He took another step, and stopped again. In this halting way, he slowly reached his father's bedside. A man ran in from a side entrance. Bald, save for a fringe of white hair around his mottled pate, he was square-built and still strong of arm. He was also the only person in clean clothing they'd seen in this place. Surely this was Ruadh, the chieftain Pedair had been ordered to find.

Lord Ruadh hurried up to Agravain's side, bowing deeply. Agravain did not seem to see him. He stood at Lot's bedside, seeming to alternately shrink and swell as he gazed on his father in the noisome bed. His face shook and spasmed as he tried to keep any emotion from showing itself.

This moment was necessary. Knowing how thorough he was, Laurel imagined Agravain had schooled himself in every possible way for it. Now it had come, and it was worse than any imaginings could have been, but he would not let it defeat him.

King Lot moaned, feebly kicking his swollen legs. The man slouched nearest the fire took a pull from his leather jack and spat into the flames.

'Clear the hall,' whispered Agravain.

The chieftain, Ruadh, opened his mouth, but had no chance to speak.

'Clear the hall!' bellowed Agravain.

The slatterns and vagabonds looked up, vaguely startled at this.

'So help me God,' said Agravain, with an icy steadiness that was more terrible than a shout of rage could ever be. 'The one who lingers here an instant longer will have my sword in their belly.'

He means it. He'd do it. That understanding touched Laurel like winter's breath. Not even in the depths of his fury would Agravain make a vow he did not mean to keep.

'You heard your prince, you sluggards!' shouted Ruadh. 'Move your drunken arses!'

Like the men in the yard, it took these a moment to realize a real order had been given. Clearly, they all considered that while staying might make for some sport, the sport might quickly become unpleasant to them. So, they rose or straightened, catching up what they cared to take, and dispersed themselves into the corridors. Not out of obedience, or even fear, but out of the pure selfish interests of those who were not quite ready to make trouble.

Grim purpose settled over Laurel. She made herself walk up to Agravain with a measured pace. They were watched, she was sure of it. She felt the inquisitive gazes glancing

backwards from of the dark mouths of the corridors, waiting
to see what happened to her.

'By your leave, my lord,' she said clearly and calmly.
'I will go see what can be made of the kitchens and work-
rooms.'

Agravain's gaze darted to hers, understanding in a moment
what she was doing. It would not do for the one who would
be mistress of this place to be shooed out with the ruffians.

'With my thanks, my lady,' he replied curtly. 'Show her
the way, Ruadh.'

Now she could withdraw, dignity and authority intact,
behind Lord Ruadh into the belly of Din Eityn. The old
woman could follow her, head erect. She heard whispers,
and the patter of sandalled feet as whoever had come down
this way ahead of them rushed to get themselves gone.

After a dozen paces, Ruadh stopped, and turned. He bowed
deeply to her. 'Forgive me, my lady, I was not given the
honour of your name.'

'There is nothing to forgive my lord. All will be strange
for a few days yet.' And far more than that. She could barely
see him in the corridor's gloom, but her impression was a
presence of strength long worn down. 'I am Laurel of
Cambryn, now wife to the prince Agravain.'

'I am most honoured.' Ruadh bowed again. 'What service
can I be to you, my lady?'

Laurel cast about, her mind racing through all that she
had seen. 'None at present, my lord, though I do thank you.
I must establish who I am in this place. If I cannot do so
alone and at once, I cannot do it.' Somewhat to her surprise,
she felt a tight smile form. 'Make a good count of who is
here among the men, and what kind they be. Your prince
will need that. Also, make note of any who quit the place
now. Make sure it's known where they go.'

Gravely, Lord Ruadh bowed once more. Despite the

shadows. Laurel thought she saw new respect dawning in his eyes, and counted that a victory. Here was a loyal man who could clearly give good service. They would need him badly.

Ruadh took his leave, the sound of his boot heels echoing against stone. Laurel stayed where she was, her hands on her hips. She suddenly missed her house keys, which she had worn so long as the lady of Cambryn's halls. Her small, light ring with its few chest keys was next to nothing. Those heavy keys had been the symbol of her authority. They had also been her way into the stores and treasury she knew so well. Whatever she needed she could lay her hands on at home. Here, God alone knew what she would have and not have.

Someone coughed. Laurel turned and saw the ancient dame she had for a moment forgotten had been assigned to her.

'And what is your name?' asked Laurel

The woman bobbed a curtsey. 'I'm called Byrd, my lady.'

'And how long have you served here, Byrd?'

'All my life, my lady.'

'So you remember this place as it used to be?'

'Oh yes, my lady,' Byrd answered, her high voice gone soft with private sorrow. 'I remember well.'

Laurel nodded, obscurely satisfied.

'Find a light, Byrd,' she said. 'We go to do our own battle.'

The little woman looked up at her keenly, and a smile spread over her wrinkled face.

'At once, my lady.' She scurried off.

Another hoarse scream drifted down the corridor. Echoing against the stone it had the sound of a wounded animal. For a moment Laurel thought to return to the great hall. Agravain should not be alone there. But she stayed where she was. She must do credit to his strength and decision now. It was her duty to begin to make this cavern fit for human habitation. To do that, she must first discover how deep the rot and neglect ran. She did not doubt Pedair or Ruadh were as loyal as they seemed, but neither had been seneschal, and there were matters that they clearly had been powerless to track or turn about.

Byrd returned shortly, holding a smoking rushlight that reeked of old tallow. But the sputtering orange flames did give out some light. It would do for now.

'The kitchens first.' Laurel gestured for Byrd to precede her. The old woman stepped up nimbly enough, whether pleased simply at this new notice taken of her or pleased that there was someone here to take charge of the place, Laurel could not yet tell. Gathering up her hems, Laurel followed the ancient dame to the kitchens.

The great keep of Din Eityn was a series of buildings and cellars connected by the ubiquitous sunken walkways. These ways were stone-lined and stone-flagged, and roofed over with indifferent skill. More than once, Laurel had to dodge puddles as Byrd led her down the uneven steps and across to the smaller stone building that held the kitchen.

Desultory voices drifted out to them, along with some sniggering laughter. Though Laurel could not understand the words, the mocking, insolent tone was plain enough. Laurel's shoulders stiffened and her jaw set.

The odours that greeted Laurel and Byrd as they entered the kitchen had little to do with food, and everything to do with filth. The place was cold as a tomb. Only one of the three hearths had any fire in it at all, and that was a pitiful pile of flickering coals, all but blocked by the bulk of a man with a leathern apron stretched tight across his middle and a blue cap slumping over his unkempt hair. His beard was crusted with grease and the remains of several recent meals. He looked up at her sharply, and Laurel knew here was the one who believed he was master of this place.

His underlings were little better. Laurel counted seven of

them. Dressed in rags and greasy wools, there were four lounging men, and two cowering girls, with one square, horse-faced dame who did not bother to hide her contempt as she glanced Laurel up and down.

Assessing the danger I represent, no doubt.

All that waited on the worktables was some peelings, scraps and bones, and what quantity of flies could be bothered to disturb themselves in this cold.

Laurel took all this in with a single sweep of her eyes.

So.

'Master Kitchener,' Laurel barked. 'Why have the fires been permitted to go out?'

The corpulent man (how did he grow fat on such scanty fare as was surely found here?) narrowed his eyes at her.

'You'd best speak up, Fergas,' said Byrd with perhaps more relish than was seemly. 'This is Her Highness Laurel Carnbrea, come as wife to Prince Agravain.'

This revelation caused Fergas to sit up on his stool a little straighter, and to lose some of his colour.

'I ask you again, Master Kitchener,' said Laurel, aware that all ears had pricked up now, and that the furtive glances cast between the dishevelled kitchen inhabitants were evidence of close and careful attention. 'Why have the fires been permitted to go out?'

Fergas shrugged. 'Naught to light 'em wi', my lady.' Then he remembered to shift his bulk enough to hide the coals sputtering behind him.

'There is now.' Laurel nodded to Byrd, who scurried forward to hold out the rushlight. 'Light the fire.'

Fergas's little eyes darted from the rushlight to Laurel, and he shifted uneasily. The stool creaked under his weight. 'Naught to burn, my lady,' he tried. 'Mist's got into the wood and it's all gone to rot.'

'All gone to rot,' repeated Laurel evenly. 'Aptly spoken,

Master Kitchener. It seems the whole of this place has gone to rot.'

The kitchener's eyes glittered angrily and he ran his fingers through his beard, muttering something.

'What was that, Master Kitchener?' demanded Laurel at once.

His underlings were all grinning now, save for the palest of the girls, and the square dame, who looked only angered at the whole scene.

'Your lady asked you a question, Fergas,' snapped Byrd. 'I'd answer if I was you.'

'Aye you would, ye old crackbrain,' Fergas spat. Then, tucking his thumbs under the band of his leather apron he said, 'All right, m'lady, you want to hear what I said. I said how I run my kitchen is no business of yours, nor of any southerner who comes back for a few days just so he can desert us as soon as he likes.'

That there was some justice to the charge was no excuse. 'You seem to think nothing has changed, sirrah,' she said, pitching every word to carry. 'You think this is some southern whim. You are wrong. Your prince is here now. Din Eityn will become a true hall again. It will show the pride of Gododdin to the Pict and Dal Riata, and whosoever else dares to come calling. You can either do your work as befits this place and your master, or you can go to squat in a fen and spit in the wind for your drink. It matters not to me.'

Fergas's lips twitched. He was attempting a grin, but some portion of whatever passed in him for thought was beginning to understand her words. 'So you say.'

'Yes, sirrah. So I say, and I am giving you your final chance. You may do with it exactly as you will.'

The kitchener was able to meet her gaze for a handful of heartbeats, but no more. All at once, he heaved himself to his feet. 'Toradan, shift yourself. Find some kindlin' ya gawper, or I'll know why!'

Toradan, a lumpish, red-headed young man, gawped to see actual movement from Fergas. Quickly, though, he shook himself, and disappeared out through the draughty back door.

Laurel faced the remaining kitchen folk. 'The cistern is empty. We need water. You and you,' she pointed at a pair of thin, spotted youths, 'find buckets and see that it is filled. Get what help you need.'

To their credit, this pair did no more than glance at each other before they sprang into motion. 'Mother,' Laurel turned to the square, angry dame. 'You will see to the ovens and be sure the fires there are made up properly. Byrd, is there a stores book anywhere?'

'None, my lady.'

It was the answer Laurel expected. 'That will be corrected in due course. Show me the stores.'

'Yes, my lady.' Byrd, sensing Laurel's dangerous humour, had the good sense not to smile at the thought of further trouble. Instead, she reclaimed the rushlight and took Laurel out a side door, through another walkway, and to a set of stairs leading down into the rock beneath the keep.

The cellars were a low warren of chambers, irregularly shaped with walls so cold and damp they might have been made of ice. Like the rest of the hall, the stores had been permitted to rot. In the flickering rushlight, Laurel could not see a single cask that was properly sealed, nor anything that was decently hung to dry or cure. The smell was more that of a charnel house than of a food store. Sacks of meal slumped on damp earth and apples lay in withered piles in the corners. Loaves of bread lay broken and dusty on the shelves. At a glance, Laurel could tell there was not enough to sustain the hall through a serious storm, let alone through a siege.

'Sorry sight, isn't it?' remarked Byrd, shaking her head.

What relish she had had for the situation had finally melted away.

Laurel put her fists on her hips, letting annoyance cloak desperation. At least two hundred souls were climbing the cliff, carrying with them enough food for a day, at most. And this was what she had to greet them with. 'Byrd, is there such a thing as a decent measure or scale in this hole?'

Byrd shrugged. 'It may be, my lady. Such things have been . . . ignored of late.'

'Find it, if you can. And anything that will do for making a tally. We must know what we have and what we lack.'

'Yes, my lady.'

A rusty sconce beside the door could hold the rushlight. A piece of sacking from a pile beside some broken casks was relatively dry and made a crude apron. Thus adorned, Laurel waded into the mess of flotsam that passed for a store room.

Their only blessing was that it was summer, and if the folk they had passed were as effusive with their tributes as they were with their cheers, they might stand some chance of replenishing this place before winter came. If not . . . it wasn't more men they'd need from Camelot, but food.

Byrd soon returned bearing an ancient wooden measure, a second, less smoky, rushlight, and, from some blessed hidey-hole, a tiny waxen tally book and stylus. It was all Laurel could do to keep from crying out in thanks. Without hesitation, Byrd made herself a sacking apron to match Laurel's and waded into the work.

For an hour or more they laboured, heaving open sacks and caskets, stamping at the rats and mice as they fled, disturbed at their feasts. It was fully as bad as it had looked at first. Half the grain was rotten, and there was little meat of any kind, and no fish at all. The only spice was salt, and little enough of that. The rats had been at everything.

Laurel carried on grimly, making the smallest notes she could, carrying running totals in her head, and trying to count weights and measures and calculate coin while a flood of questions swirled through her.

What are the levies and on whom? Is there anyone left to ask? Probably these louts take what they want when they want it . . . We must get some sort of meal together, for the hall and our people . . . Where will we sleep them? We cannot keep them in the yard or in the stables. We must have the great hall.

A hunting party would have to be organized and quickly. Judging from the boats they had seen in the village below, they should be able to get fish fairly easily. They could dry that, perhaps smoke it. Salting was out of the question, there was nothing like enough . . .

The biggest concern was the grain. It would be another month, perhaps two, before the tiny fields below would begin ripening.

How do we make shift until then?

The quick patter of footsteps sounded outside the door. Byrd squinted up over her shoulder at the silhouette that darted into the doorway. 'Ceana, what is it?'

Ceana, Laurel could now see, was the square woman she had put in charge of the ovens. She stood panting at the top of the stairs, her skirt gripped in both hands. 'My lady,' she gasped. 'Come. It's Sorcha. He's at her . . .'

Laurel did not make her finish. 'Byrd, go get Lord Ruadh.' Anger and frustration, suppressed so she could keep at her task, boiled up hard. Laurel strode up the stairs, shoving past Ceana.

Once in the kitchens, she found an infuriating but unsurprising sight. One of the youngest women was backed up against the wall by a ruffian in battered leather armour. His hand was already up her skirt and two of his fellows stood in the doorway, cheering him on.

'No!' The girl cried. She struggled and she squirmed as he planted quick, painful kisses on her face.

Fergas, squatting on his stool and struggling with flint and steel grunted. 'Oh shut it, Sorcha. Get 'er out of here, Conal if you can't keep it quiet.'

Fury burned in Laurel's blood.

'*Stop this*!' Laurel bellowed. Her voice echoed through the room. The man, Conal, did stop, looking back, startled, at this sudden interruption of his game.

Laurel stalked forward. She grabbed the girl's – Sorcha, was it? – wrist and pulled her free, sending her stumbling into another girl's arms. There, Sorcha cringed, weeping.

Laurel spared her no further glance, but instead faced the attacker, the creature Fergas named as Conal. He was no better than she'd come to expect in this place. His fair beard and hair were a tangled mess. The stench of him was strong, and he did not have a whole tooth in his head, a fact she made out easily as he grinned and bowed to her, mocking her with each movement.

'Hear that, men?' Conal inquired, his brows arching in the semblance of surprise. 'Our prince's fine wife will not have me with another woman in her presence. You flatter me, Highness.'

His words drove Laurel to that still place that is beyond anger. Her mind was perfectly clear, and she felt her own power rise within her. She knew without seeing that the witchlights shone in her green eyes.

Let this creature look on that. Let him know, and turn pale with that knowledge.

Those behind him did pale, and their smiles fell away. But Conal himself was blind. He stood before her grinning his filthy grin while the girl he'd made free with wept out loud sheltered by her friend's thin arms.

'You want to take a woman?' Laurel said, danger and anger

making her voice soft. 'Here I am.' She spread her arms. 'Come near, sirrah. I'm waiting for you.'

'Oh, my lady,' Conal answered, his own expression turning into a dreadful parody of a lover's gentle glance. 'You should not speak such words unless you mean them.'

Laurel smiled, keen as a knife. 'You think I do not mean what I say, sirrah? Come here. Come, lay your hands on me. See how you like what you find.'

He sniggered as he reached for her. Like lightning, Laurel's hands flashed out, grabbing his wrist and elbow, bending them backward. He howled in pain, but she had him already. With even her slight weight, she could bear down, hear his muscles creak, feel his joints tear.

Steadily, remorselessly, Laurel drove the creature in her hands to his knees.

'Look at me!' she ordered.

He wailed in his pain.

'Look at me!'

Panting, he slit his eyes open. The light within Laurel burned brightly.

Let him see. Let him see. Let him see the ocean at storm, and let him see himself helpless on a stone with the waters rising fast around him. Let him see himself thin and starved and naked. Let him see the wolves circling.

See what it is to be driven out to die alone.

Anger wiped out mercy. Anger at the villains in this place, anger at what had happened in Londinium, anger at Morgaine and fear for her husband alone with his mad, dying father while she must deal with brigands and filth all found release as she drove her dark visions into him.

Conal's jaw slackened and his ruddy face paled to sick grey. He cried out again, struggling to free himself, and beneath her hands, Laurel felt his elbow snap. Conal screamed.

Boots slapped against stone. A man running fast. Ruadh

burst into the kitchen ahead of Byrd, knife drawn. He skidded to a halt, almost comic in his surprise to find Laurel towering over this squeaking, squirming villain.

Laurel released Conal so suddenly, he fell backwards. He clutched his arm to his chest, huddling in on himself, whimpering in his pain. Neither of his confederates made any move towards him as Laurel drew herself up.

'Lord Ruadh, this man assaulted me, and this girl,' she nodded to Sorcha, who shrank back behind Dame Ceana, 'who was not his to touch. Prince Agravain will sit in judgment when he finds it convenient. Take him to where they may be held closely and set good guard over them.'

'With pleasure, my lady.' Ruadh put up his knife and grabbed Conal's bad shoulder, hauling him to his feet as he wailed. With a single shove, Ruadh sent him spinning into the arms of the two who had moments ago been glad to watch his assault. Laurel held her peace, lest she undermine the chieftain. But these two clutched their former leader hard. It was plain fear was already working a change in their loyalties, and they looked to Ruadh for his nod. When it was given, they unceremoniously hauled Conal away.

'And make sure the rest of them know their prince does not tolerate men about him who act like beasts. There will be law here from now on!' announced Laurel, and her words rang through the stone room.

A smile, small but bright crossed Ruadh's aged visage. 'That word will spread without my voice, I think.'

Laurel returned his small smile. 'But not without your hand to it,' she said, her anger fading slowly, leaving her feeling a little weak, and suddenly too warm. 'We will rely upon you, Lord Ruadh.'

'I will do my best, Highness' He bowed deeply.

As Ruadh departed to deal with his new men, as well as

his new prisoner, Byrd murmured. 'They are dangerous, my lady.'

'Any rat may bite, Byrd,' answered Laurel. 'It does not mean they are permitted free access to the grain.' With these words, she rounded on Fergas. 'You can quit this place now, with what you stand up in, and count yourself lucky if I never see you again.'

Fergas got slowly to his feet, his round chin trembling behind his filthy beard. 'My lady . . .' he began.

'Get out!' The lights flared in her eyes again, and Fergas lost all strength. As quickly as his bulk permitted, he charged up the back stairs. The door slammed behind him.

Laurel turned, surveying the kitchen. Those who remained were all stunned into stillness by all they had seen. She walked over to the girl, Sorcha, trembling in her confederate's arms.

'Can you stand, now?' Laurel asked gently.

Sorcha nodded dumbly and managed to push herself away from her protector a little in an attempt to stand on her own. 'Have you family nearby?' Laurel asked. 'A mother?'

Again a nod.

'Good. Here is what I would have you do. Take your friend here, and the both of you go down to your family. Say that the lady of Din Eityn is in need of honest women and men to serve here. Say that those who are prepared to work hard will find good reward for their labour. Can you do that?'

Sorcha stared wide-eyed at her, not daring to trust what she heard. Laurel let her look as long as she pleased, keeping her own countenance mild. This would be their first voice to the people outside. She must be true and she must believe.

'Yes, my lady,' murmured Sorcha.

'Thank you. Go now.'

Sorcha did not need any more urging. She grabbed up her tattered skirts and ran for the back door. But at the foot of the stairs, she paused and turned, and dropped a deep curtsey to Laurel.

'Thank you, my lady,' she said, before she vanished out the door. Her friend made the same obeisance, and moved quickly to follow.

Victory, small but genuine, sang in Laurel's heart, but there was no time to savour it. 'Byrd, we have to finish with the stores. The rest of you,' she turned her hard gaze and voice to the remaining kitcheners, 'we will have fire and water in this place before dark.'

'Yes, m'lady.' The words were murmured by half a dozen voices. The people moved like sleepwalkers at first. Gradually, they showed more energy. Indeed, it was as if they had woken up to find themselves in the midst of their own work. They looked at their own hands strangely as they picked up kettle, broom and bucket. A few cast black glances at her. They would most likely be gone before morning, and no loss. She had a pair of ambassadors now in the form of Sorcha and her companion. They would take on one or two new folk to serve here over the next few days, and permit them to come and go freely. These would soon speak the truth of the changes here. Coin given in exchange for grain and other stores would remind frightened men what it was to have an honest lord over them.

Coin. That would be a necessity as this place clearly had nothing else to give to assuage resentment for a levy out of season.

We will also deal with that in its own turn.

Fortunately, the woman she'd taken to thinking of as Dame Ceana was not only a hard-handed, hard-headed woman, but she responded well to having her opinion respectfully sought. She showed Laurel the dairy, which was in surprisingly good condition. The mistress there was Ceana's cousin and as hard-headed as she. There was cheese, milk and eggs

and even some butter. At the sight of this, the sun rose in
Laurel's heart. Pottage could be made, and oatcakes, and
posset. Perhaps even some of last year's nuts might be found
to help stretch things out. Laurel suspected that these two
cousins had been bartering the hall's produce back down the
hill. It didn't matter. The dairy mistress insisted she could
give Laurel the names of some men, good men, honest men,
who could be trusted for wild meats. Laurel sat these two
down together to create a plan for how to wage battle against
starvation. Let them benefit their friends and families, just
so long as that horror of a larder was cleaned and filled.

That left the matter of the hall. Pedair had surely arrived
with the men by now. It was most unfitting that they see
the king in his current state, even if Agravain would consent
to bring them into the hall.

'Byrd. I saw a chapel in the yard?'

Byrd nodded. 'There is, my lady, though it's in as fully bad
shape as this kitchen. The priest is long gone and no one
here prays anymore.'

'Take me. We will make a room for King Lot there.'

Byrd's gaze narrowed. Laurel could see the doubt in her.
That did not matter. 'As you say, my lady.'

The chapel had no walkway. They crossed the open court,
skirting the growing crowd of folk milling there. The clouds
scudded across the sky and the salt wind blew hard off the
bay, lifting Laurel's spirits. It smelled of clean life and she
welcomed it in this dying place.

Byrd had not exaggerated the state of the chapel. The
painted walls were battered and soot-smeared. The plain altar
table sagged in the middle and the cross on the wall tipped
to the right. There was no sign of cloth or candlestick. The
stone basin of holy water was dry and a dusty oak leaf lay
in the bottom.

Laurel's teeth ground together in pure frustration. 'We

need to clean this place, Byrd. Fetch fire and water, and find out what bed and bedding may be had. My women, Cait and Jen, should have arrived with my luggage by now. Fetch them, and whoever you see standing idle with them. We must make this place hospitable at once.'

'Yes, my lady.'

Byrd hurried away again. Laurel looked about her, despair settling dangerously near in that moment's stillness. The desolation in this place went straight through her. This was beyond her skills. She did not know how to make this ruined place holy again.

Forgive me. It will be your house again, but I must beg the loan of it this little while.

With that, Laurel tied up her sleeves, and set to work.

THIRTEEN

As Laurel walked away, Agravain made himself turn once more to his father. Perhaps the tide of Lot's pain had ebbed a little, or perhaps his strength had failed, but both the screams and the brutal contortions had eased. Lot of Gododdin lay still on his bed, breathing harshly. Sweat ran down his gaunt, yellow face.

'My father?' Agravain murmured. Lot's eyes were tight shut and he made no reply. Agravain spoke again, more loudly. 'My father?'

Lot spasmed and twisted. With an effort that seemed to involve every fibre in his frame, he opened his eyes. Agravain leaned close, his shadow falling across his father.

Lot's lips moved aimlessly for a moment. Then he croaked, 'Which of them are you?'

Disappointment sank through Agravain, but he pushed it aside. 'I am Agravain.'

'Yes.' Lot slowly closed his eyes again. He swallowed. 'Yes. Of course. It would be you.'

'I have come as I promised.' Agravain said, not understanding whether his father was pleased, or if his madness led him to rue this meeting. He almost feared to try to riddle it out.

Lot breathed deeply, once, twice, three times, searching for his strength. 'You are grown to be a man, then.'

'You could see as much, Sire, if you opened your eyes.' Agravain hated the peevish, impatient tone behind the words, but it seemed he suddenly had no other voice available to him

Lot shook his head. 'No. I cannot see. Not anymore. Only shadows and memory. There's nothing real. Nothing left.'

'Be easy, father,' said Agravain around the tightness filling his throat. 'I am here now.'

Slowly, tentatively, his father opened his eyes. They were brown eyes, and once had been deep and clear. Age and illness now clouded them over, and turned the whites dirty yellow. They flicked back and forth restlessly, nervously.

'I had other sons, did I not?' Lot whispered. 'You had brothers once.'

Agravain had to swallow hard before he could speak. 'Yes.'

Lot too swallowed, and licked his lips. They were cracked, and lined with scabs. There should be water. He should get some, give an order, but he could not move.

'How do they fare?' Lot croaked.

'They are well, Sire. Gareth and Geraint are kings in their own countries now. Gawain has fathered his first son.'

'Good. Good.' Lot nodded feebly. This seemed to drain his strength so deeply that he had to close his eyes again. 'Better than I deserve,' he breathed. He paused, and a thought seemed to strike him. 'There was a sister,' he said slowly. 'I can't see her now. Where is my Tania?'

For a long moment, Agravain could not answer. 'She is not here.'

'Not here,' repeated Lot. 'Not here.' His mouth moved, struggling for words. His hands plucked at the furs and his swollen legs kicked weakly. 'Not here. You mean she's gone trysting with her man again. Conniving slut!' The force of Lot's scream lifted him head and shoulders from the bed. 'Foul, sneaking whore! I'll kill you with my own hands!' As the words left him, his face unclenched, and his eyes opened wide in horror. 'With my own hands. With my own hands.' Those hands, with the flesh hanging loose over their bones, trembled and slowly, Lot fell back down onto his pillows.

Agravain remained still. He could offer no comfort or ease. His father had done this thing and would be judged. Should be judged. All he could do was be sure that Morgaine the Sleepless was delivered up to that same judgment for that same deed.

'Is the other still here, father?' Agravain asked quietly. 'Does she still come to you?'

But his father did not seem able to hear him. 'God, I hurt,' moaned Lot, shifting and twisting his fever-flushed frame. 'Christ and Mother Mary take me away from here, or give me strength enough . . . I had strength enough on that day, why do I not have it now? A knife, a knife. Please God. I am damned already, one more sin is no matter. Let it be clean, let it be over . . .'

'Father.' Agravain bent closer. 'Is she here? Does she still come?'

Lot's eyes darted back and forth and only slowly did his gaze find Agravain's. 'Oh yes,' he breathed, and there was a horrible, mad eagerness in those words. 'She comes. Treacherous, faithless, burning. She comes. Steals breath and flesh and leaves me burning. Bitch. Slut. I'll kill her. I'll kill her!' The words turned into a long scream and Lot's whole body fell once more into the rolling, restless grip of his pain, stretched and tossed by its invisible waves.

Agravain found he was not breathing. He drew down great

swallows of air and stumbled backwards. His heels knocked against a chair he had not realized waited there behind him. He sat down hard, running both hands through his hair, unable to stop his ears against the sound of his father's agonies.

I must think clearly. I must think clearly.

But he could not. The sight and sound of his father permeated his thoughts as surely as the stench of the illness permeated the air. It left no corner to which he could retreat, no door of self that he could close off. He should shift himself, give orders for water, clean bedding, anything. But the thought of bringing back one of those shiftless, shambling, *things* that had surrounded his father was not to be born.

Better he should . . . his knife hung heavily at his side. He could feel the hilt press against his hip as another scream ripped from his father's throat. It would be murder, but that sin could be absolved. Penance, however harsh, would surely be easier than hearing one more scream.

Agravain did not know how long he sat there, suspended between awareness of his father and awareness of the knife. At times he was only angry. At other times he felt sick to his soul. It was only the fact that his breakfast had been so long ago that kept him from spilling his stomach onto the cold stone. Helplessness pressed against him like a stone against his chest, smothering breath, hope, reason.

A footstep sounded behind him. Agravain was on his feet in an instant, whirling around, ready to strike. Laurel froze on the spot, until he could see that it was her. He drew himself up at once, tight and still.

'With your permission, my lord,' Laurel said evenly. 'I would minister to the king, your father.'

'Yes. Yes.' Agravain was shaking. This was inexcusable. Intolerable. He cast about for something to focus his scattered, wayward thoughts. Laurel held a wooden basin in her hands.

'What is that?' The words came out far more sharply than he meant.

'Clean water,' replied Laurel, setting the basin beside the feeble, flickering fire. 'Nothing more.' She faced him. Her clothing was rumpled and stained, and two locks of hair had slipped unnoticed from her braids and now made white streaks across her flushed face. 'I can have beer brought, if it seems he can swallow it.'

Of course. Of course Laurel had seen to these things, and to much more by the look of her. Her hands were stained as well, and her nails freshly broken, but her demeanour was absolutely correct and courteous. She gave no hint that she was disappointed, disapproving or frightened of this place he had brought her to.

I would minister to the king, your father.

'If you please,' Agravain said, stepping aside.

Laurel soaked a clean rag in the water, but as she approached the bed, Lot uttered a weak, keening sound of almost infantile dread. 'She is come. She is come!'

'No, father,' said Agravain hurrying once more to the bedside, in case . . . in case . . .

He could not make himself finish the thought, but neither could he stand for his father, even in his madness to be so mistaken. 'This is the Lady Laurel. My wife.'

That word stopped his father cold, opening his eyes once more. 'Wife?' Lot repeated, stunned. 'You bring a wife here?'

'Yes, Sire.'

In the space of a heartbeat, his father's hand shot out, seizing Agravain's tunic and hauling him down.

'Fool!' Lot shrieked. Flecks of spittle landed on Agravain's cheeks and mouth. 'Fool! She'll break you! She'll go over to that other one!'

Which was enough to make Agravain forget these words

were spoken in pain and illness. He dug his fingers hard into his father's wrist, amazed that a hand so strong could feel so fragile. He could snap it in two without effort. He remembered himself in time, and drew back, holding his father's hand at bay as if it were some enemy's blade.

'Father, I will not permit you to speak so of her.' No one, not even this man, this king, would deny Laurel her due.

He felt Lot's hand relax in slow, jerking stages. When Agravain dared let go, his father's arm thudded onto the bed beside him like a dead thing.

'I burn, Agravain,' Lot whispered

'I know, father.' Agravain looked up at Laurel where she waited, mute and still, but not placid, nor stupefied. Readiness showed in her stance, her watchful silence, even in the way her fists knotted about the rag she held. Ready to run, or fight, whatever was needed. She waited only to see what she would be called to do.

When Lot's arm fell, she relaxed a little, readying herself for a different kind of fight. She walked forward, without hesitation, and began to sponge down Lot's face and arms with soft, competent motions. She moistened his parched lips and dribbled water into his mouth. All this Lot bore without moving, only breathing hard against the pain that surely accompanied each touch. Laurel moved down his body, carefully examining his swollen belly and legs, returning for more water.

But something was wrong. She was doing so little. Surely there was something more she could do. Was she satisfying herself on some point? Making sure of something?

Even as Agravain thought this, Laurel returned the rag to the basin and straightened up.

'My lord, we must move him.'

'No,' snapped Agravain.

Laurel's face hardened, and he thought he saw a trace of

disappointment. That hit him harder than he would have believed possible.

'He cannot stay here,' she pointed out calmly. 'Our people must be fed and housed, and this is the only place where there is room enough.'

This is the king's hall! Agravain wanted to shout. *He will not be driven from it!*

But she was right. If there had been space in his thoughts, he would have seen that for himself. Hours ago.

'The chapel is prepared to receive the king,' she went on more gently. Agravain found that he was grateful for the sympathy while resenting her insinuation that he needed it – and then resenting himself for his irrationality.

'You and I will do it,' Agravain said. It was the only concession he found himself able to offer. 'No one else will touch him.'

It was not, however, enough for Laurel. 'We cannot move him smoothly alone. Let Pedair and Ruadh help.'

This too he would have seen, if he could see, if he could think. *God and Christ, what is happening to me?* He stood here beside his father, home at last, to wage for a war he had known for ten years was coming, and in the space of a few hours, reason had utterly deserted him.

Him, but not his wife, who stood before him, waiting for him to return to his senses.

'Very well.'

Laurel curtsied with stiff formality, and went to summon the chieftains, who, he was certain, she had waiting just outside the doors.

'Thank you,' he whispered to her back. 'My wife.'

As gentle as they tried to be, Lot screamed. It was horrible to hear. He twisted and writhed and though they had tried to swaddle him, he soon worked his way free. Twice, Laurel almost lost her grip on the sling. It seemed a mile across the court to the chapel where they could at last lay him down on the bedstead piled high with furs and fleeces.

As soon as Lot laid down, Laurel dismissed Pedair and Ruadh with soft orders to see to the feeding and quartering of the men, making sure they knew to go to Byrd and Ceana for all they needed. She hoped to spare Agravain the necessity of making more decisions at this moment. He could not seem to tear his eyes away from his father, but neither did he seem able to move. He just stood there, his hands opening and closing on nothing. Laurel shut the chapel door behind the two chieftains. When she turned, it was to see Agravain slumped down on a three-legged stool beside his father's head.

The second basin of clean water and the towel she had ordered from Byrd were laid on a small table beside the full pot and plate from the kitchen. She picked up a crockery jug from the floor and uncorked it, pouring an ample measure of its contents into the water and another into a wooden cup.

'What is that?' snapped Agravain, showing that he was not nearly so absorbed as she had taken him to be.

'Water of life,' she replied as she recorked the jug. 'How the vultures here missed it, I do not know. It will help him sleep, if he can swallow it. It is also said to be good for fever and diseases of the skin.' She sighed, brushing her hair back from her face. 'I wish Lynet were here. She is the one with the physician's training.'

But as her shadow brushed the king's bed, Lot shrank back, one hand flailing out as he tried to both fight, and find help. 'Keep them away. Keep them away!'

Laurel stopped in mid-stride. Agravain caught his father's searching hand, holding it strongly. 'No one comes here, father. You are thirsty. Let me help you to drink.' He beckoned to Laurel. She stretched her arm out to its utmost to put the cup into his hand, then retreated to the table.

Agravain cradled Lot's head with one hand and tipped the cup up to his cracked lips. Lot choked and coughed and his eyes rolled. Laurel thought for sure he would refuse the draught, but Agravain kept at the task until the cup was emptied. Lot's eyelids fluttered and he struggled weakly. This time Agravain let him go. In a short while, his father's eyes closed, and his mouth went slack, letting out a hoarse, shallow snore.

Agravain looked at the empty cup in his hand, as if puzzled by its meaning. Laurel brought the jug forward and poured in a good measure of the liquor. Agravain raised the cup in wordless salute and drank it off in two swallows.

'There is food, my lord. Will you eat?'

He looked up at her, and Laurel saw mute the gratitude in his eyes. 'An' I thank you, my lady.'

It was poor enough stuff; pottage with egg and milk stirred in, a small cake of salted oats, and a new cheese. But Agravain had been to war and surely survived on worse. He ate hungrily, and without complaint. Sitting on his low stool, the prince of Gododdin emptied his bowl, mopping the last of the pottage up with the oat cake. When he was finished, she took the bowl from him and set it aside.

'You have done much work today, my wife. I thank you.'

'It was no more than my duty, my husband.'

'It was, and I know it, and I do thank you for it.'

For the first time in all that long, dreadful day, Laurel saw Agravain's real self behind his tired eyes. Alone for this moment, with none but his sleeping father as witness, she went to him and took up his hand.

'I am sorry that you have had such a homecoming.'

He shook his head. The lines on his face had deepened, and he looked older than he should, but not beaten. He was coming to an understanding of his circumstances, accepting the reality around him so that he could begin to change it.

'Truth be told, I am glad it was no worse.' Some of his comfortable irony returned as he spoke, and the constriction in Laurel's breast eased upon hearing it. 'There are sound walls at least, and now there are men for defence.' He glanced keenly up at her. 'I trust you have eaten?'

'Before I came here.'

'Good. Good.' He scrubbed at his face, as if trying to rub off the beard that had so lately grown to cover his chin. He looked towards the closed door, distracted by some thought.

'Will you go to the hall, my lord?' she suggested carefully. 'Pedair and Ruadh would be glad of your counsel, and to learn your plans. I will keep watch here.'

Agravain glanced again at the door, and for once, Laurel found herself able to read his thoughts plainly. She offered him escape from this heavy bedside watch, but it was cowardly and selfish to even desire such escape. Yet, it was true he did need to confer with the chieftains, who must now become the captains for his dishevelled fortress and all the strange assortment of workmen and followers he had brought up with them.

'I will return before dark,' he said as he rose. He bowed to her, and Laurel answered with a deep curtsey. With one last glance of silent gratitude, Agravain left her there.

Laurel sighed, wiping her hands needlessly on her makeshift apron, grateful he had chosen to go. It would do him no good to see what must come next. Her jaw hardened, and Laurel stripped the coverings away from King Lot.

His legs were horrible. Swollen with gross humours, oozing clear matter and pus, they scarcely looked like human limbs anymore. His arms were covered in sores, and there was no chance of his back being any better.

Breathing through her mouth to keep out some of the stench, and praying that the whisky draught would hold him in its grip just a little longer, Laurel took her knife from its sheath and as quickly as she could, she began to cut Lot's clothing from his body.

She practically had to chip the stiff cloth away. The king had been left in his own filth for so long, there was hardly a patch of whole skin on him. Laurel had tended men after battle, and had seen her share of noisome infections, but nothing like this. Her heart split between pity and disgust.

Clamping down hard on both, she soaked her white cloth in the whisky water, and with the cold determination that is the shield of a nurse, she began to wash Lot clean.

She hurt him. She could not help it, and even in his sleep, he moaned and twisted. She managed to dribble some extra whisky down his throat to keep him asleep, but it was a long, slow, uneasy process. Twice Jen and Byrd came to the door, as they had been instructed to do, and twice they had to be sent for more water and more towels.

When it was finished, Laurel was exhausted. None of her other labours had taken so much from her body or spirit. In the end, she had to call all three of her waiting women to her. She simply did not have the strength to turn and lift the weight of the dying king.

But they had made a difference. The stench was all but gone now. Some of the scabs had begun to dry cleanly, and the grime was gone from the raised flesh. His legs and brow were at least a little cooler to the touch. By dint of brute force more than anything else, they had managed to swaddle Lot's waist in clean linen, followed by one of the lengths of striped wool so loved by the people of this country. She washed his hair and beard, and sent Cait running for a comb so that she might put them in order, wishing she dared find a knife sharp enough to shave him with. But she no longer trusted her tired hands to stay steady enough for such work.

He was in all likelihood no better than he had been, but

probably he was more comfortable, and his repose had at least some semblance of dignity now.

'Now, Cait,' she said, dropping the last rag onto the pile. 'You and Jen go get that chest, you know the one, and bring it here. Byrd . . .' She blinked her eyes, suddenly finding it difficult to focus on the wizened woman. 'Byrd, clean this away.' She gestured feebly at the rags and basins.

Her women scattered to obey. Alone again, Laurel paced to the doorway. She opened it a little, admitting the fresh breezes with their scents of earth and salt. The shadows were long and the sky deep blue. It would be night soon, and the night would bring thicker shadows and darker dangers. The raven was waiting out there, just past the walls, she was sure, waiting to aid its mistress however she might command.

'I remember,' said a voice behind her.

Laurel whirled around, thinking for one incredulous moment she heard Agravain. But there was no one save Lot on his bed. His eyes were wide open and clear, but they did not see her. Not truly.

'I remember when you first came to me here. I remember I worried how you would feel, so far from your home. I took you – do you remember? – up to Jove's Seat above us, so you could see the whole country you were queen of now.'

He was struggling to get his hands under himself, so he could push himself upright. Laurel crossed the room again, meaning to hold him back down, but he caught her hand before she touched him. His eyes stared ahead, blind to all but the memory unreeling itself before him.

'I remember how the wind spread your black hair out, that hair you would gift to all our children, and how your eyes shone as you looked on the river and the firth and all the valley spread out below us. I remember how you saw the beauty of it then, and how beautiful you were in seeing it.'

Laurel's throat tightened and tears pricked at the back of

her eyes. She could see it clearly, this moment from so long ago, before the war that had taken his wife and broken him. It was heart-wrenching to think of Lot as a young man, proud and brave, of that other queen, the one whose hair was as black as hers was white, who had consented to ally with him.

Who had loved him. Who had dragged him and his heirs into this war because of the blood in her veins.

'You should rest, my lord,' Laurel murmured, and began to draw her hand back.

But he held tight. 'Stay,' he whispered, and Laurel was not certain whether he spoke to his memory of Morgause, or to her. 'Stay here a little.'

A tear brimmed in her eye and fell, trickling slowly down her cheek. 'If it is what you wish.'

'Just a little,' he murmured. 'Just a little.'

She held still, sitting beside him, letting him hold her hand, letting it bring the memories of other times so long gone, while the world outside slowly darkened. Night and shadows. Night and cold creeping in on the stealthy wind's back, wrapping them both in its own blanket, setting skin and nerve on edge. This was not a wind that came to serve, but to spy, to bring the scent of danger to season the smoke from the fading coals.

'I must build up the fire, Your Majesty.' As gently as she could, she extricated her hand from his. He let her go this time. His eyes had closed. Perhaps he slept again. Good. It would give him a measure of peace. It would be brief enough.

She added fuel to the fire built in the corner beside the door. There was no place for a proper hearth. Perhaps she should tell Byrd to bring in some braziers, if there were any. She shoved her stray locks back under her veil. There was so much to do. She was sure she was forgetting a thousand things. She wanted to rest, to sleep as she prayed Lot was doing even while he stirred uneasily in his clean bed.

Then, Cait and Jen pushed open the doors, struggling to carry the weighty chest between them. She gestured for them to set it down in the corner. They obeyed and straightened, both of them swaying on their feet. Both waited, ready to obey the next order, and both, plainly, prayed it wouldn't come.

Laurel let out a long sigh. 'Very well, my women. You've done more than enough today. I want you to go into Ceana. Make sure she shows you someplace clean and safe where you can spend the night.'

Sparrow Jen looked like she might faint with relief. But Cait mustered herself enough to put up feeble protest. 'But, Mistress, you . . .'

'My place is here tonight. Go both of you. I will send for you if there is need.'

Jen curtsied, plainly a little guilty at her own eagerness to be gone. Cait followed suit, more slowly. Laurel inclined her head, and stayed where she was until they had both closed the doors behind them.

Laurel let out a long sigh. Then, slowly, like an old woman, she knelt in front of the chest, opened the lock, crossed herself, and removed the treasure she had coerced from Queen Guinevere.

'Now, Your Majesty, perhaps I can give you one night of peace.'

She had hoped to lay the scabbard across the threshold, but there was no way for it to be done without the relic being plainly visible. So, as carefully as she could, she slid it under the king's makeshift bed, and drew the coverings down to hide the gleaming silk. Then, she pulled a packet of the precious salt she had taken from the stores out of her girdle and walked three times sunward around the bed, tracing a salt circle around the king. Salt was life and cleanliness. It was a gift of the sea, and one of the most ancient protections there was. She had no idea if it would do any good against Morgaine, but it surely would not hurt.

And its presence would help disguise whatever blessing the scabbard might confer on this night.

When she had finished Laurel straightened and pressed her palm to her forehead. Weariness dizzied her.

Perhaps she cannot come here. This was once a holy place. Perhaps that is enough.

But that was only wishful thinking. Laurel went to the doors and pushed them open, standing to face the night, as if testing her own nerve.

The courtyard was settling down for the night. The cows and oxen snorted as they lowered themselves to their knees, and the horses in their stables called their good-nights to one another. The wind was filled with the homely smells of animals and straw. She could make out a glimmer of light from the doors of the hall. She hoped Ceana was managing the service all right. She wanted to be there, instructing, helping, but it was more important that she be here, so Agravain could attend to other matters. They could lose no time in establishing his authority with those who remained in the hall, and with those who had followed him so far.

The clouds scudded across the moonless sky. The salt scent of the wind was muted and the air was chilled. Rain soon, coming in over the land in all likelihood. Staring into the summer's dark, all that she had seen, all that Morgaine had forced her to see, rose before her mind's eye; the battle and slaughter, Agravain dead beside his brother, Lynet on her knees, her bloody hands raised to the sky, and herself . . . not there.

You were gone to the sea years before.

Movement startled her and Laurel gripped the doorway. A silhouette moved between the shadows of the animals and

their keepers. A heartbeat's worth of looking told her it was
Agravain.

*Oh, husband, why couldn't you have been selfish this once? Why
did you come here to face this?*

But she knew the answer. He could not do otherwise and
be himself.

Why did you come to see me fail before her? This last thought
was soft and treacherous, it prowled the back of her mind
as she straightened up and schooled her face into an expression of calm and dignity.

Agravain himself looked anything but dignified as he
stepped into the firelight. His hair was rumpled and his eyes
hollowed, but the weariness of soul she had seen before was
not there.

'How is he?' asked Agravain.

'As you see,' Laurel stepped aside. 'He sleeps peacefully.'

'Praise be.' Agravain murmured as he moved to his father's
bedside. He looked down, taking the full measure of the man
lying there in a stupor of whisky and approaching death.
King Lot twitched in his sleep, and his son's shoulders
twitched in answer.

'I have seen the miracle you worked in that blighted hall,
Laurel,' Agravain said softly. 'I cannot thank you enough.'

Laurel at first thought to make some appropriately modest
remark, but Agravain raised his head to look at her over his
shoulder. In the face of such feeling as she saw there, mere
courtesy would be an insult.

'I could not have wished for such help, or from such a
steady source.' Agravain spoke softly, as he always did when
he was at his most serious. Laurel felt a lump in her throat,
made half of need, and half of fear.

You are gone to the sea years since. What had made her desert
him? What truth was there in that lie? It must be a lie, surely
it was a lie.

But what truth made her believe she could do such a thing?

Haltingly, almost bashfully, Agravain stretched out his arm. Laurel crossed the chapel swiftly and let herself be folded into his hard embrace. For a moment, they did nothing else but stand there, each taking strength and comfort from the other's presence, reminding themselves that what lay within their hearts was real. New and confused it might be, but it was real nonetheless.

That moment was all they were granted. The wind blew hard once, laying the fire's flame sideways and sending the wisps of salt skittering like snow across the floor.

Lot's eyes flew open.

'She comes.'

FOURTEEN

Lot moaned and twisted, pain flushing his sallow skin. Laurel reached at once for the whisky jug. Lot tossed back and forth, and saw Agravain standing there. His head lifted, the muscles of his neck straining like cords to the breaking point.

'Traitor! Bastard traitor!' He cried. 'You bring her here! I should have known! You who did this!'

'No . . .' began Agravain, frozen by the ferocity of his father's sudden attack.

'Kill you with my own hands!' Lot grappled with the coverings. 'Should have killed you all! You're her children! Every one of you, hers!'

Something was coming. The suspicious, tentative wind changed, turned sour as if wafting over the midden. It grew heavy and cloying, a storm wind to bring crows and other creatures of ill omen.

Laurel forgot the whisky jug and instead moved to bar the door.

'Leave us,' said Agravain.

Laurel did not even turn. 'No.'

'You have no part in this. Go now.'

A poor time to try that lie, my husband. Did he feel it? The sick heaviness in the wind. Did he understand it was already too late?

Lot . . .

It was the softest of whispers, audible to her blood, rather than her ears. It was the voice she had heard before, but more silken now, and far, far sweeter. Beguiling, seductive, welcoming. Behind her, she felt the king straining towards it. With her own heightened awareness, Laurel could discern his fear, his yearning, his mad, desperate hope that this once, just this once, it truly was Morgause.

Lot, my lover, I am here.

But no. He knew now and his whole face collapsed into fear. It was not her. Again. Ever. It was the other one. The other one.

'No!' screamed the king. 'I beg you! Hide me!' He clutched at Agravain's hand. 'Mercy!'

They've laid a fresh bed for us. How pretty . . .

Agravain could not hear the voice. One glance at him was enough to see that. He could not hear this cold parody of a lover's greeting that made his father scream in agony.

Laurel stood square on the threshold, barring the entrance with her body and her anger. The witchlights burned in her soul, and they let her see.

A soft, silver wraith slipped through the night. Laurel knew it from the cold, skilled touch of its power. She knew the knife-sharp edge to its smile and its black eyes. Oh, she knew those black eyes.

I will not cower before you. I've seen your power. I know your power. I may fall before it, but I will not fear it. I will not fear you.

Blood and slaughter. Gareth dead. Agravain dead. Bronze and black triumphant. Lynet bloody to her elbows as she was the day their father died . . .

I will not run from you, though you walk with Death himself.

'Morgaine,' said Laurel aloud. 'You will not enter here.'

Ahhhh! It was the sigh of the winter wind through dead grasses. *You're still here, despite all. You are welcome to me, Laurel Carnbrea.*

'This is not your place. You can give no welcome here.'

'No, no. Let her in. You bitch!' screamed Lot, and Morgaine laughed, sweet and silvery as the king shuddered, groaning with helpless, twisted lust. 'My love, my love, I am here! Oh, God, it hurts. No . . .'

'She's here?' demanded Agravain. 'Why can I not see her?'

You are wrong, Laurel Carnbrea. This is my place. I have ruled here ten years and more. Behind you lies my true lover and you cannot keep me from him.

'Show yourself, Morgaine!' bellowed Agravain to thin air.

Poor Agravain. Always the ill-favoured one. You must close your eyes very tightly.

Again, Laurel felt the sick, slick touch of that knife-edged lover's smile. It slid across her thoughts, drawing the blood of her mind.

She held her ground. 'Your taunts are nothing, Morgaine. You will not enter.'

The king wept, he lashed out with his fists, and Morgaine just smiled. He screamed and groaned and begged, begged for her to stop, begged for her not to stop.

Promise me lover. Promise me you are mine, always mine . . . You want this . . . all this, which I have given to a hundred men while I was yours, a hundred men a hundred times . . . Poor Lot, are you crying for me? I am here, I am here, I will never leave you . . . you will never be without me . . .

He was hard. He was writhing in his bed, strangling on his pain and his lust, and Morgaine smiled.

'Morgause! No, Morgause!'

Let me give you what you want, lover, let me tell you how I learned so many neat little tricks . . . Let your son watch us both. He's mine next . . .

With all the might of will and power she held in her blood, Laurel seized the wind that circled them, wrenching it to her, heavy with the sea's salt as it was. It was a wind, it was a winding sheet, and a net. It was hers, and she cast it over the phantom that tormented the king, a rope, a noose, a shroud, to hold tight, to bind . . .

Morgaine just laughed, and it was only the wind once more, and Laurel stood gaping. That moment's surprise was all Morgaine needed. She lashed out, mind to mind, spirit to spirit, and the blow sent the world spinning.

And Laurel was gone, far gone, as far and as easily as she had been before. The chapel and all it held were phantoms, none more real than any other. She stood in the midst of that other battle, there but not there. She could feel nothing. She could only see the fighting, the blood, the chaos. There was no way through it. The ground held her. The air held her. She had no volition. That was all gone. She could only see the bronze knight aim his slashing blade at Agravain's throat. She knew him now. It was Lancelot, Lancelot du Lac. How had this happened?

Agravain fell, and in the smoke that hung over the battle-field she saw that the horror that would be, had been, was now, was as real as Lot's dying beside her, could not be undone. There was blood, blood everywhere, and now Lynet was dead too. Their house was torn apart and she stood behind a wall of ice. She had no flesh, no substance, she had given it all away, let it be cast away on the wind, for she had gone to the sea, gone back to the sea, back to the sea . . .

'NO!'

Agravain. His hands were on her shoulders, and suddenly Laurel was herself again. The stone around her was solid once more, her flesh her own.

The wind died. The fire shot up straight again. The

nightmare battle was gone. Laurel stood in the chapel once more, Morgaine's silvered shape before her and Agravain, as whole and solid as the stones around them.

Lot screamed as if he had been struck, and Morgaine's shade wavered, and grew strangely more solid, her face contorted for a moment in utter fury before she smoothed the look away.

She must smooth it away, for Agravain could see his enemy now. He focused on her utterly, moving to stand before Laurel, drawing his knife and balancing himself on the balls of his feet.

'No, Morgaine,' he said. 'It will not be so easy.'

Won't it? Morgaine spread her arms wide. *You want me, Agravain? Come closer. Kill me if you can. It is what you want. Come here.*

It was what he wanted. It thrummed through him, a lust as great and as painful as anything Lot felt. Agravain stepped forward. The one he hated and feared, the one who unmanned his father, stole his mother, cursed the whole of his family, robbed him of his life . . . she stood before him. Another step forward. She opened her arms, welcoming him in.

Bewitching him. His hands went limp at his sides

No!

Laurel made herself move. It took all she had; will and blood and strength, flesh and soul. She felt as if she tore herself out from the roots she did not know held her. The knife fell from Agravain's dangling fingers, and she caught it up by the blade.

It sliced into her flesh, drawing blood to spatter on the ring of salt she had drawn so carefully. The pain burned but she did not let go. Instead, she grasped Agravain's hand.

Again, the world grew clearer, and the pain diminished. Agravain shook his head, trying to clear the glamour from him. He pulled away instinctively, but Laurel held him tight. She needed him. He was the anchor here. With him she could be present and not forget herself.

With him, she could remember what was and was not true.

'Leave here, Morgaine,' croaked Laurel. 'You are not here. You never have been.'

You are wrong. The voice was dangerous, sharp as the knife that cut into Laurel's fingers. *I am all that is real here. You are the phantom, the lost, the coward who ran.*

She heard the voice, the draining, droning words, but they could not reach past the blood and iron, the touch of Agravain's hand and the sacred at her back. The sacred. *This is not your house, any more than it is mine, Morgaine.*

Laurel drew herself up. 'In God's name I banish you!' she shouted. 'By Jesus, Mary and Joseph, I cast you from this holy place!'

Oh no, Laurel. No such names here. Not between such as we. You are as like to be banished by them as me.

But Morgaine's shade was not smiling any more, nor did she move. The silver seduction was gone from her voice, and the laughter. She felt it. Laurel knew she did, the final wall before her, the power that was beyond either of them, the power that was life and hope itself. It was called down by the sacred names and willing sacrifice of life and self demanded for love's sake.

'But you will go,' said Laurel, her voice soft, low and dangerous. She felt it too. A power that that came not from the wind, not from the salt, but from the stone. She had known it was there, and she held it by right of blood. Blood to blood, her fresh blood on the stones, the sacrifice of Agravain's family going back the long generations, the other blood, shed so long ago with an open heart.

Words came, true words this time, the right words. 'You

are nothing but illusion brought here on a whim. Blood and bone prevent you. Heart and will and right prevent you. Begone from here, evil dream. Son and stone bar your door. Begone!'

Morgaine smiled and glided forward. Laurel raised the knife, cold iron wet with her salt blood, and slowly, like the chill before death, Morgaine closed her phantom hand over the blade.

We will finish this, you and I, little child, but it is not worth it now. I have what I need here. Go back to your man and wait.

The strength drained from Laurel's hand, and her arm fell, limp. The knife slipped from her fingers, clattering to the chapel's floor.

But Morgaine was gone. Gone.

On his bed, Lot groaned once, and fell back like a discarded puppet.

Laurel stood there, pain throbbing in her hand, rooted once more to the spot, but this time because she feared if she moved she would fall.

'She is gone?' whispered Agravain, amazed.

Laurel nodded. 'Can you not feel it?'

'Dimly. Lady . . .'

Laurel swayed. Her stomach heaved. 'I need to sit down.'

Agravain caught up the wooden stool at once, shoving it into place.

'What has she done to you?'

'Nothing. I am only tired.' Supporting herself on his arm, she sank onto the stool, ashamed of her own weakness, and of the fear in her heart as Agravain knelt at her side and turned her hand over, looking at the wound. She saw the blood smeared on her hand but felt nothing of it. The pain was real enough, but the hand, the blood, these were distant things, and she could not understand what they might have to do with her.

Agravain picked up one of the rags left beside the basin and wrapped the cut, quickly and efficiently, as a soldier would know how to do.

'What did you do to her?' he asked quietly.

Laurel swallowed, a new and unnamable fear shuddering through her at the cold in his voice. 'She was only a shadow, and I knew that. I just . . . reminded her of it.'

His gaze was hard. 'It was nothing so simple.'

'No.'

He was going to question her further. Laurel was not certain she could bear his cold gaze while she answered. She was already so cold. Cold as death, cold as shadows and the wind that prowled suspiciously about her ankles like a dog not certain of where its master was.

But from behind there came a low, weak, but infinitely welcome sound. 'Agravain . . .'

Lot. King Lot, speaking clearly, though weighted down by an exhaustion that was beyond anything Laurel felt now. Agravain went to him at once, kneeling by the bed so his father could turn his head and look at him more easily.

'Agravain,' said Lot again, reaching up. His eyes shone clear, his voice was steady.

Agravain caught his hand. 'Father.'

'She is gone, Agravain.'

'And will not return. It is over.'

'Yes. Over.' Lot kicked once. 'Good. That's good.' His gaze drifted a moment to where Laurel sat, tears burning in her own eyes. 'This is your wife, I think?'

'Yes, father. This is Laurel.'

Laurel rose, and gave Lot her hand. His grasp was so light it felt more like a glove lying in her uninjured palm than a man's hand.

'Good. Good,' Lot murmured, seeing her clearly for the first time. *And the last time.* 'Keep her close, Agravain,' murmured Lot urgently. 'Do not let her leave you. It is when you let them go, the darkness comes.'

Laurel could not leave Agravain to make the answer to that. The pain in her husband's eyes was past bearing. 'Rest, Your Majesty,' she said. 'It is nearly morning.'

But Lot would not rest. Perhaps he'd had too much of it. Perhaps he felt what was coming. 'You know, don't you?' he said, clutching her hand, weak as a child, but trying to hold on. 'You have eyes like my Geraint. Like my wife. You know why she was able to enter here.'

You do not have to do this, Majesty. 'She entered by deceit. It is her way.'

'Because I wanted her. I knew what she was, what she made me and I still *wanted* her.'

'Do not think on it any more. It is over.'

'She never died. Not really. I kept hoping . . .' He squeezed his eyes shut.

At last Agravain found his voice. He gently pressed his father's hand between both his own. 'Rest, father.'

'Yes,' Lot nodded, his eyelids drooping. 'There is nothing else now. Forgive me, my son. I leave you only ruin.'

Another man would have denied this, murmured some comforting lie. Not so Agravain. 'I forgive you,' he said quietly.

Lot breathed a few harsh, ragged breaths, trying to muster the last of his strength. His fingers twitched against Laurel's palm. 'Take my blessing, both of you. Poor thing that it is . . . I . . . I hurt, Agravain.'

'It will be over soon.'

Lot's eyes opened once more to gaze on his son, and there appeared over his face a look of pure trust, of utter innocence.

'Yes,' Lot murmured. 'Yes.'

His eyes closed, finally peaceful, all the ravages of pain

and madness wiped away as his frame sagged down, no breath of life left to fill it.

With his son holding his hand, Lot, King of Gododdin, died.

Laurel staggered back to the chapel doors. Once more she pushed them open and stood blinking in the light of dawn.

She filled her lungs with the sweet morning air. 'Lot is dead!' she cried out. 'God save King Lot!

'Long live King Agravain!'

And from the high walls, her cry echoed back, caught up by a dozen throats, a score, a hundred.

'God save King Lot! Long live King Agravain!'

'Long live King Agravain!'

In her own pavilion, the smoke of her brazier mingling with her misted breath, Morgaine rose slowly from her bed. No smile lightened her visage. Pain throbbed in her head and in the joints of her hands. She stumbled towards the brazier and nearly fell, catching herself on the table, rattling the wine jar there.

'How is it possible?' she whispered to the dim morning light. 'How is it *possible*!'

Laurel Carnbrea was not that strong. Morgaine had the girl's measure from their previous engagements. She had no learning, no gift of sacrifice or need. Laurel could not have held her back, not if she had drained all the blood in her veins and shouted out the whole panoply of saints in the great cathedral of Rome itself.

Morgaine's fingers curled into talons, digging into the splintering wood. She wanted to stand straight, but she was not certain her knees would hold her. The weakness was humiliating, and it fuelled her anger.

How? How did she keep him from me? How did she drive me

out? She is not that strong! Morgaine slammed her hand down. The jar rattled, turned and toppled onto the ground, spilling out the red wine like blood into the dirt. Morgaine found herself staring at it, her breath high and harsh against her throat.

Omen, whispered an unwelcome, long-buried voice in her mind. A child's mischievous voice in her ear. *It's an omen for you, sister.*

Slowly, Morgaine realized what lay underneath her anger. It had been so long, she was slow to understand.

Fear. Morgaine, the Sleepless One, the Goddess, the Fey. She was afraid.

Afraid of an untutored child who had the gall to stand before her in her ignorance and aid a bastard, a murderer and the child of a murderer.

Who had stood before her with an ordinary knife, and a little blood, and a name or two, and had driven her away from her vengeance.

She wanted to scream, to run out beneath the morning sky and call down the storm wind and the ravens, and all else in her power. It was not possible. It was not *permissible* that this misbegotten creature should keep her from what was hers by right of blood and vengeance.

Morgaine held herself still. With the strength of a well-trained will, she forced her breathing to slow. She would not act in anger. That way led to defeat. She would do nothing without forethought.

Moving slowly and deliberately, Morgaine picked up the fallen jar and reclaimed its lid. She set it once more on the table.

The action steadied her. The spilled wine had already soaked into the damp earth, leaving only a vague odour behind. Morgaine turned. One step at a time, she crossed to her chair. She sat, smoothing her skirts. Her distaff and spindle lay in her workbasket. She picked them up and let the spindle drop. The wool prickled at her fingers as it twisted. The rhythm of it, as familiar as the pulse of the blood in her veins, gave order to her thoughts, calling them back from anger and from fear.

Laurel Carnbrea did not have the strength to do what had been done. So, there were two possibilities. Either she had not done it, or she had help.

Breathing deeply, Morgaine closed her eyes to draw her concentration into herself. She searched her senses. Her fingers spun the wool and her mind spun her thoughts, binding them tightly, making a smooth, strong thread of them that would not break.

Had there been another there? A presence, a spirit or a fey? No. She had felt nothing. There had been Agravain, and Laurel, and Lot, poor Lot lying there wanting her so badly and that creature keeping her back.

It was not the *bucca-gwidden* who aided Laurel. So great a spirit could not have entered that place without Morgaine sensing it.

Now that her mind had calmed she could consider the possibilities without flinching. Even so, the next came only slowly, and her hands faltered in her work.

Was it Morgause? Reaching down through her son? The tie of blood is strong. Blood and bone prevent you, the little girl said.

The idea of Agravain accepting any aid from the invisible countries was laughable.

Not so. He is her son, and he did bind himself knowingly to this other.

Riddle me. Riddle me. Morgaine's hands found the trick of the thread again, pulling and twisting, measuring the weight of the spindle as it turned. *Did I neglect to believe you would come prepared for all aspects of this war?*

No. I did not believe your preparations would be effective. Ah, my sister. She turned her smile northwards. *You can be proud of your son, Morgause. Cold he may be, but he is not blind. Indeed, he may see the most clearly of them all.*

Very well. Morgaine set her jaw. *If Laurel did not have an ally, what aided her?*

She must know. She must know. If Laurel was able to work her will effectively over the invisible . . . then there was danger that Mordred's forces might be defeated in this war, and if that happened . . .

The thread snapped off sharply between Morgaine's fingers, and the spindle thudded to the ground. Morgaine did not even look down to it.

It cannot happen. She can raise the whole of the sea against me and it will not be enough!

Why then this fear that shook her? Why this anger that would not relent and let her think?

She closed her eyes again, swallowing, forcing herself to breathe. For a moment she thought to call Mordred to her, but what would she tell him? That she feared to be alone? That she had retreated from one small sortie, and it left her trembling like a leaf in an autumn gale?

She laid her distaff in her lap. It was cold. She was cold. The damp snaked through her skin and left her hands aching. There would be rain soon. She was hungry. Where were her women? There should be food here, and wine to replace what was spilled.

Why am I alone?

She pressed her brow against her palm. *Stop this. Stop this. You are alone because you bid them leave you. Because you could not work as you must while someone watched you. Nor is your work done.*

Which was true, but that truth sent a fresh wave of exhaustion and anger through her. She forced it away from her. She must think. She must consider clearly. She did not have the strength or the clarity of mind now to send her spirit walking again. She could not risk becoming lost while she travelled in that way. But there were other ways.

With the merest flicker of a thought, she touched a small mind, dark and restless, mischievous and ready for flight, for the hunt. She showed him the bulk of the great rock, the square, unnatural shape of the fortress squatting on top of it.

Always ready for sport, the raven launched itself. Morgaine felt the play of the wind through her feathers, the joy of flight, of the hunt, pouring through his mind. The wind above the great rock was tricky: warm and cold, weak and strong, its currents required great skill and the raven laughed for the delight of it.

What do you see, little brother?

I see nothing.

No. She pushed the raven's mind, pushed its sight. It could see, it must see, it carried her spirit's vision. It was so close now . . .

But the raven only croaked, voicing its pain and displeasure as it wheeled on the wind. It saw nothing. There was nothing to see.

Somehow, Morgaine's vision had been blinded.

Son and stone bar your doo. . . She does not have the strength!

Her binding to the raven snapped as suddenly and violently as the thread had in her fingers. She gasped at the pain of it and for a moment could only sit, dazed and blinking in her dim pavilion.

Slowly, so slowly, she gathered her spilled and scattered thoughts together.

Very well. Very well. The child thought herself protected behind her walls. She thought she had sheltered her man with her paltry words and her little workings. But what was hidden could be found, and whatever thing she had brought with her to loan her such power . . . that could be taken.

Once more, Morgaine called to her raven. *Little brother, I have an errand for you. I need you to find our friend, little brother. I have a message.*

FIFTEEN

'My lady . . . Your Majesty?'

Laurel whirled around, spoon clutched in her hand as if it were a sword. Pedair stood there, looking awkward in his bright formal clothing of leather jerkin and trailing cloak of beaver pelts.

'What is it?' She did not want to sound cross, but the truth of the matter was, she had awakened with the sun, and already felt overwhelmed by the day. It was three days since Lot's death and today at last they would hold both his funeral and Agravain's ascencion. There was barely enough food to go around, even though, thanks to the arrival of so many women in the train of Agravain's army, there were finally enough hands to prepare and serve it. Byrd, Cait and Jen were doing their best to supervise, but despite all their work of the day before, chaos still threatened the hall. To add to this, the knowledge that the king's death brought war loomed over them all as heavy as storm clouds.

She did not feel like a queen. She was stirring thin gruel over an uneven fire because every other hand was either busy clearing away the detritus of the hundred souls who had slept the night in the great hall or was busy shovelling out the stores. She was hot, and annoyed, and worried that one more thing would go wrong. That they would not find enough cups to give all the new arrivals proper welcome. That the whisky and milk could not be stretched far enough to give each a swallow. That her silk would be stained despite the thick overdress she wore, and she would look like a slovenly serving woman when she must stand in her dignity beside Agravain today. That someone else who did not relish the idea of actually working to serve their new lord had crept away and left some vital task undone.

Pedair must have seen at least some of this, because he shifted his weight from one foot to the other, looking more like a nervous boy than the sire of a clan. 'The folk have come to view King Lot and make their oaths. They wait at the gate. My lord – His Majesty – is in the chapel and has told myself and Ruadh to not disturb him.'

Laurel closed her eyes briefly, gathering her patience for what must have been the thousandth time that morning. She was in truth not surprised to hear this. Agravain had risen from their bed before the sun had risen in the sky, waving her back when she had made to follow him.

'Very well.' Laurel set the spoon back in the kettle. 'Byrd! Byrd!'

Through the milling bodies, she saw the old woman giving orders to a cluster of amused young men who carried away a board that had recently served as a table. The sound of her name made her crane her neck, causing her to look for a moment very much like her namesake. When she saw it was Laurel who called, she hurried over, looking far more spry and alert than Laurel felt.

'Go find Jen and Cait.' She drew off her overdress, revealing the gown of blue silk she had worn on her wedding day. She handed the coarse garment to Byrd. 'We need the welcome cups brought to the gate. They are to greet all

comers in our name. Make sure everyone takes a cup, and
if anyone refuses or is shorted, you are to come get me at
once.'

'Yes, Majesty.' Byrd bobbed a quick curtsey and scuttled
off once more.

Thank God for her, sighed Laurel. 'Lord Pedair, find Lord
Ruadh. Lead all concerned to the yard before the chapel.
Wait for my knock, then open the doors. I will go speak with
the king.'

The king. It sounded so strange. She had called him by so
many names now: Sir Agravain, my lord, husband, that one
more should not make any difference. But this one did, for
it made her queen, on a throne that was even more uneasy
than the one she had abdicated.

It made a difference because today was the day they would
find out if this title would be acknowledged by those who
were not his own men.

Outside the hall, the yard teemed with life and activity.
Half-a-dozen makeshift forges had been set up. The din of
hammering set her ears ringing, and the hot metal left its
tang in her mouth. Horses waited to be shod. Carpenters
worked with adzes, hammers and axes, fastening gears and
bolts and ropes to great timber beams. Soldiers worked with
their whetstones and their leather rags. Devi, wearing a tunic
of white wool belted with white leather, was arguing with an
ancient whose hands were stained grey and white with ash
and grease.

Those who saw her made brief obeisance, and went straight
back to their tasks. She in turn waved to them in barest
acknowledgement. Din Eityn would not pause to mourn the
loss of its king. This was Agravain's order. The war was on
its way. They would be ready to meet it.

The chapel's doors had been shut tight. She took a deep
breath and climbed the stairs. Laurel had spent much of the

day before in this place, washing King Lot's body and
preparing it for burial with such poor perfumes as Din Eityn
and her dower chests had to offer. There was, thankfully,
enough linen to make a proper, though plain, shroud. Ros
had been sent yesterday to sail down the coast to the
monastery of St. Joseph so that a cleric could be brought to
perform the rites of Christian burial.

Softly, Laurel opened the door. Inside the chapel was cool
and dim, the air filled with the scents of old perfume and
new smoke.

Agravain stood before the altar, his arms outstretched, his
head bowed. He held his attitude of prayer like a statue,
never tiring, making no sound.

She could see Lot's bier where it stretched between
Agravain and the altar. They had laid the corpse on a bed of
green broom, yarrow and willow. The fire was gone, and
proper lamps now supplied what light and warmth there was
in the chapel.

Agravain had changed that morning. This was no man of
the city, not anymore. This was a king in this northern land.
The wide gold torque armoured his throat as much as it
decorated him. The same might be said for the cuffs of gold
on his wrists. A cloak made of black bearskin covered the
shoulders of his saffron wedding tunic. His tightly laced trews
were also black. His only concession to what he had been
was that he had not forsaken his good boots for the sandals
the other men wore.

Laurel entered the chapel, crossing herself as she did.
Agravain did not look up at the sound of her step or the
rustle of her dress. She walked softly to stand at his right
side, so that he could become aware of her when he was
ready.

To her shame, Laurel found herself looking at the fragrant
bier to see if it had been disturbed. Excalibur's scabbard lay

hidden among the greenery, protection for Lot until the priest could come and lay the armouring of grace around his corpse. Ros would not be back for two more days, at the earliest. For those two days, the old king must lie in honour here, and it would be very like Morgaine to try to make use of him to torment Agravain.

Beside her, Agravain's mouth moved. 'Amen,' he breathed. 'Amen. Amen.'

He crossed himself and Laurel did the same. But he did not lift his face to her. He contemplated his father's shrouded form with his heavily-lidded eyes. Whatever thoughts occupied him, they drew his face into the familiar, tight lines of his carefully controlled bitterness.

'My lord,' said Laurel gently. 'The men have come. It is time.'

But he did not seem to hear her. 'I thought I knew how it would be,' he murmured instead. 'I thought I knew what I must do, what I must become. I was wrong. I did not even know how much had been stolen from me.' He lifted his hand, watching how it shook. 'Why do I tremble now, Laurel? What is this that seizes me?'

'It is only grief, my husband.'

His mouth twitched, trying to form his thin smile and failing. 'I had thought I had finished with grieving for my father long ago.'

'You saw him again, you saw that you were right. You knew all along that the man still waited beneath the madness. You grieve for the years lost to that man.'

'My brothers still do not know what he did for us.'

'You will tell them when this is over.'

'When this is over.' Agravain repeated with the lightest laugh. Then he threw his head back, his face suddenly contorted with the strength of his anger. 'God rot these sorceries!' he cried out, a child's bewilderment beneath the grinding fury. 'How can Heaven be called merciful when it leaves such witchery to torment the world!'

Laurel made no answer to this. Being who she was, what could she say?

Agravain drew one more shuddering breath, clenching his fists tightly in his attempt to control himself. 'I'm sorry, my lady.'

Laurel shook her head. 'You think I do not understand. I watched my heritage nearly destroy my sister. I watched it bring Morgaine down on my home like a plague to kill father and brother, and tempt me to betrayal. It made my people look blackly at me. It drove me from the throne I had been given, and away from my home in the end.

'Oh no, my lord, I understand your feeling very well.'

He gazed at her silently. With every breath, his face softened, the harsh lines smoothing and fading, showing the man, rather than the knight or the king.

Emotion flooded into Laurel's breast so quickly she could barely breathe for the flood of it. 'I have never known what you see when you look at me like that.'

He turned completely towards her. She could feel his warmth, smell the scent of him. He touched her veiled hair softly, drawing his hand down to her cheek, just grazing her skin.

'Beauty,' he said. 'I see beauty, and a haven that I never believed my soul would find.'

She thought he might kiss her then. She saw the desire for it in the depths of his eyes. But instead, he stepped past her. 'I have . . . I suppose it is a gift for you. I don't know why I brought it in here . . . Perhaps I needed some blessing for this.'

He opened a lumpish package of soft leather which had been laying on one of the small tables and drew forth the gleaming contents.

It was a crown. A delicate circlet wrought of silver and sapphires. The craftsman had fashioned dozens of glistening ribbons to frame the midnight blue stones, the smallest of which was the size of her fingernail.

'It was my father's marriage gift to my mother,' said Agravain turning the beautiful thing over in his hands. Memory made his voice distant. 'It is yours now. I am sorry there are no more worthy hands than mine to place it on your brow.'

'Your hands are most worthy,' she answered. She had not paused to think there might be a real crown for her head in this place of stone and scarcity, and certainly not one so rich.

'We will do this in the great hall, as it should be.' Agravain folded the leather around the circlet again. 'And now, it is time I ceased this self-indulgence. You have come to call me to my duty.'

She inclined her head, straightening her shoulders and putting on the mask of dignity that had served her so well up to this time. 'If you are ready, Your Majesty.'

'I am.'

'Then let us begin.'

Laurel moved to the chapel doors and hesitated, listening. Outside, she heard the rumble and murmur of voices outside. She knocked three times, and then took her place beside Agravain at the foot of the bier.

The chapel doors open. Pedair and Ruadh entered, solemn and dignified, attired in fine woollens and rich furs, with Cait, Jen and ancient Byrd right behind. They had found a drummer, and they walked to the slow, steady beat. An ancient man who might have been Byrd's older brother walked with the drummer. His voice rang out high and clear as he called to heaven above, for blessing, for peace, for forgiveness.

For all to witness that King Lot was dead.

With drum and song circling about them, Laurel nodded to her women. They lifted the white linen shroud with careful hands and folded it aside, exposing Lot's resting corpse to the flickering lamplight.

Devi, clad in white, was the next to enter the chapel, and behind him came the men of Gododdin.

It was not only the folk who had their holdings at the foot of the rock, but those who had been travelling this way for days, since Pedair and Ruadh were able to send out word that Agravain had indeed returned to Din Eityn. They came to get a look at Lot's heir, to speak with him and determine what sort of man he had become away down in Camelot. They walked in slow procession to see that it was indeed their king laid upon the bier. They saw he had been treated with honour, that his sword lay at his side, and the wealth of kingship decked his wrists, hands and throat. They saw that merciful death had erased the madness from him.

Then each one of them turned their eyes to Agravain, and to her. This was no time for words of any sort. In silence these men with their hard, weathered faces, their long beards and moustaches, their gold and bronze ornaments and cloaks of striped woollens took their measure. They looked Agravain up and down with eyes the colour of earth or mud or sky. They had to satisfy themselves that he was a whole man, and that he could indeed be the son of Lot. Whatever the shade of their eyes, however young or old, their expressions were all the same. In each face waited doubt worn deep by too many years of uncertainty.

Agravain did not flinch from a single one of them, but returned calm strength to all those men now stood in silence before him. He marked each of them, noting the ornaments, sigils and tattoos that surely told what valley or clan they came from, measuring each of them as they measured him.

Laurel wished she felt half so calm as Agravain seemed. This was a necessary part of the ceremony, and she should be used to being on display by now. But it still chafed at her. The awareness of the hidden scabbard, the approaching army, and the poor showing her house was making unnerved her. Perfume and smoke, and the smells of sweat, earth and leather crowded the small room and prevented fresh air from reaching her, despite the open doors. The beating of the great drum echoed her heart and disordered her thoughts. The steady drone of the singer's doleful hymn vibrated through her bones. Here was all the solemnity and dignity of death, but here was all the fear and distraction of it as well.

But there was nothing to do but stand and be still, and try to match Agravain's cool expression until the last of Gododdin's men had satisfied themselves that Lot was dead, and that Agravain was alive.

When the last man had made his respects to the corpse, and made his stony inspection of Agravain, Jen and Cait covered the body again. Ruadh would stand guard here, with the hymn singer and the drummer, watching over his king in death as he had in life. Byrd gestured urgently to Cait, who took up the crown beneath its loose wrappings, and then took her place with Jen and Squire Devi in front of Laurel and Agravain so that they might not walk unescorted into their own hall.

Out in the yard, the work went on unabated. By the time they reached the bottom of the chapel steps, the smith's ringing hammers drowned out the mourning drum. The shouts of the men assembling the strange engines of war, the whickering of the horses and the lowing of the oxen overrode the lonely hymn.

It was wrong. The whole of Din Eityn should have stopped, not for a moment, but for days, to make solemn notice of Lot's passing, and then to allow Agravain to ascend the throne with all due honour and homage. Messengers should have been sent to the approaching enemy, asking for time so that all ceremonies could be properly observed. It could not be done. She knew that. But she still wished for it, and could not silence that wish. The right order of things was violated by this unseemly haste.

And Laurel knew after looking in all those weary, earthen eyes, she was not the only one who felt this way.

Laurel and Agravain and their company reached the great hall, and the crowd parted slowly for them, making an aisle for their small procession. Laurel kept her gaze focused on Pedair's back. Let them stare.

There was no dais in the hall. There was only a chair, carved from oak that had gone dark with age. Generations of use had worn its arms smooth and had polished the carvings of ribbons, wolves, cattle and warriors until they shone like silk.

Across the chair's arms lay a spear. Its tip was white bone, and its shaft carved with more signs and sigils than Laurel could read. The kings of Gododdin wore no crowns, Agravain had told her. This spear was the true sigil of kingship in this place.

But Agravain did not take it up. That was Pedair's place in this ceremony. Agravain stood behind Pedair, while Laurel stationed herself at his right hand with Cait and Jen behind her.

Pedair lifted the spear reverently, and raised it high over his head, turning so that all could see. The men of Gododdin closed their ranks, watching in silence.

'Here stands Agravain *mach* Lot *mach* Lulach!' cried Pedair, his old man's voice sounding thin in the cavernous hall. 'If any man is not satisfied he is a whole man of true lineage, let him speak!'

A rustling of wool. A cough. The sound of heavy breathing,

and in the distance the tinny ring of the hammers heard through wood and stone, but no word was raised.

'Here stands Agravain *mach* Lot *mach* Lulach. If any man is not satisfied as to his right to bear the name of his fathers, let him speak!'

Three score pairs of eyes watched them. Hard eyes that had seen the ravages of war and nature, and all the hardships that could be visited on a people. Men who starved and fought in the winter and feasted in the summer, who knew flood and illness, sun and joy, and had not broken. They looked at Agravain, weighing and measuring his lean form and his unflinching expression. They measured him against themselves, and against their fathers and their heroes. They measured him also against Agravain's own father, who, for all they knew, had broken down and fallen into the depths.

'Here stands Agravain *mach* Lot *mach* Lulach. If any man is not satisfied as to his right to claim the seat and the spear of his fathers, let him speak!'

Laurel could not breathe. Her lungs seized tight within her. Her blood had turned sluggish in her veins, and her heart beat as heavy as the funeral drum. The moment stretched out. Surely it had already been long enough. It must end, but it did not end, and they all stared at Agravain like the stranger he was, and the hammers rang in the courtyard, reminding them all he had moved with too much haste.

But no word was raised. Pedair turned and knelt down before Agravain, holding out the spear of kings. Agravain wrapped his long hand around it and lifted it, holding it high. There was no roar of approval, but there rose from the men of Gododdin a bass rumble; a recognition that what happened here was right and just. Laurel found she could breathe again.

Pedair bowed his head, and placed his hand over his heart.

'My king,' he said. 'I beg the right to be the first to swear my fealty to you. My soul and self are yours, to do with as you see fit.'

For the first time, Agravain's cool expression flickered. His eyes brightened the smallest amount.

'Rise up, Pedair who has served so faithfully.' Laurel doubted any but she and Pedair heard the tremor in his voice. 'Take your place at my side, as you stood at my father's.'

Pedair did as he was bid, and again, the bass rumble of approval lifted from the gathering. This too was as it should be.

A man stepped out of the gathering. He was like an elm tree, tall and gnarled by weather and time. His moustaches hung down to his chest. His brown eyes were keen, and his hard face showed his relief clearly, as he too knelt at Agravain's feet, laying his right hand over his heart in salute, and his left upon the spear.

'My king. I am Kolad *mach* Kade. I speak here for the men of the Red Stone, and I do swear my fealty to you. My soul and self, and all that I hold are yours to do with as you see fit.'

Agravain nodded. 'The men of the Red Stone are well known for their courage and their honour. Rise up, Kolad *mach* Kade, and be welcome.'

With Kolad's oath, the dam broke, and the others came forward. Some chiefs came alone. Others stood with their sons or brothers at their sides. All swore fealty; hand upon heart, hand upon the spear of kings. They spoke warmly, and hope shone in their eyes more strongly as they saw their oaths acknowledged by this man who bore himself with so much pride. Laurel's heart swelled with her own pride, and her own relief.

Then, up stepped a young man alone. He looked to be Agravain's match for years. His face was tight, controlling some deeply felt emotion. His beard and moustaches were sparse, but his auburn hair was long, and he wore it in two braids down his back. His eyes were green as the sky during the sea's worst storms. He knelt as the others had, and laid his right hand over his heart, but when he stretched his left hand out to the spear, he hesitated.

'No,' he said, and he stood, backing away. 'No. I will not swear fealty here.'

'The time for debate is over, Bryce *mach* Deuchan!' cried Pedair, stepping forward. 'If you had doubts as to His Majesty's claim, you should have spoken at the right time!'

'I have no doubts as to the claim made here,' replied the man, Bryce, calmly. 'I am certain that here stands the son of King Lot, and that he is a whole man and that the right of inheritance is his.' He looked at Agravain as he spoke. He did not blink or falter. He did not raise his voice. He did not need to. The hall had gone absolutely silent. Even the distant ringing of hammers had fallen away.

'But I ask you, men of Gododdin, what will be gained by placing the son of such a father over us all? This is Arthur's man, and Lot's son. The one has ignored our straits, the other languished for years in madness and waste while we were left to make our own way, without protection, without judgment or intervention.' Until then, he had spoken to Agravain and Pedair. Now, he swung around and addressed Gododdin's men. 'I say the rights of these kings are forfeit, for they did not hear the pleas and petitions of those over whom the right had been given. I say we owe them no oath and no allegiance. I say that had they desired such from us, they should have come before and restored the peace and justice that was theirs to give and hold!'

Laurel's breath caught in her throat, and it seemed as if the stones shifted beneath her. But Agravain was not moved. He had been expecting something like this, she realized, and unlike her, he had not let his guard down. Like the warrior he was, he had held himself ready until his opponent had shown himself.

'I hear your rebuke, Bryce *mach* Deuchan,' Agravain answered coldly. 'It is well spoken, and it is not without worth. But I ask you this: where were these pleas and petitions?'

This took Bryce aback, and for a moment, Laurel thought he might laugh out loud. 'The men of Gododdin for ten years have lifted their voices.'

Agravain raised his brows. 'Have they?' he asked in mock surprise. 'For those ten years I and my brothers have been at Camelot. There was not a chieftain in all these lands who did not know that. We went there obedient to the command of our father, and not once in those ten years has a man of Gododdin come to any of us.

'If you wished to speak of right, of justice, why have you waited so long, Bryce? Why wait for the moment when Lot is dead and the spear passes to an unknown hand? Why wait for the time of greatest weakness to make your fine speech about the rights of the ruler and the ruled?'

Murmurs of approval rippled from the assembled men, and a lone chuckle from near the back. Bryce folded his arms. 'I came to witness the actions of a king, not to hear a scholar mincing words.' But this sounded petulant, childish, and his words only glanced off Agravain.

'Then you shall witness the actions of a king,' Agravain answered calmly. 'And so shall all men here.

'Gododdin, an army is coming. It is on the move, now. You all know this, and you came here in part to learn what would be done in the face of it. You looked to find a gathering of soldiers and knights. Instead you have seen strange engines being built in the yard, and strangers' hands at work upon them, broken men, half men, ancient men. You have smelled sulphur as well as the honest scents of the forge. And you wonder if what you do is right.

'Let me tell you what I know of this army. It outnumbers us five to one, at the very least. Its ranks include the Dal Riata and the Picts, and they do not mean to leave a man among us standing. We cannot take our lesson from the bear or the boar and stand to face our foe sure of our strength. But we can take our lesson from the hawk, which hovers silently, waiting for the moment its prey relaxes to strike, and from the wolf which stalks and watches and waits until it is ready to attack.

'The engines my men build are strange to our eyes, but would not have been to our grandfathers'. It was such engines that allowed the Romans to take this rock from our fathers.'

This raised a mutter of unease from the assembly. Agravain did not give it time to grow.

'The Romans took this place,' he went on. 'But they could not hold it, because it was not theirs. God would not permit their hold over this place of ours. Now, once again, an invader comes. They come from the west, and deceit is in their vanguard. They think to play upon our pride and tempt us into a fight we cannot win.

'But we will not be fooled. We will not fight with strong arms alone. We will fight with the cunning our grand-fathers bequeathed us, using the lessons from the history of our people. We will take the tools from those old thieves and turn them against the new, and we will hold, for this place is ours, by right, by blood and by the unbending will of God.'

This was what Arthur could not match; the soul-deep pride of place; the understanding that this single stretch of stone was like no other. It was here that the blood and bone, story and history of all the generations lay. That was the cord of sympathy that bound Agravain tightly to these men.

Arthur had severed that tie in himself to become an emperor, and Gawain had done the same. But not Agravain.

Nowhere and nothing was more important to him than this one place.

Bryce did not move. He stood, turned half towards Agravain, half towards the men of Gododdin, who watched him now, waiting to see how he would respond.

Bryce nodded once. 'Well spoken, King Agravain,' he acknowledged. 'But it is only one way. If we fight this war, the loss to all standing here will be great. It will be greatest to those who have given their oath, for with your defeat they lose their honour with their blood.'

Bryce smiled, sharp and grim. 'But why should we make war at all?' He spread his arms wide, making the words ring against the stones. 'Why should we not treat with those who come this way? The word of the men of the north and west is as sound as that of Arthur and of Lot. Their kinship with us is as close, if not closer, than that of the men from further south, and their power is as fair. Their quarrel is not truly with us, but with Arthur. Why should we not let them pass us by and leave our fields, our cattle and our people un-molested?'

No one moved to answer the question, not one voice lifted itself in either agreement or dissent. But Bryce was not prepared to wait until someone did make an answer. His needle-sharp gaze flickered to Laurel, and Laurel felt fear touch the back of her neck. She saw what he meant to say in the curl of his lips and the cold gleam in his eye.

'And why, should we permit another sorceress of the Dumonii to hold sway over our land and king?'

There it was. Spoken aloud in the great hall, and the stirring and the murmuring answered it. The tension in the air thickened. Many here wished to hear the answer to this question, and, surely, there were as many who expected a poor answer as hoped for a sound one.

Over the beating of her heart, Laurel heard Byrd suck in

a sudden breath. 'Her doing,' the old dame murmured. 'Should have known.'

Agravain's cold anger brushed Laurel's skin, but she could not permit him to make this answer.

She stepped forward, unafraid, closer to the assembly, closer to Bryce, whose smile faded with each step of her approach.

'I am Laurel Carnbrea, the Lady of Cambryn,' said Laurel. 'I am kindred to Queen Guinevere. It was at the request of King Arthur and Queen Guinevere that I came in marriage to King Agravain. It is beyond me to bring dishonour to this marriage, or to his person. If it is my presence that stands between the men of Gododdin and this fight, then I will remove it immediately.'

She faced Agravain, dropping at once to her knees, head bowed and both hands over her heart, for it would not have been seemly for a woman to lay her hand on the warrior's symbol. 'I am Laurel Carnbrea, the Lady of Cambryn, wife to Agravain of Gododdin, and I do swear my fealty to you. My soul and self, and all that I hold, are yours to do with as you see fit.'

She lifted her eyes to Agravain, and saw a crowd of emotions there: anger, relief, pride, and love. Oh yes, hidden, unspoken, but most definitely she saw love there and her heart constricted.

Now she saw that Cait stood just a little behind him, holding out the crown of silver and sapphires. Agravain took it into his hands, and set it gently on Laurel's brow.

'And may God bless the wearer and the wearing.' Agravain reached down and raised her up, putting her at his right hand.

'So you have heard the oath of my queen,' said Agravain evenly. He spoke over Bryce's head, to the waiting assembly 'And now you shall hear mine. I swear before God Almighty and Jesus Christ Our Saviour that all I do, from this day until the day I die, will be for the strength, the honour and the preservation of this land of Gododdin. No king, no emperor, no force under Heaven will change this.' He lowered his eyes and met Bryce's gaze. Bryce's smile was gone, and there was only anger shining in his storm-green eyes. 'You have heard my oath, Bryce *mach* Deuchan. You have heard that of my wife and queen. What oath do we hear from you?'

They stood like that, facing each other as if they stood alone, Agravain strong, and absolutely assured, Bryce trying to shore himself up with his anger and his righteousness.

To her, it was no surprise that Bryce shrank in on himself and took a step backwards.

'I will take no oath in this den of wolves!' Bryce shouted. Turning on his heel, he marched from the hall.

One man followed him out. Then, another stumped after him, trailing a pair of sons who looked nervously over their shoulders at the remaining company. A third man humphed, wavered, and then he too walked out.

But that was all. Three men and two boys, no more, and not one who had taken the oath of fealty.

Agravain did not permit minds to linger over those who had left, nor over what they had said. 'There should be a feast at this time,' he admitted. 'But our enemies will not wait while we fulfil that ritual. My lords and chiefs, you must come sit with me so that we may discuss our resources and our plans. All others, you shall be made as welcome as my house is able. When peace and safety are ours, we will feast in celebration. Not before.'

The growl that answered was a low and dangerous rumble. It was the sound of approaching thunder, and yet there was clearly approval in it. The assembly dissolved, the chiefs giving orders to their followers and their sons. These took their leave, while their lords moved towards the throne. Laurel feeling keenly the new weight of the crown circling her brow, turned to the duties of lady and hostess. Food and drink, the laying of the tables and the filling of cups. These were all her arena. Outside, the sound of the armourer's hammers rang once more.

That was Agravain's concern now. Her concern was as it had been when she laid down last night and rose this morning. The food. Every hand that was not turned to the work of arms must be turned to the provision of food, and that work must begin at once. Starving men could not fight. An empty fortress could not hold, though it had the finest weapons in the world.

As soon as she was able, Laurel retreated to the kitchens and the dairy. The mistress there had rallied ten lean, brown huntsmen. Every one of them had bright eyes and clever hands. These hunters all boasted of their prowess with net, snare and arrow, but when she spoke plainly to them about the amount of game required, they blanched. To their credit, under the hard eye of Dame Ceana, they rallied and faced the facts.

She gave them cider to drink and a small jug of whisky to carry down with them. These were paltry gifts, but necessary. Din Eityn's reputation would begin to mend on the strength of such small gifts.

Along with the food, they would need herbs too, and all the resources required for tending the wounds of war. Standing in the midst of the dairy, surrounded by crocks of milk, butter and cheese, Laurel tried to rally herself against despair. It was a list of needs that would grow longer as the days progressed, not shorter, and she could not fail, even though her feet ached and her head was spinning.

'Ceana, go make sure all things are in hand in the kitchen, and send Byrd to me here.'

Ceana made her obeisance and left. Laurel sat abruptly

down on the dairy's plain stool, glad for a moment's peace.
It was likely to be the last she would have for many days to
come. Laurel pressed her hand to her brow and felt the hard
metal of the crown she had forgotten to remove.

With a sigh, Laurel lifted the beautiful ornament from her
head. It felt so foolish to be sitting here now in her finery,
consumed with worry about quantities of meat and cheese.

She turned it over in her hands as Agravain had done,
watching the play of lights on the silver. It should have
tarnished after all this time. Agravain must have had one of
the smiths polish it. It was very like him to see to that detail,
even in the midst of all the other, more vital tasks that he
must complete now.

What had Queen Morgause felt when this beautiful thing
was placed on her head? A draught curled around Laurel's
hems, and wrapped itself around her neck. Had Lot crowned
Morgause as Agravain had crowned her?

Was Morgaine there in disguised flesh or spirit, watching
her sister, her soul brimming with its unspeakable gall?

*What would you tell me, if you were here? What would you say
I should do to help my husband, your son?*

What was it you tried and failed to do, Morgause?

The patter of Byrd's footsteps sounded on the walkway
outside, and the ancient dame hurried in, bending her knee
as far as she was able.

Laurel looked up to see that no one else lingered in the
doorway. She listened hard for a moment longer to be sure.

There was another battle that was Laurel's responsibility,
and that she did not forget.

'Byrd,' Laurel murmured. 'When Bryce spoke in the great
hall, you said it was "her doing". What is it you meant?'

'I think Your Majesty knows.' Byrd peered up into Laurel's
bewildered face. Her eyes were tiny, black and cunning. 'Look
at you,' the old woman clicked her tongue. 'Did you think

you drove her out the other night? You've been listening too hard to your own hopes.'

Byrd shuffled closer. 'Forgive me Majesty, but I will say what I know. She is still here. That was a distraction that night, so she could work her true will. That's what we saw in the hall.'

'Byrd, how . . .'

Byrd snorted. 'You think you are the only one with eyes that see?' She wagged her head heavily back and forth. 'Oh, there were plenty of us once who knew, about the black-eyed ghost in the queen's shape. I am the last.' Her mouth quirked up, finding some irony in that truth. 'I only stayed because I had nowhere else to go.'

Laurel looked again to the empty doorway. Softly, so softly that Byrd had to shuffle even closer to hear her, Laurel whispered. 'Byrd, do you know what became of Queen Morgause? How she meant to defeat Morgaine?'

'No, Majesty.' Byrd's face fell. She stood so close that Laurel could see that her black eyes were rimmed with red. 'I would that I did. No one here could answer that now. Save . . .' Her head lifted, questioning, as if she had heard her name called from a distance.

'Save what? Who?'

'No.' But Byrd did not look at her. She was seeing some other place, hearing some other voice in her mind. 'It is too much.'

'Speak, Byrd. We cannot win this war if we remain in ignorance.'

Slowly, Byrd lowered her gaze, meeting Laurel's eyes. Her own glittered, knowing and dangerous in the dim light. 'King Lot would know.'

Understanding she did not wish to possess rose in the pit of Laurel's heart. 'He is dead, Byrd.'

Byrd shrugged her crooked shoulders. 'What matter? The

oldest blood sings in you. For you, he would speak of what he sees in Death's realm.'

'I cannot do that.'

'I know,' the old woman answered simply.

'We will find another way. Morgause too can be made to speak.'

Byrd shrugged again. 'By what relic would you call her? That crown? This is a working that requires far more than figured metal.' Byrd straightened for a moment. Then, weariness overtook her and she settled again, small, bent, and so old. 'Ah. I wish this had happened when I was younger, when I could still walk these hills. But I am old, and half-blind now, and I've made too many of my own bargains . . .' She blinked rapidly, remembering where she truly was, and to whom she spoke. 'I am sorry, Majesty. You do not need my regrets now.'

Laurel waved her hand. 'It is no matter, Byrd. Go. Make sure everything's all right in the hall. I'll be along shortly.'

Byrd shuffled forward, and to Laurel's surprise, laid a light, wrinkled hand on her hair, a gesture of conciliation, and understanding. 'You'll do as you must, Laurel Carnbrea. Never fear that.'

Byrd left, and Laurel looked again at the lights that played in the crown's precious gems.

The vision took her so strongly and suddenly that Laurel had no chance to prepare. She saw a woman, saw Morgause. There was no mistaking her, for she knew the shape of her face and her form, and she saw Agravain in the depths of her blue eyes.

Morgause lifted the crown from her black, unveiled hair, and pressed it into a man's hands. That man was Lot. But not Lot as she had ever seen him. This man was broad and blunt, and as solid as the stone cliff that held Din Eityn. His hands were thick from the strength of the sinew within them.

Morgause pressed the shining crown into those hands, and it suddenly looked as fragile as a dream.

'You must hear me, Lot. If I do not return, another will come. You will know her when she does. You must tell her what you know. All of it. She will finish what I have begun.'

And Laurel was back in the dairy again, watching, aghast, as the crown slipped from her numbed hands and clattered onto the floor.

'Byrd!' she cried. 'Byrd!'

Light footsteps, more shuffling than running, sounded along the passageway, and Byrd scurried back in, the trailing ends of her head cloth flapping like wings behind her.

'What is it, Majesty?'

Laurel swallowed, trying to collect herself, and failing. Her thoughts were filled with Agravain's stern image, with the knowledge that she had already lied to him. She saw him once more as he stood beside his father's bier, heard him cursing the sorceries that had plagued his family.

She knotted her hands into fists. 'I need a bowl of water, Byrd, from the sea. I am going to ask King Lot what became of Morgause.'

She did not look up to see the smile on Byrd's face as the ancient dame made her obeisance once more. 'Yes, Majesty.'

SIXTEEN

The silence of the chapel fell over Laurel like a veil. After all
the endless noise and hurry of the preparation that filled the
outside world, it felt as if some essential element was missing
from the air.

Laurel found she was cold too, for the first time in a long,
hot day.

King Lot lay shrouded on his wilting bier. Laurel had
already sent away Ruadh and the hymn singer, telling them
she would keep vigil here for a while. They went with gratitude. The hymn singer because he was exhausted, Ruadh
because he could no longer bear to keep still in the chapel
while around him his home, and his living king, prepared
for war.

Laurel had seen little of Agravain for the past two days.
She had heard his name attached to orders, some praise and
some grumbling. Every so often, she would catch a glimpse
of him talking, usually with this captain or that group of
workers, while around them the angled, attenuated timber
frames of the war engines rose to the sound of straining ropes
and thundering hammers.

Once, she had seen him as she was hurrying across the

yard, dodging men and oxen. He had been standing high on the parapet over the cliff. He leaned on the stones, not moving, just staring out across the valley. It was not the direction from which Morgaine's army would come.

With a shudder, Laurel realized where it was he must be standing, and what he must be thinking on.

Much later, Agravain had climbed reluctantly into their bed. He was sent by Pedair, he said, who had insolently claimed his king could no longer see straight for exhaustion. She had pressed herself close to his side.

'What became of Tania?' she asked quietly.

He started at that, shifting in the darkness. 'She died. What else?'

'No, what became of her body?. Where is she buried?'

She heard him swallow, and felt him tense. 'I do not know. I went down . . . as soon as I could, with some . . . others. But her body was already gone. No one then was willing to admit they had buried her, and I cannot blame them for it.'

'It may be time to ask again.'

He lay in silence for a long time. 'When this is finished,' he whispered at last. 'When I have finally avenged her, then I will go, and I will bring her home.'

He had said nothing more, and she had not asked any further. But those words had followed her into sleep and out again. They were with her now as she stood alone beside Tania's father, and murderer.

Laurel had hesitated to the last instant. It was a dire thing, seeking to speak with the dead. It was far beyond anything she had ever done, or ever thought to do. But each time she tried to turn away she felt again the force of the vision. Everywhere she went, she heard the endless hammering and shouting. She saw the men out upon the cliffs and the pass, working until they dropped from exhaustion, getting up and working more.

The army was coming and Morgaine was already here, perhaps watching all their preparation, readying her own.

No.

So many dead. So much blood and destruction. No more. It stops here.

Mindful of where she stood, as well as what she came to do, Laurel set the basin down. She crossed herself and bowed her head.

'In nomine Patris, et Filii et Spiritus Sancti. Pater noster qui es en caelis . . .' she prayed, letting the familiar syllables play softly across her tongue. *Our Father who art in heaven . . .* It seemed most appropriate.

When she finished the pater noster, she looked again at the still figure beneath its white shroud. Even as she did, she felt the presence of her own father and brother at her shoulders, cold, expectant.

Mother Mary look down on what I do and have mercy upon it. God forgive me for disturbing this rest that should be peaceful until your Judgment Day.

Grandmother, let this work.

With a glance back to make sure she had closed the chapel doors completely, Laurel stepped up to the bier.

Since the ascension ceremony, the shroud had been wound securely around Lot's corpse. Wrestling that wrapping from about the dead man's head was an awkward and undignified process wholly unsuited to either the reverence due the remains of a king, or the atmosphere of a chapel. The only fortunate point was that as she had helped lay the corpse out she was ready for the surprising weight and chill of it. The stench was harsh, despite the careful washing they had given him and Laurel tartly cursed the priest for taking so long to come and lay Lot to his much-deserved rest. She held her breath as best she could, and tried to be gentle. It was difficult. Flesh and sinew, even bone, shifted alarmingly in her hands. Her fingers and hands shrank at the touch of the slack, too-soft clay flesh as they never had at the touch of offal or other rot.

At last she bared Lot's face and torso. The look of peace had left him and decay had set in. His skin was grey and mottled now and emitted foul air. Laurel's stomach churned. The urge to flee prodded at the back of her mind.

Laurel steeled herself. She needed what only Lot knew, if she was to keep her own vow to Agravain. She would have spoken to him in life if she could. Denied that, she must resort to older, darker means.

But she could not do this while he remained guarded. Laurel reached beneath the bier's withering greenery, searching impatiently until her hands closed around the silk-shrouded shape of the scabbard. As carefully as she could, she lifted it free, and laid it at the foot of the altar where the bier concealed it from immediate view.

Then, Laurel picked up the basin and the cloth. Six days ago she had washed him to bring him comfort. Four days ago, it was to lay him to rest. Now she must wash him a third time to bring him back to life.

A draught curled around her ankles, patient and inquiring. Laurel stepped through it, took up the cloth, dipped it in the sea water and wrung it out. The droplets made a sound like clean rain falling.

Gingerly at first, and then with more confidence, she began to dab at the king's face, washing his corrupted skin with the essence of the sea, the source of life and power, her essence, her root and protection, her channel to the world, her way. The draught stirred her hems, wrapping closer. Warning her? No warning could stop this. She needed to discover what knowledge Morgause had left with her husband.

Lot. King Lot. Lot mach *Lulach, Lot father of Tania, Gawain,*

Agravain, Geraint, Gareth. Lot husband to Morgause. Lot of Gododdin. I call you back. I call you here. You know my touch, King Lot, you know my voice. You called me daughter, now I call you back.

Laurel stretched her thoughts out from herself. It was cold, so cold. The stench of death grew stronger. She breathed it in deeply, taking its essence into herself even as she laid her own salt essence upon the corpse. Death was a yielding thing. It waited just beyond the fine membrane that was Life. Death was not a king in a crown, nor a skeleton with a scythe, nor any other figure of man's imagining. Death was a place, patient and waiting. Death was soft as the womb. It was the promised refuge. Empty and yearning, it waited to receive the weary and the weighted down.

Come back, come home, Lot of Gododdin, Lot of Din Eityn. Agravain needs you. Your kin below need you. There is danger here, Lot. You are needed.

No. Confusion filled Laurel's mind. She felt another presence fill the room, struggling, confused as a newborn babe. But this was not birth. This was not homecoming. This was too warm, too hard, too filled with blood and motion. It hurt, it hurt after the softness, the dark stillness. It burned too bright. It moved too fast.

Come back, King Lot. Your son needs you. The people you sheltered so long need you. The place you protected with body and soul needs you.

Death. Cool, soft, shapeless, completely yielding but completely binding. All encompassing, yet smaller than the eye of a needle. So much there, so many. Father here, drenched in red. Colan here, drowned and dissolved in salt that would have saved him had he but asked. Mother, mother swollen with her illness, slick with sweat, her head lolling against the pillows because she had no strength to lift it anymore. Agravain, slaughtered on the battlefield, herself lying on the shingle, half-in, half-out of the waves, reaching with one hand towards the shore . . .

No!

Lot's eyes flew open. Laurel jerked her hand back, and the corpse turned its head to face her.

No, it was not a corpse that lay before her now, but neither was it a living man. The eyes were occluded with a pearlescent sheen masking the warm brown that had been theirs in life. The jaw slipped and gaped, falling open to show the grey teeth and the slick, slack tongue.

'Laurel,' he rasped. 'Laurel, why do you do this to me?'

For a moment Laurel stood paralyzed in fear. The sound of death, for it was death, calling her seized her heart in an icy grip. *Run, run, run!* Panic thrummed through her sinews, but her own working held her in place. She had brought this soul here with her own hands. She was bound to it, and could no more leave before this thing was done than it could.

'Forgive me, Your Majesty,' she whispered. She could not have made a louder sound had she wished to. 'I need answers that you only can give.'

'I am dead, Laurel. I have neither questions nor answers.'

'But you lived once,' she reminded him, it, him. 'You know what you did then.'

'No. No more.'

Laurel clenched her fist around the cold rag. Water dripped against her skin, like a handful of tears. 'King Lot, you held for fifteen years against Morgaine the Sleepless. This is not gone from you, not yet.'

Lot did not fit this skin any more. It had changed its shape, its nature, too much, as his soul had changed. The two were no longer kin, could not knit together anymore. But power and need held them tight for this moment, and in the dimming, rotting memory that was all that was left of life. The dead king smiled. 'No, no. That remains.'

'How, Lot? How did you stand against her?'

Lot spoke again, but it was not only his harsh, breathless voice now. This time Laurel heard other voices, far older voices, dragged back from the darkness and bound up with him.

'Strength of stone. This stone, this place, this is mine. Lived and died a thousand times here. Came crawling out of the valley to the burning tree. Held the fire until I died. Born again, I held the forge to heat the stone, and died to make the bronze, and died to make the iron, and died to see the army come and died to beat them back again. Life and death and life and death and over and over and Lot is dead and Agravain lives and the rock is beneath their feet, accepting life, accepting death and God watches over all . . .'

Laurel's mouth was dry. With each word she felt herself dragged deeper, sinking further into the soft, slack darkness. She could not see, could not feel anything but the current of years, of life and death, winding around her, separating her from herself, from her own power, sinking her beneath its infinitely giving weight.

Lived and died here a thousand times . . . Strength of stone . . .

And she remembered how she had taken Agravain's hand and how all had become clear again as she faced Morgaine.

Yes. Yes. Of course. So much sacrifice poured out on this great rock to keep and hold it. The rock had accepted it all and granted the ancient blessing that could come only from earth and life itself. That blessing was strength for the sons and daughters of this place. Bound up and bolstered by the blood of the greater sacrifice which she had brought here.

Lot had never left this place, never slept a night anywhere else since Morgaine first came. He barricaded himself in here to wait for her, and so trap her though she did not know herself to be trapped. She thought she was tormenting him, torturing him for the sins of her sister, but he was the one who lured her back time and again. Distracting her.

Weakening her.

It was truth, but it did Laurel little good. Her blood was not of this place, not of this unyielding rock. Her thoughts struggled, floating and sinking again in the darkness of death.

'She has a weakness? What is it?'

'Not my place. Let me go. Let me rest.'

Desperation crowded into Laurel's mind. The dark was so close, so thick. There was nothing beyond the darkness, but she must find her way out. 'She threatens your son. She is coming here now. Help me. How can she be defeated?'

'No.'

Anger stiffened Laurel, broadened her, lent her shape to hold steady. The softness curdled, slipped, rippled around her. 'You cannot leave your son to her mercy. Must he live in death for all these years as you did?'

'Never knew. Couldn't learn. Could only hold. Trapped. Alone.'

'You are not alone now. Eternity is with you. I am the one your wife told you would come. Speak, Lot. Tell me.'

'She did not . . . she never . . . she never . . .'

'What?'

'Never spoke. Never left. Never died. Not really.'

She knew those words. She had heard them before, but it seemed a long time ago, at some impossible distance, where there had been light and warmth and her eyes could see, when she was not sinking into this sick, slick, cold pool of nothingness, back beyond the thin membrane. Back when she walked in life.

'The answer is here, Lot.' The words fell clumsily from Laurel. They were wrong. Her insistence was wrong. She had the truth, it swirled around her like the wind once had. Yet it was nothing, another nothingness, so much emptiness. 'Tell me . . .'

'WHAT IN THE NAME OF GOD HAVE YOU DONE?'

The shout was like a bolt of lightning blazing into darkness. It tore through her, ripping apart death's stillness, letting all the harsh, frenetic movement of life pour in. Lot cried out once in gladness, and fell back into darkness, swallowed up, drowned, gone.

Laurel screamed, hurled suddenly backwards. Stone slammed against her back and skull. Her legs buckled under her and she slid to the cold floor, blinking in her confusion.

She was herself again. Her head spun. Her lungs heaved. She was in the chapel at Din Eityn, sprawled ridiculously on the floor. Pain blossomed at the back of her head.

Agravain, swollen in rage, stood over her.

Agravain had seized her and thrown her away from the bier, against the wall, so that she fell in this ridiculous, crumpled heap.

Why are you here? She could not speak. She did not have enough breath in her.

'I ask again,' Agravain said through his clenched teeth. 'What were you doing?'

Threw her across the room, shattered her working, sent Lot back to death, left nothing but the corpse and no answer. The corpse with its eyes sunken shut once more.

Never spoke. Never left. Never died. Not really.

Anger surged through her and brought her to her feet again. *You surely have not forgotten the part you hoped I would take in this war?*

'I have, my lord, done neither more nor less than I was bid.' Laurel instantly regretted the words. She must reason now, not accuse. What he saw . . . what she had done, was difficult to comprehend, especially when his feelings were still so raw.

Agravain seemed stunned by how straight she stood and how calmly she answered him. He walked past her to the bier. His hands shook as he reached out and clumsily, but carefully, attempted to replace the shroud. Without thinking, Laurel moved to help him.

'Stay back,' he snarled.

Laurel froze. The pain at the back of her skull throbbed sharply.

As gently as he could, Agravain smoothed down the fine linen. There was no mistaking it, however, the shroud had been disturbed. The king, his father, had been disturbed, disordered, desecrated. He stood there, leaning over the bunched and wrinkled shroud, his breathing so loud and so harsh, Laurel's own breath caught in her throat in sympathy.

'Fifteen years, he dwelt in madness and torment. For ten years he held his ground alone in hell so that his sons might live. He sacrificed all he was, all he had, hoping only that he might have some peace in the end, that at the last God's mercy would not be denied him.'

Agravain turned slowly, and Laurel's heart constricted hard to see the naked fury in his face. 'And you dragged him *back*! You forced him to serve your need. You confounded the will of God, and you denied him the only peace he could know!'

'My lord . . .' Laurel faltered.

Agravain was closed, shuttered not behind the old, bitter mistrustful walls of his self. He had gone still further, behind a wall of anger and hard righteousness.

'There was knowledge that only he had,' said Laurel, forcing herself to speak. 'Things he could tell about Morgaine that no one else could. It was the only way I could aid your victory.'

'There is no victory from such knowledge!' Agravain's voice was level, and utterly certain. 'There is only damnation and death and confusion. How could you do this?'

In the face of that furious, plaintive question Laurel had no choice but to hold her ground. 'You said you trusted me.'

'Yes, yes, I trusted you.' Agravain ran his hand through his hair. 'God forgive me.'

'Then trust me now.' Laurel took one step forward. 'Let me have but a little time . . .'

He looked at her again, and the blood ran from Laurel's heart. His face was not merely stern, but contemptuous.

'Time, my lady?' he inquired, the sneer in his voice making a mockery of the polite words. 'Time for what? To torment my father's soul further? Do you next wish to quiz my sister's bones with your ceaseless riddles? Or just my mother's? Is it your father's head you carry in those great trunks you have guarded so jealously? Perhaps I do not suit you alive as I am, and you need time to take my head, to make use of what wisdom death can bring such a fool.'

'Agravain, this is beneath you.'

'You, you witch, you necromancer, you have the *gall* to lecture me on right conduct!' His fists knotted and she remembered the raw strength of his lean arms. For a moment, Laurel was purely, physically afraid. If he struck her . . . if he beat her . . . if he killed her . . .

But he only stood there for a moment, anger drawing his face tight and sharp, his eyes as shining and hard as amber. Then, resolved, he whirled around and flung wide the chapel doors.

Outside, the harried activity of the courtyard seemed almost comic compared to what was happening within the chapel's walls.

'You! You!' Agravain shouted at two men in leather corselets.

They halted their conversation at once and came forward to kneel in front of him.

What are you doing? What do you mean by this?

'You will take Her Majesty to the gates,' said Agravain. 'And you will throw her out.'

They stared. Laurel stared, unable to comprehend what she heard.

One of the two soldiers, the younger and bolder of the pair licked his lips. 'But, Sire . . .'

'You will do as you are commanded or you will bear the whip for your insubordination.'

The soldiers bowed their heads, and rose.

'Will you come out, Majesty?' asked the one who had spoken before. He was very young, scarcely more than a youth, for all his gangly height. 'We cannot bring arms into the holy place.'

Laurel looked to Agravain. He met her gaze without hesitation, without change of his stance or expression.

'Agravain . . .' she began again. She must try. She must explain. He had to hear her.

'Go with them, or I will drag you from here myself.'

His shuttered eyes had sunken deep into the recesses of his skull, turning them black. The bones of his face pressed hard against his skin. The people outside, coming and going, had stopped, and turned to stare. At her, at him.

She could make a scene. She could shout and scream and throw herself to the floor. She could lay her hands on the altar and claim sanctuary.

But there was no protest she could make, no word or movement that would reach him and crack open those walls. She would only serve to make herself ridiculous, and that she would not do.

Laurel's hands shook. Her blood had turned to ice. Good. She needed the strength of ice to prevent her bones and sinews from collapsing under her. Her feet still seemed able to move, and they directed themselves to the chapel door without her intervention. This too was just as well, for she

needed all her concentration to keep her gaze pointed ahead
of her. She could not turn and look at Agravain. She did not
want to see the burning hatred levelled at her.

Go with them or I will drag you from here myself.

She walked down the chapel steps to stand between the
soldiers. She saw people, men, women, soldiers, workmen,
saw their mouths moving, but could hear nothing. They
should have knelt. She was the queen. Their queen. For all
of two days. But no one moved to bend their knee, or to
doff their hood. They stared. She had not stopped walking,
flanked by these two soldiers like two of the great shaggy
hounds so beloved by these people.

In the midst of the whole staring crowd, one face was
clear. Back in the shadows, beneath the wall, watching
intently, black eyes glittering, Laurel saw Byrd.

Black gaze. Round black eyes, bright and shining, red-
rimmed with age and weariness, but bright and steady. They
watched her without blinking, tracking her slow, numb
progress.

Throw her out . . . Where am I going? Din Eityn's first gate
opened before her. The men surrounding it stared. Men on
ladders ceased their hammering and stared down; confused
and dirt-smeared angels watching over her as she passed
through this earthly gate into the second circle. This place
was packed with sweating, shouting men toiling at the earthen
berms, labouring at the strange engines Agravain had caused
to be made. She walked patiently between her escorts, waiting
for this last gate to be opened. It was a little portal to the side
of the great one. It opened, and Laurel walked through into
the surprisingly green and sunny hell beyond.

She heard the solid sound of wood slamming against stone,
and the sliding of the bar into place. The wind brushed her
cheek, a mother's sympathetic touch. There were more
people before her. They popped up among the rocks and on

the sloping hillsides to see who had come down to join them. She could have lifted her head to speak to any of them, requested anything as they stared, their tools loose in their hands, their eyes too large in their heads.

But she could not speak. She had been struck dumb and cast out. The path that had been opened for her descended further, and her feet followed it without interference. She stumbled here and there, but she did not fall. There were voices, there was movement. She could not understand any of it. It was as if there were only three words left in the world.

Throw her out.

He had done so, and it was a very long way down.

Agravain stood on the chapel's steps and watched Laurel, under guard, walk away. She did not turn around. She would not. She would not turn and look at him with a plea in her eyes. She would not turn to argue, or beg.

She would not turn.

All the while he heard the voice of his father's corpse, the harsh, flat whisper of cold and fear that was like no living voice. The pain was there. The pain beyond description that he had heard before, in Merlin's shadowed hut as the grisly oracles had spoken to him.

Laurel walked through the first gate. She stood for a moment in the shadows, swaying, before she found her stride again, and walked beneath the walls. The men on duty swung the great gates shut behind her. The sound of them reverberated through the yard.

Silently the workmen began to move again, picking up their bundles, or continuing their tasks. Slowly, in a strangely muted way, hammers once again began to strike wood and metal. The oxen snorted and strained as their drivers touched them up.

Mordred's army, Morgaine's army, was a day away at best. A day away, and they were far from ready. That was the only thing that could be important right now. The red tide that clouded his vision must be made to recede.

Laurel had betrayed him. She had committed blasphemy. She was gone. That must be an end to it.

He must leave these steps, walk out into the yard. He take up his duties once again. Now. He must go now.

A movement, nearer and smaller than all the others, caught at the corner of his eye, dragging his vision around. There at his right hand stood little Byrd.

He had been in the shadow of Tania's wall when she had come to him, conferring with Devi as the winch on the great trebuchet was wound. They needed time to aim the machines. Men were already down in the valley, setting up the first of the target flags, but would they be ready in time? Their runners reported the enemy was making good time through the low hills, driving themselves hard. But the Pictish men could run for days and be as fresh as when they'd begun . . .

'Majesty!' Byrd cried, breathless from her shambling run, her eyes wide with fear. 'Majesty! You must come at once. The queen . . . in the chapel . . . the queen . . .'

Thinking some ill had befallen Laurel, he had gone at a run, to throw open the door, and see her necromancy.

Byrd, the bearer of this foul news, stood before him once again. He had not seen her approach, and he should have. But he could not see anything. The sight of Laurel walking away blocked out too much of the world around him.

Byrd's hands fidgeted with her filthy apron. 'I'm sorry, Your Majesty.'

Agravain stared at her, mute. His own hand itched. He wanted to raise it, to strike her, to beat her bloody for bringing him word as she had. For showing him that Laurel was not as he had believed her to be; as he had trusted her to be.

What the ancient dame saw in his face, Agravain did not know, but she had wit to make her obeisance and flee down the steps into the sea of activity that filled the yard.

I must move. I must get back to work.

Carefully, methodically, he shut the sight of Laurel's stricken face as she pushed herself away from the wall away, along with every word of love he had ever spoken to her. It was over and done, as dead as if it had dropped from the cliffs. He had been a fool and he had paid for it.

Oh, he had paid the bitterest price of all.

Agravain strode down the steps. He needed to speak with Devi, and with Cador. They had to begin the aiming while there was light to see by . . .

A grey-headed figure strode through the yard's hive of activity.

Pedair. Agravain cursed inwardly as he turned towards the old chieftain. Pedair's face was contorted by anger and confusion, and the effort it took to smooth them away as he planted himself foursquare in front of Agravain. 'What have you done?'

I grabbed my wife by her arms, just like Gawain did. She flew so lightly away. She drew herself up so proudly as I confronted her with her crimes.

'I ask you again, Majesty, what have you done!'

'Less than I should,' Agravain answered, noting that Pedair did not kneel.

Pedair strangled on his own words, forcing them out with difficulty. 'They say you have expelled the queen, without hearing her.'

'This is not your business, Pedair,' Agravain answered curtly. *I will permit this questioning just once, my lord.* 'We have no more time to waste.'

He pushed past Pedair, who stood stock still in his path. 'It's happened already,' the old man murmured. 'God help us all.'

Agravain stopped in mid-stride, and slowly he turned around. 'I do not understand you.'

'No, my king?' Pedair drew up his slumping shoulders. 'I will be more plain. You have not been returned for seven days, and you have already expelled your wife from this place.' He stabbed his finger toward the gates. 'Your wife, our queen, who had eyes that might have seen the workings of our greatest enemy and the power that might have worked against her.' Pedair's own eyes gleamed with the kind of desperation that could overcome men in battle when they saw death waiting for them on the top of the next hill. 'I had hoped you would be able to put up more of a fight than your father.'

Agravain stared at the old man as if he had suddenly become a stranger. He saw Pedair's crooked hands and his narrow eyes, his pinched face and his trembling shoulders hunched up like a hooded crow's.

'Do not speak of what you do not know, Pedair,' he said softly.

'Very well. I will speak only of what I do know.' If Pedair noted Agravain's barely contained fury, it did not deter him. Pedair came forward, moving in close to his king, whose coming a handful of days before had left him weak with relief. Now, Agravain could see the bitter disappointment in the old man's eyes. 'I know that by your actions we are weakened. I know that by your actions we may suspect that the madness that haunted your father has got its first claws into you . . .'

Red, red anger swamped Agravain's reason. He could barely cling to the memory that this was a friend before him.

'Pedair, use the wits I credit you with having and be silent.'

Be silent, do not force me to strike you down. Do not force me to call you traitor as well. 'You have work enough to do.'

Pedair stepped back, his body trembling as he straightened it. 'As it looks to be the last work of my life, yes, Your Majesty.' Pedair turned, without obeisance or acknowledgement, and walked away.

Agravain looked up and found the crowd staring at him again. They dropped their gazes, turning away hurriedly, but he heard the whispers, and the breath of them fanned the anger burning in him.

For Agravain, anger had always been a cold thing. It lent precision to thought and to word. It calmed his blood and made him still. He did not understand this fire in him that made him want to lash out, to scream and curse and destroy whoever or whatever was nearest at hand. It sent his frame shuddering and drove out the reason he so desperately needed.

Agravain looked towards the gate again, and saw Laurel standing in its shadow, swaying, trying to gain her stride. Not looking back.

What have I done? What have we done?

With all the strength brought by years of keeping his heart and his counsel absolutely to himself, Agravain drove down the flame in his blood. He could not quench it, but it would be contained. He had a war to win, and it must be won. Too much depended on this for him to doubt his eyes or his actions.

He strode into the crowd of his people, trying not to hear the whisper of that part of mind and self that lingered behind, gazing at the gate, whispering one word.

Laurel.

SEVENTEEN

Laurel did not know how long she walked. She only knew her path led downward, following the slope of the hill to the plain of the valley. She thought she passed clusters of houses and pens for animals. Perhaps people spoke to her. She could not hear them. She could only walk on, passing through the green and silver world like a ghost.

She felt the sun on her skin, felt the wind wrapping around her. Her sandals turned and skidded on the stones, making her stumble. She righted herself and walked on. There was only one place left for her to go.

The long shadow of the rock fell across her shoulders as she stood at last on the curving shore of the sea. Salt filled the air, stinging her throat and lungs. The setting sun turned the restless waves opaque silver and blinding gold. The sound of the waves pounded against the walls of her mind, bringing them down, releasing the flood of emotion so that the tears could run freely.

Laurel collapsed onto the salt-crusted stones, weeping out her fear and rage to the eternal sea. Unchanging, the sea rushed and roared, the tide pulling back, laying bare sand and stone. She felt its retreat in her blood, and longed to follow, to fall into her other home. She could dissolve with the foam into the living waters, be forgiven and accepted.

You are gone to the sea years since.

The burning chaos of the war spread out before her mind's eye, blotting out the silver sea. She saw again Agravain's corpse upon the bloodied earth of her home, and that sight was nowhere near so terrible as the sight of his shuttered eyes in the chapel as he sneered at her protestations and called for the guard.

And so why not go? I am bid to go and never to return. In my failure, where else is there for me? The foam crested the retreating waves before her, cool as snow, ephemeral as dreams. It wore away the world, and yet lasted no more than a moment. It was a byword for weakness that water, and yet no stone, no steel, could stand before it.

Gone to the sea, years since.

Laurel drew her knees up under her chin, huddling on the stone, watching her grandmother, her other place. She could not move. She could not go forward or back. The land's shadow crept across her flesh, stretching out past her, moving towards the sea.

After a time, she felt a change in the air behind her, a little warmth that had not been there before.

'Majesty?' said a soft voice. It took her a moment to place it.

'Bryce,' she said without turning around. She could not take her eyes from the dimming waves and their wordless roar. They did not compel, nor did they call. It was she who yearned. 'What brings you here?'

'Word from Din Eityn, Majesty. I have kin there.' He walked around into her field of vision and went carefully down onto one knee. 'Let me take you to shelter.'

The wind from the sea blew hard, whipping laces of hair back from her stinging cheeks. 'Why would you do that?'

He pulled back, honestly surprised. 'Because you have been wronged. Because I would have men know what sort of man calls himself our king.'

Slowly, she shook her head. 'No.'

Confusion flickered across Bryce's face, and wariness, like a man who felt the sands shifting beneath him. 'You say the charges are true?'

'No. But I will not go with you.'

Setting his jaw, Bryce reached out and laid his work-hardened hand over hers. The chill in her skin went too deep, and she could not feel the warmth of his touch. He spoke fervently, willing her with all his might to understand. 'This is not justice. This is madness. We cannot let another mad king take the rule over us.'

She lifted her face to him for the first time, and she knew the cold lights now shone in her eyes. He was the one who did not understand. 'And the one who brought on this madness is waiting on the other side of this night. She will not spare you, Bryce, nor any other man of this place now that you have failed her.'

He swallowed, his words lost to him. He drew his hand away from hers, as if he could no longer bear the touch of her flesh.

As if the corruption of death clung to her.

'Go back to your home, Bryce.' Laurel said turning her face once more towards the sea. 'Sharpen your sword. Either fight with Gododdin, or slit your own throat. It will be kinder than what Morgaine will do to you.'

She could hear his breathing, even over the rush and crash of the waves. She did not look at him. He had ceased to be important. Eventually, he walked away and left her sitting there in the twilight, watching the sea.

Will you do as I said? She wondered idly. He was a good man. She felt it. Agravain could use him.

Why should I care? She had no answer. She could still feel the ache against the back of her skull where she had hit the wall, could still taste the blood in her mouth where she had bitten her lip. Rage blackened her heart with its heat. She had trusted him! Had given all she had and all she was to him, and this was how he repaid her! After all they had done and seen and been, how could he think . . .

But there was something else, something shining like a broken coal, its heat making it dangerous to grasp.

Gone to the sea years since. The words Morgaine spoke over the vision of Agravain's corpse. Her future in red and black.

She is still here. Her work . . . was a distraction . . .

Laurel's head lifted. It was not her own thoughts, nor Morgaine's taunting words. That was another voice, another memory.

Byrd. Wizened, black-eyed Byrd.

Byrd convinced her to speak with Lot. Byrd laid a hand on her head just before the vision assailed her. The vision that told her it was Lot who held the one piece of knowledge she could not remain in ignorance of.

Byrd who said she made too many of her own bargains. She, her mind full of empty stores and fish and cows, had thought Byrd meant the kind of earthy bargains a woman might make with the least objectionable men around her, the sort that could help her keep her place and stay alive. Even as Byrd had spoken of the other ways, the ways that skirted the invisible countries, Laurel hadn't thought of what the true nature of those bargains might be.

And there, alone with the sun setting against her back and the sea retreating in front of her, Laurel remembered Byrd's round, red-rimmed eyes and remembered where she had seen them before.

They were the eyes of the raven who had carried her soul for Morgaine to make sport with.

Byrd was Morgaine's spy, her hand in the fortress that was held against her. When Laurel could not be defeated, Byrd had contrived to disgrace her. Byrd had told Agravain she was speaking to his father.

Byrd was still inside the fortress. Byrd now held Agravain, her husband, in the palm of her crooked hand.

Byrd had the scabbard.

Laurel was on her feet, but did not remember having moved. Her lungs strained and pulled and her ice-cold hands knotted into fists.

She must run. She must fly. She must get back to the rock and warn him, warn him . . .

And who would listen to her? She had made her own appearance of guilt with her thoughtless obedience to a false vision.

Why should I care? He banished me. He would have struck me. He betrayed me in the end. Why should I care?

Because it was not he who did these things. Because he had been used and played with as she had been, for Morgaine's games and Morgaine's hate, and Morgaine's end.

She has taken my father and my brother; she will not have my husband!

But there was only one way to gain the strength to meet this promise, and Laurel saw again the battle and the death it must bring. Even if she did not care for Agravain, going to the sea would mean she destroyed her sister, destroyed her home . . .

But it was Morgaine's vision, and it clouded her own, as it was meant to. Laurel faced the memory before her.

I am gone to the sea. I am not in this future you spin. But you are not there either. The thought moved slowly, almost sluggishly against the tide of her despair. *You did not show me your triumph. You did not show me yourself, not at Camelot, not in Din Eityn.*

If I have gone to the sea, Morgaine, where have you gone?

The moon was rising over the waters, a perfect crescent against the blue-black of the sky. It lent her enough light to see where to put her feet, as she finished making her way down to the foaming waves.

Laurel had often thought of her mother's choice. She wondered how her mother felt in that moment when she chose to take on the cloak of mortal flesh and leave the sea, to give her love to an earthly man and give life to his children. Did she know it must only be for a short time? Did she feel it was worth the sacrifice?

Laurel reached the water's edge, but she did not stop. She waded on. The waves swirled around her hems, cold and harsh.

How did one measure the worth of such a sacrifice? Christ on the Cross, soldier on the battlefield, or woman in labour, how did one measure the worth of giving of one's own life?

She did not know. She could not know. She could only choose.

Laurel waded deeper. The waves surged and sighed, pushing and pulling at her. The spray drenched her face, throat and arms. Laurel raised her hands, holding them out in supplication and in so doing she opened her soul.

The immensity of feeling staggered her: anger, wariness, sorrow and love. They dragged her spirit under, rolling it over in a flood-tide stronger than any force the physical waters might produce.

Be sure. Be sure. the waves said.

'Grandmother,' Laurel called out. 'Grandmother, *please*.'

Slowly, her blood yielded. It was as if a wall battered by the sea began to buckle, then crack. At last it crumbled apart while the flood rushed into the breach. The force of her heritage, the whole of the other, invisible world that Laurel had held at bay for so many years tumbled freely through her. Laurel cried out in pain and in shock at the wild freedom pouring through her veins.

Then, the ocean's song changed. The roar and rush dimmed, and the cresting waters slowly stilled. Flat and silver as a pond in the moonlight the ocean pooled around her knees. The silence and beauty caught her breath in her throat.

In the next heartbeat, a horse climbed from the waters.

Awkwardly, it emerged snorting and panting as if mounting a steep hillside. It stood before her, silver rivulets cascading from its gleaming black hide, and looked down at her. It shook its black mane, scattering diamond droplets everywhere, and snorted again. Its eyes were so dark they might have been holes in the great beast's head. No light of moon or star was reflected there.

'Kelpie.' Laurel breathed the word.

The creature regarded her from one black eye and stamped its heavy hoof. Laurel felt suddenly cold. She should have been brimming with relief, and gratitude that her grandmother had sent such an answer to her. She should be pouring out her thanks, but she could not. In her bones, she understood the deeper message. Where Laurel went now, she went of her own will. There was no more shelter, no more blessing from the sea. For her, there was only power, and such power as she possessed would take fully as much as it gave. She had been warned, and she had made her choice.

But where could she go, to learn what she must know? Laurel closed her eyes, stilling the tumult inside her. She had to think. She had to hear the truth, not the lies, not the fear.

She heard the voices, all the voices, all the answers she had already been given. They coursed through her mind, unknotted and rewoven with the sound of the tide and the cold touch of the moonlight.

Why didn't you kill her? . . . She never died, not really . . . I took

*you – do you remember? – up to Jove's Seat above us, so you could
see the whole country you were queen of now . . . she never died . . .
Why didn't you kill her . . . my mother vanished . . . why didn't you
kill her? . . . Stone and son prevent you . . . This stone, this place,
this is mine . . . up to Jove's Seat so you could see the whole country
you were queen of . . . Never died, not really . . .*

Why didn't you kill her?

Laurel swallowed and walked around the kelpie. The great
black beast held still while she clumsily heaved herself up
onto its bare back. The kelpie's hide was cool and smooth as
river water and the strength beneath was just as great.

Laurel knotted her cold fingers in the kelpie's wiry mane.
'Kelpie, take me to Jove's Seat.'

The kelpie snorted once and sprang forward. The rush of
icy wind, the bunch and release of the muscles beneath the
cool hide combined to form a single flowing current to carry
her away, and all Laurel could do was hold tight and pray.

Stillness came at last to Din Eityn.

Reluctantly, Agravain ordered the men to sleep. The forges
were quiet and the powerful, angular war machines waited
still in the darkness. There remained much to do to prepare
the defences. He needed to review the preparations for the
bridge, and the pass. It was still not sure that all the engines
had been correctly aimed . . .

But this battle could not be fought with his men worn
past endurance. They had more than earned this one night
of sleep. One more night before the war came on them.

Agravain stood on the parapets and willed the morning to
come. He did not want stillness. He did not want to have to
fight the fire still burning in him. He wanted to give it free
rein, let it pour out of him to overwhelm his enemies. He
did not want to stand here and burn, and think on where
and why this had come to him.

Laurel.

She would not leave him be. No matter what task he turned his hand to, no matter who he stood with, her eyes watched him, confused, betrayed, though she herself was the betrayer. She brought forth every memory of every moment they had shared to nag and whisper in the back of his mind, incessantly distracting him, and making him see again and again how she had walked away without looking back.

His hands gripped the ancient stones and he stared out into the night. It was clear and winter-cold. The crescent moon hung amid the stars like a curving silver blade. He knew where he was. He knew the feel of the stones under his hands and under his boots. He knew the sigh of the wind past the cliffs below. This was the place. He had come here once again, unknowing, or perhaps knowing far too much.

This was where Tania had died.

Oh, it was clear as moonlight that moment, after all these years. He remembered the bite of the wind against his skin. He remembered the frenzy in his father's face as he bent Tania over the stones, his fingers dug into her hair and her arm to hold her down. He remembered Gawain's fear turning him white while begging for mercy, trying to appeal to their father's honour.

He remembered himself. A youth, awash with sickened horror. Aware that he held the secret that could save her, that she had made him swear to reveal to no one.

He'd learned it a year before her death. She'd come to him in early morning, while their father and his men still sat at their meat. He was in the stables, looking over the horses that would be used for the coming journey.

'Agravain, father takes you to Rhegid tomorrow?' Tania had pale skin and raven-black hair, and blue eyes just like their mother. Like her she was usually filled with grace and confidence. Not then. As she entered the shadowed stone enclosure, she was breathless, and she looked over her shoulder. 'Will you give this letter to King Owein?' She pressed a tiny packet into his hand, a single piece of parchment, folded over and tied with red thread until it could fit into a man's palm.

He remembered looking at it, and how cold dread had run through his veins. 'Tania, what manner of letter is this?'

She'd smiled, attempting careless mirth. 'Do not ask, my brother, it is better that you do not know.'

Agravain looked up into his sister's blue eyes and saw doubt there, and fear. Tania was taller than he was still, slender but not fragile. She too had endured their mother's loss and their father's decay. But more, she had taken their mother's place as mistress of the hall. Agravain had seen how she stood between her father's wrath and her brothers. He saw the bruises on her face and arms from his blows, and burned with shame that he could not spare her.

And for all her too-intimate knowledge of their father's strength and fury she was giving him such a missive. 'Tania. You cannot be doing this. You are promised to . . .'

She cut him off, her face going cold. 'I know full well to whom I am promised, Agravain.'

'Then why?'

She laughed, a bitter sound, and hung her head. 'You think to hear me tell some besotted tale of maiden's love, don't you, my brother? Like one of Gawain's romances. Well.' She brushed a wisp of straw from her skirts, her tone and demeanour going strangely brisk. 'I fear I will disappoint. I do love him. Owein is a great man and a great king. But it is more than that. The wealth and position of his land will do us greater good when father dies than any other.'

She stepped forward and took his hand, folding it around her letter. 'You are the clever one, Agravain. You have seen the truth. I've heard it when you've tried to reason with him.' Their father. There was no need to name him. 'We are growing weaker every day. We can do nothing here while father lives. We must be ready for the time he is gone, and then you and I, Agravain, you and I together, must be ready to raise fallen Gododdin up.

'This is where it begins. There is more than one way to make a marriage, and I mean to take advantage of the law if I can. A child in my belly undoes any other bargain.' She held his closed hand in both of hers now. Her touch was cold, but steady. 'Take my letter, Agravain, please.'

His mouth had gone dry. He felt weak and far too young for this burden. 'Tania, he will kill you if he finds out.'

'Then we must see that he does not.' Her smile had been small and hard, taking no delight in conspiracy. 'It is you who will be king one day, Agravain. Let this be your first undertaking in that office.'

His first undertaking, begun in a stable and ended on this wall. Tania had scrabbled at the stones, Gawain dived for her, seeking to snatch at her sleeves and skirt where they fluttered in the breeze, but his fingertips only brushed the cloth and she fell, screaming long and high.

Gawain leaned over the parapet, calling her name again and again, until the scream was gone.

Agravain had not moved. Could not move. Strength and heart were shattered. No word, no breath, no thought was left to him.

Agravain realized his cheeks were wet. He wiped at them. He had not wanted to come here. He had been forced, by the burning within him, and by the knowledge that threatened to crack his mind in two. He felt himself reeling, reason teetering in precarious balance, and terrible understanding clinging hard against his back.

Had Laurel been up here rather than in the chapel below,

he might have done it. Might have thrown her to her death. He had been angry enough. There had been a heartbeat, more than a heartbeat, when he could have, would have done it, and called it justice.

I know that by your actions we may suspect that the madness that haunted your father has got its first claws into you.

It was Morgaine who killed her not father. It was Morgaine who killed Tania.

And who was it who moved you to betray the one secret she gave you to keep?

Never had he felt so alone, not even in the first days, when Gawain had left and Tania's corpse had not been found, and he and Gareth and Geraint had hidden in the cellars to keep out of their father's way. Then he had his brothers beside him. Then he had a purpose. He had to protect Geraint and Gareth. Now, all purpose seemed hollow, burned away by the fire that would not cease. The rage had served him well, but now he could not close it off. It tortured and tormented, as fearsome as the memories that fed it.

When will the battle come? When will Morgaine and Mordred be here? When can I draw my sword and cut free these hollow memories?

Make amends for that betrayal. For the one committed in the chapel below.

No, it was she who betrayed! She did!

I know that by your actions we may suspect that the madness that haunted your father has got its first claws into you.

It cannot be. God Almighty. Agravain lifted his eyes to Heaven. *I did right. She was . . . she had . . .*

Oh, Christ. He squeezed his eyes shut, praying from the depths of his battered soul. *Mother Mary, give me a sign. Give me succour. Please. Show me the right. I can't see anymore.*

Look then, brother.

Agravain spun around. He stared about wildly, fear and

the most painful hope strangling his breath. As he did, his eye caught movement in the moonlit yard.

Below, he saw a dark figure, little more than a shadow among shadows. Only its motion rendered it visible, and that motion was hindered by the presence of so many men camped out beneath the stars. It clearly did not want to disturb any of them, and picked a careful path to the chapel steps.

Who was going to the chapel at this hour? What could they want there? It came over Agravain that something else might be done to the king's body, some new desecration . . .

He did not pause to consider whether this was a logical thought at all. He had been driven by the whips of fear and doubt all this night, and this final scourge sent him running. Careless of his ankles or his neck, Agravain ran down the narrow steps and across the yard, stumbling over the sleeping bodies, earning curses from the men so rudely woken and not knowing by whom.

Agravain vaulted up the steps, and into the chapel, throwing the doors open wide to let the starlight pour through.

The cloaked figure whirled around, hugging its arms to its chest. The shadows clung so thickly to this place, it took even Agravain's dark-adapted eyes a moment to make out little, wizened Byrd. Ruadh, slumped against the wall, asleep on his feet, struggled to wakefulness.

'Wha . . .' Ruadh began, and horror sent his jaw slack as he realized he had fallen asleep, and that Agravain stood there with him.

But Agravain did not attend Ruadh. He only watched Byrd, as she moved to kneel, still huddling in on herself.

'What are you doing here?' Agravain spat.

'Forgive me, Majesty,' Byrd gasped. 'I only wanted to see if my lord Ruadh needed anything on his vigil. I wanted . . . to make amends if I could.' She bowed her head. 'I wished to pray for forgiveness.'

Agravain wiped at his eyes. This would not do. None of this. Pedair was more right than he knew. Madness. Replaying old wrongs, screaming at old women. What had happened to him?

His father's corpse lay shrouded in moonlight. Father would have understood exactly what was happening to him.

No. Morgaine drove him. I drove her out. I am not . . . I have not . . .

'Sire?' murmured Byrd. 'Sire, is there . . . how may I serve?'

Something wrong. Something missing. Something he was not seeing. It knocked on the walls of his mind and skittered off the edges of his thoughts. Her voice brought it back. Byrd's voice, that had summoned him to the chapel, as urgently as that other voice had called him to look down from the murderous parapet. Voices, voices, speaking secrets, speaking truths, speaking lies . . .

His own voice, croaking more harshly than any crow. 'How did you know what she meant to do?'

Byrd frowned. 'Who, Majesty?'

'My . . . the lady Laurel. How did you know she meant to desecrate my father's body?'

Byrd bowed her head, her hood falling over her face. She still held her arms tight to herself, as if praying, or huddling against the cold. 'She told me, Majesty. She had come to trust me and she said what she meant to do.' When she looked up again, her black eyes were bright, as with tears. 'I'm sorry. I should have come to you at once but I was afraid.'

Certainty rose in Agravain, a great ballooning mass buoyed by a wealth of feeling that began and ended with anger. As if from a great distance, he watched himself straighten, and take one step forward. Byrd swallowed, which set her dewlap wagging, but held her ground and her humble pose.

'You lie.'

That snapped her head up. Her round, black, red-rimmed eyes turned fearful for a moment, but for a moment only.

'No, Sire,' she said sadly. 'I was afraid. I beg your forgiveness, I . . .'

'No.' Agravain shook his head slowly. 'She would never have told you such a thing. She kept her secrets to herself.' A hundred memories flitted through him: Laurel choosing her words with great care. Laurel deep in her own thoughts, taking her own time, waiting for her moment, keeping her counsel.

Byrd had made her mistake, and she knew it. The humble, helpful mask of her countenance slipped just the tiniest amount. Agravain returned to himself with a rush. Whole again and at one with his solid flesh, his thoughts both clarified and quickened.

'She lied to us all, Majesty,' Byrd said softly. 'Forgive an old fool for believing in her.'

It was a good feint, meant to bring his mind back to Laurel's perfidy, and take his attention from what was in front of him. It might have worked, but for that tiny slip, that moment when she had to put her mask back into position.

If it had not been for Tania's voice that had come in answer to his prayer.

'Yes, there has been more than one kind of fool awake this night,' he made himself say. 'You may go.'

'Thank you, Sire.' The relief in her voice was palpable. She got up to her feet with difficulty, because she would not put her hand out to steady herself. Agravain watched her from half-lidded eyes.

'What have you there, Byrd?' he asked softly.

Byrd started. It was a moment's hesitation. It did not leave enough time for eye to blink or heart to beat.

But it left time enough for Agravain to lunge forward, to grab her skinny hand and wrench it out from under her cloak, sending the flag of white silk flying into his face.

Time enough for the scabbard to clatter to the floor.

Agravain stared. The scabbard. The moonlight lit gently on the flaking leather and battered bronze, and the long, dark stain that was black even against the old leather in the shadows. He met Byrd's gaze, words dying on his lips.

She threw back her head and she laughed, a screeching bubbling sound. She yanked her arm from his grasp with surprising strength and raised her arms wide. White silk fluttered to the floor. Ruadh dived forward, but it was too late. The woman was gone, and a black shape streaked past, cawing and rattling its wings. The raven flew unerringly for the door, and out into the night.

Leaving the men behind, gaping.

Shaking, Agravain knelt. Shaking, he crossed himself, and reached for the scabbard.

'Sire, what is it? What happened?' gasped Ruadh.

'She brought it. I told her not to, I commanded her, but she brought it.' The holy thing, the humble thing lay in his hands.

'But what . . .'

'Worth ten of the sword. He who carries it will not bleed. She brought it to this place, and laid it here.' Agravain looked up at Ruadh. 'God stood beside her while she worked, and I did not see it, Ruadh.'

Ruadh stared speechless, and crossed himself.

Agravain stood. He carried the scabbard to the altar and laid it there, then stepped back, around his father's bier. All that he had remembered, all he had thought, all he had done that hellish day came back to him with a clarity that cut through his soul.

He had been deceived by Morgaine's spy. Laurel had only

been trying to do as he himself had bid her. And she had sought the aid of Heaven to protect him, and his father.

And he had not seen. She had walked so proudly from this place, unbowed by all his words, all his violence. He was the one who had been struck down then. Struck deaf and blind.

Agravain knelt and crossed himself. He clasped his hands to his chest, and struck his breast.

Forgive me. Forgive me.

He struck again, and again, and again. Pain warmed his blood with its fire. Pain's fire burned him black and red.

Forgive me. Laurel. Tania. Laurel. God and Christ and Mother Mary. Forgive me. Laurel.

Again and again. One blow for each sight of Laurel. One blow for each wrong, for each slight, for each word heard and not believed. One blow for Arthur, and one for Gawain. A blow for Father, for Tania, for Mother. Blows for all the dead, Morgaine's dead, his dead, called back and cast aside.

Agravain beat his breast until he crumpled senseless onto the stones. It was Ruadh who caught him before his head could crack against the floor.

EIGHTEEN

It was cold.

Despite the layers of leather and wool that Mordred wore, the dew had already soaked through to his skin where he lay flat on his belly among the heather and bracken staring across the great valley that cradled his prize. Beside him, Durial shifted restlessly. His remaining captain had been against the idea of going uphill, on foot, under cover of darkness, to overlook a land they could see next to nothing of. As a reward for his protest, Mordred had made him come along. They must do whatever scouting they could, whenever they could. Their fractious allies would not hold together for any more long encampments.

Although the sky brightened steadily, he could still see precious little. Thick, patient mists filled the valley. From here, Din Eityn looked to be floating in a sea of clouds. Away on that island, Agravain *mach* Lot, King Agravain now, made his preparations to prevent Mordred's progress.

What are you about down there? Mordred's jaw worked back and forth. *You and your hundred men. What are you planning?*

He could see no spark from any fire, but he could not believe Agravain was wasting a single heartbeat's worth of daylight. Birdsong and the far distant rush of waves punctuated the still morning, and something else. Mordred strained his ears until they ached, and heard something like the faintest ringing of bells. A forge at work, hidden by mists, and perhaps by walls.

No, King Agravain was not idle.

Mordred considered. If he were the one rattling around in the shell of Din Eityn, he would station part of his host at the base of its pass. He would try to begin the battle in the broad lowland and then retreat slowly up the narrow, rocky way to the fortress. He would sell every inch of ground dearly, take as many enemy lives as possible to make maintaining a siege that much more difficult. According to the spy, Agravain had all manner of folk up and down that pass. They piled stones and dug traps for both horses and men.

No. I think we will not come to your doorstep so easily, Sir Agravain.

Agravain expected Mordred to be impatient. Expected him to go directly for Din Eityn, knowing it was weak and being eager for the prize. Yes, he was impatient, but not to the point where it clouded his judgment. He would not loose his hounds until he knew for certain what his enemy was doing.

There were only so many places where Agravain could advantageously make his stand. He must keep Din Eityn at his back to secure his retreat. Cut him off from that single safe haven, and the battle was ended.

Agravain, would, of course, know this and take precautions. Mordred's task would be to make Agravain spread himself too thin, and then to cut off that retreat before he knew it was gone.

'Well, my lord?' inquired Durial impatiently. 'Your eyes surely see farther than mine. What are we to do?'

'We divide the men into three,' replied Mordred softly,

gazing at the mists, willing them to roll apart and show him Agravain's fortification. 'One third to march along the shore and take the landings. Loot what's there. Burn the ships, if possible. It will be footwork mainly, so I think we can leave it to the Dal Riata. I'll put them in your charge. You know this country. Once the boats are dealt with, you must find the back way up over the rock. We know there's a bridge there. You must take it as quickly as you can.

'Our second host will be the main force, and will have most of the horsemen. I will lead them around east of Lucifer Hill, up the valley. Agravain will have a signal and a watchman there. Let's let him get a good look at us. We'll take the village and whatever else we find there, bring Agravain and his hundred men right down to us, thinking we're about to fall into their trap.'

Durial grunted. The plan was settling into shape in his thoughts, and he was not displeased. 'And the third?'

Mordred felt himself grin. 'This will be the task for the Pict men. They will come in from the north, climb the back of the ridge onto the pass. That's quiet work for knife and hammer. Kill the defenders, wreck whatever engines he's got stationed there. Burn them if they can. We can trap Agravain between the sea, and stone and fire. Even if they cannot hold it, they can destroy some of these careful preparations, and draw at least some men out of Din Eityn to die defending their king's retreat.'

Durial gazed out over the heavy mists toward Din Eityn, considering, seeing the plan Mordred had given him, turning it over once, and again, looking for flaws. Despite the cold numbing his face and the dew soaking through his sleeves, he did not hurry Durial. This was what he had brought the man up here for.

'What about these engines?'

'Catapults, trebuchets. Terrible, but not overwhelming. If

he wants to lob stones at us, we can always withdraw and wait, until his men are gnawing on beams for food.'

'And the lady?' Durial inquired softly. 'Where will she be?'

Durial was one of the few who would speak to him openly about the depth of his mother's role in the work they pursued.

'Where her secrets take her,' he answered. 'But I think she'll want to be with the horse, to meet Lot's son face-to-face.'

Durial nodded again thoughtfully. If there was the smallest sign of distaste in his expression, Mordred pretended not to see it, much less understand it.

'It's sound,' Durial said at last. 'It's a risk to divide your men in the face of the enemy, but in this case it may win us the day. If nothing else, it'll help keep those fools from each other's throats.'

'Well, let us get back down and tell them the news. Their wait is over. The war begins tomorrow.'

Quietly, cautiously, Mordred and his man crept back down the hillside to rejoin their force and give them the orders.

The war begins tomorrow.

'Majesty, the runner from the north is come.'

Agravain looked up from the map table he had caused to be set up in the great hall. A rangy young man came forward from the corridor. He was gasping, dew-wet and dishevelled. He – Eadan, that was his name – had been picked for his duty because all in the village agreed there was none to surpass him for speed. He made to kneel, and Agravain gestured for him to keep his feet.

'What did you see?'

The youth shook his shaggy head. 'Not much, I fear, Majesty. The mists are bad. But a host comes out of the hill, down the near bank. They'll be here by noon, at the latest.'

'Down the shore?' Agravain turned again to his map, laying

a finger on the deep, crooked, blue intrusion that the firth made into the coastline. His hand was still sore and weak from his penitence of the night before. Scabs blossomed on its side and on the knuckles. The pain of movement found a bright, eager answer in the centre of his chest each time he breathed.

He ignored all this. 'How many?'

'A hundred men, maybe more, but not many more.'

Agravain pictured the shore in his mind, the lay of the land, and the hazards it offered. These were few, but they were hidden by the mists that showed no signs of lifting. 'Horse or foot?'

'Foot. There are only a dozen horse with them, if that many.'

'Do we give the word, Sire?' asked Pedair. He stood beside the fire, rigid and correct. Agravain did not miss the wariness with which the old chieftain watched him though, nor could he blame him for it. He had been right. Disaster had come too close, and it was Agravain's fault.

If he was glad to hear his king talking like a warrior, Pedair still cast too many black looks at the stained and empty scabbard Agravain had strapped to his back. Agravain had not found the words to explain this. It was Laurel's last gift, one of the great and holy mysteries in most humble guise. Unrecognized for what it might truly be. Like the word of a faithful woman. He would not reject what she gave him, even if he could never see her again.

Do not think on that.

'We do not give the word yet,' Agravain looked down to the map again. 'With only a dozen horse coming that way, there will be another runner coming soon.' He set his jaw. 'They're dividing themselves. The question is how. Eadan?'

'Sire?' The boy straightened himself. He was clearly tired and chilled, but he still offered the fastest means for getting

over the rough ground that could easily take down a rider
on horseback.

'Get down to the ships. Tell the guards they're to get up
here, and the sailors they're to put to sea, round the point
and wait there. If they do not hear from us in seven days,
tell them to set sail south to take the news to Camelot.'

Eadan blanched to hear his king planning for the possi-
bility of defeat, but he swallowed his qualms with reasonable
speed and straightened his slouching back. 'Yes, Sire.'

Agravain nodded and Eadan hurried out the door, leaving
himself, Pedair and Ruadh with the maps and the knowledge
that the war was coming closer. The air was heavy with the
cloying damp the fires could not dispel. People came and
went in as much silence as they could manage.

Pedair stood still beside the table. Though he looked down
at the broad map, Agravain wondered what he really saw.
Ruadh, by contrast, paced. He circled the fires, not questioning
the orders Agravain had given, but plainly not wanting to wait.

Agravain did not want to wait either. The need for movement was like an itch inside his veins. He also wanted to pace,
to be outside with his engine men and his smiths, urging them
to their work. But he did not move. The men were already
working as quickly as they could. They knew full well their
own lives depended on being finished in time. Devi oversaw
them, and Devi could be trusted absolutely. There was no word
he could add that would make them work more quickly.

But more than that, Agravain could not now show himself
less than calm and in control. His heart was shattered, but
his mind could not be. He could not, he must not, fail in
this thing, whatever came afterwards, be it Judgment Day
itself. This much Laurel would understand. He was certain.

Agravain saw Laurel's face before his mind's eye again and
his fists clenched. He needed to show his people what he
truly was. Show her. She waited out there somewhere. He

had no one to spare but boys who should have been hiding behind their mother's skirts, but they were out looking. She would be found. The war would not wait for him and his wrongs, but when it was done . . . when it was done he would beg forgiveness, from her or from God, whichever would face him first.

Sandals slapped rapidly against stone, and Agravain turned. A lean boy, barely old enough to be called a youth, rushed into the hall to drop to his knees before Agravain could move to stop him.

'I saw the signal off the hill beacon!' the boy cried. 'A host of men come up the valley. Near two hundred of them!'

Agravain nodded, and waved the boy out. The boy gulped air, bowed his head quickly and ran, no doubt to tell father or uncle or brother what he'd seen and so spread the news like wildfire throughout the fortress. It didn't matter.

'There is it,' he said to Pedair and Ruadh. 'They mean to flank us, draw us down and then cut off our retreat. If they separate us from Din Eityn they carry the day, and they know it.'

'And if we sit here any longer, they will converge outside the wall and lay their siege. Then we may sit here until King Death comes to fetch us,' said Ruadh flatly.

'Aptly spoken, my lord Ruadh.' Agravain looked down at his map. He had studied this parchment for years on end, working through every scenario his imagination and training could invent. In mind and in sinew, he felt the lay of the land around him.

'Who do we choose to meet?' He tapped his aching palm against the table's splintered wood. 'We cannot let ourselves be divided for long. We are too few. And we must draw them within range of the pass. So, on which side of this scale do we throw our weight?'

'Better to face a hundred than two hundred,' said Ruadh.

He looked old, as if he was feeling each and every one of his years. He was not afraid, Agravain was sure of that, but he was tired. He wanted to find hope, but the strangeness of the engines and their masters had bewildered him. The stinking, poisonous jars that now waited in neat lines beside the trebuchets filled him, and many others, with fear.

Agravain had no comfort to give him nor any time to explain more than he already had.

'Facing the smaller force will put us on the backside of the rock, and we'll have to double back against our own force in retreat.' Agravain tapped his hand again, making a rhythm for his thoughts. 'As it is, we cannot trust that all of us could make it back across the bridge.' *And what's the reason for that?* Ruadh was plainly thinking. Agravain chose not to answer that thought.

'If we face the greater force, we have the straightest line back,' he went on. 'Which no doubt the Black Knight has also considered. So, he's doubled his numbers there to frighten us off.'

'And has made a fine job of it,' remarked Pedair mildly. A rebuke for Ruadh, or just the plain truth?

'So, we meet them in the valley.' Agravain pressed his fingertips against the place on the map, as if he thought the pain in them would burn some mark on the lined parchment. 'Let their other men break against the cliffs and try as they might to open our back door. It will bring them what they deserve.'

'We will have only one chance,' said Pedair. 'If we cannot keep the course of the battle as we need it, they will slaughter us.'

'I did not ask if this would be easy. I asked that it be done.' Agravain lifted his hand from the map again. The pain filled him, reminding him of how much he had done, and of all he had yet to do to atone.

It ends here and begins again. God help me. 'It all depends on how much the Black Knight knows. We had a spy with us a long time . . . did she really understand the engines? What exactly did she see?' He lapsed again into silence.

'Shall I give the word?' asked Pedair.

Agravain nodded. 'Let it be done.'

Pedair bowed and left to give the orders. Agravain's fingers curled, trying to dig into the wood beneath them.

So, we know where Mordred is. Where is Morgaine?

And where are you, my wife? Now that war has come, where have you gone?

He could not believe she had gone meekly away like some disgraced daughter sent to a nun's house. That was not Laurel's way, not even now. But what had she done? Where had she gone?

That he had no way to answer these questions tightened his jaw and gut. He could only make his first moves, and wait until Mordred countered, and pray with all his heart and soul that Laurel would not hate him so much that she would turn against him.

This was to have been his moment of strength, but Agravain found he had never felt more weak. He could only see half the war arrayed in front of him. All around there was a second field that he could not even begin to chart.

He felt the scabbard press against his back, a warning hand, urging him on. Her last gift to him.

Agravain closed his eyes. 'Laurel,' he whispered. 'Laurel, where are you?'

The shadows made no answer.

Darkness whirled about Laurel. She could see nothing but a chaos of blackness cut by silver light. The rush of icy wind, the bunch and release of the kelpie's muscles beneath its cool hide combined to form a single flowing current. She could hear nothing but the wind in her ears. It tore away her breath and forced itself into her throat. She was drowning on air and motion.

There was no time. There was only the struggle to hang onto the slick mane that cut into her fingers and the struggle to keep breathing. Blind, deaf and cold, she held on. Were it not for the current rushing over her, Laurel would have feared she had died.

Then, unthinkably, the current lessened and stilled. Hearing and vision returned, and Laurel was able to drag in long, gulping draughts of air. They stood on a stony hilltop. Stubborn grass and lichen grew between great, grey boulders. At the hill's crest waited a single thorn tree. Though it was summer, the twisted branches bore no leaves, only scraps of cloth and ribbon that had been tied there by people seeking blessing or to avert curses. The moonlight glinted on coins and silver pins tucked in between the tree's roots or into the cracks of its bark.

The wind blew hard around Laurel's head. She felt the trickle as her blood eased itself from the stinging cuts in her hands to run down the length of her fingers and drop onto the exposed earth and stone.

Pit. Pat. Her blood fell.

This was an ending place. This was death. The tree was dead and dry with no water to feed it. The hard, pitiless wind should have broken it long ago, but here it stood. Something stronger than the wind kept it there.

How is it this place is not guarded?

But it was. By dry silence and dry wind and the boundless reaches of the night. There was nothing to grasp here, nothing to strive against. Only the isolation, and the dry thorn tree. Nothing to reach towards or for. No sign of trap or tomb.

Tick. Tick. Her blood fell onto stone.

The thorn tree rattled its branches. Laurel lifted her head.

The wind fell away, leaving behind silence as thick and binding as any shroud. It was cold, cold as the grave and dry as a bone. The stars shone overhead, hard, brilliant and distant.

Tick. Tick. Her blood fell onto stone. Nothing moved but her blood dropping down. The kelpie stood like a statue. Time had ceased. There was nothing and there would be nothing here but darkness, and the drops of blood. *Tick. Tick.*

Blood. Blood to blood the strongest call. This whole, long nightmare had been about blood. Goloris's blood, shed to free Ygraine, Morgause's blood that ran through the veins of her sons. Morgaine's blood burning with the need for vengeance against the world.

She never died, not really. But she was kept forever apart. Morgause had not killed Morgaine, and Morgaine had not killed Morgause. But she had trapped her where she could not hear, could not answer.

What call would be strong enough to reach her? The call of blood.

'Morgause,' said Laurel. 'Morgause, Ygraine's daughter, I am come from your son Agravain. I am come to aid all your sons; Gawain, Agravain, Geraint and Gareth. Morgause, in their names, will you speak to me?'

Laurel felt light as a feather, and dry as dust. There was nothing for her to hold here, no way for her to find purchase on the dry, dead stone. No cloud, no mist to bring her the water of life and hold her in place. There was only dust and stone, and nothing more. Nothing at all.

'Morgause, I come in your son's name. Will you speak to me?'

The thorn tree shifted.

Laurel blinked. There was no wind. *A trick of the light?*

No. The branches moved, but not like a tree's that is blown

by the wind. They drooped and bent. They bowed in to wrap around the trunk which hunched and thickened. The ribbons tied to the twigs blurred and stretched, darkened and lengthened, until they were an ancient woman's white hair and black robe, its hems spreading out around her feet, and yet somehow remaining the roots of the tree she had been, held tight by the dry stone.

'Who calls me?' she rasped, her voice rattling like dead leaves. 'Who can call me?'

Laurel stood frozen. She had spoken to the dead, but the sight of this captive robbed her of the power of speech. She could still see the tree this woman was. Part of her heart wanted to believe that this was a dream. The ribboned tree had to be the truth, not this old, worn woman, her blue eyes gone cloudy with despair and the dry chains of enchantment that held her.

'I am Laurel Carnbrea, daughter of Morwenna, who is the daughter of the sea.'

'Ahhhh!' sighed Morgause. Her arms waved vaguely. Her clouded eyes searched the heavens, the hilltop that sloped away into shadow.

She's blind, realized Laurel numbly. Had Morgaine blinded her deliberately, or was that just one more curse levelled by her imprisonment?

'You call out the names of my sons.' Like the movement of her body, her voice was vague, almost careless. Each word seemed to stretch up like a child, reaching for some object it wanted, but could not understand. 'What are you to my sons?' The question was light, not amused, but vacant, empty, as if she could not believe it was real.

I want her to be a dream. What does she want me to be?

'I am wife to Agravain.' *Despite all, I remain so.*

She did not answer for a long time. Her blind eyes moved, this way and that. Her mouth opened and closed soundlessly, as if tasting the air. Her crooked fingers stretched out to nothing. Did she know where she was? What had happened to her? Was her prison some terrible dream Morgaine had laid upon her from which she could not wake?

Or had she gone blind trying to see through the tangled web of the invisible countries to where her flesh was trapped into the mortal world?

'Yes,' Morgause said at last, letting the word fall slowly as a sigh. 'It would be Agravain who would cleave to such a one.' She cocked her head and smiled just a little. The sadness of that smile went straight to Laurel's battered heart. 'How does my son?'

Laurel swallowed, licking her lips, and trying to find the strength to speak words that would be true. 'He is sore pressed, my lady,' she said. 'He goes to battle against Morgaine and her son Mordred.'

'Then . . .' Morgause reached out with one hand, stretching it to its limits, caressing the empty air in front of her eyes. 'Lot is dead.'

'Yes.'

Morgause held still for a moment, eyes, hands, mouth all frozen. Then, she sagged down, her head slumping to her chest, her body curling and buckling. In unfettered flesh, she would have fallen to her knees, but her transformation, her prison, held her upright.

'Ah! Ah!' Morgause wailed. 'My husband. My husband!' She lifted her head up to the star-filled sky, straining her blind eyes to see what was gone. No tears shone on her cheeks. This place was too dry even for tears.

'Wait for me, Lot!' Morgause pleaded. 'Wait for me!'

Laurel hardened her heart. 'There is a question I must ask you, Morgause.'

It took some time for her words to reach through the fog of grief and enchantment. But Morgause did lower her face, turning an ear more closely to Laurel. 'What question?' It was as if she could not help herself.

What use has Morgaine made of you here? Have you been made to be her oracle for all these years? Oh, Mother Mary preserve us, did she make you tell of the downfall of your husband and sons?

'What is Morgaine's weakness? How can she be defeated?'

'Ahhhh! Ahhhh! It's come to that. It would come to that.' Morgause's pale eyes darted back and forth, seeing phantoms of nightmare and memory. 'I tried. I tried. But I was too slow and far, far too late.'

'Please, my lady,' Laurel took a step forward, holding out a hand that could not be seen. 'I must know, so I can tell your son Agravain how to strike.'

'It cannot help him. But it can. But cannot.' Morgause shuddered and twisted, her arms swaying, buffeted by tormenting winds that came from nowhere but her imprisoned heart. 'My heart is gone. I have nothing left. Lot is dead. Lot is dead!' Her voice broke piteously upon the words. 'I had so much,' she whispered. 'But it is all gone now. My fault,' she whispered and the words were the sound of heartbreak. 'My fault.'

'No,' said Laurel. 'Not gone. Stolen. Your sons live still, Morgause. Let me help them. Let me help Agravain.' She stretched out her hands, pleading, for every good moment they had shared, for every glimpse of the man he was and the king he could be.

Morgause wavered, swaying back and forth, a woman who wanted to faint and fall in her weakness but could not, a tree that would bend and break, for its heart had long ago rotted away, but could not. Trapped. Trapped and made to serve until she was uncertain whether she could, or should, defy her captor anymore. The thought of failure sickened her heart as badly as the sight of so much pain. At the realization that she had been willing to do this much to Lot Luwddoc.

No, no, I would have let him go at once.

But for how long? Surely I would have needed him again . . .
Oh, power was a dread thing.

Laurel took the queen's hand, kneeling down in supplication, in remorse. She felt bark and stem, and she felt a woman's bones. 'Do not leave Agravain to her.'

It was as if a storm shook her. Morgause threw her head back, twisting and turning, caught in an invisible gale. She would have screamed, but she could only whimper. Laurel heard her limbs crack, saw the pain contorting her face as her joints bent and turned, cramped and crabbed. Her gnashing teeth bit her withered lips. Laurel held her hand, held tight, not daring to let go, to break the cord of human sympathy, the only such that had come to Morgause in ten years.

Remember your sons. Remember your husband. You say their suffering is your fault, then act now to end it.

But to save the sons, to avenge the husband, she must again betray the sister whose suffering was caused by the death of their father, caused by their mother. Suffering that Morgause must feel as keenly as if it were her own, for that sister was her other self.

Which treason would she choose?

Morgause slumped down in her cage of enchantment, borne up only by confinement. She lifted her head, and for the first time, her blinded eyes turned towards Laurel.

'It was early days,' Morgause said, and she laid her other dry, light hand over Laurel's and Laurel at once remembered the touch of her mother, wasted by illness and ready to die. 'The twelve battles were won. The Britons were safe at last. But Merlin gave Arthur one last prophecy. Merlin told him his unlawful child would bring all the Britons to their knees. But it was not only Merlin who learned this truth. My sister, my twin, her soul broken and bleeding after all the long years, she also knew, and she acted.'

Vision gripped Laurel, and she saw a war-ravaged town, its surviving people, all of them Britons, swarming about to greet the bloody and mud-covered victors. They shouted their praises, and fell at their feet, and . . . and . . . and . . .

'Great king. Great king, will you have me?'

Black-haired and black-eyed, older than she had been, he did not recognize her. Her dress was torn, but nothing of her manner was broken. She was full of life, and the lust that is raised by battle made it easy. He grabbed her hard by the waist and she came with a laugh to press against his chest and answer his kiss boldly, bawdily. The soldiers around cheered, as he pressed her against the wall, and then swept her laughing through the doorway.

In a fever pitch, he took her there on the dirt floor, tossing aside his armour and his restraint. She laughed hard and urged him on, crying out his name. When it was done, he backed away on his knees, suddenly ridiculous in his nakedness and shaking with spent lust.

'Are you . . . did I hurt . . .'

She smiled at him and rose gracefully. 'You did magnificently.' She crossed to him, drawing his head back and kissing him. 'Great king.'

And she left him there in the darkness of the hovel, to gather his armour and wonder why he was so afraid.

'Arthur didn't know where the child was or who he might be, but he would not take the risk. Flush with his victories he lost caution, but not all mercy. He thought . . . he thought he could do an evil which was no evil.'

Merlin she saw now, his beard shorter, his face less lined, but the beginnings of the sadness that would carve those lines deep in his eyes.

'You have fathered a son,' said Merlin flatly. 'That son will be your death and the undoing of your life's work.'

He was still thin, his beard scanty. A youth become king in battle, but now with a king's work to do, and not yet grown to that work. 'What do I do?' he whispered.

Merlin turned his face away. 'I don't know, my king.'

'You must know.'

'He is near Durnovaria, but more than that I cannot see. He is being hidden from me.'

Arthur faced the horizon, looking out over the vast plain, where the ravages of war were being buried by the plough. That was his victory, and there was a kind of greed in him as he watched it. Dreadful decision took him.

'Take the boys there, send them hostage to Joyeux Gard in Normandy. When it becomes clear which is . . . which is the one you spoke of, we will know better what to do.'

Merlin held out his hand, a gesture halfway between pleading and warning. 'You cannot cheat destiny this way.'

The habit of command had came swift to Arthur. He would not abandon his victory, his great peace so dearly bought. 'I cannot leave it. Do as I have said!'

Merlin bowed his head, before his king could see the tears in his eyes. 'It shall be done.'

'He did not want any to know which was his son, to protect him from being the kernel around which an uprising might grww, or to protect himself should the child come to learn his nature, I do not know, but he had a hundred boys, babes, that were about the right age, brought together. There were plenty of willing hands, but it was his order, and they were put to sea in a ship, to be sent to Brittany and Languedoc, for fosterage he insisted. To be murdered, others said.

'In the end, it mattered not, because a storm came up and the boat went down, and all those children sent to sea at Arthur's word died.'

Morgause threw her head back once more, and it seemed to Laurel she was pleading for tears, for release. 'It was Morgaine who raised the storm,' she whispered. 'She called on the *morverch* and she made a bargain with them. They could take every life on that ship if they spared but one. Her son, Mordred.' The blind eyes searched, restless, frightened, and found her again. 'It was her doing that took the innocents that might have lived.'

And that was it. That was the deed, the way and the door to Morgaine, and she held it in her hands now. She had thought at such a moment she would feel triumph, but she knew only a sick horror at the deaths, so much death, that could be assuaged and bought off only by yet more death.

For the death of the innocent there was always a price. It was a fell bargain, and it would exact its cost.

This was why she wanted to keep me from the sea. So that I would not learn this, because this is the deed for which she must answer, and for which there is no answer.

'God have mercy,' she whispered. 'Oh, grandmother, God have mercy on us all.'

'No,' Morgause shook herself. 'There is no mercy for such as we. Ah, Lot! Lot! Forgive me! Forgive me my sons!' She hung again, limp, helpless, a butterfly in the web, forgotten by even the spider.

'Why didn't she kill you?' whispered Laurel.

Morgause lifted her head, looking right at Laurel with her blind eyes. 'How could she? She gave me half her power, when we were still girls.'

'You don't understand, Morgause. What we are. What we can be.' Her twin gripped her hands. 'Come back to me, sister. Let me show you.'

It was like light. It poured into her, stronger than wine, stronger than love. It filled her with terror and with beauty. It was the wild rush of freedom Laurel had felt when she stood up to her knees in the sea and let it suffuse her. It was a thousand wondrous things, but most of all it was the gift from one twin to another, one half of a soul to the other. From Morgaine to Morgause.

'Now we are together again,' said Morgaine. 'No one will ever separate us again. Now you understand everything.'

But Morgaine was wrong. Morgause did not understand everything. She understood power, but not hatred.

Morgause also understood the one thing Morgaine did not. Morgause understood that love could heal as well as wound.

She never died. Not really. Of course not. Morgaine needed her alive. Here was half her power, half her spirit. The blessing and the curse of those born twinned. That bond made closer by Morgaine herself, thinking she could win her sister over by bestowing some of the power she gained upon Morgause.

But when the time came, she found that the link she had forged could not be broken. Morgause had learned that lesson earlier. That was why Morgaine had never died. Guinevere and Merlin between them were ready to undo Morgaine, but not to kill Morgause in the doing. So, she was imprisoned only.

For that they had paid, and Morgause herself had come to this place to make the end she could not make before. But she had failed then, and this was the price. The price for failing to see the sacrifice required of her before. The price for the simple, all-too-human wish to live instead of die.

'How can I free you?' asked Laurel. 'Let me take you back to your son.'

But Morgause only shook her heavy head. 'I cannot be free until death comes, and death will not come to me here.'

Laurel swallowed and nodded. She had feared as much. She stood, drawing away from the imprisoned queen. Her legs weak and shaking, she made her way back to the black horse that waited so unnaturally still and patient. 'Kelpie,' she murmured. 'May it be that you and I can bring release here?'

The kelpie whickered and rolled one blank, black eye towards the sky. The wind blew hard, and Laurel nodded.

With her hand on the kelpie's cool neck, she faced into the wind. It brushed past her ears, blowing her hair out, tugging at locks and hems. It knew where the clouds waited. It could fetch them here, fetch them all with their heavy load of water. Water enough to wash away all the sins of the world. The clouds closed over Laurel's head, blotting out the stars and moon. Pregnant with their water, they collided grumbling together, crowding, merging, lowering.

Rain showered down upon Laurel's head. Hard, fat hard drops struck her head, shoulders, arms. Drops turned quickly into threads of water, then whole streams falling from the sky. The rain ran into the dry stone beneath her feet. It trickled into the cracks, drizzling down to seek the water hidden far beneath this rocky crust that had been still and stagnant for years. The rain filled up the cracks opened by the roots of the tree, forcing the stone apart like a wedge. Rivers of rainwater tumbled down the hill. The wind blew hard. The tree swayed and creaked, the queen whimpered and wailed. Laurel, drenched by her own storm, did not permit herself to move.

The cracks widened and the water rose to the tree's dried roots that could drink no more. They could only weaken and waver. The split trunk that held the nails and the coins trapped could not absorb so much so suddenly. It could only give way.

Slowly, slowly the thorn tree bent and screamed and snapped in a long, splintering tear. It toppled into the new river of water that flowed down the stony hillside to be swept up in the freshening current.

For a moment, Laurel saw not the broken tree, but Morgause, arrayed in the raiment of a queen, eyes closed in the last sleep.

Morgause, queen of Gododdin lay at peace and was carried away by her river.

Laurel's knees gave way and she fell to the ground, gasping and shivering under the weight of the water that poured down.

Mordred stood in his mother's pavilion, holding back the door, and looking out at the darkness. The summer nights in Gododdin waned so short that it seemed a man could barely lie down on his cot in twilight before the morning slipped over him, but for Mordred this night had been a season long. It was not worry that made the hours pass so slowly. His company was in good spirits. Each of the peoples sang in their separate languages, telling one another great stories and great lies. Old heroes were brought out and made to live again in the brief darkness.

They made their camp amid the empty huts and animal pens of Gododdin's village. They had crept through the lowering mists at evening, only to find the houses had already been abandoned, for a day, perhaps two. Anything of any value had been packed off with the inhabitants.

While his men cursed, and kicked at cold ashes in extinguished hearths, Mordred had smiled. So. Agravain had indeed seen this much coming. So could a blind man. It was of little consequence. Less if the air stayed as still as it was and the mists held until past dawn.

Now the eagerness for battle, so long held at bay, made him champ at the harness. At last, at last, this was his war. His beginning. With the dawn he truly became a man and able to stand among men. Tomorrow he earned the title of lord and of knight that had been laid over him.

Tomorrow he would begin to avenge his family: grandfather, grandmother, mother, self. With the dawn, as soon as his horse could see to put one foot in front of the other, it all began.

'You'll wear yourself out.'

Mordred turned to look at his mother, sitting calm and clear-eyed beside her brazier. No night journeys for her now. She was fully present, saving her omens and her skills to support the battle once dawn came.

'I thank you for your concern, lady mother.' Then he winced. He had not meant the words to sound so much like a complaint.

She smiled at him with a mother's fond indulgence and Mordred felt his hackles rise. A heartbeat later, he saw the glint of humour in her eyes.

'Forgive me, Mordred, if I take the mother's part one last time. My hours to do so are short. With the dawn you will be leader of our people, and I will be . . .' she hesitated. 'Priestess, old woman, unneeded.'

'You will always be needed, Mother. It is you who brought this into being.'

'So I did. And tomorrow, we begin to harvest what was sowed so many years ago.' The glint in her black eyes grew sharper, the humour melting into steel. 'Your hands shall seal it, my son. I am proud of how you have grown.'

He bowed, the compliment warming him. 'I will show I am worthy.'

'You already have.' She touched his cheek briefly, and he felt how dry and rough her palm was from so many years of spinning and weaving and all her other works. 'Now,' she stood back. 'If I may give one last order. It is not good that you spend these final hours in the company of your mother. You . . .' She paused, and Mordred felt his smile fade. 'You . . . what . . . who are you?' She took a step toward him, confusion in her face.

'What is it?' A vision was coming over her. She did not speak to him, but to it. Cold threaded through Mordred's blood.

'No,' whispered Morgaine. 'You cannot. You cannot. She is beyond you. You cannot touch her!'

Her voice rose to a nearly hysterical pitch. She stumbled blindly forward. Mordred heard worried calls outside.

Mordred grabbed his mother's arms. 'Morgaine!' A name had power to reach deep, she had taught him. 'Morgaine, it is Mordred. What do you see?'

'How! How does she reach her!' It was as if the strength went out of her, and she slumped in his arms, her eyes wide with agony. 'Stop! Stop her!'

'Morgaine! Mother! I can do nothing unless you tell me what is happening!'

But she began to tremble, then shudder, then shake, her whole body contorting with its spasms. She screamed, wordless with pain and the horror of whatever her staring eyes saw. It was all Mordred could do to hang onto her as her seizure bore them both to the ground. Sweat poured down her as if she were drenched in sea water and she bit her own lips frantically, mindlessly, until the foam and blood came.

'Morgaine!' he cried as if to a sick child. 'Morgaine, mother, what do I do? What do I do!'

Then, she screamed. It was the deafening sound of pure agony ripped unwilling from her ravaged throat. It bent her body like a bow in his arms, and then she dropped back, senseless, still, her eyes wide open and staring.

She did not move. She did not breathe. Outside men were calling his name. Asking questions he could not hear properly. Mordred, shaking, laid her down, backing away as if he saw a ghost.

His throat closed. His hands shook. She did not move. She did not breathe.

Dead? Dead? It cannot be. It CANNOT be!

'My lord? Lord Mordred?' Durial. Just outside the door. 'My lord is . . . are you well? We heard . . .'

But if he finished his question, Mordred did not hear it. In front of him, his mother moaned, twisting weakly. In an instant, Mordred was on his knees beside her, clutching her hand, which had gone as cold as the grave.

'Mother? Mother?'

Morgaine's eyelids fluttered, and opened. He looked into her black eyes, and saw nothing there but seething hatred.

Slowly, Morgaine sat up, and Mordred fell back onto his heels. This was not his mother, this was some demon of hate made flesh.

Morgaine rose, a figure of white and black in the brazier's light.

'She thinks she has beaten me. She thinks she can kill me.' Morgaine smiled, cracking the patina of blood and foam on her lips. 'She thinks she can undo me with such a little thing. Oh, no. No. No, my son. She will pay.'

She raised her arms and threw back her head, shouting out three words that Mordred could not understand. They sank through his skin, clawing at blood and seizing bone to twist and change.

In front of Mordred's bewildered gaze, his mother flew into a thousand pieces of darkness, a flood and flurry of wings and raucous laughter making a hurricane to fill the pavilion. Mordred hid his head in his arms. Beating wings and unforgiving claws grazed his back and skull, until the birds found the pavilion opening and burst free.

A storm of ravens rising up to blot out the stars.

Mordred had no idea how long he sat there, head cradled in his arms, unable to do anything more than breathe and shake. Then, slowly, he heard someone calling his name.

Names are powerful. Names reach deep. Mordred lifted his head, and saw himself alone in the pavilion. A single, black feather lay on the trampled grass before him.

'Lord Mordred?'

Durial again. He stepped hesitantly into the pavilion. Mordred could not turn to look at him. He could not tear his gaze away from the feather shining in his hand. Behind him, the pavilion opening flapped loose, and Mordred could see nothing but the solid wall of mist reflecting the brazier's feeble light.

'Lord Mordred, where is the lady?'

'She . . .' Broke into a thousand pieces, flew away as a flock of ravens. Died and came back to life again. 'She goes to defend us from Merlin's treachery.' It sounded possible. It might even be true. 'She told me we should not waste any more time.' He closed his hand around the feather. 'Get the men together, Durial. Light the fires. It's time we made ready.'

NINETEEN

Dawn. Harsh and bright, and life-giving. The sun touched Laurel's skin with warm fingers, searching for life. It touched her eyes gently, to find if there was still sight. She stirred, shifting from the night's cold into the day's warmth, unwilling to move, unwilling to be drawn from oblivion after all she had done. The kelpie, still beside her, as fresh and steady as it had been in the nighttime, whickered once.

Then, she heard the raven's cry.

It woke her like the sound of her own name. She sat up at once. Bruised and battered as she was, she felt triumph pouring through her. It warmed her from within as the sunlight warmed her without.

'Kelpie,' she said. 'I need you to take a message to my grandmother.' The beast turned a displeased eye towards her. Its purpose was to be beside her, to speed her on her way and protect her in danger.

Laurel met its midnight gaze and told it what she needed. She could not do this without the last secret, the one the sea held so close that even Morgaine had forgotten it waited there.

The kelpie stamped its hoof, and whisked around. Without

a sound, it sped down the hill, a blade of night cutting through the day.

Laurel was alone.

She knew what she must do. For the first time since the night of her marriage, she knew what she must do and knew she had the strength to do it. The water had washed away her doubts. Her communion with Morgause had taught her how Morgaine could be drawn out. For Morgaine believed she understood her own power, and the nature of her power, fully. Morgaine believed there was no one she could not deceive or seduce.

Not even her own sister who knew her best.

Laurel rose to her feet and turned her face towards the clear, blue sky.

They came from the east; a cloud of ravens, carrying the storm of war behind them. Morgaine had felt her sister's freedom, and now she came to wreak her revenge, thinking to find Laurel alone on this dry hilltop, far away from her blood's home and power.

'Come to me, Morgaine!' Laurel shouted. 'Let us make an end, here and now!' She spread her arms, in summoning and in prayer. She felt the wind wrap itself around her, clothing her in its life and power.

'Are you the raven, Morgaine?' Laurel cried. 'Then I am the falcon, soaring high to strike!'

The whole world changed then, and Laurel changed with it, rising up on her own wide wings.

Now. Now we make an end.

With the sunrise, Agravain and his men descended into the mists. Cold fog surrounded them, muffling breath, footfall and the jingle of harness. The horses snorted, disconcerted. They whickered to one another, reassuring themselves that their mates had not suddenly vanished in this opaque, grey world. Beside Agravain, Ruadh carried the hawk banner that had been his father's standard. It hung limp on its pole, weighed down by the still mists.

As an omen, thought Agravain grimly, *it cannot not bode well.* The empty scabbard rode uneasily on his shoulders, pressing him to vigilance.

Keade, headman for the holding at the rock's foot, led them down the treacherous path on a shaggy pony. The headman could guide the way down this hillside in the dead of night, and his sturdy mount trusted him. Seeing the pony's calm, Agravain's stallion followed willingly, and all the rest came after him, nearly nose to tail. They'd make a proper formation when the slope evened out.

If we're given the chance. Agravain gritted his teeth. *Where are you, Black Knight?* He narrowed his eyes, willing his sight to pierce the mists farther than the rump of Keade's pony.

'Sire?' breathed Keade. He eased his pony up slowly, giving Agravain plenty of time to bring his horse around his right side. 'Do you see?' He pointed out into the mists.

Agravain strained his eyes until they ached, and then he did see. Pale sparks wavered in the fog. Fires. Camp fires. Torches perhaps.

There you are. A grim warmth spread through him.

'So now we know where we're going,' he murmured. 'Eadan.' Agravain looked down. They'd taken the swift boy with them for a messenger. Nervous as he was, Eadan was holding steady. If they came out of this alive, he'd make Devi a good squire. 'Pass the word back. We fan out as soon as the ground gets level and every man is to hold his tongue. The enemy is camped in the village, we do not want to give them any warning of our coming.'

Grey and white and storm wind. Laurel's limbs spread wide, alive to each current, each ripple beneath them. It was good.

She knew the wind well and it had answered her need faithfully before. It lifted her high above the tiny, dark, paltry thing that was the raven below. Oh, it came in an unkind mob of its fellows, but there was only one she hunted.

One in the centre. One that shone more darkly than all the others.

She spread herself broad and her blood surged. She folded herself tight and plummeted down, beak open to grab warm flesh and warm blood, and the raven screamed in its pain.

But there was something else, something that had no place in this world where they wheeled together, hunter and prey.

Something that rent a sharp wound through her triumph.

Are you the falcon, Laurel of Cambryn? Then I am the eagle and my wings cast their shadow far above you!

Her prey was gone. Laurel spread her wings, catching the wind, just in time. She soared high again, suddenly bereft.

Alone and afraid she drifted on the wind.

Agravain caught the scent of smoke moving sluggishly through the mists. If he stared hard, he could see that the misted shadows around him were stone and thatched houses, and the lines of wicker fences.

And nothing had happened. He rode up to a fire that drove back the fog just enough to show muddy, trampled ground. He stood in the middle of straw stubble and the prints of dozens of feet, both human and animal. There waited a grey stone wall. There a stick fallen crosswise to their path.

All around them was mist and silence. Agravain's horse shifted uneasily underneath him. His company waited at his back, just as uneasily.

'Where are they?' For a moment Agravain thought he'd spoken aloud. But it was Ruadh, staring at the fire they could now see clearly.

The brightly burning, completely unattended fire.

In the back of his mind, Agravain heard the trap slam shut.

'Back!' he shouted, reining his stallion around. 'Back! Everyone back!'

The sound of a strange horn shivered the mists. 'Back!' he bellowed again. *Too late, too late.* The words sang in his blood even as he hauled on the reins and dug his spurs into his stallion's sides to send the beast leaping forward.

He heard the hoofbeats now, thundering against the ground. Hoofbeats enough to make the whole world tremble as the Black Knight's army poured out of the mist.

The falcon knew she was hunted. She felt it through the length of her body. The world was too dark, the wind too weak. She tried to flap her wings and gain some height, but it was too late, far too late.

This is wrong. Wrong. This is not how it should be. But she couldn't think. She was too small. Too afraid. Something waited above. It usurped the wind. She had to think. She couldn't think for the fear. She could only fly. She could fly far away, seek the broad salt waters. The waters were safety. They were part of something she had been once, before she changed, before all things changed.

Pain slammed against her neck and she screamed as hot blood ran down her feathers. Her body flailed and struggled and the world darkened before her eyes. And she remembered who brought the pain . . .

Eagle, I am the arrow loosed from the bow, and I fly to your heart, bringing you down!

Mordred leaned low across his stallion's black neck, baring his teeth to the rushing wind. The jolt and thunder of the mad ride drummed into him, setting his blood pounding in eager answer.

'Run! Run!' He laughed towards Agravain's fleeing form.

Here it began, here was the first great victory. Here was the hand of vengeance that had waited so long to smite down the bastard, traitor brood whose son fled before him.

He knew what they meant to do. Their outriders had seen the loose fence of sharpened pickets set in the shadow of the cliff. Agravain thought his men would impale themselves on those stout stakes, run up on their pikemen and their spear throwers.

Oh, no, Your Majesty. We will not be caught so easily!

Most helpfully, Agravain's men had set a course of flags up to mark the distance to the pickets. Blue, red and yellow; yard after yard of cloth hung from stout posts. It was as if they thought to mark a festival day rather than a war. A wealth of brightly dyed cloth to be wasted on the battlefield.

Durial had wanted to tear them up, deprive the enemy of their road. Why? Why not use it for themselves and deprive him of the dead he hoped to make with his little fence and pathetic surprise?

Agravain and his men were already dead. They were surrounded and they did not know it. This plain was just the killing ground. The Picts scaled the back of the hills to take the pass. The Dal Riata climbed the cliffs to take the narrow bridge that was the last retreat of the kings of Din Eityn. The mists made the war engines useless, because the operators could not see whether they aimed at their own king.

It was all over but to see Agravain's head rolling at his feet.

The red flag flashed past on his right. 'Now!' cried Mordred to Durial. Durial reined up short and raised his horn to his mouth to blow three sharp blasts. As neat, swift and sure as any Roman guard, his horsemen wheeled. They turned to the right, running back and fanning out to make a living wall in front of Agravain's picket fence.

To make their battle line, and hold it there.

Mordred's grin broadened. The sun had lifted the mists just enough that he could see the picket fence from here. There dark and lumpish mass of pikemen arrayed before the shifting line of horsemen. One figure gleamed red and black in the grey fog.

Mordred urged his horse forward a few steps. 'King Agravain!' he called out to that straight, proud, doomed figure. 'King Agravain! Surrender now and I swear that none of your men will suffer for their allegiance to you!'

Agravain also moved his horse, coming forward to the very edge of the fence that was his chosen battleground. Mordred sat back in his saddle, waiting for whatever curse of defiance Arthur's kindred could muster.

But only one word came.

'NOW!'

Bronze horns, and the frenzied pounding of drums split the world. Mordred stood at once in his stirrups, staring wildly around to look for the attack, but there was nothing. No cloud rising from the fog, no blur of motion from the picket in front of him. Only the rush of wind, the blare of horns.

Then, the stars began to fall.

The arrow flew fast and flew high. It was long and keen, with one purpose only. Her shadow nemesis, her target, the focus of all her will, soared aloft. It thought itself safe on the winds, but these winds were her winds and they propelled her forward. They rushed and sang about her, keeping her path straight and true.

When at last the shadow saw her, it was too late.

She bit deep, sinking hard, revelling in the blood that flowed free. She was falling, falling towards the green and stony ground. She fell short of the surging waters. It did not matter. The shadow, her prey, her enemy fell helpless with her.

Arrow falling to earth, I am the badger, and I catch you up in my mouth and crush your body in my jaws.

Earth beneath her. Green trees overhead. Light and shadow playing with the wind that glided over her body. The wind was weak here without the salt sea to strengthen it. She lay helpless on the soft loam.

She could not move.

The mists shifted and blurred before Agravain's eyes as he spurred his stallion on. The horse whickered its terror but it obeyed, racing forward half blind. The wind blew the stink of sulphur, piss and burning flesh to them. The horn sounded, again and again, urging the men to follow. For the first time since the battle began, Agravain could see as well as hear the men tearing along with him on either side. Fire burned ahead, terrifying the horses, terrifying the men. But the men swallowed their fear, and forced their beasts to do the same, and they ran.

The whooping, jeering cries burst out of his company, the sounds of courage and feral cheer, and his cold heart warmed as he bent low over his stallion's neck.

The stinking wind blew and the mists shredded, and he saw for one brief moment where they were, and the chaotic mass of the enemy that was before them. They ran from the fires, ran from the approaching enemy. Ran without thought or plan or command. Horses screamed and mud flew, men shouted to each other and to God and heaven and curses rang up with the sounds of the horns.

Cold calm descended, and Agravain lowered his spear.

'Gododdin!' he cried. 'Gododdin!'

Digging his spurs hard into his horse's sides, he charged towards the darkest shadow, all the roar and thunder of his men echoing off the great rock at their back.

Battle in all its fury surrounded him in an instant.

A confusion of shouts and clashes, men and horses careening in and out of thinning mists. The jolt of blow on shield, the jarring as his lance drove against shield, against flesh. The screams; triumph, fear, pain, the hoarse shouts of the crows. He could see nothing but the men around his knees, and Ruadh holding the banner at his right.

The arrow, spent upon the ground, could not move. She had no limbs, no will and the wind was not strong enough to lift her up.

Something, some animal snuffled nearby. Its nose touched her, wet, caressing, imperious, intruding. It cared nothing for her fear as it prodded and probed. Hot spittle dropped onto her rigid form. She could not even shudder at the burning breath that wafted over her, or the teeth that closed around her.

Wrong. This was not as it should be. She could not allow this to be.

Badger, I am the wolf, and I am far swifter and more silent than you; my teeth longer, my senses more keen.

She was great and strong, and her blood sang strong within her. The wind blew hard, bringing her all the news of the green world around her. So much life. So much death. Turmoil, treachery, peace and struggle surged around her. But none of it was what she sought.

She crept forward, hunting.

Pedair stood on the battlements, straining his eyes to see through the tattered mists. Sometimes he saw the battle below, sometimes he only saw the most persistent clot of white fog rolling this way and that. He clearly heard the thunder, clash and the roar that was louder than the ocean in the midst of a gale, but the fog would not clear. How the hell were they to fire these ungainly, dishonourable engines with their smouldering, stinking missiles if they couldn't see!

His fingers clutched at the stone until he felt his bones would split.

'My lord Pedair!'

Pedair whirled around, coming within an inch of losing his balance. Lawren, greying, slump-shouldered, skinny-legged, one of the few who'd stayed the long course of Lot's decline, came pounding up the parapet's stairs.

'My lord,' he wheezed. 'The Pict men . . .'

Pedair did not need to hear any more. Forgetting the ache in his bones, Pedair raced along the narrow way to the western wall that overlooked the precious pass. Devi, Sir Devi, knighted and given charge of the battle engines, was already there. For a moment, their eyes met and Pedair saw the younger man was grey with ashes and fear.

Together they leaned out over the parapet.

The wind blew hard, dragging open the curtain of mist. Pedair saw the Picts with their brown skin and blue tattoos. He saw how their hands and bare chests were spattered with red blood. He saw how the ground beneath them and the stones around them was splashed with yet more blood.

He saw the corpses at their feet. Two, six, ten, a dozen. All.

All done in the blink of an eye, and without a sound.

The blood drained from Pedair's heart as he looked down on defeat. The pass was taken. The retreat was gone. The thing they had most feared was already done. The king and all his company was cut off.

'Can we re-angle your damned engines?' He demanded.

'Not without killing our king and all the men down there.' Devi clutched at his head with his one good arm. 'When the retreat comes, we have to be able to fire onto the plain again, especially now.'

Pedair's thoughts raced. The clashes, screams and bellows beat upon his skull. It was the oldest of his hard-bought soldier's instincts that enabled him to push all that aside and think.

These were the Picts. He'd fought them off before, fought them long and hard. He knew these bloody-handed men. He knew what they were, and what they weren't.

What they weren't.

He had it. Pedair faced Devi, wishing with all his heart this was Ruadh who stood beside him now, as he had for so long. 'Get me every man who can hold a sword and break open the treasury. We're going down there.'

Devi gaped at him, his withered arm twitching as he jerked back. 'We'll leave the fortress open. Who . . .'

'If our king cannot get back here, what will it matter?' Pedair roared. 'Find me ten men who can hold a spear and get them armed! I don't care if it's with carving knives and buckets! But deck them out with all the gold and silver they can wear. And get me one of those stinking jars of yours, one small enough for a man to carry.'

Realization that there was a plan behind this insanity flickered in Sir Devi's eyes. 'What are you doing?'

Pedair licked his lips. 'Those are the Picts down there. I'm going to show them some plunder, and then I'm going to pray to God they forget whatever training that Black Knight of theirs has given them and come after it. Right into the gates, which I'm going to foolishly open behind me.'

Not enough. What else do we need? What else? God grant me some of my king's wit, just for a moment . . .

'Get some of those spare ropes in use. Every man you don't need this instant, every boy, every girl, if that's who can do it, goes over the walls out of their sight and comes up behind the Picts while they're looking at my company. If we can distract them, we can make an ambush. Turn their game against them. There's still a chance.'

Devi met Pedair's eyes, both of them making the swift and terrible calculation of slender chances done by every fighter in every war since the first man lifted the first stone against his brother.

'Yes, my lord.' Sir Devi turned, and led the way down the stairs.

Ferns and bracken touched the wolf, tickling the ends of her fur as she slunk low beneath them. She must not be seen. She could make no ripple in the wood's shadows. Her prey was sly, but slow. Her prey had a bolt nearby, but her prey was near. The wind, her friend and advisor, told her that. It brought her the rank, blood-tinged scent of the deep earth that clung to her prey.

One cautious step after another, she crept forward. She paused between each silent stride to listen and to drink in the changing news that the wind brought her. Her prey was closer now. The earth smell grew heavier, drowning all the smells of green and earth and more distant life.

There. Its bristling, striped back showed plainly behind the screen of ferns and herbs. It thought the green scents would keep it hidden as it worried at the earth. It did not know the wind was her ally. She bared her strong white teeth and gathered up her muscles to spring.

But her prey whipped around with a speed it should not have possessed, snarling in fury as it bared its yellow teeth.

Wolf, I am the bear, and there is none on land stronger than me.

The world shrank down. She was small and weak, and whimpering as she backed away from the mountain of hair and teeth and claws. The bear rose up over her like the night itself given form.

*   *   *

Fool! Fool! Mordred cursed himself. He should have known, should have seen. Agravain retreated too fast, too easily, and now with the fires blazing in their midst these fool northmen who knew nothing of the Romans and their war engines were screaming about witchcraft and were more interested in running than fighting.

But Durial and the rest had got behind the cowards, and lowered their lances. So those who would retreat had to choose quickly to either fight the enemy and live, or fight their allies and die.

It was a weak feint, but it worked, and the raging sea of battle crashed and crowded around them. They held this new line. Barely. But the rain of fire had stopped now that the melee tossed the men of Gododdin together with his own. It would not do to kill your own.

Mordred stood in his stirrups, straining his eyes, looking up the pass. Had the Picts done their work? Had they? He made a target of himself and he didn't care. Everything depended now on whether the Picts or Agravain's men held the pass.

There! There! The flash of blue, and the soaring black of a raven's wing. Mordred dropped onto his horse's back again. He wheeled his mount around and plunged back into the thick of the fight, one eye on Agravain's distant figure, bobbing like a cork above the sea of battle.

All they had to do now was hold. Agravain's clever engines had not been enough. He, Mordred, had been right about that after all. Agravain was still in Mordred's net. That net could still be drawn tight. For all the hellish damage the fires had wreaked, his company still outnumbered Gododdin's pathetic hundred horsemen.

It would be hard, but it could be done. They just had to hold. Just a little longer. They just had to wear Agravain down until he had to retreat, and found out there was no place to go.

Grinning behind his black helmet, Mordred set his will to his work.

The bear spread its brown and wicked claws, and the wolf backed away, whining. She dodged, but felt the hot pain as a claw caught her silver coat.

Run. Run!

The bear's crashing charge and its roar filled the world. The scent of it was pure panic driven into her senses by the wind turned suddenly traitor.

Run. Run! Only speed could save her now. Only speed.

Speed. She needed speed. She could be speed . . .

Bear, bear, I am the boar, and my tusks are sharp and my feet swift. Not even you can stand against me.

And she was sleek and small no more. She was a mountain herself, heavy and unyielding. Why should she run? There was nothing to run from. Her very teeth were curving swords, and it was only bear; a lumbering coward.

She turned, bearing her needle-sharp teeth, showing her stained swords so eager for the fight. Her enemy slowed, uncertain now that it saw her. She shrieked in her delight.

This time. This time she would have her prey.

Pedair rode out of Din Eityn's gates adorned as a warrior in the old style. He was the image of the man his father had been, so long ago, before Arthur, before Uther, before the southerners and their damned grasping hands had come up to seize hold of this land. Gold cuffs weighed down Pedair's wrists, and gold chains gleamed on his breast. Even the spear in his hand was gilded. He had to guide his sway-backed mount with his knees, because his other arm cradled an undecorated jar of plain, red clay.

Slowly, Pedair rode down the narrow pass. Heaps of stone rose up on either side. He felt, rather than saw the old men behind him. He ached. The gold was too heavy. His arm hurt as he tried to keep his horse's rocking gait from jarring the urn he carried. He fixed all his attention on the Picts.

They did not even bother to keep watch. Instead, they were busy heaving corpses aside to give themselves more room to maneouvre.

There was Barra. There, Oisian. Machan lay over there, and young Torradan with him, waiting to be tossed aside like inconvenient driftwood.

Pedair filled his lungs. 'Halt!' he bellowed.

The Picts did halt. Startled in the midst of their gory work, they turned to see what old man raised such a feeble shout. For a moment, he saw fear on their sunburned faces. But it was only for a moment. They soon saw who had come down to face them in this too-narrow pass. They saw a dozen men on horseback, all too old, or weak or sick for battle, all decked out like princes in gold and silk and silver. As a final joke, their leader carried a ridiculous clay pot.

One of them, a squat, broad fellow with a maze of ribbons on face and arms, grinned.

Look, look, thought Pedair towards the Pictish captain. *Here's a body to strip. Rich pickings for the one who can take it. Come on, come on, you bastards. Come get it!*

The squat fellow shouted something, and another Pict sauntered forward. Taller than the first, he wore a wealth of white scars over his swirling blue ribbons. Leather banded his throat and wrists, and his bronze sword was in his hands and his stone hammer hung from his belt. Behind him, another Pict straightened his back, and brought up his knife. Another hefted his hammer, and another and another.

Pedair's horse snorted, and strained to back away, to take shelter among its skinny, lame, broken-winded herdmates.

Hold, hold, just a little longer. Let's see who will join these stout fellows.

Look, look, we've left the gate up. All this gold came from in there. There must be more for the taking. Those southerners down below will just keep it for themselves if you don't get it first. Come on. Come on.

The lead man grinned, showing all his yellow teeth, and raised his bloody stone hammer. Pedair let his horse back up a full four paces.

The Pict shouted something to his followers, and they charged up the hill, a roaring wave of brown and blue, leather, bronze and stone.

Slowly, slowly, Pedair backed his sweating horse, and the Picts screamed in delight. There was no room to fight, barely room on horseback to turn. They were engulfed, a wave of bodies and terror and the maddening stench of offal. Bloody hands grabbed Pedair's reins as his horse tried to run. He clutched the ungainly jar to his chest and fought to keep his seat. His horse screamed and tried to rear, but there were too many of them. He was trapped in the flood of bodies, and his spear was gone and his horse bucked and danced and screamed.

The brown river poured up the pass, into the waiting shadow of Din Eityn.

You must finish it for us, Sir Devi.

The hands got hold of him, fingers digging into leg and arm, neck and chest. As the world began to shudder and his grip began to loosen, he saw the first of the hands come up over the mound of boulders that lined the pass. The youth and the aged of Din Eityn clambered into the pass. Untrained, unblooded, too young and too old together, sisters beside brothers, wives beside husbands. But they'd armed themselves with knives and smith's hammers and meat hooks and the courage born of fighting for their home.

Enemy hands dug into his arms, clawing at the gold to tear it from his body.

With the last of his strength, Pedair raised the jar he had brought. The stench of it was like the sulphurs of hell. He flung the jar down at his feet, and those same fires erupted around him.

'Gododdin!' he screamed as agony and fire took him. 'Agravain!'

Fire ahead and Gododdin behind, the Picts tried to fight, and, swiftly, they began to die.

The bear retreated before her. The whole world stank with its fear. She narrowed her eyes and squealed in her delight. The bristles on her back stuck out straight and proud in her ecstatic fury.

She began to run. Head down, tusks out. Faster, and faster she barrelled forward. Nothing could stop her. Nothing could turn her. She had her quarry that had eluded and tormented her for so long. She would spit the cowering mountain of stinking fur on her tusks, toss it past her shoulders, trample it with her hooves . . .

Boar, I am the hunter, and my spear is as stout as my heart.

There was no mound of hair before her. The scent of fear vanished as if had never been. There was a man, a pathetic little man, kneeling calmly behind a sharpened stick, the end of which glistened with black iron. Black iron pointed at her onrushing heart.

And she could not slow down.

They were being driven back, one slow, bloody, cacophonous inch at a time. Through the sweat and blood that stung his eyes, Agravain saw the Black Knight on his black horse, here and there, death's own shadow wielding a bloody spear. Agravain struggled to turn his horse towards the knight, towards the youth in a man's disguise who did Morgaine's will. Anger turned his vision red as he strove to reach that shadow. But a world of battle blocked his path time and again, forcing him to duck and strike, wheel and plunge forward again, only to find he had lost sight of his quarry.

The clouds were gathering overhead and the cold wind was damp against his sweat-drenched skin. There'd be rain soon, making more mud to mix with the stench and screams and blind them all as surely as the morning's fog had.

Didn't matter. Stay alive. Stay alive. His spear had shattered long ago. He gripped sword and shield, raining blows down on every side, protecting horse, protecting self, one eye on the rising ground behind him. Agravain marked where he was, and cursed.

He had to let the Black Knight go. For now. For now only.

'Now!' Agravain shouted.

Three blasts on the horn, the wave of the red flag. Ruadh was sweating and blood-spattered, raising the hawk banner high to show the rallying point.

Follow the standard! Agravain prayed to his own men through his gritted teeth. *God Almighty, let them keep together and follow the standard!*

He couldn't wait any more. He had to turn his horse yet again, and retreat. Shift the course, move fast, bear around to where the ridge was low, to the cleft where they'd dug so hard to clear a way that was wide enough and smooth enough for the horses to get through.

Agravain risked a look over his shoulder, squinting to try to make out the picture on the jolting landscape behind him. There was no way to tell how many had managed to follow him. The pack looked fairly tight. He caught flashes of colour that might have been banners for his men. It might still be all right. They might be dragging Mordred's army around behind them, putting their flank to the ridge.

He faced forward again. The ridge was near. In another

few heartbeats the ground would rise and he'd have to swing around again to force his tired, balking horse up the pass.

It could still work. It had worked so far. It could still work . . .

Laurel ran towards her death, squealing in her shock, but unable to stop, unable to slow or turn. The path was too tight, her hooves too slick, her speed too great. The hunter grinned, holding his spear steady. She must run towards him, and he held, and as long he held she must die. She ran, a bare arm's length from him now and he held . . .

Hunter, I am the stone that slips and turns your ankle, throwing you helpless to the ground.

Small, tight and hard, round and smooth and treacherous. Blind and senseless, knowing only the unbearable pressure from above. Then, the pressure shifted just the tiniest amount, and she was free. She rolled, and the pressure was gone, and she flew into the dark.

Stone, I am the sea where you fall, plummeting, helpless to the bottom.

Now! Now! Pain burned up Agravain's arms as he gripped the reins. He clamped his aching knees to his stallion's sides, forcing the whickering, whining animal up the rough ground. The makeshift walls of stone and timber were too high for him to see what was happening above. His ears were so deafened by the clash of battle he could hear nothing.

Come on! Any further and you won't have a clear shot at them! They'll run right past . . .

Cold dropped hard against Agravain's mind. Had he missed something? Had there been a third arm? No, no, they didn't have enough men for that surely . . . He wheeled around, and his horse screamed as he dragged at the beast's raw mouth. He ignored it. He had to see below and read the flags and shields in the pounding churning mass struggling to overtake him, his mind and sight a blur.

The Picts. Where are the Picts in this horde?

God, no . . .

But the thought had no time to complete itself. A shout came from above, and a new sound, a creaking thunder that began low and picked up speed. Agravain's head snapped around in time to see the logs of timber cascading down onto the great fantail of Mordred's army.

Horses and men screamed and fell, toppling down the steep hills. Dying, crushed by the logs, by the hooves and falling bodies of their comrades' horses.

Then, one man after another popped up from behind the barricades of earth, and the bolts and the stones began to fly down.

His men cheered, and Agravain lifted his sword, turning again, following the path of the timber, grinning fiercely as he roared out his wordless battle cry.

She flew free. The air brushed her, tumbling her over. There was joy in her flight, but it was wrong somehow. Too long, too far, curving, tumbling, endless. A shock of cold. Pressure now on all sides, a cold embrace, guiding her down and down, without stint or measure, no ending, cool turning to cold, the warmth of light fading fast as she fell and fell and fell.

But this too was wrong. The touch of this embrace was not right, was not true somehow. The current was wrong, the flow, the cold not enough, too much was missing. False, false, false . . .

Like all things made by Morgaine.

Morgaine.

And Laurel remembered and strained and changed.

* * *

Devi, his hand gouged open by splinters and his eyes stinging from sweat, backed slowly away from the catapult. His weak arm trembled and spasmed and he lacked the strength to control its frenzied dance.

'Try it now!' he cried to his crew.

The men, old sailors and miners used to the ways of ropes and pullies, bent their backs to the wheel, chanting slowly.

'Bring her round, boys!

'Hard now, haul now!

'Bring her round, boys!'

Devi barely heard them. All his focus was on the trebuchet's arm, slowly lowering. The timbers sang out sharp and angry as the gut ropes forced them down.

They had to be ready. The army below was in retreat. The king's men would pursue them back to the shattered pickets, and then it would be their turn up here again. They must be ready. They must be able to finish this. To show Sir Agravain – King Agravain – that his faith and planning had not been misplaced. That all those years Devi had spent grubbing through Londinium's ruins, all the gold he had paid out for the scrolls from Rome and Byzantium so he could ferret out their mysteries, had not been a waste.

That Pedair had not given his life in vain.

I might die today and here I am worried about my honour. The thought moved through him with a tremulous laugh. *Ah, God, pride makes us all fools.*

The armature reached the level of his nose. The timber and gut creaked, slowly; complaining, but not shouting.

'Brake!'

The man standing by shoved the great bar into place, jamming the gear, taking the strain off the ropes. For a single heartbeat, Devi could breathe.

'Sir Devi! Sir Devi!'

Devi swung around to see Abel, a broad, stunted boy

pelting across the yard. He'd been carrying buckets of water and grease all day and much of the night. Devi had set him with the watchmen over the cliff walls, so he could get some rest.

'They're coming for the back door!'

Devi felt the blood that flushed his cheeks run down to his heart. 'Are the men still in place there?' His voice cracked. His throat hurt. Everything hurt. His skin and eyes burned from the corrosive firing compounds, and sheer lack of sleep.

But Abel was nodding. 'They've all held their places.'

'It's up to them, then,' Devi whispered. 'Keep good watch.'

He turned back to the engines. These were his charge. He could not think too much on the narrow bridge that was Din Eityn's back door, or the men waiting hidden in its shadows. They'd crafted the hinges and stops as carefully as they could. It would either work or not work. There was nothing he could do now.

This for Pedair, Devi told himself and whatever god old or new might be listening. He clutched his weak arm to his chest as he remembered the scream and the stench and the old chief calling out their king's name. *One last gambit to keep us safe.*

Laurel's change flung her high, lifted her to float neatly above the false waves.

Sea, I am the boat that rocks upon your waves, the boat that holds the children crying for their mothers. The children set adrift for dreadful purpose.

For the first time in this long, strange war, Laurel heard Morgaine laugh. The laughter came from every side, enveloping her even as the waves buffeted her timber sides.

You think to shock me with my own deeds? You think I do not know what I have done?

I will be the morverch, *cold daughter of the sea's longing. To take up the babe promised me.*

Laurel rocked hard, buffeted by Morgaine's blows on every side. Water poured in an unbroken stream from the sky, pushing her down so that she could not swim, could not float, could only founder. Morgaine filled the whole world, her power dragging the water down, pushing it up. Laughing, laughing over Laurel's screams as she tipped slowly over, pushed and pulled by the weight of the water too strong to fight.

Laurel sank beneath the waves.

Behind Mordred, his army was being routed. The rush and thump of the stones hurled from the fortress above filled the air, punctuated by the desperate cries of men, the screams of the horses, the endless clash and clang of sword, shield and spear.

Mother, where are you? Why aren't you here to break them down!

Some of his men managed to follow him out of the heart of the carnage. Not too many, he didn't think. He could not spare strength to look back. He had to ride, ride hard, ride fast, trust the smoke of the stinking fires to hide him as he raced his horse the long way around, to find the Dal Riata, to see how they took the bridge. Last gambit, last game.

At last he rounded the ragged outcropping and reined in his horse, too hard; the beast shrieked and tried to rear. Up on the walls, he could just see the Dal Riata, moving cautiously along the ridge, their shields high. Bolts and stones rained down from above, clanging like hailstones. But they kept their formation, each man pressed tight against his neighbour, the whole of them moving slowly forward, the bolts doing no more damage than pebbles against a stone wall, for all the rattle and clangour.

They'll do it. They'll do it.

Agravain had let the bridge over the cliff's gap stand. Probably, he thought it could be used in retreat. Perhaps he had gambled that Mordred had not been able to find out about its existence.

Movement in the shadows caught Mordred's eye. Mordred stood high in his stirrups as his horse danced beneath him.

Beneath the bridge, Mordred saw men moving.

Mordred screamed in wordless, helpless warning. All the shouts and clash of battle turned in an instant to cries of horror as the bridge's supports neatly separated from its planking, and the Dal Riata, like so many straws, fell screaming into the ravine.

It was over in a moment.

Shaking as if fever overcame him, Mordred dropped back into his saddle.

It was over. Over. If he had a third of his men left, he had a great deal. He'd been crushed and burned and broken, spitted and cleaved. He'd failed. Utterly and completely. His mind was stunned, unable to contain the enormity of it. All the whirlwind of battle that he had somehow managed to keep at bay sank into him, buffeting him to his bones, pounding against his very heart.

He turned his horse; his trembling, sweating, nigh-on dead horse. He could not think what to do. He had no plan for this. This should not have been. Could not be. How had this happened? How in the name of all the gods had this come to be?

'Mordred.'

Mordred's head jerked up. His mazed ears couldn't identify the voice, and for a single wild instant, he hoped it was his mother.

No. Before him waited Agravain, sitting on a mount flecked with foam, blood and mud. His sword was drawn, his helmet gone, shield gone, face and hands spattered with drying blood.

Mordred grinned. Not done yet. Not yet. There was still a chance.

His sword sang as he freed it from the sheath. He nodded to Agravain.

Agravain charged.

Come now, little one, come to your home.

All of Laurel's awareness had dwindled down. This was not her change. This was change made for her. She was flesh and bone again, small and struggling, weary and hungry. Gentle arms wrapped around her, cold but living. It was so good to be held again, she did not fight. She could not fight, even though it was still cold and dark, and the world was too heavy for comfort. The dreadful noise had stopped now, and the element all around her was deeply familiar somehow.

Home, her small, weary mind whispered. She stirred in the arms that held her so gently but so firmly. Morgaine's arms.

Home in the depths. I will sing you to sleep. Come down, come down, come away with me.

Breathe. The flesh she wore could not, did not, refuse, but the soul it clothed stirred again.

Morgaine, this is no home of yours.

Hush, little one. Little one. Small and helpless, and longing to be held. Nothing more. No one else. Just the tiny bundle in the dark. No name to remember, no wish for anything but to be held. *Hush. Breathe deep. I will take you home.*

Swing again, and again. All art, all science gone. Only bloody, brute force left. Hammer hard, like a smith breaking iron. Wear the other down, beat him, break him until he fell. The whole world had come down to this; blow for blow, ducking, wheeling, fighting pain, struggling to see, to sense the next fall of the enemy's blade. Struggling to bring his own arms up, again and yet again.

But the ground underneath was mud and stone. The horses were as overtaxed as their riders, and had no fury or fight for life to sustain them. The black war horse stumbled, and its foreknee buckled, just for a moment, but it was enough. The Black Knight lost his seat, sliding hard to the ground, landing with a squelch and a thud.

Agravain slashed down, but his reach was not long enough. He swung out of his saddle and stumped over to his enemy.

It ends, here and now it ends.

He took aim at Mordred's exposed throat, and stabbed down.

Mordred moved. A flash, a ringing clang as the Black Knight's blade knocked his own aside. Jolted into awareness, Agravain tried to step back, but fire lanced through his knee, and he fell. His shoulder hit stone and pain burned, robbing him of the ability to roll aside for a crucial instant. Mordred was above him, his teeth flashing white beneath the black guard of his helm. Mordred's sword flashed down, burying itself deep into Agravain's chest.

And pulling out again.

There was surprisingly little pain. Just a strange pressure. His hands were warm and wet from the dark blood fountaining over them. It was hard to breathe. Very hard. The darkness was coming. Agravain was not so confused as to think it night. No. This was a darkness far older and eternal, and it laid itself down lightly on him.

Laurel.

The darkness closed down and took all thought with it.

Darkness surrounded Laurel; cool, calming darkness that was infinitely familiar to the deepest part of her soul. The deeper they dived, the more familiar, more intimate that touch became, the more clearly she heard her name in the currents that whispered past her ears. It was the arms that held her that felt wrong. This was a stranger's touch, it had no belonging here. It borrowed the flesh of a beloved and mischievous daughter. It was an abomination. It would be cast out.

Grandmother was angry. Laurel stretched, holding the form she had been given with difficulty, as the sea's grip closed. *Where are you taking me, Morgaine?*

Down to your brothers and sisters. Down to where daylight will no more trouble you.

Pride. It poured from her in ripples. Laurel made the babe in her arms go limp. *Are we almost there, Morgaine?*

Almost there, little one. It was so gentle. So much like what a mother would say to soothe a restless child. Laurel could bear it no more.

Yes. Yes. Here we are, you and I Morgaine. And we are not alone.

Morgaine laughed, flinging herself wide. You think your grandmother will save your mortal flesh, little one?

I do not speak of the bucca-gwidden, *Morgaine. I speak of the other ones. You called them my brothers and sisters, but you never knew their names.*

Names. Names were powerful. Names cut deep. Her grandmother knew the names of all the souls who rested in her body, and she whispered them in Laurel's ear.

Shall I call them for you? Bran and Tor, Caden, Austell, Masin, Piran, Daveth, and Ian.

Laurel felt Morgaine's pride and certainty waver. *What are you doing?*

Calling my brothers, Morgaine, she answered calmly. *You brought me here. Made me one of them. One more babe drowned to buy your son's life. How can you refuse to see the others who you murdered in this darkness? Garen and Eloweth, Worth and Rhys and Kevern . . .*

More shadows, shapes made of a darkness beyond darkness, but as the list of names tolled they grew clearer.

The ghosts of the children came.

They walked on thin legs. They were bloated and black-eyed, heavy with the water their skins had drunk. Their mouths hung slack from the choking screams that had been their last sounds. The remains of their clothing and the coils of their hair swayed in the current like strange water weeds.

Come, my brothers. Come, my sons. Come and meet the one who brought you here. Come meet Morgaine the Sleepless, Morgaine the Goddess, Morgan the Fey.

Fear. Fear, deep and black as the waters that surrounded them boiled out of Morgaine. This she had not seen. This she had never looked for.

Morgaine, Morgaine, the little ghosts' whispers were filled with wonder. *We never knew your name before. We called and called, and you could not hear, because we did not know your name.*

Morgaine.

Morgaine.

She rallied, anchoring herself to the strengths that had held her so long. She drew deep on the bottomless well of hate and need that had sustained her heart and soul and strangling power for all the long years. *You cannot call to me. I accepted this deed long ago. My soul will pay when I die, and I am not dead yet!*

You accepted this deed, but we did not, Morgaine. You never asked us. It was not with our consent you made us sacrifice. We said this to you over and over, but you never heard us. Because we did not know your name.

You did not hear us call our mothers and our fathers.

You did not hear us cry for the cold and the sound of the thunder overhead.

You did not hear us weeping all these long years in darkness.

They closed, those dreadful ghosts, grinning grins that

belonged to no child. These were the ghosts of hate and fear. These were the last, lost wishes of the human soul. They wanted to know why this had happened, to find the hand that bore them down.

To strike back. Even a child could wish so very hard to strike back.

No! Morgaine cried, cringing. *These are baptized children. God took them!*

He reaches out His hand, Morgaine but we do not go. We cannot forgive, Morgaine. We waited here in the dark for you, to show you what you have done.

No!

She tried to run, tried to fly. But this was not her place. This place belonged to Laurel, and to the White Spirit of the Sea who had sheltered these smaller spirits for so long. There was no escaping them. They permeated the element all around her.

Hear the storm, Morgaine. Hear what we heard.

Feel the cold, Morgaine. Feel the cold arms that take you from all you know.

Know that you are sacrifice, Morgaine, to another's need. To another's hate, another's fear.

Come down into the dark, Morgaine, down where all your fear and all your sorrow mean nothing

Come down, Morgaine.

Come down to us.

They rose up, light as the foam on the waves far overhead. They knew her name and she knew not one of theirs. She could not call out, not really. She had nothing to hold them with, nothing to bind them, but they held her chains tight, and she screamed, and screamed and screamed again until they smothered her. Smothered her and dragged her away.

She was gone. Gone. And Laurel was alone.

Laurel swayed back and forth. She was blind and cold, her

self both fully at home and utterly lost.

Where am I? she wondered dazedly. *Where am I really? Is this flesh or spirit here?*

Grandmother? She whispered. Perhaps it was not flesh. Perhaps she could still find herself again

I'm sorry, Laurel. The sorrow was as gentle as the spring rain. It washed away her hopes and fears as easily as that rain would have washed away her tears. She had made her bargain willingly. She had purchased a victory, for herself, for her family and her husband. Like Morgaine, she could not refuse to pay the price

Love and understanding carried away the pain, making the rest easy. All she had to do was let go; let go of breath and mortal being. All her work was done. She could sleep now. Slip into easy dreams. She could remember another pair of arms around her, lean and strong, sheltering her and taking shelter. Remember eyes looking to her and seeing beauty and precious trust.

Remembering, Laurel Carnbrea drifted down into the further deeps.

Mordred watched Agravain drop into the mud, and fall still. Panting, aching in every muscle, he wiped sweat and rain from his face. It was not victory, not as he had hoped, but it would become victory in time. When they found their new king was dead and without an heir, these northmen would tear themselves up trying to replace him. Arthur might even come and wear himself down in the conflict.

All he had to do now was bide his time. He had done that before. It would be a hard thing to turn now and leave so many dead, and this rock unbroken, but he could do that because he must. He must remember the greater prize, the greater battle yet to come.

Mordred heaved himself to his feet. *You almost won.* He

picked up his sword that Agravain's fall had wrenched from his hand. *You almost won because you fought with the whole of your wit as well as your heart.* He looked down at the corpse, the blood pooling on its breast and on the sodden ground beside it. *I will not forget that,* he promised.

But I will have your head. I'll need to prove you are dead, and my mother will have her own uses for you. In the pit of his heart he added, *And it will buy me her forgiveness for this debacle.*

Mordred raised his sword. Its swing sent a giddy wave of anger and mischief through him. But as that swing reached its apex, Agravain sat up.

Mordred froze, sword aloft. Slowly, trembling, Agravain climbed to his feet. His blood made a black stain across his chain mail and soaked the torn leather underneath.

Reason vanished, stolen by the irresistible force of fear that must take hold in the face of the terrible and the impossible. Agravain faced him, arms loose, weight forward, in a wrestler's stance. Agravain faced him, silent, implacable, his life's blood drying on face and hands, death's own darkness like shadows in his gaze, the chaos and the fires of his victory rising up behind him.

Agravain, whom he had struck dead, stood and faced him.

The last shred of Mordred's courage melted away. He dropped his sword and vaulted onto his sweating stallion. He wheeled his horse around hard, and fled. Tears streamed down his face, stabbing into his soul like spurs. But he could not stop, could not turn and face the man he had killed.

You've lost! You've lost! You failed! The voice gibbered in the back of his mind, each word stabbing straight to his heart.

Driven by shame and by fear, Mordred rode away.

Agravain rode, abandoning the waning battle. There was no doubt of its outcome now. Discarding reason, he whipped his horse forward, racing to catch his enemy, racing to put the last of death's smothering shadows behind him. The scabbard was a blaze of warmth at his back, and he lived, he lived, he lived.

He could feel his stallion's exhausted breathing, feel the killing strain in its muscles as the foam flew from its ravaged mouth. He was running it to death, and it did not matter. All that mattered was catching Mordred, stopping this here and now.

The horse's drumming rhythm missed a beat. The world slipped. A vision of Uncle Kai leaning on his crutch warned Agravain what was happening half a heartbeat before the saddle lurched and turned beneath him. His horse screamed, and Agravain threw himself sideways, slamming full-length – shanks, back, head – against the ground.

Stunned, he couldn't move, even though he clearly heard the fading sounds of Mordred's fleeing hoofbeats.

'No!' he screamed to the steel-grey heavens overhead. 'No! Why would you do this! Why bring me back to this!'

There was no answer, save for the soft fall of the rain. Shaking badly, Agravain slowly pushed himself into a sitting position. His horse lay on the ground, not even bothering to try to rise. If the creature was not dead now, it would be shortly. Agravain scrubbed at his scalp, and waited for his men to come to find him, to take him back to his castle and his kingship and leave his battle unfinished.

But he was alive. He was alive, and he had won. He could seek Mordred out another day. He was alive.

Laurel. Where are you? I need you to give me good advice. I need you to chide me for my arrogance. For believing that this could be done in one day.

Where are you my wife?

He looked up, letting the soft rain bathe his fevered face, waiting for Heaven and earth to bring him some sort of answer.

* * *

He did not have long to wait. It was Devi and Ruadh who came to find him, the men and their mounts battered and bruised, and with the bemused air that is the shock of finding oneself still alive.

They dismounted as soon as they came near, and looked at each other, uncertain. Beyond pride, Agravain held out his hand and let Devi help pull him to his feet. He could be king later. Right now he was too tired for ceremony.

'How does Din Eityn?'

'We held, Sire.' A world's worth of weariness could not keep the echo of pride from Devi's voice. 'We took some losses, but we held all the same.'

'Who?'

'Pedair,' answered Ruadh. He was holding back his grief with all his remaining strength. Tears would come later, beside the fire, as they drank to the dead and the living in equal measure.

'He will be honoured,' said Agravain. It was all the promise he could make for the good old man who had stood for so long. *I deserve none of this.* His hand strayed to the strap that held the scabbard. *None of this.*

'Sire?' said Devi softly. Agravain realized he was staring back towards the rock.

'Yes?' Too tired. Too many long days. The fires were still burning, there were a thousand details to be seen to in victory that did not come with defeat. He was just too damn tired.

'Sire . . . they . . . they've found the queen.'

Devi led him to the shore. He had to. Agravain moved like a blind man. He could not make out the trail in front of him enough to guide his pony. He could not tell whether night had fallen or whether this was the darkness of his soul. He could not tell the roar of the sea from the roaring of his own blood in his ears.

But then, the sea shimmered in front of him, and his vision cleared. He raised his eyes, and there, there she lay. Just beyond the touch of the waves like any bit of flotsam, tossed aside carelessly. By the sea. By him.

Agravain all but fell from the back of his pony. Someone caught him. He shook them off. He felt the turn of stone and sand under his boots. He could not see. There was only Laurel, her white hair spread on the sand, her skin whiter than it had ever been, her face so still, too still.

Agravain dropped to his knees. With his two hands he lifted hers where it was flung out at her side. He pressed it against his forehead. Cold. So terribly cold.

No. No. Your time is not yet. God is merciful.

He scrabbled at the strap that held the scabbard to his back. It had saved him. God's grace borne here by Laurel's hands, her greater understanding. It would save her. It must. It could not be that he was meant to live and she to die.

'Sire . . .' said someone. Devi. 'Let us . . .'

'Do not touch her!' he shouted. His numb fingers finally found the trick of the strap and he tore the scabbard from his shoulders. He laid it onto her still breast, and carefully, gently folded her arms, so that her hands were laid on top of it.

'Live,' he whispered. 'Laurel, live. Death is not for you. It is too cold, too dark for you.' A wave surged up wetting his boots, teasing her hems. 'God, I beg you. Take the life you have given me. I do not need it. Only let her live.'

Another wave came, rolling over her, wetting her to her breast. Agravain wept, his tears falling into the salt water. He could not move her away from those taunting waves. He had no strength left.

'Please. Please. Let her live.'

'Sire . . .' began Devi again.

Agravain gripped her hands, pressing them against the

scabbard. A third wave, cold and salt, surged around them. Agravain dug his boots into the earth, the earth that had known his family down the generations, that earth that claimed him and called him back to the service of his land, the earth that was his very bone. Agravain cleaved to it and reached with all his heart and soul to the retreating sea. With all the love that could be held in the chambers of a broken heart, he reached towards the final darkness.

He reached and he reached, and he prayed, and he believed he touched the softness of his wife.

Laurel. Laurel come back. Come home.

And underneath his hands, Laurel's breast stirred. Her hand moved, and lifted and grasped his.

A wordless cry escaped him. All his strength returned in a rush and he pulled her back from the salt sea, back to the land, to life, to his arms. And as he knelt there, her eyes opened.

'You came,' she murmured.

He wrapped his arms around her, bowing his head, suffused with gratitude beyond the ability to pray. 'Forgive me, Laurel. I was wrong.'

'Agravain.'

He kissed her, and she returned that kiss, and there was nothing else in the whole world as he held her, warm from the sea, warm from the sun, warm with life and love.

Neither of them noted the scabbard, now sea wet and salt scrubbed. Neither of them saw then, nor for a long time to come, how the dark stain on it had been washed clean away.

EPILOGUE

I, the monk Elias, least of the brothers in Christ, write these words and ask forgiveness from God Most High. For in so doing, I commit the sin of pride, and I defy the orders of my father abbot.

Today we found the body of the old man, Kai ap Cynyr, once called Sir Kai, who had long lived in sanctuary here among the holy brethren. He lay in the orchard, peaceful and at rest, with the fallen leaves of the hawthorn lying on his breast. He has now been laid in his grave to await the Day of Judgment which must come to all. Father Gildas ordered that I should write the day of his passing in this last record of his, and nothing more.

But I will write what I saw, even as Kai did.

Kai's mind has been wandering of late. He was often seen in the orchard talking and laughing with himself as the oldest of men will. We left him alone at these times, for he did not seem inclined to violence or fits, although we prayed frequently for the ease of his mind and soul. He spoke sometimes of a holy brother who came to visit him, a man with stout arms and a warrior's build who wore a monk's plain habit. No one else could ever say they had seen this monk.

But I have.

I was fetching water from the river and as I straightened up with the yoke on my shoulders, I saw a broad man in monk's habit. He carried a white staff in his hand and came striding down the hill towards me. Beside him walked another man, a young man so tall that the monk's head came only up to his shoulder. They made no answer to my hail. They only splashed across the river and began to climb the hill on the other side.

On the top of that hill, I saw yet another man, a man of straight and noble form with a king's crown on his head and a golden torque around his throat. He held out both hands to the tall man, and that man broke into a run, leaving the monk far behind. They embraced, the king and the tall man, and the monk leaned on his staff and watched them fondly.

Then, that tall man turned to me, and gave me a broad wink, and I saw it was Kai ap Cynyr.

This was in the instant before they all three vanished into the sunlight.

A great fear came upon me. I dropped my buckets and ran back to the monastery, where all had discovered the mortal shell of Sir Kai.

I have read his writings, as has Father Gildas. Father Gildas has pronounced them an old man's dreams, but despite that, it is plain he is more than a little afraid of them. He has ordered they should be burned.

God and Mary forgive me but I disobey my father abbot. I will wrap these pages up in leather. I will take them to the town. I will give them to the first trustworthy sailor I can find to take across to Gododdin. I think the king there will look on them more kindly than Father Gildas, for his name is Gawain, and his father's name was Agravain, and his father's name was Lot.

It is the sin of pride I commit, but I will do this thing. For it seems to me that dreams and miracles are close cousins. If such men as Arthur Pendragon, Agravain ap Lot, and Kai ap Cynyr can be declared merest dreams, and word of them burned away, what then can become of the rest of us?

Brother Elias
At the Monastery of Gillean,
Eire